I0694819

Beast of the Bronx

Rowan K. Lake Jr.

To my wife, daughter, family, and friends: thank you for all the support. I couldn't have done this book, or anything, without you. I love you all and thank you from the bottom of my heart.

ONE

The heavenly sound of bells filled the clear sunny air, signaling the
school's dismissal. Flocks of high schoolers flooded the concrete sidewalks
as some piled onto the cheese-colored buses. To a passerby, it was a
beautiful spectacle. But to the driver: it was a nightmare. One boy managed
to walk away from the site, with his green backpack weighing him down.

Andrew Roberts stood at average height. With a lean body and youthful
face, Andrew looked like he was still in middle school. His short brown
hair had bangs that hung right on top of his green eyes, and he wore baggy
jeans and a blue T-shirt.

His mind seemed to be elsewhere as the sounds of cars and people passing
by became fuzzy. Everything to him was boring: boring school and boring
life. All Andrew ever wanted was a bit of change to make his mundane life
more meaningful.

Crossing the street was no problem, thanks to the new traffic light set in by
the city. As he walked past a *Fred's Wings* restaurant, he saw two guys
dressed in suits beating up a kid in an alley. He watched their fists pound
the kid's face like a baker kneading dough. Blood splattered everywhere as
the kid's face caved in with each blow. His Chiclets-size teeth popped out
like a busted piñata and his nose became flat. In Andrew's heart, he wanted
to help him, but his mind knew the outcome. Andrew quickly walked off,
trying to forget what he saw.

That's how it is in the Bronx nowadays. Life has changed ever since this
new drug-lord came into town. They see guys in suits beating up punks and
other drug dealers. Now they're trying to hurt the elderly with their
protection program.

Back then, the Bronx was peaceful. Even though Andrew was living in Co-op City, the people there were friendly and always looked out for each other. The apartments there were like skyscrapers. He used to envy the people who lived on the top floors since they could see everything the Bronx had to offer. The smell of the bus fumes always followed you no matter where you were, and the cries of the pigeons seemed to tell a story of their struggles here. Andrew remembered going up to the rooftop of his apartment building, watching the sun hide behind other apartment buildings, as it approached the evening. Back in those days, the Bronx was considered beautiful and safe. Now, Andrew wonders why he lives here.

Andrew turned onto his street, De Reimer Ave. A gentle breeze blew across the grassy field of his twelve-story brick apartment complex. Suddenly, he saw a familiar face, eating a sandwich.

"What's the word for today, Toby?" Andrew asked with a smile.

Toby was the neighborhood hobo. He was a wise Asian man in his sixties and stood at five feet. He wore dirty blue jeans with a shabby red polo. His brown shoes seemed to be as weary as he was.

"Darkness approaches, Andrew," he said staring at the sky. "The world's gonna be in some deep doo-doo if you don't stop it."

"C'mon Toby, I can't save the world," Andrew replied chuckling. "I know you like to prophesize to people, but this is way beyond you."

Toby looked at Andrew with serious eyes. "Don't question God's plan. Just be ready for that time of change."

Andrew sighed. "I will, Toby. See ya."

As Andrew walked past him, he felt a cold chill run down his spine. He began wondering if Toby was right.

Me, save the world? That's impossible. But...what if...

The elevator ride up seemed non-existent as Andrew continued to drown his mind in Toby's words. Like a routine, Andrew walked down the second-floor hallway while pulling his keys out of his right front pocket. He reached the green painted door and unlocked it. When he got inside, he sighed and pretended to be cheerful.

Andrew and his family were living in a four-bedroom apartment with white walls and ceilings and red carpeting. Andrew walked a couple of steps and turned to the right, staring at the kitchen.

The kitchen wasn't big. It looked like a narrow hallway with cupboards on each side, a refrigerator, an oven, and a sink, but it had enough room for two people to cook.

"How was school Andrew?" his mom asked while cooking dinner.

"It was good, Mom. I got an A on my History test."

"That's good to hear."

Lily Roberts was two inches shorter than Andrew. Her blue eyes were filled with warmth and love while her dirty blonde hair draped most of her back. She wore her pink pajama bottoms and the white polo she wore to work earlier.

"Hey Andrew," a voice said as he came out his room.

"Sup William," Andrew replied.

William Roberts was Andrew's younger brother. He was the same height as Andrew with short flat brown hair and handsome blue eyes. He wore blue jeans and his favorite Einstein t-shirt.

"Andrew, are you going to the football game tonight?"

"I don't know William. I have homework to do."

"Don't worry, I'll help you."

"At a price, right?" Andrew asked, seeing through his little scheme.

"If you'll let me hang with you and your friends," William answered with a grin.

"I think I can do it myself," Andrew replied walking to his room.

"Andrew?" William whined.

"Under one condition."

"You name it."

"That you don't do your joke routine."

William felt embarrassed. He muttered, "My jokes are fine..."

"Take it or leave it."

"Alright, fine, I won't make any jokes."

The roar of the crowd filled the clear Friday night air as William and Andrew went to their school's football game.

PS 78 was the name of their school, located on Baychester Ave. It was a minority populated high school. There were some whites and other races, but blacks ruled this school. The building itself looked like it was built in the seventies. The outer walls were cracked and some of the windows were broken. The inside was much worse. The hallways were filled with long jagged cracks and some of the lockers were banged up worse than front end collision. Parts of the ceiling had holes in it with roaches randomly crawling in and out. Some of the lights kept on flickering, giving the hallway an eerie feel. Even the description of the bathroom would make newcomers hurl.

At the football field, William and Andrew sat down near the back, next to William's friends. Andrew sighed, seeing that his friends were nowhere to be found. Andrew glanced at Leon, one of William's friends.

Leon was just like William: smart yet so clueless about life and sports. He was an inch shorter than William and Andrew, but a year older than them. He had a chubby body and face, like the Stay Puft Marshmallow Man, and he wore thick soda bottle glasses. Leon's mop-top hair was a black color, had deep dark brown eyes, and his semi-wide nose could suck in air like a vacuum.

"I'm glad our quarterback didn't throw the ball at a 48.5° angle, or we wouldn't have scored," said Leon, who was calculating the trajectory of the last play.

"Whatever, Leon," William replied. "If Terrel ran four seconds slower, after catching the ball, the other team would've creamed him."

Andrew sighed as he looked at the scoreboard. Their school was up by seven. He let out another sigh. It's not that Andrew didn't like sports: he just felt bored and fed up with life. Even with his circle of friends, Andrew kept to himself. He stared at the stars for a moment. He smiled. It really was a perfect night for football. Not a single cloud was in the sky and the moon was full and bright. Andrew's thoughts slowly drifted towards Toby's words once more, drowning out the sounds of the game. If this night was going to be a night of change, where was his sign?

 Suddenly, the whistle blew, bringing Andrew back to his senses. He looked at the field and saw that his school had the ball from the kick-off. The quarterback threw the ball with great trajectory. The receiver caught the ball and held it tightly, running as fast as he could to the end zone. He dodged left. He dodged right, shaking off the oncoming opposing team. With only five yards remaining, the receiver took it into overdrive. BAM! The receiver felt weightless for a moment. In that moment, all he could see were the floodlights and the starry sky. A loud thud came as his face met the ground. The whistle blew and the referee called for a time-out.

"That…had to hurt," William said with his eyes wide open.

"That's what football is all about," replied Andrew, "getting hurt just to get a ball onto one side of the field."

"Hey, Drew!" someone called out.

Andrew looked down into the stands. He saw his best friend, Mark Rivers, waving to him.

Mark was three inches taller and the same age as Andrew. He had curly black hair in a fade with a mocha complexion. His dark brown puppy dog eyes managed to get him the ladies. Minutes later, Mark made his way to where Andrew was.

"Sup son," said Mark as he bumped fists with Andrew.

"Sup kid," replied Andrew.

"Yo, have you seen the chicks down there?" Mark asked pointing to the group of girls sitting near the front row, "The one in red is fine."

Andrew took a good look at her. She seemed to be two inches shorter than Mark and her curvy body was proportionate. She had short black hair, smooth light brown skin, a cute smile, and of course gorgeous emerald, green eyes behind her small square glasses. She wore a red spaghetti strap top with skinny leg jeans that advertised her curvy butt.

"Damn, she fine."

"I was thinking of talking to her, but some guy beat me to it," Mark said with a disappointed tone.

"You'll get your chance," Andrew said trying to cheer him up.

Soon, Mark noticed William.

"Sup Big Will," Mark said bumping fists with William.

"Sup Mark," replied William.

Mark turned his attention back to Andrew. "Yo Drew, I hear there is a new club in town for teens sixteen and over. Wanna check it out?"

Andrew was surprised. "When?"

Mark grinned. "After the game. It's a good way for you to holla at some girls."

"Sure…" Andrew said sarcastically.

"Can I come too?" asked William looking at Mark.

"Sorry dawg, but you're still a baby," answered Mark. "They don't allow fourteen-year-olds in the club."

"Besides, you have to do my homework," Andrew added with a smile.

"Fine," William muttered. "I'll ask Leon to drop me home."

"You better hurry," replied Mark watching Leon walk towards the exit, "Leon's leaving."

"But...the game's not done," said William as he ran after Leon.

Andrew smiled as he sat next to Mark for the remainder of the game. The game was fierce. Both teams went all out to score on each other, bashing, dashing, and crashing into each other. The sound of the whistle blowing filled the night air as the scoreboard's lights flickered with excitement. By the end of the last quarter, PS 78 was declared the winner.

"Great game," Mark said as he got up.

As the stands slowly emptied themselves, Andrew followed Mark to his car. Out of all of Andrew's friends, Mark was the only one to get his driver's license early. Suddenly, a hand reached out for Andrew. Andrew turned around to see a familiar face.

"Hey, Hime," he said as he hugged her.

Emily Singleton, aka Hime, was three inches shorter than Andrew. Her long blonde hair was in a ponytail and her big brown eyes are always cheerful. She wore a pink tank top with a white cardigan over it and boot cut jeans.

"Guess what?" she asked with a huge smile. "I finally got that pink cell phone I always wanted."

She pulled it out of her pink purse and showed it to him. Andrew couldn't believe how small her flip-phone was. It was literally half the size of his hand and had a sleek look to it. And the pink color seemed to shine in the light.

"That's really awesome, Hime," Andrew replied with a smile. "How much did you spend?"

"Less than five hundred dollars," Emily said in a bubbly voice. "It's got texting, a camera, mp3 storage, and Bluetooth capability. And the color is sooo cute!"

Emily jumped up and down with excitement. Although Andrew didn't want to stare, her large chest seemed to bounce along with her.

He averted his eyes towards the field as he smiled. "I'm glad to see you happy about it, Hime."

"Hey, Drew, what's up with the 'Hime' word?" Mark asked, interrupting.

"To me, Emily is like a princess," Andrew answered. "So, I decided to call her Hime, which is Japanese for princess. Found it in a Japanese dictionary."

"And only Andrew can call me Hime," Emily added with a stern look. "I'll get really mad if you do, Mark."

"Why?"

"Because, when you say it, you sound like you're making fun of me."

"But…"

Andrew grabbed Mark's shoulder and shook his head. "Let it go, man."

Emily looked at the time on her cell phone. "I better go. My family is probably looking for me. See you tomorrow in Science class, Andrew. Bye, Mark."

"Later, Hime," Andrew said, waving.

"Bye," Mark replied, also waving.

They both watched Emily run off towards the east parking lot. Then, they headed for Mark's car.

The road to the new club, *Fire & Ice,* located in Manhattan, seemed long and uninteresting. Mark's dark blue car zoomed down the highway, seeing that traffic was clear. Silence filled the air between them as the hip hop beat boomed in the car. All Mark was thinking about was getting some digits. Andrew, on the other hand, felt that Toby's words were about to come true. As they passed the club, they noticed how incredibly long the line was. Getting in would take them hours. Mark parked behind the club, on the corner of East 37th Street. It looked shabby, but it was the only place left for parking and you didn't have to pay.

As they got out of the car, something caught Andrew's eye. He noticed this abandoned-looking house with the name *Madam Renee's Fortune House* written above the door. Something inside Andrew was telling him to check this place out. Andrew hesitated, staring at the building. The outside was filled with cracks and some of the shutters were off their hinges. Even the steps looked worn and rotten. He clenched his fist tightly, summoning enough courage to move. Slowly, he approached the door.

Andrew tried to turn the knob. *Locked…*

"What the hell are you doing?" Mark asked, sounding concerned. "You trying to go to jail?"

"I'm not trying to rob the place!" Andrew exclaimed in a whisper.

"Enter," a voice called out to them.

"You heard that?" Andrew asked Mark.

Mark nodded. Andrew turned the knob. The door suddenly opened. As Andrew went inside the dark house, Mark slowly followed. It was too dark for them to see what was inside the house, but Andrew knew the room was huge. Their hearts were beating like drums as they cautiously approached the center. They felt like turning back, but their bodies were too stiff to move. Suddenly, blue smoke covered the room. Their eyes widened as they tried to figure out what was going on. Then, a huge spotlight shined in the middle of the room, revealing an old lady sitting on a hovering wheelchair holding some kind of deck of cards. They couldn't see her eyes, since she wore shades, and her face was wrinkled. She had gray stringy hair that was in a ponytail, and a small thin nose. She wore a black dress with a purple shawl over it and matching purple bandana.

"Who…are you?" Andrew asked, feeling frightened.

"The question is: who are you?" the lady asked pointing to Andrew.

"Yo grandma, what gives?" Mark asked.

"You must defeat the man you never knew," she said looking at Andrew.

"What the hell are you talking about?" Andrew asked.

"Andrew, you know you're adopted and have been seeking the answers to your questions. Mark, you too have been seeking the answers to your questions. You two have the power to change this city. But to do that, you must seek the power inside both of you."

Suddenly, Toby's words came back to haunt him. This was the sign Andrew needed and now he didn't know what to do or think. Excitement and confusion both occupied his mind.

"How…do you know our names?"

"You ain't God, are you?" Mark butted in.

"I'm just a fortune teller with amazing psychic powers," the lady answered calmly. "My name is Madam Renee. You two were brought here to receive a gift."

"What would that be?" Andrew asked.

"The power to meta-morph," she answered looking at her cards. "Only you two can stop this evil man."

"Meta…what?" Andrew asked with a confused look.

"Meta-morph. It is an ability given only to God's chosen warriors. You two have this ability and need to harness its power soon."

"Who is this evil guy?" Mark asked.

"That…I do not know," Madam Renee answered, feeling ashamed. "I have tried to seek out his face, but there's an evil force blocking me from getting any further."

"Okay, so how do we get this power?" Andrew asked.

"You will receive it soon," Madam Renee answered with a smile.

Immediately, she pulled out two cards from her deck and showed them to Andrew and Mark. Mark's card was a picture of a panther while Andrew's was a picture of a wolf. They stared at their respected cards with unenthusiastic looks. To them, they were amazing drawings on cards. Madam Renee took both cards from Andrew and Mark. She placed the cards on their foreheads. Suddenly, a weird light began to surround them. They freaked out, but soon began clenching themselves tightly. They dropped to their knees as their backs began to burn. Sweat rolled down their cheeks and dripped onto the hardwood floor. They cried in pain as the burning sensation increased. They really thought they were going to die. Soon, the light faded. The cards on their foreheads had disappeared, along with the burning pain.

"Mark, you have the spirit of Pansā, the Japanese panther. And you Andrew, you have the spirit of Ōkami, the Japanese wolf."

Mark and Andrew slowly rose from the floor, facing Madam Renee with cold stares.

"So how…do we…use it?" Mark managed to ask.

"You will know soon enough," Madam Renee answered.

"This still…doesn't make any sense to me," Andrew replied, struggling to stay up. "How do you know that I'm adopted…and how is this evil man related to me and this city?"

"That's a good question," answered Madam Renee. "In order to answer that, you must trust me first. I can reveal to you most of your past, but everything else will be revealed to you in due time."

Andrew nodded. For once, he wanted to know the truth behind his birth. He and Mark sat down on the floor and listened to Madam Renee.

"This is all I know: Andrew Roberts, you have been alone ever since you were born. Your real parents lived in Japan and abandoned you because they were two irresponsible people who thought they were in love. Once you were born, your father left, and your mother made the ultimate decision: putting you up for adoption. Under the cover of night, your mother left you on the doorstep at St. Mary's Orphanage, in New York. You were raised there for five years, until the Roberts family took you into their home. Their story was that after having a difficult birth with William, their real son, Lily Roberts couldn't have any more children. Since then, you have been part of the Roberts family."

Andrew was stunned. His throat became dry, and no words could come out. For sixteen years, he felt empty, alone, and unsure about his birth. Even though he was surrounded by loved ones, he still felt incomplete. But now, he truly felt whole. Tears rolled down his cheeks as he continued to wipe them away. Mark could see how happy Andrew was and patted his back.

"What about me?" Mark asked. "Don't I get a turn?"

Madam Renee sighed. "Mark, your life has been full of disappointment from your parents. You may get decent grades, but you don't apply yourself to anything. Your parents worry that you'll bum off them for the rest of your life. And forget about getting a girlfriend. Until you can take a stand for others, you'll never overcome your weak mentality."

Mark felt ashamed. It was like someone punched him in the gut with the truth.

"Andrew, Mark, now do you trust me?" Madam Renee asked.

They both nodded.

"Good. For now, live your lives normally. I will call upon you when the time comes."

Suddenly, a blue cloud of smoke covered them. Mark and Andrew coughed as they tried to see what was in front of them. The smoke cleared. They looked around and quickly realized they were back outside, behind the club. Mark looked at Andrew with a "what the hell just happened" look. Andrew shrugged his shoulders. He looked at the Fortune House's door for a moment. Mark knew what Andrew was thinking as he placed his hand on Andrew's shoulder. Mark pointed to the car, signaling that they should go home instead of checking the club.

Andrew got home to find Lily and her husband, Mike, in the living room watching TV.

Mike Roberts was four inches taller than Andrew and had a small gut. His short brown hair covered his forehead while his thin mustache barely covered his lips. His face was sort of round, and his blue eyes were filled with insight. He wore his blue striped pajama bottoms and a white raggedy T-shirt.

The living room was the largest of all the rooms. On the left side of the living room stood three cabinets filled with glass and china. Down a small narrow hallway, behind the living room, were the bathrooms and bedrooms. They're small rooms, but comfortable. Mike usually would sit on the black leather couch and watch the news on a twenty-four-inch TV screen. Lily would join him after she finished getting tomorrow's lunch together.

"How was the game, Drew?" asked Mike, still looking at the TV.

"It was great," Andrew answered calmly.

"William told us you went to a teen club with Mark," replied Lily with a stern look. "Is this true?"

"Well…yeah…" Andrew answered, averting his eyes elsewhere, "But the line was too long. So, we headed back home."

"That's good to hear," replied Lily with a smile. "You're too young to be going to clubs. Even your father and I didn't go to clubs until college."

"I understand, Mom," said Andrew. "Night, guys."

They waved as he went straight to his room. Andrew lay on his twin-sized bed, staring at the ceiling.

Andrew's room was like any typical teen male: it had pictures of sexy models plastered on the walls, a game console next to his small TV, a large drawer filled with clean clothes and a large closet filled with dirty ones.

That night, Andrew couldn't stop thinking about what Madam Renee said to him about his past and defeating a man he never knew. As Andrew kept on asking himself more questions, his eyelids began to close. Soon, Andrew fell into a deep sleep with the full moon shining down on him.

TWO

Andrew woke up to the sound of Lily's voice.

"Time to wake up, Andrew!" she yelled from the kitchen.

Andrew sat up in his bed. He rubbed his eyes before looking at his Sports Illustrated Swimsuit Calendar. There was a red circle around today's date. Andrew smirked. Today was a special day. Seconds later, he got out of bed and headed for the bathroom. After a nice, warm shower, Andrew headed back to his room to get dressed. Minutes later, he was in the kitchen with Lily.

Lily smiled, as she handed Andrew his plate of food. "It's just you and me today."

Andrew smiled back as he took the plate.

Bay Plaza was sort of a mall, but more like an outlet center. Originally, it was the size of a small baseball stadium with twenty small stores, including an enormous supermarket. Since then, it has developed. They have added big department stores like *Sears* and *K Mart*, a popular toy store, *Toys R Us*, and *Barnes & Nobles*, one of the larger bookstores. Even popular restaurants, like *Rib Shack* and *Silver Spoon*, have claimed a spot in the now spacious Bay Plaza. At least Lily doesn't have to go to White Plains as much as she did.

Andrew and Lily stopped by *Sears* to buy new work pants for Lily. Andrew watched Lily comb through the Women's Section, searching for the perfect pair of pants. Being a Court Clerk meant that you had to look professional. Andrew stood there a bit longer before helping.

Afterwards, Andrew and Lily stopped by *Barnes and Nobles* to see if DC's latest Outsiders comic finally arrived. The place was packed. Even the registers had a long line. Andrew sighed heavily.

Lily placed her hand upon Andrew's shoulder. "We can try next time."

Suddenly, Andrew heard something. It sounded like…crying? It was faint, but Andrew heard crying. He closed his eyes, trying to pinpoint the sound.

"Andrew, is something wrong?" Lily asked with a confused look.

"Do you hear someone crying?" Andrew answered with a question.

Lily tried to listen but could only hear the various noises from the store. Lily shook her head. Andrew cupped his ears and listened closely. He could hear the crying very clearly. Andrew opened his eyes.

"Follow me, Mom," Andrew said, as he pressed through the crowd.

Minutes later, Andrew was in the Bargain Section (on the other side of the store). He looked around until he found a little boy, crying. Lily brough up the rear. Her eyes widened as she stared at the crying child. Soon, her motherly instincts kicked in. Lily knelt beside the little boy and gave him a warm smile.

"It's okay, Little One," she said calmly. "My son and I will help you find your parents."

The little boy stopped crying. He wiped his eyes and quickly clung to Lily. Andrew smirked. Suddenly, his ears picked up another faint sound. It sounded like someone was calling out someone's name. Andrew looked around. Soon, his eyes began to zoom in on various people, even from far away. He couldn't believe it! Andrew continued to scope around the area, until he spotted a tall, scrawny man with a frantic look on his face.

That must be the dad, Andrew thought. He faced Lily. "I think I found this kid's dad."

Lily looked puzzled. "Already? But that's…"

"Trust me, Mom," replied Andrew.

Lily nodded. "I'll follow your lead."

They went through the crowd once more, heading towards the Kids' Section. Andrew spotted the man, who was standing in the center of the section. Andrew quickly ran up to him.

"Excuse me, Sir," said Andrew. "Are you looking for your kid?"

"Yes!" the man exclaimed, with a concerned look. "Have you seen him? We were in the Magazine Section, and I looked away for just a minute and…"

Suddenly, Lily and the little boy appeared. Tears ran down the man's face, as he ran towards the little boy and hugged him tightly. Even the little boy was overjoyed to be reunited with his father. Andrew smiled. The man held onto the little boy's hand as they approached Andrew.

"Thank you for finding my son," the man said with a warm smile. "How can I repay you?"

Andrew shook his head. "There's no need: I'm glad I could help."

"Are you sure?" asked the man.

Lily approached the man with a smile. "There's no need."

The man nodded. "Thank you."

Minutes later, the man and the little boy left, holding each other's hand. Lily hugged Andrew.

"My hero," she said kindly.

"Mom…" Andrew whined, feeling embarrassed.

Lily linked arms with him. "Let me treat my hero to a reward."

Andrew lay on his bed, recalling what happened earlier at *Barnes and Nobles*. How did he do all of that? Then, he pondered about what Madam

Renee said to him that Friday night. Was he and Mark really chosen warriors to save the world? He sighed heavily as he placed his hand upon his brand-new comic Lily bought him. Andrew sat up and began opening the comic. Suddenly, his phone rang. He looked at the screen and saw Mark's name.

"What's up?" Andrew asked, answering the phone.

"Yo, did you check you back this morning?" Mark answered, sounding frantic.

Andrew was confused. "Why would I?"

"Check your back, Dawg!" exclaimed Mark.

Andrew took off his shirt and checked his back in his full-length mirror. Andrew's eyes widened when he saw the wolf tattoo clearly on his right trapezius. Andrew wanted to scream, but held it in. He quickly grabbed the phone.

"I…have a tattoo on my back…" Andrew said, trying not to cry.

"You think the old lady did it to us?" Mark asked. "If so…did we gain any powers?"

Andrew pondered on that question for a moment. Suddenly, his eyes widened.

"I think my sight and hearing got heighted," Andrew answered. "Earlier today, I helped a man find his son at Barnes and Nobles, using my eyes and ears. Even Lily didn't know how I was able to find the man and his son so quickly."

"For now, let's not tell our parents anything," Mark replied. "After school, we can try and figure out what kind of powers the old lady gave us."

Andrew nodded. "Sure."

Andrew couldn't concentrate that Monday morning. All he wrote in his notebook for every class was today's date: *3/19/07.* Andrew headed straight for the gym. The gym was rather large, but still had that old moldy look to it. Long jagged cracks ran along the off-gray walls and the hardwood floors had dents in them. Andrew sighed as he went downstairs to the locker room.

The locker room was much worse. Leaky pipes ran along the cracked walls and the smell of sweat and soap filled the air. Even the concrete floor had seen better days.

Andrew opened his dark gray dented locker and began changing into his gym clothes. As he took off his blue collared shirt, one of Andrew's classmates stopped behind him. He examined Andrew's back. It was Josh.

"That tattoo is tight Andrew," he said enthusiastically. "Wish I had the balls to do it."

Josh Taylor was an inch shorter than Andrew with shaggy dark brown hair that would cover his deep dark brown eyes. His lean stature made him appear fragile. Josh wore blue shorts and a white T-shirt.

"Uh…thanks," replied Andrew, feeling embarrassed.

Andrew continued to change. Suddenly, Mark, wearing a green T-shirt and blue shorts, came downstairs. He was about to ask Andrew something, when Coach Myers appeared, blowing on his whistle several times.

"Alright ladies, it's time to do some laps!" exclaimed Coach Myers.

Andrew could hear the enthusiastic moaning of his classmates as they walked onto the field. At least outside was warm. It was a perfect day for running, not that any of them wanted to run.

"I want you ladies to do four laps around the track in less than eight minutes," said Coach Myers. "Begin now!"

It started off as a big blob of people running, but soon began to spread out. Mark and Andrew were in the middle running as fast as they could. They both began to wheeze, knowing they couldn't catch up to the fast-paced runners. Even the chubby kid was slowly catching up to them. Their minds were filled with embarrassment as they soon realized they were trailing behind everyone.

If only I were faster, filled their thoughts as they felt like giving up. Suddenly, their legs began moving faster. Their wheezing slowly disappeared, becoming more rhythmic. Time seemed to slow down as they passed the slow runners and quickly approached the average runners. Seconds later, Mark and Andrew were ahead of the class. They passed Coach Myers. Coach Myers looked at his stopwatch and noticed that only a minute had passed. Soon, Mark and Andrew were on their fourth lap. They bent over, breathing hard as everyone finished their last lap. No one could believe how fast Mark and Andrew had become. Even Coach Myers was amazed.

"May I see you both for a moment?" Coach Myers asked, approaching Mark and Andrew.

"What's up Coach?" Andrew asked.

"Have you two ever thought about joining the track team?"

"C'mon Coach, you know that Mark and I can't run."

"Did you know that you both clocked in at three minutes flat?"

Their eyes widened. They couldn't believe what they were hearing.

"You're joking, right?" Mark asked.

"I wish I was, but you boys should try out," Coach Myers said. "With some practice, you boys can lead this school to Nationals."

Andrew thought about the tattoo on his way home from school with Mark. They couldn't believe that their tattoos gave them the chance to run track. Still, it seemed too good to be true.

"What do we do now, Drew?" Mark asked with a frantic look. "We can't reveal our powers to the world. The government will find us and experiment on us. I don't want to be experimented on!"

"Calm down, will you?" Andrew replied. "No one's going to experiment on us."

As they crossed the street, something in the air smelled off. Their noses twitched as they sniffed the air. They detected a faint smell of cheap cologne, and it was coming from a nearby alley. Andrew ran over there as fast as he could. Mark trailed behind him. Two guys in suits were coming out from the same alley. Andrew and Mark slowed down as they walked past them, trying not to show any interest. From the glimpse Andrew got of them, they seemed pleased as they wiped their hands in a handkerchief from their back pockets. They left. Andrew and Mark immediately went into the alley. Even though the light grew dim, they were able to see where they were going (their eyes turned yellow as they went further in the alley). Suddenly, Andrew saw a teenage boy, about his age, dead on the floor with a bloody streak on the alley wall behind him. His body was covered with multiple stab wounds to the chest, his eyes were rolled back, and his tongue was cut off. Blood leaked from his mouth and dripped slowly onto his ice blue T-shirt. Mark saw the body next. Seconds later, he began to throw up. Andrew stared at the body with clenched fists. Angry, Andrew's fist pounded the wall as everything Madam Renee told him became clear.

Friday was a boring day, especially in Mr. Smith's Algebra class. The guy sounded and looked like Ben Steiner. Andrew couldn't listen to him as he talked about inverse functions. All he could hear was "blah-blah-blah." Andrew covertly yawned as he mindlessly stared at Mr. Smith. Sometimes he wished he were in another class. The bell rang for dismissal. Andrew immediately ran out the door before everyone, leaping for joy.

As he exchanged books in his locker, Mark walked up to Andrew with a grin on his face.

"What are you so happy about?" Andrew asked, looking at him strangely.

"I saw the girl today, dawg," he answered shaking Andrew's shoulders. "I was walking to the bathroom when I saw her in her Art class, painting a picture of a cat. I think her name is Tracy."

"That's nice. Can we go now? I need to go to the store to get some milk for Mom."

As they walked down Baychester Ave, the warm March weather kicked in. Mark and Andrew's backs were filled with sweat as their backpacks clung to them. Mark continued to talk about the Tracy-girl while Andrew ignored him, watching people and cars go by. They approached a small park with a metal slide and monkey bars on the grassy field. Something was off.

"Hey, you listening to me?" asked Mark angrily.

Andrew stretched his arm out, blocking Mark. Andrew wasn't familiar with this area, but he knew kids would be outside playing. Something caught his eye. He signaled Mark to look left. Mark looked and saw four thugs dressed in sweat-clothes, bothering a small kid in the park.

The kid looked like he was in elementary school. He wore black jeans, a white T-shirt and a Sixers jersey over it. He had very short brown hair, large dark brown eyes, and a round face.

It seemed those guys were after the kid's money. Mark looked at Andrew with a "don't make me do this" look. Andrew looked back at Mark, giving him the puppy dog stare. Mark knew he couldn't resist that look. He sighed, praying they would make it out alive. Quickly, Mark and Andrew ran across the street.

"Hey dawg, leave the kid alone," said Mark to the thugs.

The thugs turned around simultaneously. They stared down Mark and Andrew with evil eyes. Mark gulped as he stepped back.

"Wanna start something, runt?" the leader asked.

Mark nervously showed his fists. "Let the kid go."

"Looks like we got to teach these runts a lesson or two," said the leader as he snapped his fingers signaling his men to fight them.

Mark and Andrew stood there, with their fists ready. Mark's legs trembled as two guys came towards his right. He dodged, rolling onto the ground. He felt a hand grab his shoulder as he was hoisted up. A blow came to his stomach. Mark fell to his knees and began coughing up blood. Andrew rushed over to help, but felt a blow to the cheek, knocking him sideways. He regained his balance. Andrew spat into the ground. His green eyes burned with determination as he stared at them. He charged towards the thugs. He swung wildly, trying to connect to one of their bodies. Mark watched in horror as Andrew was being tossed around like a beach ball. Andrew collapsed, battered and bruised. His body twitched and ached with pain. The thugs surrounded him. Their evil grins were all he could see as they cracked their knuckles. Their leader grinned with glee as both Mark and Andrew were going to meet their demise.

Can't let it end like this. Damn, if only I was stronger, Mark thought, trying to summon the strength to move.

He slowly rose to his feet, clenching his stomach. Suddenly, his back began to burn, with the imprint of his animal spirit glowing brightly. The thugs stopped and quickly looked at Mark. Mark vanished from their sights. With unprecedented speed, Mark charged at the thugs, knocking them down one-by-one. Blows to their face, chest and stomach came at all angles. One felt a powerful blow to his chin, knocking him backwards. Andrew watched in amazement as Mark's jabs and kicks connected fluently. The ground rumbled as each thug's face met the hot cracked concrete. The leader's eyes widened as his men were on the ground moaning and groaning in pain.

"What the…?" the leader managed to say.

"Let the kid go or I might pound your face into the ground," Mark said cracking his knuckles.

Without hesitation, the leader handed the kid over to Mark. The leader helped up his comrades and quickly ran off. Mark walked over to Andrew and helped him up. He could see the huge gash on Andrew's forehead and left cheek.

"I never thought I would actually beat them," said Mark sarcastically. "Forget that: your mom's gonna flip when she sees you."

"Shut up," Andrew replied angrily.

He wobbled as he got up. Mark stood by him, giving him support. Andrew clenched his right arm as he slowly approached the kid.

"You a'ight, kid?" he asked looking at the boy.

The kid nodded. "Thanks for your help. Next time, don't swing so wildly. You'll leave too many openings."

Andrew's heart sank. A mere kid was giving him fighting advice, after he risked himself to save him. He hung his head low and kept his eyes on the ground. Mark smiled as he told the kid to hurry home. The kid smiled and waved goodbye. They watched as the kid left the park, heading down Baychester Ave.

"Cheer up, Drew," said Mark, patting Andrew's back. "You did your best."

"Easy for you to say," replied Andrew grumpily. "You're the one who sent those thugs running. And you were able to harness your powers. I still can't do that."

"Hey, I don't know how I did it. All I know, I just wanted to save you and the kid. And the next thing I knew, I was Bruce Lee on speed. Kinda felt cool."

Andrew limped away, giving him the cold shoulder. Mark ran after Andrew and apologized. Andrew was reluctant, but soon forgave him.

As an apology, Mark bought the milk and bandages. They walked out of the store, heading for home. The sun began to hide behind the apartment buildings. Andrew looked up at the sky as the red mixed in with the blue and a few stars twinkled brightly. With each passing minute, the blue slowly engulfed the red and moon's face began to poke out. Andrew smiled, for it was the most beautiful paintings God could have ever created. What a way to end the day.

THREE

"**W**hat in the world happened?" Lily asked Andrew, touching his face.

"Mark and I got jumped by some thugs," Andrew answered, freeing himself from her motherly grip. "We sent them running, so everything's okay."

"No, it's not! You could've been killed. You don't know if they have guns or knives. Please, don't fight them. I don't want to lose you."

Andrew's heart sank. This was the first time he ever saw Lily sob. Tears rolled down her cheeks as she struggled to keep her voice to a minimum. Andrew quickly embraced her with her head buried in his chest.

"I'm sorry, Mom. It won't happen again."

Mark and Andrew headed for Bay Plaza Cinemas, next to Co-op City, on a clear Saturday night to see *Spider-man 3*.

 Bay Plaza Cinemas was a spacious place. Originally, it was a three floored parking deck for the water treatment plant across the street. Ten years ago, the mayor decided to remodel the old parking deck, changing it into a cinema. Andrew had to admit, the architect and designers really outdid themselves. Because of the original design, twelve medium-sized screen rooms were able to fit nicely and still have room for a large game room and concession stand.

 As usual, Mark would scope the girls while Andrew got the tickets. The line wasn't too long and was filled with mostly high schoolers. There were a few diehard fans, either dressed up as the characters or just reciting lines from the comic. While waiting, Andrew admired the interior.

Suddenly, Andrew felt a hard tap on his shoulder. It was Mark, who wasn't even looking at Andrew while he tapped him.

"What?" Andrew asked as he took the tickets from the dealer.

"There she is," Mark said sort of pointing at her.

Andrew looked closely and noticed that it was the same girl Mark tried to holla at when they were at the football game. She seemed to be with a group of girls, giggling and talking amongst themselves.

"Go for it," said Andrew.

"You crazy? You don't tell a brotha what to do. He must do it on his own."

"So, what's stopping you?"

"Nothing, a'ight," Mark answered feeling bashful, "I'm…uh…I'm…"

"Scared?"

"I ain't scared," Mark replied, trying not to look at the girl. "Yo, when does the movie start?"

"Hey guys!" someone called out to them.

Mark and Andrew turned their heads over to their right and saw Rosa Sanchez waving at them. Andrew's heart raced and a huge grin spread across his face.

Andrew had known Rosa since they were kids. In fact, they lived in the same apartment building. Rosa was a fine Spanish chick. Her body was what most guys consider perfect. Her oval-shaped body was able to support her curvy butt and cantaloupe-sized breasts. Her long brown hair always smelled like lavender and her hazel eyes shined brightly in the light.

Andrew snapped back to reality as Rosa approached him and Mark. Soon, they fist bumped her. Andrew took a moment to admire Rosa's attire.

"Well, aren't we a bit dressed up," Andrew said, trying to hide his feelings.

Rosa attire was a bit dressed up. She wore dark blue curvy jeans that seemed to cling to her. Her yellow top was wide and puffy. It had a low U-shaped neck that exposed her cleavage. The only thing that looked normal was her brown sneakers.

Rosa felt embarrassed. "I have a right to dress up."

"Trying to pick up a guy or something?" Marked asked, winking at Andrew.

Andrew felt flushed, as he averted his eyes.

"Anyway, what movie are you gonna see?" Rosa asked, dodging Mark's question.

"*Spider-man 3*," Andrew answered, "You?"

"Same here."

"Well, we better bounce," Mark said leading the way, "the movie's about to start.

 Man, was it packed! The room was flooded with people of various ages. Small pockets of empty seats were scattered throughout the room and was a battle to get to them. Andrew watched a young couple desperately squeeze through the middle aisle as various heavy people blocked their path. Suddenly, Rosa spotted some seats, next to two familiar faces. They scurried towards the middle section and began their fight for their rightful seats. Moments later, they sat down. Emily and Josh looked at them and waved.

"I'm surprised you guys got in here," Emily said.

"Yeah, we got here three hours earlier," Josh added. He pointed to the front section. "When we got in, that whole section was already filled up."

"Damn," Mark replied with a surprised look. "See, I knew I should've waited 'til next week."

"And miss all this fun?" Andrew asked sarcastically.

"Quiet, you two," Rosa said with her finger over her lips. "The movie is about to start."

As if on cue, the lights began to dim, and the blank screen became bright.

The movie finished around eleven. Hungry, they walked to *McDonald's*, which was across the street from Bay Plaza. Andrew ordered a Big Mac with medium fries and a large soda. Rosa ordered chicken nuggets with medium fries and a medium soda. Mark ordered the usual: two cheeseburgers, chicken nuggets, super size fries and a large soda. Andrew watched Mark munch happily on his food. Even to this day, Andrew wondered where all that food went. As they ate, Rosa kept on talking about the movie.

"That was a big waste of my time."

Andrew's eyebrows rose. "What's wrong with the movie?"

"First off," Rosa began, "there wasn't much character development with all the characters, especially Eddie Brock. And what was up with Venom? They didn't do him justice."

"You know how Hollywood is," Mark answered after swallowing the bit of his food. "Any time they make a movie from a novel or comic, they always take what they want from it and shorten it to fit that two-hour slot. I get what you're saying, but it still rocked."

"The only thing that *rocked* was the sound effects," Rosa replied. "And what's up with MJ? Is it just me or did she look like a stick in the movie? I know comic MJ has curves, but they made her look anorexic."

"Again, Hollywood's interpretation of the comic," Mark said before sipped some of his soda.

The conversation continued for another thirty minutes, filled with laughter and a bit of arguing.

Walking back home from the movies something Andrew enjoyed doing with Mark and Rosa. But this time the streets were quiet, a little too quiet. Torn fliers and loitered trash jaywalked across the cracked street as the cries of the alley cats filled the air. A chill went down Andrew's spine. Usually, prostitutes and drug dealers would be walking the streets around this time, trying to make a quick buck. Something didn't seem right. Even Mark knew something was off.

"Man, I should've driven us to the movies," Mark whined. "This ain't good."

Without thinking, Andrew grabbed Rosa's wrist and stayed close to her. The scent of his cologne was much stronger up close. Rosa gazed at Andrew's serious look. Confused, she quickly let go of his grasp and stepped backwards.

"What's your deal?" she asked Andrew with an irritated look.

"I just thought…" Andrew answered but was cut off.

Suddenly, footsteps from a nearby alley began to get louder. Morphing from out of the shadows, ten guys dressed in suits stood near the alley with evil intentions. Each of them had some sort of weapon in their muscular hands.

"You kids shouldn't be out here this time of night," one of them said grinning.

"Yeah, just for that, you should pay a fee," another guy said pointing to them with an aluminum bat.

They were surrounded. Andrew gazed at their Hulk-like bodies. This was one fight he wished he didn't walk into.

"Maybe you can give me some tender love and care," a tall guy said to Rosa grabbing her by her waist.

"Let go you bastard," Rosa said elbowing him in the stomach.

"Little…bitch," he managed to say, clenching his stomach.

"What do we do, Drew?" asked Mark with a frightened voice.

Andrew was trying to come up with a plan. SMACK! Rosa's eyes widened as her whole body was overcome by pain. She dropped to her knees, clenching her stomach and gasping for air. Andrew quickly charged towards the guy and swung, aiming for the face. The guy flew backwards. He tumbled to the ground, but quickly regained his balance. The guy wiped the blood from his mouth and grinned. WHACK! Andrew was hit from behind. He felt gravity suck him towards the ground. His face met the ground, scratching his skin up. Blood slowly oozed out from the small torn up skin patches on his face. Andrew tried to get up but was attacked from both sides. He felt every kick and stomp they threw. His forehead began to bleed as the blood splattered on the ground. Mark tried to save Andrew, but his effort was useless. One of the other guys quickly grabbed Mark by the throat and slammed him into a wall. Mark cried in pain as his entire back cracked the wall. It sent pain all over his body. POW! Mark's eyes widened as the sounds of his ribs cracking filled his eardrums. He coughed up blood. The guy tossed Mark aside like a rag doll, watching him crash into the pile of garbage.

"We can't…fight them…" Mark moaned, trying sit up. "These guys are too strong."

Andrew wanted to help them, but he couldn't even protect himself. He struggled to get a good grip on the ground, but soon realized it was pointless. His body was too battered and bruised to move. He slowly looked to his right and saw Mark struggling to breathe. He slowly looked to his left and saw Rosa laying still. Andrew clenched his fist tightly and gnashed his teeth. All Andrew could think about was protecting Mark and Rosa. He didn't care how it was done: he just wanted a miracle.

"Seek the wolf inside of you," a voice called out to Andrew. *"Seek out Ōkami."*

Andrew looked confused. *Huh, Ōkami? Who's…?*

Andrew suddenly remembered the tattoo on his back. The tattoo was a picture of a wolf, named Ōkami. Maybe the voice was telling him to summon Ōkami. At this point, Andrew didn't care. He just wanted that miracle. Andrew mustered all his strength to get up. With all his weight on his left leg, Andrew glared at the men with a slight wheeze. He inhaled deeply.

"ŌKAMI!!!" Andrew shouted.

Suddenly, a massive wave of light exploded from below, blinding everyone. The light quickly faded. Everyone was both awestruck and frightened at Andrew's appearance.

Andrew's muscles bulged and his back hunched a little. His body was covered in brown fur, and he grew a bushy tail. Andrew still stood on two legs, but his feet were in a tiptoe position. Andrew's nose and mouth were extended, and his ears had shifted upwards, changing to a triangular shape. Andrew had razor-sharp claws, glowing yellow eyes and drooling sharp fangs.

He stared at his claws for a moment, wondering what he'd become. He noticed his reflection on the glass window. Andrew had become a werewolf. To his surprise, his clothes remained intact. The hems of his jeans were ripped and there was a hole to let his bushy tail be free. Even his shirt had rips on the sleeves. This wasn't the miracle Andrew had in mind, but it was good enough.

"Touch my friends and I will kill you," Andrew growled angrily.

"S-Stay away, you freak!" The guy with the bat stuttered.

"Not until you tell me who you are and who your boss is," Andrew said.

"I ain't telling you nothing!" he exclaimed as he charged at Andrew.

"Fine, we'll do it the hard way," said Andrew.

The guy swung the bat, but Andrew caught it just inches from his face. Without any effort, he snapped the bat in two. The guy's eyes widened as

Andrew threw the top part of the bat aside. Andrew grabbed the guy by his neck, holding him in mid-air.

"Tell me or die," Andrew said staring at the guy with his glowing yellow eyes.

Fear took over the guy as tears rolled down his cheeks. Even the smell of the guy's urine filled Andrew's highly sensitive nose. Andrew ignored it and continued his interrogation. Suddenly, the sound of a car roaring filled Andrew's ears. He turned around and saw a black sedan coming towards him. Andrew hesitated. He was at a loss of what to do next. Winging the situation, Andrew leaped over the speeding sedan, throwing the guy in front of it. The guy's body made a loud thud against the windshield. The sedan skidded as it tried to stop. It tumbled several times, slowly crushing the roof and both sides. A loud boom filled the air as the sedan crashed into the wall, killing everyone. Flames sprouted from inside the sedan. BOOM! The sedan lit up like a Christmas tree. Andrew stared at the flames with a small grin. He never felt so powerful. The flame in his heart burned bright as his eagerness to fight grew. His ears twitched with excitement as another sedan approached. Andrew got down into a track runner's pose, waiting.

"What the hell are you doing?!" Mark cried with his eyes wide open.

"Trust me," said Andrew.

It became a game of chicken as the sedan sped towards him. Andrew dashed, vanishing from their eyes. The driver mashed the brakes, skidding to a stop. He slowly got out of the sedan, looking around. His heart raced as beads of sweat formed on his forehead. Suddenly, something caught his ear. The sound of a soft whistle filled the air. The driver spun around trying to locate the sound. The sound grew louder with every passing second. WHAM! A brownish object came crashing down onto the sedan's roof. The driver watched as metal and glass scattered everywhere and the sedan's middle caved in. The sound of his comrade's cries rang in his ears as blood and a few body parts flew out of the sedan. To him, it was like watching someone bite into a cream-filled doughnut with cream gushing out the other side. Andrew's yellow eyes glared at the driver as the driver slowly backed away. The driver spun around and dashed. He smacked into something hard, falling backwards. He looked up and saw those same pair of yellow eyes stare him down. Fear took over. His body froze as his pants became wet. He wanted to scream, but no sound came out. Andrew grabbed him by his shirt, holding him up in the air.

"Tell me who you work for now and I'll spare your life," Andrew said angrily.

"Alright! Alright!" he said, covering his face. "We work for Mr. Hidishi. He is a notorious drug lord in Japan."

"Why is he here?"

"He wants to use the Bronx as a base for his drug shipping. Why do you think all the other drug lords here are gone? We freak'n killed them! He wants his company to be a monopoly. He already owns Japan. Other countries have heard of him and do business with him. The U.S. is the only place that hasn't been invaded by him yet. But you can't stop him. Mr. Hidishi is a very powerful man. Your power alone can't stop him."

"Perhaps, but I will still try. Tell Mr. Hidishi that a new force is in town and ready to kick his Japanese ass. Now, get out of my sight."

Andrew let him go. He watched as the driver ran down the street. Mark clenched his stomach as he slowly came up to Andrew. Andrew could see how much pain Mark was in and quickly grabbed Mark's arm, placing it around his neck. Mark looked at him with a smile.

"That was tight Dawg. Now, we have a fighting chance."

"Yeah, but I don't know where to start," Andrew said as they slowly walked towards Rosa.

Mark stopped. "Uh, Drew, you do know how to change back?"

"No…"

"Well, I don't know either."

"Thanks…" Andrew replied sarcastically.

 "I didn't mean it like that. Uh…maybe you could try thinking of yourself as a human."

"It's better than nothing."

Andrew shut his eyes, picturing himself as the scrawny kid he once was. He thought about his brown hair and green eyes, his average height and weight, and his handsome smile. He opened his eyes. He looked down at his hands: he saw fingers, not claws. Andrew was back to normal, despite his clothes looking trashed. Andrew gave a sigh of relief. He saw Rosa lying on the ground. He walked over to her and crouched down next to her. Andrew stared at her. Rosa's skin gleamed under the streetlight, as her chest rose and fell rhythmically. Andrew's heart raced as his face flushed bright red. He quickly shook his head and scanned her for any injuries. A small smile sprouted on his face as he saw no injuries towards her. Andrew placed his hand on her warm cheek and gently woke her up. Her eyelids fluttered a little as they slowly opened. She stared at Andrew for a moment.

"What…happened?" she asked sitting up.

"Well…" Andrew began as he helped her up.

"This brotha came out of nowhere and saved us," Mark filled in, slowly walking towards them.

"What's his name?" Rosa asked.

"I don't know. Drew, do you know?"

"I think he called himself, Ōkami."

"We better get Mark to a hospital," Rosa said grabbing Mark's other arm.

"You ain't taking me to a hospital," Mark replied, freeing himself from her grip.

"Mark, you're injured," Rosa said, grabbing his arm again. "We don't have time to argue."

Sirens filled the streets.

"She's right, Mark," replied Andrew. "We better act fast or face the police."

Admitting Mark to the hospital was the easy part. But when Lily and Mike came to pick up Andrew and Rosa, explaining what happened was brutal. The entire car ride home was an interrogation scene out of a detective movie. Although they bought Andrew's "mysterious person saved them" explanation, Andrew could feel Lily's worries mount up. He hung his head low until he got home.

At home, Andrew stared at the ceiling in his room for a moment, wondering how he became Ōkami. It was something he had never experienced before. He felt powerful and fierce. He could feel the animal instincts within his veins. But one question still puzzled him: Where would Mr. Hidishi hide?

FOUR

"HOW can ten men get killed by one child?" Hidishi asked angrily.

He gnashed his teeth as the driver, the only surviving man from the battle, relayed the bad news. He sat in his chair facing the window with the lights dimmed.

"This wasn't an ordinary child sir," said the driver nervously. "This green-eyed, brown-haired kid turned into a werewolf and attacked us."

"What!" Hidishi exclaimed rising out of his seat still facing the window. "How is this possible?"

"I don't know Sir, but we are looking in that."

"You better or else…"

Hidishi's shadow elongated, casting itself onto the wall. A pair of blood red eyes illuminated the driver's periphery as the shapeless and spacious shadow began to slowly transform into a hideous creature. Beads of sweat ran down the driver's cheek as eerie sounds filled the room.

"Y-Yes Sir," the driver stuttered as he ran off in terror.

Hidishi sat back down. Suddenly, his phone rang.

"Yes," Hidishi answered.

"This is Sgt. Gregs of NYPD," replied Sgt. Gregs. "I did a forensics sweep, like you asked, and found a few blood spots around the scene. I'll call you with the results."

Hidishi grinned. "Excellent…"

Compared to Saturday, Monday seemed so mundane. Rosa and Andrew were in Algebra class silently talking about Saturday's incident. While Mr.

Smith wasn't looking, they passed notes to each other. It was easy since Andrew sat in front of Rosa. Upon replying to Rosa's question, a young man with spiky red hair and blue eyes whispered to him.

"When I used to date Maria, we used our phones to write to each other."

"Shut up, DJ," Andrew whispered back.

DJ was short for Dennis Jr. Almost everyone called him DJ.

"Hey, Captain Planet wants us to save the trees," DJ joked.

Andrew chuckled as he continued to write. As the day went on, Andrew couldn't stop thinking about how he transformed into Ōkami. He felt stronger and faster, but one question ran through his mind: How did he manage to keep his clothes from shredding? Andrew knows from watching horror movies, when people transform into creatures, their clothes are shredded. However, his clothes stayed on.

Maybe I'll ask Madam Renee that question.

As the bell rang for dismissal, Andrew walked up to his locker and exchanged a few books. He looked down at his watch for a moment. He wondered if he'd have time to ask Mark's teachers for their assignments before catching the next bus. Andrew looked up and looked down the hallway. There was Rosa, walking down the hallway. Her hips swayed to and fro with every step and her hair shined brightly, like those shampoo commercials. Andrew's face became flush.

"Hey, Drew," Rosa asked as she opened her locker.

"Hey," Andrew replied bashfully.

"Let's go see Mark, okay?"

"Wait, I never…"

"I know, but I figured you would," Rosa replied and grabbed Andrew's arm.

Andrew's face turned bright red.

"Let's go now," she said as she dragged Andrew down the hallway straight to the Metro bus stop.

Our Lady of Mercy Hospital was in downtown Bronx, near Yonkers and White Plains. It was a large old building with cracks on the outer walls and on the pavement. Inside, the walls were painted in an off-white color and the floors were tiled. When Rosa and Andrew arrived at the hospital, they both saw Mark's parents sitting in the waiting room.

"Hey Mr. and Mrs. Rivers," Andrew said waving to them.

"Hey Andrew," said Mr. Rivers getting up from his seat to shake Andrew's hand.

"How's Mark?" Rosa asked.

"He's fine, the doctor took him to the X-ray room to check on his progress," Mrs. Rivers answered.

Mr. Rivers was a big and tall kind of man. He had an oval face, a wide nose, curly black hair and dark brown eyes. He wore his usual khaki slacks with a white dress shirt and a blue tie.

Mrs. Rivers was two feet shorter than Mr. Rivers and had the same characteristics as Mr. Rivers except for the hair. Her hair was short and brown. She was still wearing her green scrubs, since she just finished her day shift.

Nearly an hour passed when the doctor suddenly came to them and told them they could see Mark. Rosa grabbed Andrew's arm and led him to Mark's room. Mark was already sitting up on the bed watching TV. Rosa and Andrew greeted him as they sat down on the couch next to his bed. Of course, Mrs. Rivers was constantly asking him if he was comfortable. Mark looked at Andrew for a moment before he looked at his parents.

"Mom, Dad, Rosa, I would like to speak to Andrew alone."

"Mark, you're not hiding something, are you?" Mrs. Rivers asked with a concerned look. "You and Andrew aren't…"

"Mom, please!" Mark exclaimed. "It ain't like that. Can ya just leave the room for a sec, please?

Mr. Rivers touched Mrs. Rivers' shoulder. "Sure Son, whatever you want." They left the room, closing the door behind them.

Andrew looked at Mark. "So, what's up?"

"Check this out: Doc took another X-ray of my ribs and noticed that they recovered by fifty percent. I ain't a doctor, but ribs don't heal that fast."

"Maybe the tattoo is healing you."

"Maybe…" Mark said and paused for a moment.

Silence filled the air.

"Yo, did you find out anything on Hidishi?" Mark asked.

"Nah, I don't know where to start," Andrew said looking outside the window. "He could be anywhere. Listen, I gotta go. I'll talk to you later."

They bumped fists. Suddenly, Mrs. Rivers opened the door. Still concerned about her son's behavior, she glared at them.

"Mom, we don't swing that way," Mark said as he clasped his hands together. "So please stop giving us the glare. If you wanna know, I was asking Drew to tell me what my assignments were, as well as my test scores. I didn't think I passed two of them and I didn't want you worrying even more. Okay?"

"Have it your way," replied Mrs. Rivers. She looked at Andrew. "So, Andrew, how are his test scores?"

Andrew paused for a moment, trying to recollect the tests. "Uh, he got an A on his History test and a B on his Chemistry test."

"Yo, for reals?!" Mark asked with a surprised look. "I thought I failed that Chem test."

"Well, I gotta go," said Andrew as he headed for the door. "Unlike Mark, I'm grounded and can't stay out past nine. I'll see ya later."

Andrew waved good-bye and left the room. Irritation slowly built up inside Rosa. She quickly said goodbye to Mark and Mr. and Mrs. Rivers as she tried to catch up with Andrew. There she found him waiting for an elevator.

"I see you were going to leave me," Rosa said looking at him with an angry face.

"I thought you were going to stay longer," Andrew said, trying not to sound mean.

"And how would I get home?"

"Have you ever thought about asking Mr. Rivers?"

"You can be such a jerk sometimes," Rosa said angrily.

"A jerk! You're the one who insisted on coming with me when you could have gone with Ms. Sanchez."

"Is it wrong to have someone protect me, after what happened on Saturday?" she asked, almost crying.

Andrew didn't answer. He could see fear in her eyes and see her body tremble. She was right: he was being a jerk.

"I'm sorry," Andrew said softly. "I didn't mean to..."

Rosa quickly walked off. Andrew sighed heavily before trailing behind her.

Three days later, Mark was released from the hospital. Since Mr. Rivers was at work, Mrs. Rivers came to pick him up. After eating an oily breakfast at *McDonald's*, they went home.

Mark lived on Hill Ave, three blocks from where Andrew lived. The house was a red brick two-story house with a huge window on the first floor and four smaller windows on the second. The inside was beautiful. The walls and ceilings were painted tan and green with sand colored carpeting, while the ceiling fan and chandeliers gave the house that homey feeling.

Even though Mark was tired, he wanted to get his homework done. He went upstairs to his room and found the list with the homework assignments. Luckily, Mark had History homework to do.

"This stuff is mad easy," he said to himself as he started at his History homework.

Hours later, Mark woke up to his stomach growling. He decided to make a turkey sandwich, seeing that Mr. Rivers hasn't finished the turkey deli meat. He went downstairs to the kitchen and headed straight for the refrigerator. He noticed a note stuck on the refrigerator door. It read:

Mark,

  I'm at work now. Try to get something to eat and make sure to call your dad. I'll be home tonight around 10 or 11.

Mom

Mark sighed with a smile. He opened the refrigerator door, looking for turkey meat, mayo, cheese, and pickles. Grabbing each one, he set them on the counter. He went to the bread pantry to get white bread. Minutes later, Mark made his sandwich. He gazed upon its beauty and felt proud of his masterpiece. This sandwich consisted of three fine slices of turkey meat, two thin slices of cheese, two juicy dill pickle slices, and a light coat of mayo on two fresh pieces of bread. But something was missing from his artwork. He went to the pantry, found a bag of potato chips and poured some next to his sandwich. He grabbed his plate and set it down on the table. He stared at his plate some more and still felt something was missing. He grabbed a glass from the cupboard and set it on the counter. Mark opened the fridge door, searching for the perfect drink to complement his masterpiece. He saw water, orange juice, cranberry juice, and milk lined up in the front. Mark stood there, indecisive of his drink. He rubbed his chin, staring at his limited choices. Suddenly, like a blessing from God, he saw the neck of a glass pitcher in the far corner of the fridge. He cast aside the other drinks and found a pitcher of purple juice. Tears of joy came upon his soul as he grabbed the pitcher and poured it into the glass.

"Nothing goes better with a turkey sandwich than a glass of purple stuff," he said as he walked over to the table.

After eating, Mark looked at his watch and noticed that his mom would be home in another hour. He found a pad and pen on the counter near the phone. He scribbled down some words, grabbed his keys from the counter and closed the door behind him.

A young girl walked to the subway alone, after having so much fun with her friends. A cool breeze slapped her face, sending a chill down her spine. Nervous, she turned around and saw no one. Suddenly, distant footsteps rang in her ears. The girl pressed forward, picking up the pace. The footsteps grew louder. She trotted, but soon jogged. The footsteps grew even louder. She could faintly hear voices calling to her. The girl ran for dear life, zigzagging in the maze-like alleys.

Mark walked to Seton Falls Park, located on the east side of Baychester Ave., with his hands in his pockets. The cool breeze seemed to bring an eerie feeling to him. He noticed the streets were kind of quiet, especially around the usual drug spots. As he waited for the traffic light to change, he noticed four guys dressed in blue-colored street clothes surrounding a girl across the street. At first glance, Mark thought it was a prostitute trying to get some money. But as he stared closely at the girl, his eyes widened.

It's that girl I saw at the movies on Saturday. I don't know who those guys are, but I'm not gonna let them mess with her.

Mark ran across the street and pushed one of the guys off the girl.

"What the hell ya doing, Playa?" he asked angrily.

"It ain't any of your business," the guy answered.

Mark stood there with his fists ready. He could tell these guys were going to be difficult to beat. Not only were they tall but were muscular. Mark took a good look at his opponents. Each of them wore the same blue bandana and blue jacket. Mark's body froze in terror, realizing he was messing with the Crypts, a notorious gang in the Bronx.

"Looks like this runt wants to protect his girl," another guy said.

The others laughed. Mark clenched his fists tightly while gnashing his teeth.

"You want to make something of it, punk?" the guy asked.

"I don't want to fight you guys," Mark slowly answered. "Just let the girl go."

"This bitch is willing to give me the satisfaction I need," he said grabbing her waist in one hand and unbuttoning her blouse with the other, "and I don't need you to ruin it for me, a'ight?"

Mark watched helplessly as the guy opened her blouse revealing her lacy navy-blue bra and cross-shaped birthmark above her left breast. Mark wanted to help her, but his legs remained glued to the ground. Mark knew he would get beat up if he helped her, but he couldn't shake the feeling of watching her get raped. The girl struggled to get free, kicking and crying out in fear, but the guy's grip was too strong.

The guy chuckled with delight as his hand cupped her right breast and began to caress it. Tears ran down her cheeks as embarrassment and shame pierced her heart. Mark's body trembled with both anger and fear as he watched the guy press the girl against the wall, holding her wrists over her head with one hand. The girl felt her jeans become loose as her matching panties were slowly appearing. She felt his hand rub in between her thighs. She turned away, hoping the uneasy feeling would subside.

Mark had enough of this horrible scene. He dashed forward and punched the guy in the face, making it cave in. The guy flew backwards and smacked the ground hard, leaving a small bloody trail. Mark walked over to the cowering girl and knelt beside her. He took off his jacket and covered her, gently holding her in his arms. The trembling stopped as she looked up at Mark. Everything about him seemed to make this horrible event slowly disappear.

"Touch her again and I swear I'll kick your ass," he said furiously.

"You're gonna get a serious ass whooping, kid," another guy said as he cracked his knuckles.

Mark stood in front of the girl with his fists ready.

"Nice knowing ya kid!" he cried as he threw the first punch.

The tattoo glowed. Mark dodged the blow, countering with an uppercut. The guy staggered backwards. Mark dashed forward and punched him in the face. The guy's cheek caved in as his body became weightless. He smacked the ground hard, tumbling past the girl and crashing into the wall. SMACK! Mark felt a hard blow from behind. He fell to the ground. Mark struggled to get up as the remaining two guys began kicking him in the ribs. Mark tried to fight them off, but their strong blows were too much to bear. With one strong kick, Mark was tossed aside like a rag doll. The girl's eyes widened in terror as she slowly crawled to him. Mark twitched as he slowly came to. He struggled to get up as blood ran down his cheek and dripped onto the ground. Suddenly, he felt a warm hand wipe away the blood. He looked up and saw the girl struggling to make the bleeding stop. Mark smiled and knew what he had to do: he had to meta-morph. He slowly got up and glared at the gang members. The girl quickly hid behind a dumpster.

With all his strength, Mark shouted, "PANSĀ!!!"

Instantly, a bright light illuminated the area. Everyone shielded their eyes, trying to make sense of their surroundings. The light faded. Mark looked down at his hands and realized they transformed into claws.

Huh? What was that weird feeling I just had? Andrew thought as he stared at the wall.

He laid his pencil down on his notebook and walked over to the window. Andrew peeked through the blinds, staring at the sky for a moment. He wasn't sure what was going on, but he had a strong feeling Mark was in on this.

Andrew quickly changed his pants and put on a jacket. He transformed and snuck out the window, leaping around until he landed onto the ground.

Mark, please don't be there. Andrew thought as he dashed towards his best friend.

Mark's transformation was amazing. He was covered in black fur and had a long skinny tail. His muscles bulged and his feet were in a tiptoe position like Andrew's. Mark's mouth and nose extended outward a little and his triangular ears had moved upward to the top of his head. He had glowing

yellow eyes, razor sharp claws and drooling fangs. To Mark's surprise, he
was still wearing his clothes.

"Oh snap!" he growled loudly. "I've become Pansā and my clothes are still
on. Now that's tight!"

"Get away you freak!" cried one of the guys.

"I'll stay away after I kick your ass," Mark said grinning.

He dashed forward at the nearest Crypt member and began his assault.
With one punch, the guy tumbled to the ground and crashed into a store
across the street. Absorbed by fear, the remaining Crypt members drew out
their guns and began firing. A hailstorm of bullets headed straight for
Mark. Mark froze. He knew he was strong, but not bulletproof. He raised
his hands to shield himself. He could feel his life flashing before his eyes,
yet his mind was focused on having some kind of shield. Suddenly, a
shadow-like wall rose in front of him and absorbed the shots.

Did I do this? I wonder what else I can do...

The shadowy wall vanished to the ground. Mark stared at the guys with his
yellow eyes and grinned.

"My turn," he said. "SHADOW FANG!!!"

Instantly, a shadowy rug rose from underneath Mark's feet. It began to
transform into a giant mouth with sharp fangs and white eyes. Shocked, the
Crypt members ran for their lives. They screamed in terror as the shadowy
rug chased them down the alley. To the girl, the chase scene reminded her
of an old Scooby-Doo cartoon. She giggled as she clenched Mark's jacket,
keeping it from falling off. The shadowy rug rose into the air and came
crashing down onto the Crypt members, covering them in a dark purple
shadowy blob.

"Help...us...man!" one guy cried trying to breathe.

"Get us...out of here!" exclaimed another guy waving his arm furiously.

"Mess with her and I'll make sure you guys won't live to see another day," Mark said staring at them angrily.

"We won't, we won't!" the guy exclaimed. "Just get us out of here!"

Mark removed the shadowy blob. They got up and scurried down the alley. Mark de-transformed. He walked over to the girl to see if she was all right. At first, she was afraid to look at Mark. She stepped back, bumping into the wall. Mark stopped. He could see she didn't trust him. He kept his eyes fixed to the ground. Suddenly, he heard footsteps. He looked up and saw her walking towards him. She looked at Mark with her green eyes and smiled.

"Thank you," she said in a low voice.

"Hey, I couldn't let those bastards hurt you," replied Mark with a smile. "By the way, what's your name?"

"My name is Tracy."

"My name is Mark. So, you're the girl from Art class."

Tracy raised an eyebrow. "Are you in my class?"

"No, I watched you present your piece out in the hall. I would've stayed for the whole thing, but I had to go to the bathroom."

"Uh…"

"Don't get me wrong, I ain't no stalker. I just…"

Tracy giggled. "I understand. No need to apologize."

Mark smiled. By the grace of God, Mark finally got his chance to talk to Tracy. It was like a dream come true. Still, Mark was nervous. As much as he wanted to ask her, no words would formulate. Suddenly, Andrew came from around the corner to find Mark and Tracy unharmed. Mark was surprised to see him and yet Andrew had a feeling Mark didn't want him there.

"Great timing…" Mark said sarcastically.

"Sorry, but I had a feeling you were in trouble."

"Nothing I couldn't handle."

"You didn't? You meta-morphed?"

"I did."

"Did anyone see you?"

"I did," Tracy answered shyly. "If he didn't…umm…meta-morph, I would have been raped and Mark would have died."

Andrew looked at her for a moment and realized she was the girl Mark was trying to holla at.

"Drew, this is Tracy," Mark said introducing her to Andrew. "Tracy, this is Andrew."

"Nice to meet you," Andrew said shaking her hand.

"Can you also meta-morph?" she asked Andrew.

"Uh…yeah," Andrew answered feeling embarrassed. "You're not going to tell anyone?"

"Don't worry, your secret is safe with me," Tracy answered.

One of the Crypt members told Hidishi about Mark's transformation. Anger overwhelmed Hidishi. Glass scattered everywhere as he crushed his cocktail drink with his bare hand. The Crypt member trembled with fear, feeling Hidishi's demonic aura. The guy fled. Hidishi sat in his chair and pondered for a moment. A smile spread over his face as he slowly came back to reality. He picked up the phone on his desk, pushing the speed dial button.

"Hello?" asked the desk clerk.

"Get me Professor Yen," Hidishi answered.

"One moment please," replied the desk clerk.

Two minutes passed by. Then, a voice answered the phone.

"This is Yen," he said.

"Ah, Yen, this is Hidishi," Hidishi said. "I have a job for you."

"What is it?" Yen asked sounding curious.

"I need some reinforcements. When can they be here?"

"In six days, Sir."

"Excellent," Hidishi said grinning. "Notify me when they arrive."

Hidishi hung up. He placed his elbows on the desk. A huge grin spread over his face as he folded his hands and rested his chin on top of them.

"It's only a matter of time before I claim the world," he said and laughed psychotically.

FIVE

Mark stared at himself in the mirror as he got ready for his date with

Tracy. He decided to wear black slacks with a blue dress shirt and black

shoes. He even left the top button unbuttoned, exposing his white

undershirt. To him, this was going to be an interesting Sunday night.

Seeing it was his first date, he made sure his hair was groomed and even

put on Mr. Rivers' cologne. The plan was simple: take her dancing, get

some food, and then do some star gazing. What could go wrong? The very

thought made Mark nervous. He looked at his watch and realized he

needed to leave. He made a dash for his car and headed straight for Tracy's

house.

After a few wrong turns, Mark made it to her house. Living a few miles

away from school (and a block away from a subway station), Tracy's house

was large. Mark guessed the house to have four beds and two baths with an

average basement. He walked up to the gray colored door and rang the

doorbell. Instantly, someone answered the door. It was Tracy's mother,

Mrs. Hamilton.

Tracy and her mother looked very similar. You would almost believe they

were sisters. There were two differences between them: their hair length

and body shape. Mrs. Hamilton kept her hair long and was round shaped,

while Tracy's hair was short, and her body was more pear shaped.

"You must be Mark," she said with a smile. "Please, come in."

Mark entered the house. He got that homey feel but knew that they were

artsy people. Paintings and sculptures filled the house, along with flowery

walls and tiled floors. Mark sat down on a very comfy sofa in the living

room. He almost felt like sleeping in it.

"Tracy told me about you," Mrs. Hamilton said. "Thank you for saving her. I don't know what I'd do if she were gone."

Mark stood up. "Don't worry, I'll protect her."

She smiled. "I'm glad you're different from her previous boyfriends."

Mark was stunned. All that ran through his mind was the word *boyfriends*. Suddenly, he heard footsteps. He looked at the stairs and saw a shadowy figure slowly coming down. His eyes widened as he watched Tracy elegantly walk down the stairs.

"Is this too much, Mom?" Tracy asked.

Tracy wore a short red halter dress with a small V-neck. The dress itself covered her butt but exposed a little too much cleavage. Mark's face became flush as he averted eyes elsewhere.

"It's fine, dear," Mrs. Hamilton answered. "It's not every day you get to wear that dress with a cute boy."

"Mom, don't embarrass me."

"I'm not. Besides, your last boyfriend didn't appreciate the dress. At least Mark has a reaction towards it."

"Mom!" exclaimed Tracy, feeling embarrassed. "Let's go, Mark."

Mark nodded nervously and quickly left the house with her. Mrs. Hamilton waved goodbye as they got in the car.

Inside the car, Mark kept quiet. Tracy looked at him with a sad look before she stared at the car floor.

"Sorry about my mom. She tends to blab things to people that she likes."

"So…you've had boyfriends?" Mark asked nervously.

"Yeah…" she answered. "That was during my Freshman and Sophomore year. I was naïve and thought they really liked me. Turns out, I was nothing more than eye candy to them. My first boyfriend cheated on me and my last boyfriend…well…he seemed to keep his distance."

Mark looked puzzled. "Keep his distance? I don't follow."

"It was his anti-social behavior that drove us apart. We barely went out and trying to get him to notice me was a lot of work. I just couldn't take it anymore."

"How long were you guys together?"

"I guess that would be almost a year."

"I'm sorry…"

"Why are you apologizing?"

"Cause…no woman should be treated like that. It pisses me off when guys with cute girls treat them like playthings."

Tracy placed her hand on top of his and smiled. "You're sweet, Mark. That's why I like you."

Fire & Ice was packed. Mark's heart sank as his plan started to crumble. They got back into the car and headed toward the Italian restaurant, *Gardenia*. Luckily, the place wasn't packed. They sat down near a large family and a young couple. After looking at their menus, they were ready to order.

"I'll have chicken alfredo," Tracy said, closing her menu.

"And I'll have chicken scampi," replied Mark, closing his menu.

The waiter nodded as he wrote down their orders. He took their menus and left. Tracy looked around the restaurant with a smile. She fixed her eyes upon Mark, who was sipping his soda. He looked up and blushed.

"What?"

"Can't I look at you?"

"Yeah…" replied Mark as he averted his eyes.

"Am I embarrassing you?" Tracy asked.

"No. It's just…"

"It's just what?"

"I've…never had a beautiful girl give me the time of day. It's all new to me."

Tracy was stunned. Although they met through a bad situation, she truly was glad for their meeting. The longer she stared at him, the more her heart yearned for him.

"You really are sweet…" she muttered.

Suddenly, the waiter appeared with their meals. He set their food down and left. They both stared at their food, letting the smell entice them. Tracy grabbed Mark's hand and began to say a small prayer. Mark quickly shut his eyes and bowed his head. Afterwards, they picked up their utensils and dug in. Mark smiled happily with every bite. As they ate, they talked about various topics. They even sampled each other's food. The night was going well. That is, until the bill came. Mark's heart sank further as he quickly realized he couldn't afford the bill. Tracy looked at bill and quickly opened her purse.

"You don't ha-" Mark began but was quickly silenced by Tracy.

"Just handle the tip, okay?"

The waiter came by and took Tracy's card, along with the bill. Minutes later, the waiter came back with her card and two slips of paper. She signed the merchant copy and handed it to him. The waiter smiled as he glanced at the tip underneath the napkin. He left.

"So, where to next?" asked Tracy with a smile.

Mark drove to a spot near a construction site. The site was where the new *Sears* building would be built. They both got out of the car and stared at the site. Although it was dark, they could make out the different construction vehicles, as well as the framework.

"Mark, why are we here?" asked Tracy, a bit confused.

Mark smiled. "Just look up."

Tracy looked up and her eyes widened. The night sky was lit up with countless stars. Even the crescent moon shined brightly tonight. Mark stood next to her, staring at the stars.

"Sorry about tonight," he said. "It seems I can't plan a date right."

"You really need to stop apologizing," Tracy replied angrily, looking at him.

He looked at her. "But…"

"Did I ever complain about our date? Have I once given you a look of boredom?"

Mark shook his head.

"Well then, that should tell you something. I really had a great time with you, Mark. It's been a long time since I got dressed up and went out. Thank you for making me feel beautiful again."

Tracy kissed his cheek. Mark's face instantly turned bright red.

Suddenly, he gave her a serious look. "You are beautiful: don't you ever forget it."

Tracy's face became flushed. Without thinking, Mark held her close to him. His embrace was warm and gentle. Tracy embraced him back, pressing her head against his chest. Their hearts began beating in sync. They gazed into each other's eyes with smiles. Mark gently lifted her chin and leaned forward. Their lips touched. Warm, gentle feelings flowed through them with each passing second. They unlocked their lips and stared at each other again.

"So…are we a couple?" Mark asked.

Tracy didn't answer with words, but with a long kiss.

SIX

"Spring Dance this Friday?!" Andrew exclaimed, looking at the bright yellow paper.

What a way to start a Monday. Andrew continued to stare at the paper with great despair.

"Yeah dawg, didn't you know?" Mark asked, approaching Andrew.

Andrew shook his head. "When was it posted?"

"Last week. Hey, aren't you grounded?"

"No, Lily let me off for good behavior and a good grade on my Algebra test. Anyway, why is there a dance when Seniors have prom coming up in May?"

"It's for everyone, idiot," Mark answered.

"I'm not an idiot," Andrew replied angrily. "I'm just out the loop."

Mark laughed.

"What's so funny?" Andrew asked angrily.

"You're wondering if you should take Rosa to the dance."

Andrew's face turned red. "Am not…"

"Just ask her," replied Mark. He looked down the hallway. "Here she comes now."

"Hey guys," Rosa said cheerfully. "Hey Drew, are you going to dance?"

"Yeah…"

"You want to go together? I'd rather go with you than these clowns. Pick me up at seven, 'kay?"

Andrew watched as Rosa walked off to her class. He couldn't believe that Rosa wanted to go with him to the dance. He felt like jumping for joy, but he had to keep his cool and not embarrass himself in front of everyone.

"Way to go Romeo," Mark said sarcastically, grabbing Andrew's shoulder. "You really know how to get the ladies."

"Shut up Mark," Andrew said shoving him a little.

"Hey, you guys going to the dance?" a voice suddenly called out.

It was DJ, along with Josh.

"Yeah, we're going," Mark answered. "You guys going?"

DJ nodded. "I have to: I'm the one who made the Spring Dance."

"Really?" asked Andrew with a surprised look.

"Yeah," DJ answered. "It was a miracle that I could get it done by myself."

"You da man, DJ," Josh replied.

"Please, call me Yeshua," said DJ, taking a bow.

Andrew laughed while Mark and Josh both raised an eyebrow.

"At least someone gets the reference," replied DJ with a disappointed tone. "Shows how religious you are."

During fifth period, Andrew tried to pay attention to his Art teacher. He still had a lot on his mind. Besides Rosa, Andrew wondered what Hidishi was planning. He began to remember what one of his goons said to him.

"Mr. Hidishi is a very powerful man. Your power alone can't stop him."

His words seem to play back in Andrew's brain over and over. If this guy is as powerful as he says he is, then Andrew and Mark might be in trouble. As Andrew slowly came back to reality, he could hear his Art teacher calling his name.

"Andrew!" she called out and pointing to a painting on the projection screen, asked, "What is the name of this painting?"

Andrew stared at it long and hard. He wasn't sure what it was. It looked like a blurry jukebox with a disfigured guy standing next to it. Andrew took a guess.

"Jukebox by Lawrence," he answered.

"Correct," she replied.

Andrew gave a sigh of relief.

Hidishi got off the phone with Sgt. Gregs. According to the results, the blood from the scene matched Andrew's. Hidishi ordered Sgt. Gregs to send the remaining blood to a special lab, while he waited for the DNA results to come in. Seconds later, there was a knock upon the door.

"Enter," said Hidishi.

The door opened, revealing a guy in a suit.

"You wanted to see me Sir?" a guy in a suit asked.

"Gather your best men, I have a job for you," Hidishi said staring at the window.

"What is it?" he asked.

"You will know soon enough," Hidishi answered. "Now go!"

The guy left the room, closing the door behind him.

"Time to test a theory," Hidishi said evilly.

School ended with a loud ring. Waves of teenagers flooded the hallways and quickly flowed out into the streets. On their way out, Mark and Andrew saw Emily and Josh talking by the front gate. Emily quickly approached them.

"I can't believe Josh," she said with a displeased tone. "He has the nerve to ask me about my sex life."

Mark and Andrew both raised their eyebrows.

"I wasn't trying to be nosy," Josh replied with a laugh. "I just read something from a magazine and wanted her opinion on it."

"Still, you don't ask women about that," said Andrew. "Hime isn't that kind of woman to kiss and tell."

"You're right, Andrew," replied Emily. "What I do with my boyfriend is none of your business."

"But you don't do *anything* with him," said Josh. "You're still a vir-"

POW! Josh fell to his knees, clenching his stomach. Mark and Andrew both watched as Josh struggled to get up from Emily's powerful blow. For the first time, Andrew feared Emily.

"I'm sorry, Josh!" Emily exclaimed, with a flushed face. "I don't like it when people make fun of me about *that*."

Mark squatted next to Josh and poked his cheek several times.

Mark glared at Emily. "Great, I think you killed him…"

Lily and William were watching TV in the living room. As Lily went to the kitchen to get something to drink, the doorbell rang. Confused, William got up and answered the door. He turned the knob. SLAM! The stranger broke the door off its hinges, flinging William backwards. Four guys in suits entered the apartment and began destroying it.

"William, run!" Lily shouted.

William ran out the door as fast as he could, but one of the guys grabbed him. Squirming, the guy carried him off to the elevator.

"Let go of my son!" Lily exclaimed, hitting one of the guys with her fists.

SMACK! The guy backslapped Lily across the face. He grabbed her by the throat, slamming her against the wall. Blood ran down her mouth as she tried to get free.

"Stay down," he said as he punched her in the face.

Lily fell to the ground unconscious. A note was left on the wall, saying:

If you ever want to see your bro again, come to the warehouse on Library Ave. Come alone or else.

Hidishi's gang

Mark's kitchen was filled with laughter and lip smacking as the boys ate. Mark was giving Andrew the highlights on his date with Tracy.

"So, you tried to take her to *Fire & Ice* for a little dancing," Andrew said repeating Mark's statement. "Then what happened?"

"I took her to *Gardenia* to get something to eat," Mark answered rubbing his stomach. "I can still taste the chicken scampi."

"Then what?"

"This is the good part. After *Gardenia*, I took Tracy over to the construction site where they're building that new *Sears*. You know, the one in Yonkers."

"I know, but how is that romantic?"

"You can get a better view of the stars! Dawg, you really suck at dating." Andrew huffed at Mark.

"Anyway, there we were, sitting on the hood of my car staring at the stars. Tracy and I began to talk about the different constellations. Suddenly, Tracy stares into my eyes and smiles. I smile back. Without thinking, I lean forward and lock lips with her. I'm telling you, Dawg, it was the greatest kiss in my life."

"It's the only kiss you ever got in your life.

"Very funny," replied Mark shoving Andrew a little.

Andrew looked at his watch and realized how late it was getting.

"I better go," Andrew said walking towards the door. "I'll see ya later."

The night air brought an ominous feel to Andrew senses as he walked home. Trusting his instincts, Andrew ran towards home at top speed. He leaped from roof-to-roof, until he was near his apartment complex. Minutes later, Andrew arrived home. He was awestruck by the damage. Andrew saw Lily on the ground and immediately went to her aid. Her face was bruised and a little swollen on her left cheek. She also had a cut on her lips and a gash on her temple. Andrew held her in his arms as she started to come around.

"What happened?" Andrew asked franticly.

"They…took William," she answered in a low voice.

"Who are they?"

"I don't know. A group of guys dressed in suits."

Andrew gnashed his teeth. They were going to pay. Suddenly, Andrew noticed the note on the wall. He read it with tight fists.

"I'm going to get William," he said.

"I don't want to lose you too," she said, almost crying.

Andrew squatted next to her with a smile. "I'll come back safe: I promise."

He helped Lily to the couch in the living room and even got her a cold, damp wash cloth to help wipe her bruised face and reduce the swelling. Once Lily was situated, Andrew ran out the door. Andrew ran back to

Mark's house with determination in his eyes. He knocked violently. Mark opened the door with a scared look. Relief and anger came upon him when he saw Andrew standing at his doorstep. Before Mark could utter a word, Andrew told him what happened. Mark eyes widened. He really wanted to help Andrew. He began to move upstairs. Quickly, Andrew grabbed Mark's shoulder, telling him to watch over Lily.

Mark refused. "If anything goes wrong, I got your back."

"All right, but you have to be inconspicuous," Andrew said with a sigh.

Library Ave. was located on the south side of Baychester Ave. The wind blew fiercely as they slowly approached the abandoned-looking warehouse. Andrew told Mark to hide near the warehouse while he went inside.

Andrew walked up to the door and knocked. One of the guys looked through the peephole with a glare. He opened the door. Andrew walked inside the dark room. He could barely see his hands in front of his face. Suddenly, a light illuminated a portion of the room. Underneath the blinding light was William, who was tied to a chair, and the leader of the group.

"Welcome," said the leader, "I see you got our message. Let's get down to business. My boss wants you gone. I will spare the boy's life in exchange for yours."

"Sure, why not," Andrew replied with a smirk.

The leader untied William, telling him to walk to the middle of the room.

"Now, walk over here," the leader called out to Andrew.

Andrew followed his direction, walking next to William. Suddenly, the sounds of guns being drawn filled the air. The lights went up. Andrew looked around and realized they were surrounded with guns aimed at them.

"Did you think we would spare the kid's life?" the leader asked Andrew.

"Well, the thought crossed my mind," Andrew said sarcastically.

"End of the line, Kid. Now, you die!"

"Well let me change into something more comfortable," Andrew said smiling. "ŌKAMI!!!"

Suddenly, the same light energy illuminated the warehouse. Mark realized it was time for him to join the party. The light faded. Everyone was frightened. Even William couldn't believe his eyes.

"Who…are…you?" he managed to say with terrified eyes.

"It's me, Andrew," Andrew growled. "I'll explain later. Right now, I must get you out of here."

Immediately, Andrew attacked the nearest guy. His fist met the guy's face. With one punch, the guy went flying. A hailstorm of bullets came towards Andrew. Andrew froze. He dodged at the last moment, leaping and side stepping in a rhythmic dance. While Andrew distracted them, William escaped, running to a nearby bush.

Suddenly, glass shattered everywhere. Everyone stopped and saw Mark (in his were-panther form) rise from the ground. He smirked as glass continued to fall around him.

"Nice entrance," Andrew said.

"A brotha gotta make his entrance in style," replied Mark.

The remaining guys continued to fire at them. Mark quickly waved his hand to the side. Instantly, they were covered by a shadowy wall. The wall absorbed the bullets, suspending them in mid-air. Andrew was amazed to see that Mark could control his powers so quickly. Silence filled the air, followed by rapid clicks. Mark and Andrew both knew the guys were out of ammo. Mark quickly lowered the shadowy wall. Andrew jumped into the air.

"STRIKING CLAW!!!" he shouted with his hand raised in the air.

Andrew's hand turned bright yellow. He waved his glowing hand sideways. Five boomerang-shaped energy waves came crashing down on the guys, flinging them everywhere as the waves exploded. The remaining guys he hit were unconscious and bruised badly. The battle was over.

"That was fun," Mark said sarcastically.

"We must find William and tell him everything," said Andrew.

Surprisingly, William was in the bushes with his head between his legs. Mark and Andrew quickly de-transformed.

William looked up at them. "How the hell did you do that?"

"It's a long story," replied Mark. "You might want to sit down."

Andrew explained everything to William. He told him about the tattoos on their backs, Madam Renee, their incredible fighting abilities, and of course, their transformations.

"Andrew is a werewolf?" William asked with his eyes wide open. "I knew you were weird, but this takes the cake."

Mark just stood there and laughed.

"Oh, like you're normal!" Andrew shot back.

SEVEN

"**W**HAT!!!" Hidishi yelled. "You let those kids beat you!"

"I'm sorry, Sir," the guy replied trembling, "but they were too strong for us."

"TOO STRONG?!!!" Hidishi yelled. "I'LL SHOW YOU STRONG!!"

Hidishi extended his hand. The guy's eyes widened as he felt a sharp pain. Blood oozed from both sides of the guy's body. Hidishi removed his hand. The guy dropped to his knees, falling face first. Hidishi wiped the blood off his hands, asking his secretary to send in a cleanup crew. Just then, someone knocked on the door.

"Enter," said Hidishi.

It was his secretary, carrying a manila folder in her hand. She was tall, pretty, and didn't take anyone's bullshit. She wore professional business attire and kept her brown hair in a bun.

"Sir, here's the DNA results you wanted from Sgt. Gregs," his secretary replied.

She made her way to Hidishi's desk and placed the manila folder on it. Then, she took a few steps back. Hidishi took the manila folder and carefully read the contents. A smile spread across his face.

"Also, your reinforcements have arrived," his secretary said.

"Excellent and in good time," Hidishi said. "Send them in."

"Right away Sir," she said as she closed the door behind her.

A few minutes later, five guys dressed in black jumpsuits stood in front of Hidishi. A huge smile spread over his face as he looked at them.

"You guys must be the best of the best?" he asked.

"YES SIR!" they shouted in unison.

"Excellent," Hidishi said grinning evilly.

Clattering sounds filled the back alley. From an outside perspective, one female was surrounded by five brawly men. But from the inside, it was a bad idea.

This young girl had all the right curves in all the right places. Her mocha complexion made her look a little Hispanic. She had dark brown shoulder length hair and dark brown eyes. She wore blue jeans shorts and a baby blue tank top with a yin-yang symbol on the front.

She dashed forward and hit the nearest guy in the face with her knee. Blood squirted out from his broken nose as his body let gravity carry him to the ground. Pissed, another guy stepped up with a jab. She dodged and countered with a left hook. He clenched his stomach as he fell to his knees.

"Hmph, barely a warm-up," she said.

The remaining three stared at her, each with a pulsating vein on their forehead. They teamed up and quickly charged towards her. She leaped forward, stepping on one of their faces. The extra boost flew her into the air. She could see over the rooftops, feeling she could grasp the moon in her hands.

"KICUNE!!!" the young girl shouted.

Suddenly, light began to swirl around her as she plummeted back to Earth. The light crashed into the ground and quickly dispersed, revealing someone different.

The young girl's transformation was like, damn! Her body was covered in golden yellow fur with white fur around her chest and abdomen. She stood in a tiptoe position and had a bushy yellow tail with a white tip. Her nose and mouth had extended out and her ears had moved to the top of her head. She had green eyes, a small black nose and razor-sharp claws. Even her clothes made her furry body look fine.

The three guys froze in terror. She grinned as she leaped into the air, crossing her arms over her chest.

"NEEDLE STORM!!!" she shouted.

Instantly, a shower of needle-shaped energy came crashing down onto the guys. They dodged but couldn't keep up with the fast pace. The needles hit their marks. Tiny explosions filled the back alley as the guys flew in different directions.

"So, are you guys ready to talk?" she asked, towering over their bruised bodies.

Rosa and Tracy were at *Macy's* shopping for the Spring Dance. Although Rosa and Tracy were classmates, they never spoke to each other in Gym class. It was after Tracy's first date with Mark that they got to know each other and quickly became friends.

"This blouse will go nicely with this skirt," said Rosa picking out a red long-sleeve blouse from the rack.

"What do you think of this outfit?" asked Tracy holding khaki pants and a black tank top.

"Girl, it's cute, but you need something better."

Rosa showed Tracy a black skirt with a blue off-the-shoulder blouse.

"I think Mark will like that better," Tracy replied with a smile.

Silence filled the air. Then, Tracy asked Rosa a question.

"Hey, why did you choose Andrew as your date?"

"I told you before: the other guys in our school are jerks."

"Maybe, but is that the real reason?"

Rosa averted her eyes and didn't answer.

The young girl arrived home to find her mother sitting on the couch in her robe. She looked at her mother and quickly averted her eyes. She could feel a lecture rising from her mother's throat.

"Where were you? It's already eleven and way past your curfew."

"Mom, I…"

"Don't 'Mom me', Shanta Shepherd! I know you've been going out and fighting those thugs. Just 'cause you got some strange powers doesn't make you a superhero."

Mrs. Shepherd looked like an older version of Shanta. She was the same height as Shanta and had the same mocha complexion. Even the dark brown eyes, semi-wide nose, and shoulder-length black hair were the same.

"You expect me to hide my powers and never use them?" Shanta asked angrily. "You were there when Madam Renee gave them me."

Mrs. Shepherd began to recall the event in her mind…

It was a cold winter night ten years ago. The snow had fallen the night before and the city sweepers hadn't made their rounds yet. On their way towards the grocery store, Mrs. Shepherd noticed a figure slowly approaching them. It was Madam Renee, but she was walking instead of sitting in her chair. Shanta, who was holding Mrs. Shepherd's hand, couldn't stop staring at Madam Renee. It almost felt like meeting a celebrity for the first time. Madam Renee stopped and stared back at Shanta through her dark shades. Mrs. Shepherd stepped in front of Shanta, glaring at Madam Renee.

"I mean you no harm, Mrs. Shepherd," Madam Renee said with a smile.

"How…do you know me?" Mrs. Shepherd asked with an astonished look.

"Your child is one of the chosen few to save this world," Madam Renee answered. I know it is hard to believe, but it is the truth. A dark force is slowly approaching. There is no time to waste."

Quickly, Madam Renee pulled out a deck of cards from her pocket. She shuffled the deck. She slowly pulled out a card from the deck and revealed it to Mrs. Shepherd. It was a picture of a fox. Confused, Mrs. Shepherd took the card from Madam Renee's hand.

"Please, give the card to Shanta," Madam Renee insisted.

Mrs. Shepherd did what she was told. Shanta held the card in her tiny hands. Instantly, a swirl of light surrounded her. Mrs. Shepherd stepped back, shielding her eyes from the intense light. Cries of pain rang in Mrs. Shepherd's ears as she heard Shanta screaming. Try as she might, she couldn't progress further to save her daughter. The light faded. Mrs. Shepherd ran towards Shanta, who was lying on the ground face first. She held her in her arms. Shanta's eyes fluttered and opened. Mrs. Shepherd embraced Shanta tightly.

Even after all that, I still can't get over the tattoo, Mrs. Shepherd thought as she slowly came back to reality. "Just be careful, okay? You know I hate worrying."

"I know, Mom," replied Shanta and kissed her mother on the forehead.

Three days came and went. Soon, the School Dance was only five hours away. Andrew waited anxiously for the bell to ring for the two o'clock dismissal in his Algebra class. He looked at Rosa for a moment and then back at the clock. The bell rang loudly as everyone scrambled out of the seats. As Andrew placed some of his books into his locker, he couldn't help but think about Rosa.

She is pretty, but will she enjoy dancing with me?

Andrew knew he acted differently around her, like he didn't want to be bothered by her. But Andrew just didn't know how to tell her how he felt.

"Yo, Drew, you ready for tonight?" a voice called out to him.

It was Josh with a huge grin. They bumped fists.

"Kinda," Andrew replied shyly.

"Aren't you going with Rosa?"

"Yeah…"

"Dude, you are so crush'n on her, right?"

"S-Shut up, man!"

"Dude, it's cool. I think Rosa's a sexy chick too. You should totally hit that."

"Josh, stop saying childish things," another voice called out.

It was Emily. "Andrew, I think it's cute that you like Rosa. You should tell her how you feel."

"But…I…" Andrew started.

"Just let it come out natural," Emily replied with a smile. "I'm sure she likes you too."

"I hope so…" Andrew said with a sigh.

Andrew got home, placing his backpack down on the bed. He quickly took a shower. Andrew wiped away the steam from the mirror, staring into it. He really wondered if Rosa really saw him more than a friend. He sighed as he put on a yellow-collared shirt with blue horizontal stripes, blue jeans, and his new Tims he bought last week. Andrew walked to the kitchen to get something to eat. The smell enticed his nose as Lily had already made dinner for everyone.

"Thanks," Andrew said with a smile, "It looks great."

Lily smiled back. "Eat up before it gets cold."

William came into the dining room wearing a blue-collared shirt with gray horizontal stripes, blue jeans, and blue and yellow *Reeboks*. He even combed his raggedy brown hair.

"You look tight, Will," Andrew said before he ate another bite of his food.

"You too, Drew," William replied. He moved closer towards Andrew. "So, I heard you're taking Rosa to the dance."

"You are? That's great Drew!" replied Mike walking into the kitchen. "You and Rosa make a cute couple."

Andrew stopped chewing and ignored Mike's last comment. With a mouthful of food, he said to William, "Yeah…so?"

"Oh, nothing," William answered. "I just wanted to know if it was true. Oh yeah, you might want to hurry up since you're picking her up, right?"

Andrew looked at his watch: he had ten minutes before he picked Rosa up. Andrew rushed to the bathroom and quickly brushed his teeth. He put some cologne on his neck. He took one last look at himself in the mirror. With enough satisfaction, Andrew jogged towards the door. He kissed Lily goodbye and ran outside the door.

Andrew arrived at the Sanchez apartment with two minutes to spare.

The Sanchez's tenth floor apartment is like the Roberts' apartment: small yet comfortable. Andrew didn't know if they redecorated since the last time he came over, which was around age ten. He mostly remembered the living room. It was the same size as his, but it had beige carpeting. Ms. Sanchez always kept her rosaries in her oak cabinet, which was on the left side of the room. The TV and couch were on the right side and were tilted a little. The bathrooms were always clean while Rosa's room was always dirty.

Andrew rang the doorbell and waited for someone to open the door. A few seconds later, Ms. Sanchez opened the door.

Ms. Sanchez looked like an older version of Rosa. She was the same height as Lily and was a little plump. She had brown shoulder-length hair and hazel eyes.

"Rosa will be out shortly," she said sweetly. "Please, come in, Andrew."

Andrew stepped inside. It was the way he remembered it. Minutes later, Rosa walked out of her room.

"Aren't we sexy tonight," Ms. Sanchez said in a slick tone.

Man, Rosa looked hot. Rosa wore a red long-sleeved blouse showing her belly button and some cleavage, a blue jeans skirt that made her butt look bigger, and her blue shoes. She even wore red lipstick to match her outfit. Not only that, but her hair was up in a bun which made her hazel eyes glow a little more.

"You look hot," Andrew said bashfully.

"You don't think it's too much?" she asked, not listening to him.

"Oh no," he answered with a flushed face. "It's just perfect."

As they walked to the gym entrance, Rosa held Andrew's arm. His face turned bright red. Once inside, they stood there in awe looking at the decorated gym.

It was awesome. Streamers and balloons hung everywhere. Over in the left corner was the DJ playing the hottest hits. In the middle of the gym was a huge disco globe that glistened all over the place. Even the colored spotlights added a nice touch to the décor. The gym was crowded with people, even though most of them were sitting down talking. When the music got crunk, everyone got up and danced.

Andrew quickly found Mark and Tracy on the dance floor. Boy, were they having fun. They were bumping and grinding to all the hits. He even saw Josh trying to impress this cute girl with his moves. To his surprise, Josh managed to get the girl to dance with him longer. Emily, who wore a pink halter dress with a white cardigan, waved to Andrew and Rosa. They waved back and stared at the dance floor. Andrew looked at Rosa, asking her if she wanted to dance. She nodded, leading Andrew to the dance floor. As Andrew danced with Rosa, he realized he wasn't half-bad.

"You're getting better," she said to Andrew as they continued to dance.

"Thanks," Andrew said trying not to lose his concentration.

As the night went on, Rosa and Andrew danced to almost every song the DJ dished out. Even William joined in, dancing with a girl in his class. The place was jumping! But when the DJ said it was time to find that special someone for a slow song, Andrew immediately freaked.

"I uh…I uh…" he managed to say.

"What's wrong?" Rosa teased. "You're not afraid to dance a slow song with me?"

"Me…noooo," Andrew answered trying to act cool.

"Good, now I want you to lead," she said smiling.

Andrew gulped. "Sure."

He placed his hands on her hips. She wrapped her arms around his neck. Andrew began to feel flush. Rosa rested her head on his shoulder, turning Andrew's face into a tomato. As the music played, Andrew led the way. Suddenly, he felt calm. Andrew wrapped his arms around Rosa's hips and let his body get closer to hers. Her face grew hot. Andrew wasn't sure where he got the courage to do this, but he liked every minute of it.

Meanwhile, in a black sedan, the five guys in jumpsuits waited for the right moment to strike. One of the guys looked at his watch.

He nodded. "Let's make this fast."

As the song continued to play, Rosa and Andrew looked into each other's eyes. Andrew smiled.

"What?" she asked in a sweet voice.

"You're so beautiful," Andrew answered. "And I can't take my eyes off of you."

Rosa's face turned red. *Why am I so nervous? Is Tracy right: do I really…?* She gave Andrew a warm smile. Andrew smiled back. Soon, they both slowly leaned their heads forward, and closed their eyes. Andrew couldn't believe he was going to kiss Rosa. BAM! The gym doors flew open revealing the five guys in jumpsuits. Rosa held Andrew tightly as the guys walked closer to the dance floor.

From the looks of these guys, they were elite. Mark and Andrew knew Hidishi sent these goons to stop them. The only problem was how were they going to transform without everyone knowing?

"We're looking for two high-schoolers who can meta-morph," the leader said. "Have you seen them?"

Nobody answered. Nobody had a clue what they were talking about. Tracy and William both glanced at Mark and Andrew.

"I'll ask again nicely," he said angrily. "Where are they?"

"Dude, what the hell are you talking about?" Josh asked, looking confused. "And what's meta-morph? Is that some code word for selling drugs?"

The leader sighed. "Look, have you seen them or not?"

Josh shook his head. The leader looked around. Everyone was shaking their heads.

"I guess they haven't seen them," the leader said, shrugging his shoulders. He looked at his team. "We can't have any witnesses. Torch the place, Flameboy."

A short skinny kid with black spiky hair, a long face and dark brown eyes stepped forward from the group and instantly lit his hands on fire. He raised his fiery hands towards the ceiling and began firing flames. Everyone ran for safety, screaming at the top of their lungs. Soon, Mark, Tracy, Rosa, William, and Andrew were the only ones left.

"That was easy," said Flameboy as he extinguished the flames surrounding his hands.

"William, take the girls to safety," Andrew said still focusing his eyes on the group.

"On it," replied William.

"Are you crazy!" Rosa exclaimed, still holding onto Andrew. "You can't fight them."

"Don't worry about me," said Andrew, looking back at her. "I can take care of myself."

"You better go too," replied Mark looking at Tracy.

Both William and Tracy quickly grabbed Rosa.

"Come on Rosa, let the boys handle it," said Tracy. "I know they can take care of themselves."

Rosa looked at William. William nodded, agreeing with Tracy. Once William, Rosa and Tracy left the gym, Mark and Andrew were ready for business.

"Who the hell are you guys?" Andrew asked.

"We are the Meta-Morphic Five," the leader said.

"Well, at least their name is original," said Mark sarcastically.

"I'm Big C," the leader said. He introduced the rest of the gang by size. "Next to me is Rampage, Gyro, Sparks and you already met Flameboy, the youngest of the group."

Big C was as tall as Shaq and was very muscular. He had brown hair with bangs that hung over his ice blue eyes. His long face made him look older even though he was a teenager.

Rampage was the heaviest one in the group. Even though he was made of muscle instead of fat, he still looked like a giant ball of blubber. He was bald, had a round face and brown eyes.

Gyro was a weird guy. He had long blue hair that covered his brown eyes and smiled, in a psychotic way.

Sparks was the quiet one. He had white spiky hair and a small face. His eye color was a mystery since he had very narrow eyes.

"The name's Mark and this is Drew," replied Mark. "AKA Pansā"

"And Ōkami," Andrew filled in.

Andrew and Mark quickly meta-morphed. With their claws ready, they waited for the Meta-Morphic Five to strike. To their surprise, the Meta-Morphic Five just stared at them.

"Haven't you seen a were-panther and a werewolf before?" asked Mark.

"We were expecting a challenge," answered Big C. "You guys are weaklings compared to us."

"Say what!" Andrew exclaimed.

"You wanna start something?" Mark asked, raising his claws. "We can take you on."

"I don't think so," replied Big C. "You wouldn't last five minutes with us."

"We'll see," Andrew said sounding confident.

"Sparks, I want you to fight these punks," Big C ordered.

Sparks stepped forward. Electricity surged around him. He looked at Mark and Andrew and grinned evilly.

"Give up or face my wrath," he said.

"We'll wait for you outside," replied Big C as he and the others left the gym.

"C'mon Mark, let's show him what we can do," Andrew said dashing towards Sparks.

William, Rosa, and Tracy were hiding in the Home Economics classroom. They had the door locked and kept their heads down.

"What the hell just happened?" Rosa whispered. "And why are you guys so confident in Drew and Mark?"

"Well…uh…" William began.

"I just am," Tracy replied. "You should always have faith in your man."

Rosa's face became flushed. "Drew's not my man!"

"You sure?" William asked. "From what I saw, you two were about to…"

Rosa quickly covered William's mouth, as she glared at him. William began to panic.

"Say anything else about it, and I'll kill you myself," Rosa said in an almost demonic voice.

William nodded frantically, with beads of sweat running down his face.

Andrew threw the first punch. Sparks vanished. They couldn't find him. Mark turned around and saw Sparks leaning against a wall.

"You're doing it all wrong," he said grinning, "Let me show you how it's done!"

He opened his narrow eyes, revealing his colorless eyes. Instantly, Sparks was behind Mark and Andrew. BAM! They both felt a hard blow to their backs. Their bodies became weightless, gliding across the gym floor. They both somersaulted to regain balance. They dashed forward.

Mark began the assault with several punches. Andrew came in with some kicks. To their surprise, Sparks blocked all their attacks. BAM! SMACK! Mark and Andrew skidded on the ground and crashed into a wall. They both got up slowly, gnashing their teeth. This time, Andrew led the attack. He tried slashing Sparks, but Andrew couldn't touch him. Sparks' movements were so fast, it was like Andrew was fighting light. SMACK! Sparks kicked Andrew in his chin, making him fly into the air. With no time to react, Andrew felt a hard blow to his back. He came crashing down. The gym floor cracked, and a cloud of debris rose into the air. The debris settled with Andrew face first on the floor.

"SHADOW FANG!!!" Mark shouted as the worm-like shadow rose into the air.

Sparks stretched out his hand and blocked the attack, splitting the shadow into five smaller shadows. The ceiling turned into Swiss cheese. With the same hand, Sparks fired a jolt of electricity at Mark. Mark cried in pain as his body began to feel numb. Soon, his body couldn't take much more. Mark fell to his knees and de-transformed, falling face first onto the gym floor. Sparks laughed hysterically. His laughter woke Andrew. With blurry eyes, Andrew could make out Mark's body. He clenched his fists tightly and gnashed his teeth. Anger overwhelmed him. He stood up, placing all his weight onto his left leg.

"You bastard!" Andrew shouted. "Try this on for size! STRIKING CLAW!!!"

Andrew jumped to the air with his glowing claw, outstretched towards him. Sparks immediately reacted with a jolt of electricity. The jolt hit Andrew, but his glowing claw kept pressing on. It was like his body wanted him to go through Sparks' attack despite the pain he was in. All Andrew knew, he wanted to get Sparks for hurting Mark.

What! Sparks thought. *I can't lose to a runt like him!*

Sparks added more electricity to his attack. It pushed Andrew farther away from him. With Spark's added power, Andrew's body couldn't keep up with this struggle. Andrew cried in pain as Sparks' attack surged through his body. Andrew crashed into the ground hard cracking the gym floor. He slowly got up trying to keep his eyes focused on Sparks. Electricity discharged from his numb body, as his body grew tired. Andrew de-transformed, collapsing to the ground face first. Sparks walked over to Andrew and towered over him.

"What does the boss see in you?" Sparks asked the unconscious Andrew while making a face.

Sparks left the gym and headed for the main entrance. As he passed the Home Economics classroom, Sparks heard a loud gasp. He peered inside and saw a foot sticking out from behind one of the stations.

"What do we have here?" Sparks asked himself.

He raised his hand and blasted the door down. William, Rosa and Tracy shrieked in terror as Sparks entered the classroom. They quickly split up, trying to reach the classroom door. Sparks looked at them evilly, knocking the girls out with a small jolt of electricity. William, on the other hand, made it out of the classroom. Sparks grabbed them by their waist and began hovering towards the main entrance.

Back on the gym floor, Andrew tried to get up. Soon, William met up with Andrew. He was out of breath.

"Drew…that guy…took Rosa and Tracy away…!" William cried out, in between breaths.

Andrew was stunned. Despite all their efforts, they couldn't save the ones they loved. Out of anger, Andrew slammed his fist into the ground.

EIGHT

On a nearby rooftop, Shanta watched the black sedan drive away from the school. Quickly, she transformed and followed. Leaping from roof to roof was nothing for her as she stealthily tailed the sedan. Suddenly, a nearby neon sign began shining brightly. Shanta shielded her eyes from the intense light. The light faded. Shanta looked down at the street. No sign of the sedan.

Shanta smirked. *They sensed my presence, from this distance. Looks like I'm up against some strong people…*

"Head to my place ASAP," Madam Renee said.

"What for?" Shanta asked.

"Now's the time to meet the other members," Madam Renee answered. *"You all must train in order to beat the true enemy."*

Shanta nodded as she headed for the Fortune House.

Mark woke up to the sound of Andrew's voice. He sat up and looked around the gym. Even William was there.

"What happened?" Mark asked. He looked at William. "Where's Tracy and Rosa?"

William hung his head low.

"They…got captured…" Andrew answered in a low voice.

Mark was pissed. "Aw, hell na!"

Andrew clenched his fists tightly. "If only we were stronger…"

"I can help you with that," a familiar voice said.

"It's the old lady who gave us our powers," replied Mark.

"Watch your mouth!" Madam Renee exclaimed angrily. She calmed down. *"You need training. Those men you fought are four times stronger than you two. You boys need to train, using the Inter-Dimensional Gateway."*

"What the hell is that?" Andrew asked.

"You'll know soon enough," she answered.

Her voice vanished. Mark and Andrew stared at the ceiling for a moment before they looked at each other. William cleared his throat.

"Who were you two talking to?" he asked with a raised eyebrow.

"The lady that gave us our powers," Mark answered. "Anyway, you should go home where it's safe."

"Mark's right," Andrew chimed in. "From here on out, this matter involves only Mark and I."

William didn't like the sound of that. However, he understood the situation and trusted both Andrew and Mark.

"Just be careful," William said before leaving the gym.

Moments later, Mark realized where they were heading.

"Great, just what I need, to go back to her little pet shop of horrors," Mark said sarcastically.

Andrew chuckled and said sarcastically, "Do you want me to hold your hand?"

"I ain't scared, a'ight," Mark replied.

"C'mon fierce warrior, let's go the Fortune House," Andrew said helping Mark up from off the floor.

The Meta-Morphic Five drove up to Hidishi's hideout with both Rosa and Tracy gagged and blindfolded. The security guard let the guys in. He quickly phoned Hidishi of their arrival.

"Excellent," Hidishi said with a grin.

Hidishi put down the phone and waited for them to walk in his office. A few minutes later, the door opened. The Meta-Morphic Five formed a straight line in front of Hidishi.

"We have defeated those kids, Sir," Big C said. "And we brought you guests."

"Well, this is great news," Hidishi said smiling.

"Uh, what should we do with them?" Big C asked.

"Lock them up for now," he answered. He looked at Rosa and Tracy with an evil grin saying, "I have big plans for them."

Mark and Andrew arrived at the Fortune House. They walked in, looking like two bums begging for money. Their clothes were torn, their bodies ached, and they were tired. Madam Renee gave Mark and Andrew new clothes: like the ones they had on and fed them food. As they ate, Madam Renee explained to them what the Inter-dimensional Gateway was and why they had to use it.

"So, we're going to another planet to train?" Andrew asked, trying to understand all of this. "What, are we in some kind of Anime cliché?" Mark asked sarcastically.

"I don't understand your question, Mark," Madam Renee answered. "But know you will train there for three months."

"THREE MONTHS!" Mark shouted. "We don't have that much time to train. By then, Rosa and Tracy would be dead!"

"Three months in their time is equivalent to nine days in ours," Madam Renee explained, calmly. "You will have plenty of time to rescue the girls."

"Where is this place?" Andrew asked.

"On the planet Macu, thirty light years away from Earth," she answered. "The planet is divided into five huge regions. You will stay with the Nebtans in the central region of the continent, known as the Forest Region. They are a strong, friendly race that live like the Ancient Japanese. Even their language is exactly like the Japanese, except for their dialect. A good way to view their dialect is a New Yorker speaking Japanese. They can teach you how to master your powers. Also, I have taught them many of our Earth customs. You might be surprised to see what they have learned."

"What about our parents?" Mark asked. "They're going to know we're gone."

"Not to worry, I have already taken care of it," Madam Renee answered. "Even William has helped out on the matter."

"Hope so," he said folding his arms.

"When do we leave?" Andrew asked.

"In four hours," she answered. "Get some rest, you guys need it."

Madam Renee led them upstairs to her spare rooms, in a huge attic. Mark and Andrew picked a room, jumped into the bed, and drifted off to sleep. Four hours later, Madam Renee woke them up. She quickly prepared the gateway. The gateway was a huge stony circle with zodiac symbols that hung a few inches above the ground. Madam Renee had to place a small ramp in front of the gateway, for Mark and Andrew to walk through it. As they came downstairs into the basement, they saw another person standing next to her. Mark's eyes widened as he realized who it was.

"I can't believe she's here," Mark said smiling.

"Who is it?" Andrew asked.

"Shanta, my cousin," he replied.

"Sup, Cuz!" Shanta exclaimed as she hugged Mark.

She looked at Andrew asking, "Who's this guy?"

"Oh, that's Andrew, my homie. You can call him Drew."

"So, I heard you can meta-morph too. And here I thought I was the only one in our family who could."

Mark and Andrew's mouths dropped.

"You…can meta-morph too?" Andrew asked.

"Yeah, I meta-morph into Kicune, the Japanese fox," she answered.

"Does Aunty and Uncle know?" asked Mark.

"Just my mom," Shanta answered. "Mom was there when I received it, but she doesn't like it, even to this day. Although, she told my dad that the tattoo on my thigh was a birthmark."

"So that's why you always wore shorts to the pool or the beach!" Mark replied, with a surprised look. "And here I thought…"

"Enough with the chitchat, you guys have work to do," Madam Renee interrupted, staring at the open gateway.

"She's right, we have to train hard in order to defeat those guys," Andrew said.

"Then let's kick some ass!" Mark shouted as he walked through the gateway.

"Wait up yo!" Andrew exclaimed following behind.

"I'll take care of them," Shanta said to Madam Renee before walking through the gateway.

"We have to get out here," Rosa said staring at a small window in a large room.

"Don't worry," replied Tracy, "Andrew and Mark will save us. I know it."

Rosa smiled a little as she stared at the floor. She thought about Andrew for a moment and how she nearly kissed him. Her face grew hot. Rosa couldn't believe she was falling in love with Andrew, the guy who used to take baths with her and always needed her protection when they were kids. She stared at the crescent moon from the small window for a moment.

Please be safe.

Mark, Shanta and Andrew arrived on planet Macu within seconds. They stood there in awe looking at their surroundings. This was a beautiful planet. It was like the rainforest on Earth, but lusher. There were unknown animals of different sizes, colors and species. The water was crystal clear and was filled with sea life. Even the fruits here looked different.

"So where do we start?" Andrew asked, looking for a clear path.

"Over there," Shanta answered pointing to a path going into a forest.

As they walked through the dense forest, red eyes popped everywhere. Even though they were scared, they kept their faces composed. Suddenly, a huge creature jumped in front of them.

It was a creature that was part reptile and part human. It had a Komodo Dragon's head, green scales, bulging muscles and a tail with spikes at the end of it.

"What the hell is that?" Andrew asked with his eyes wide open.

"I don't know, and I don't want to find out," Mark answered with his eyes wide open.

Shanta shook her head. "Boys…guess I'll get rid of it."

White light illuminated the forest. Even the creature had to shield his eyes. The light faded. Both Mark and Andrew's mouths dropped. It was their first-time seeing Shanta in her were-fox form. Shanta jumped into the air. She crossed her arms over her chest as she smirked.

"NEEDLE STORM!!!" she shouted as she stretched out her arms.

A hailstorm of white energy came crashing down onto the creature. A smoke cloud filled the air. Shanta landed onto the ground thinking the creature was destroyed. The smoke cleared, but the creature was still standing. The creature opened his mouth and lashed out his tongue at Shanta. Shanta dodged and attacked. Mark and Andrew knew she was in trouble. They both transformed, giving her a helping hand.

"STRIKING CLAW!!!" Andrew shouted.

"SHADOW FANG!!!" Mark shouted.

Both of their attacks knocked the creature backwards. They bumped fists. The creature got up, lashing out his tongue at them. They all dodged, watching as a tree turned into dust.

"We have to cut that tongue," replied Shanta.

"How?" Andrew asked.

"Someone has to be a decoy while the other two cut the tongue," she answered.

"You ain't getting me to do it," replied Mark. "You know my people don't mess with animals in the wild."

Andrew raised his eyebrow. "You are so pathetic…"

Andrew sighed as he dashed towards the creature. He punched it in the face. The creature stepped backwards. It used its spiky tail to smack Andrew into a tree. The creature opened its mouth, lashing out its tongue at Andrew. Andrew shut his eyes. SLASH! The sound of sliced tongue filled Andrew's ears. The creature screamed in pain. Andrew opened his eyes, staring at the decapitated tongue.

"Hey Drew, wanna finish the job?" asked Shanta.

"Oh yeah!" Andrew exclaimed as he rose to his feet.

He dashed forward to the wounded creature with his glowing claw.

"STRIKING CLAW!!!" Andrew shouted as he thrust his claw through its body.

Blood squirted everywhere. Andrew pulled his claw out of the creature's body, watching the creature fall to the ground. Andrew flicked the blood off his claw before he de-transformed. He walked over to them.

"That was tight Drew," Mark said, bumping fists with Andrew.

"I agree, but we have to find the Nebtans," replied Shanta.

Suddenly, a small giggle echoed in the trees. They looked around trying to pinpoint the sound. Out of the trees, came a small boy wearing a dark blue sleeveless garment. He had a small face with huge eyes, a small nose and an innocent smile. His black hair was in a ponytail with small bangs that covered his forehead.

"Aw, he's so cute," replied Shanta waving at him.

"Yeah, but what's up with the spots on his cheeks and arms?" asked Mark pointed out. "He trying to be a cheetah or something?"

The small boy ran towards Mark, hugging his leg.

"Aw, he likes you," Andrew said sarcastically.

"I see…" Mark mumbled.

"Maybe he can help us find the other Nebtans," Andrew replied looking at the small boy.

The small boy spoke to them in Japanese. Andrew didn't know what he was saying, but the small boy kept on pointing towards the path.

"I think he wants us to follow him down the path," Andrew said looking at both Mark and Shanta.

The small boy grabbed Mark's hand, signaling him to follow.

"Lead the way, Kid," Mark said.

As they walked down the path, the forest started to clear. Rays of sunshine poked through the dense trees. They exited the forest. Their mouths dropped in awe.

"This place is beautiful," replied Shanta with a smile.

Standing in front of them was a huge stony temple with an area of about 80,000 acres. Suddenly, a crowd of Nebtans surrounded them. Some stared at them while others talked amongst themselves.

"Welcome friends," a voice said from the crowds, stepping forward.

"Wow! He's hot!" exclaimed Shanta with her eyes wide open.

"Down Girl…" Mark said trying to act cool.

"My name is Ching, I'm King of the Forest Region," he replied. "Welcome to my kingdom."

"Say what!" Andrew exclaimed.

Ching was a handsome young man, around the same age as our heroes. He was an inch taller than Andrew and was toned. He had short black hair with small bangs, a long face, dark brown eyes and a smile that seemed to twinkle whenever he smiled. Ching wore a black garment like what Ancient Japanese Buddhist priest used to wear. His crown was thin and circular, with a large red diamond in the center.

"I know I'm young, but I'm the only male in my family to take the throne," he said.

"You know why we're here, right?" Andrew asked.

"Yes, Madam Renee told me everything," said Ching. "We will help you in every way we can."

He smiled. Instantly, his mouth twinkled.

"Is his mouth supposed to do that?" Mark whispered to Andrew.

"I don't know," Andrew answered shrugging his shoulders.

"Thank you for your kindness," Shanta said holding Ching's hand. "Let me know how I can repay you."

Mark grabbed Shanta's ear and pulled her away. Ching stood there, baffled.

"You'll have to excuse them," Andrew said feeling embarrassed.

Ching led them into the temple, where the Nebtans lived. Many of Ching's servant-girls, who were wearing short-sleeve kimonos, smiled at Mark and Andrew. They giggled amongst themselves. Of course, Mark enjoyed the attention.

"Yo Drew, these cheetah girls love us man," he said grabbing Andrew's shoulder.

"Don't you have a girl?" Andrew shot back. "Remember her?"

"I do remember Tracy," Mark replied with a sigh. He looked at Andrew and grinned. "What, are you afraid of losing Rosa to a girl from another planet?"

Andrew face felt flushed. "Rosa and I are just friends…"

Mark gave Andrew a look that said he was lying.

"These are the guest rooms, you are welcome to choose any room you would like to stay in," Ching said. "My servants will call you for lunch in thirty minutes."

Ching left. Mark and Andrew chose the rooms next to each other while Shanta chose the room across from them.

The rooms were amazing. Every bed was made from oak trees and draped in silk cloth. The floors were made of black marble. There was a closet in the upper right-hand corner filled with garments of different colors. Over the bed was a huge tapestry of a dragon. The walls were made of stone with a small window on the left side of the bed.

Andrew went into the closet and pulled out a blue garment from off the rack. He noticed a drawer at the bottom of the closet. He pulled it open and found several pairs of moccasins. Andrew changed his clothes and put his "Earth" clothes into the closet. Suddenly, a knock came upon the door. Andrew opened the door. One of the servant-girls was standing before him. She signaled him to follow her to the dining hall. She kept on looking back at Andrew, smiling and giggling as they walked. This girl was hot, but Andrew couldn't stop thinking about Rosa.

They arrived at the dining hall. Both Mark and Shanta were already eating.

"What took you?" Mark asked and ate a piece of meat.

"I was just admiring my room," Andrew answered as he sat down next to him.

Another servant-girl came out of the kitchen and brought Andrew his food. Even though Andrew didn't recognize anything on his plate, the food smelled good. He grabbed his fork and knife and dug in. His eyes widened as the taste reminded him of steak and chicken. Andrew wolfed down his food since he hadn't eaten for nearly half the day.

"The food was delicious," Andrew said rubbing his stomach.

"I'm glad you like it," replied Ching.

"Uh Ching, I got a question," said Mark.

"What is it?"

"Why do the children and servant-girls have spots on their cheeks and arms?"

"With our race, every child, boy or girl, is born with spots all over them. The spots symbolize our connection with animals and how we are one in the same. Unlike your planet, we do not see ourselves as superior beings. We treat everything with respect and equality. I believe you call it Animism."

"So, what happened to your spots?" asked Shanta.

"My spots vanished when I turned sixteen," he answered. "Males lose their spots around the age of sixteen while females keep theirs. Their spots change from black to blue at age fourteen. When that happens, the males must find a bride. Many of the women here have changed their spot color, but not one I like."

"Why?"

"I don't want to marry someone that I don't love or understand."

Shanta smirked.

After lunch, Ching showed them around the temple. There are so many rooms within the temple even Ching didn't know what some of the rooms were. What caught Andrew's attention was the courtyard. It was about the size of three football fields. There were trees planted everywhere and the grass was lush and green. The courtyard reminded Andrew of Central Park, only it was cleaner and had no muggers.

As Ching continued the tour, Andrew noticed two young girls, one was wearing a purple kimono and the other was wearing a light blue kimono. They were walking towards the courtyard. Ching ran towards them. Minutes later, he brought them over to Mark, Shanta and Andrew.

"These are my sisters, Hibika and Aiya," he said introducing them.

Hibika was the older of the two sisters, being younger to Ching by a year. Even though Andrew had just met her, her aura reminded him of Rosa. She was the same height as Andrew, had long black hair, dark brown eyes and wore a purple kimono.

Aiya was the younger sister. Even though she was sixteen, she looked like she was in middle school. Aiya was two inches shorter than Andrew, had long black hair in pigtails, and dark brown eyes. Of course, Aiya was wearing a light blue kimono.

"My name is Andrew," Andrew replied introducing himself, "and this is Mark and next to him is Shanta."

"It is nice to meet you all," Hibika said in a sweet voice.

"Would you like to join us with our tour around the temple?" asked Mark.

"I'd love to," she answered sweetly.

"Ching, did you show them the garden yet?" Aiya asked in a babyish voice.

"Not yet," Ching answered. "We're heading over there now."

"You're going to love our garden," Aiya replied to them.

Mark, Shanta and Andrew were amazed at the size of the garden. The garden was in a dome-shaped greenhouse behind the courtyard. Most of the men worked here in order to keep the temple's food supply in stock. Inside, were trees filled with fruits, various plants, and strange vegetables. One Macuan tree was filled with blue-green swirled fruit that tasted like apples. Of course, Mark was interested in the Macuan vegetables, particularly the orange lettuce.

"As you can see some of our fruits and vegetables taste like yours," replied Ching picking up a Nebtan fruit. He looked at Shanta. "Would you like to try it?"

"I'd love to," answered Shanta taking the fruit from Ching's hand gently. Shanta bit into the fruit and began to blush.

"This is the best fruit I've ever tasted," she said with her hand on her cheek.

Ching smiled. Another twinkle came out of his mouth.

"Wish my mouth could do that," Mark whispered to Andrew.

The tour concluded with dinner. Once again, Andrew didn't recognize anything on his plate. Hungry, he wolfed it down and asked for seconds.

Even Hibika was amazed. Mark, on the other hand, tried to eat his food but felt a pair of eyes staring at him. He looked through his periphery, noticing Ayia silently gawking at him. Nervous, he managed to finish his plate. Of course, Shanta continued to talk to Ching, asking him about Macu and his people.

"If you go by Earth's time, we are ten years older than we appear," Ching explained. "We Nebtans age very slowly."

Shanta was intrigued. "Is it because of your DNA or something else?"

"Both actually. Our DNA makes us age slowly by about seven years. But according to our Nebtan scientists, the fruits and vegetables we consume also have an anti-aging compound in them, slowing our aging by another three years."

"So, if my friends and I continue to consume your food, would we also slow down our aging?"

Ching rubbed his chin. "I'm not sure. But I guess it's worth experimenting."

Shanta grinned with delight. Yup, dinner time was lively.

That night, Andrew decided to take a bath. According to Ching, there was a hot spring for everyone in the temple (and a private hot spring in the temple for Ching, Hibika, and Aiya). Andrew walked down the hall, holding a towel, a washcloth and soap bar in his hands. For five minutes, he searched aimlessly for the hot spring, passing the public hot spring several times. Finally, Andrew found it located near the dining room, on the east side of the temple. There was a large door with the words *For The Royal Family*, written in Japanese. Andrew looked at the door, before walking in. The changing room was very large. Andrew quickly took off his clothes and placed the towel around him. He stepped out of the changing room and into the enclosed hot spring.

The hot spring stood in the center with tiled floor surrounding it. Just above him was a very high glass ceiling and the stony walls added a nice touch. There was even a stone divider, separating the hot spring. The place seemed empty. Andrew approached the steamy water.

Suddenly, the water began to bubble. Andrew stopped to examine the bubbles. With a splash, Hibika rose out of the water. Her voluptuous body exposed every blue spot she had to him. Andrew's eyes widened and his nose bled.

"Oh…my…God…" Andrew managed to say.

Hibika screamed as she covered herself in the water. "Get out, you pervert!"

"I didn't mean…" Andrew started but was hit in the forehead with Hibika's soap bar.

Andrew fell backwards, crashing to the ground with a huge red lump on his forehead. Hibika clapped her hands, calling for the servant-girls. They came and immediately carried Andrew, who was still dazed, back into his room.

A shadowy figure sneaked down the hall and had picked the lock in Mark's room. They got into Mark's bed with Mark sleeping in it. Mark turned over, holding the person in his arms with a smile on his face.

The next morning, Andrew woke up in his bed with a headache.

"That girl can throw," he said rubbing his bruised forehead.

Andrew got out of bed. He went to Mark's room. Andrew rapped on the door. The door slowly opened with each rap.

That's odd, thought Andrew as he looked around the room.

Mark slowly woke up. He was shirtless. He saw Andrew standing by the door.

"How'd you get in here, Drew?" he asked rubbing his eyes.

"The door was unlocked," answered Andrew.

"That's impossible," replied Mark placing his right hand on the other side of the bed. "I know I…"

Mark gently tapped the bed with his right hand. He felt a body. Mark jumped up, holding onto the chandelier. It was clear to Andrew that Mark slept only in his underwear. Andrew pulled the covers off the bed. Andrew freaked when he saw Aiya sleeping in Mark's bed. At least her nightgown was still on.

"I didn't do nothing," replied Mark, who was still hanging onto the chandelier. "I don't do kiddie love, yo!"

Suddenly, Aiya woke up as her left nightgown strap fell off her shoulder. "Good morning, Andrew. Where's my lover?"

Andrew pointed to the ceiling.

"How the hell did you get in my room?" Mark asked.

"I picked the lock," she answered with a smile. "Nothing can come between us."

"Dude, she's got a major crush on you," replied Andrew. He started to crack up.

"Not funny, Drew," said Mark.

Suddenly, Hibika entered the room. "Aiya! What are you doing in here?"

"I wanted to stay with my lover," answered Aiya.

"Why do you want to stay with him?" Hibika asked, pointing at Andrew.

"Not him," replied Aiya. She quickly pointed at Mark. "Him. Mark is the sexiest guy I've seen in my life, and I want to marry him."

"This is what I get for being sexy," Mark said sarcastically.

"Aiya, Mark is an Earthling who probably has a lover on Earth," replied Hibika. "You can't marry him."

"So, what!" Aiya shot back. "It is destiny that brought us together. You can't defy destiny. If you will excuse me, I'm going to take a bath."

Aiya winked at Mark and headed for the hot spring.

"That child has some serious issues," replied Mark.

"Poor Mark," said Shanta, who came out of her room, "can't even handle a little crush."

"Shut up Shanta!" Mark exclaimed.

The chandelier hinges came apart and he crashed onto his bed.

After breakfast, Ching told Shanta, Mark and Andrew that today began their training, and they would be trained under Master Dao. Ching said he would teach them Animism. Learning it would take months, but they were ready for the challenge.

NINE

Ching walked Mark, Shanta and Andrew to the training area. It was a huge area, about the size of a large university. Inside, were many rooms: half of it was classrooms while the other half was the training ground. Some of the men were inside the classrooms teaching the kids Math, Science, English and Art. Ching pointed Mark, Shanta and Andrew to the training ground, where they met Master Dao.

"This is where you will be training for the next three months," said Ching. "I wish you guys the best."

They stared at Master Dao for a moment. Master Dao was a short man, only reaching to Mark's hips. He walked with his hands behind his back and had narrow eyes. Master Dao had a bald head, gray eyebrows, and a wide nose.

"Good morning," he said in a calm voice. "Before we begin, I want you to put on these clothes."

Three pairs of training clothes were piled on top of a box next to him. Mark stepped forward and grabbed the first pair. Next came Shanta and finally was Andrew. Master Dao pointed to a changing room on his left side. A few minutes later, they came out of the changing room wearing their training clothes. They wore blue sweatpants, a V-neck sleeveless shirt with a picture of a dragon on the back, a white karate belt, a pair of blue wristbands, and dark blue moccasins with white socks.

"Anyone up for searching for some Dragon balls?" Mark asked sarcastically.

"Now the training will begin," said Master Dao. "Your first task is to fight me in your human forms."

"Say what!" Andrew exclaimed.

"This task will show me where each of you stand," Master Dao said.

"Alright Gramps, it's time to give you an ass beating, Bronx style," replied Mark cracking his knuckles.

"Whenever you're ready," Master Dao said.

Mark, Shanta and Andrew dashed towards Master Dao in unison. With their fists ready to strike, Master Dao just stood there. Andrew broke from the group, somersaulting into the air. He leg-dropped Master Dao. Andrew's eyes widened as he saw Master Dao block Andrew's leg with his index finger. Suddenly, Mark jumped into the air with his hands clasped over his head. Master Dao smiled as he vanished before Mark could strike. Mark looked around the training area but couldn't locate him. SMACK! Master Dao elbowed Mark in the face. The blow knocked Mark sideways. Mark skidded on the ground, crashing into a wall. Debris kicked up into the air and quickly settled. Irritated, Shanta kicked Master Dao. She missed. BAM! Master Dao punched Shanta in her stomach. Shanta clenched her stomach, falling to her knees. Andrew dashed towards Master Dao and began throwing punches at him. Master Dao dodged every punch. He quickly countered. SMACK! Andrew became weightless. Master Dao had uppercut Andrew into the air. Master Dao vanished, quickly reappearing above him. Andrew felt his stomach cave in from Master Dao's attack. Andrew crashed into the ground hard, cracking the ground a little. Andrew watched Master Dao land onto the ground on one foot.

"Looks like we have a long way to go," he said. "Training will resume in two hours."

Mark and Shanta slowly got up and went to help Andrew. They walked back to their rooms, bruised and achy. They tried to get as much rest as they could but couldn't close their eyes. Even Ching and the others didn't know how to help. Two hours flew by quickly. They got back to the training grounds.

"From what I've seen, you guys have the power, but lack control," Master Dao said as he paced back and forth. "I will teach you how to control your powers, as well as increase your strength and speed. I'm not an easy teacher. But if you trust in yourself and work hard, you will achieve greater power. Here, this is going to be your daily schedule."

He handed each of them a list with their task and chores. Mark's eyes widened when he realized he had to wake up at dawn.

"For your next task, I want you to meditate for three hours," Master Dao said. "This will keep your mind focused and heighten your other senses."

"Man, this stinks!" Mark whined.

"I know, but we have to do it in order to get stronger," Andrew said looking up into the sky.

"You guys sound like quitters," replied Shanta sitting on the ground in an Indian-style position.

"I ain't quitting," replied Mark, sitting in an Indian-style position.

Andrew sat down in an Indian-style position, in between Mark and Shanta, and closed his eyes. For three hours, Andrew focused his mind on getting stronger. He even thought about Rosa and how she was doing. He knew this training was going to be intense, but he was willing to try anything to get stronger in order to protect her. Andrew had a feeling Mark was thinking about protecting Tracy.

"Time's up," said Master Dao coming out from one of the rooms.

They opened their eyes and looked at Master Dao. But Mark noticed someone standing next to him.

"Hey, it's the same kid we saw when we first came here," he said.

"This boy is my grandson," Master Dao said. "His name is Rei-Rei."

"I didn't know Nebtans had ghetto names like us," Mark whispered to Andrew.

Rei-Rei ran towards Mark and hugged him. Mark smiled as he patted his small head.

"He can't speak your language Mark, but I'll be happy to translate for you," replied Master Dao.

"Ask him how he's doing," said Mark.

Master Dao asked Rei-Rei in their native tongue. Rei-Rei answered quickly. Master Dao translated.

"He said he is okay and what about you," Master Dao replied.

Mark gave Rei-Rei a thumbs up. Rei-Rei smiled, giving Mark a thumbs up. Then, he turned his head to Master Dao. He asked Master Dao a question. Master Dao smiled before he looked at Mark.

"Rei-Rei wants to know if you would like to take him to the courtyard," he replied.

"Sure," answered Mark. "But what about…?"

"Training will resume in two hours," Master Dao said. "Have fun."

Rei-Rei raised both his arms towards Mark. Mark lifted him up and carried him on his shoulders. Both Shanta and Andrew watched as Mark and Rei-Rei headed for the courtyard.

"Mark has really changed," replied Shanta. "I've never seen him act this way."

"Mark always had a good heart, he just hid it from everyone," Andrew said.

"Rei-Rei looks so happy with Mark," she said.

"Indeed, he is," said Master Dao. "Ever since his parents died, I've been the one to take care of him. He was a very lonely boy. He had neither siblings nor any friends. Mark would be the only friend he has ever had."

"At least Mark will know what it feels like to have a younger brother," Shanta said with a smile.

"And I know Mark will take good care of Rei-Rei," Andrew added.

At the courtyard, Mark was teaching Rei-Rei how to fight. At first, Mark had trouble communicating with Rei-Rei, but eventually he knew what to do.

"This is a punch," said Mark showing how to do it.

Rei-Rei followed. Soon he was punching like Mark. Mark raised his hands, signaling Rei-Rei to punch his hands. Rei-Rei understood and began punching Mark's hands. Suddenly, a familiar person walked up to Mark.

"Hi Aiya," Mark muttered.

"Hello, my lover," Aiya said sweetly. She looked at Rei-Rei. "Hey Rei-Rei, how are you today?"

Rei-Rei ran towards Mark and held him tight. Rei-Rei covered his face in Mark's leg.

Aiya sighed. "After all this time, he still doesn't like me. Well, I must go. I'll see you later, my lover."

Aiya left. Mark gave a huge sigh of relief.

"It's okay: the monster is gone now," Mark said to Rei-Rei. "Now let's continue punching."

High in a treetop stood a creature wearing a black chest-plate. He watched the people in the temple with his keen eyes. Suddenly, he spotted Hibika and Aiya sitting near a pond talking. An evil grin spread over his face. He signaled another creature to tell the boss what he spotted.

Mark, Shanta and Andrew resumed their training. This time, Master Dao wanted them to gather and release energy by focusing their minds and bodies. They spent hours trying to gather energy. By the time they gathered any energy it was already nightfall.

"Now that you know the routine, I want to see you guys here every day at dawn for the next twelve weeks," replied Master Dao. "Have a goodnight."

Later that night, Shanta sat in her bed thinking.

It's funny…here I am on another planet training to save the world from a guy I don't even know. Why did I come here and why did Madam Renee choose me to save the Earth?

She sighed. *I remember when I first meta-morphed. It was on a summer night in 2005. I remember walking home from my friend's house when I saw two guys in suits beating up Nick, a guy I had a huge crush on. At first, I was scared to face those guys, but I knew I had to do something, or Nick would've been killed. So, I meta-morphed. I felt strong and powerful. After I kicked some butt, I de-transformed in front of Nick. Bad move. I could see it in his eyes: he was afraid of me. He ran away and left me alone. I vowed never to use my powers in front of people I like again. I mean, what's the point of having powers when you can't find anyone to tell them too? I just wish there was someone out there who understood me…*

Shanta walked down the hallway to get a glass of water. As she made her way to the stairs, she saw Ching sitting by the window looking at the three moons.

He seems depressed. I wonder what's bugging him.

Shanta walked over to Ching.

"Hey Ching," she said and sat next to him. "Is something wrong?"

Ching looked into Shanta's eyes and back at the moons. "It's nothing."

"C'mon, you can tell me," Shanta said, gently pressing his hand.

Ching felt a little embarrassed. He cleared his throat. "I think I've found my bride."

Shanta looked surprised. "Really?"

Ching felt bashful. "Yes, I have…"

Shanta smiled. "See, I knew you'd find her. So, who is this mystery person? Is it one of the servant-girls…or is it someone else?"

Ching gazed into Shanta's dark brown eyes and replied, "It is you, Shanta."

Shanta's face turned bright red. "M-Me?! But…"

"Say you will be my bride," he said looking into her eyes.

"Whoa! Slow down," she replied. "I hardly know you. How can you be sure that I'm the one?"

"When I first met you, I knew you were different from the other girls," Ching answered. "You always spoke your mind and you're not afraid of other people's opinions. Many of the girls here only see me for my status and wealth. But you…you saw me as a person. Not only that, but you're strong, independent and caring. Maybe that's why…"

"I too understand how you feel," Shanta replied, feeling bashful. "I used to think that no guy would ever love me because of my powers, because he could never understand it. To find someone who understands and means it…"

Ching placed his hand on her cheek. Shanta's face became flushed. He gazed into her dark brown eyes and smiled. Ching leaned forward, ready to kiss her.

Shanta backed away. "This isn't right. You can't just kiss someone like that. On Earth, we keep lasting relationships by taking things slow. Let's start off as friends first, okay?"

"So, just friends?"

"For now: I want to get to know you better and you should get to know me better."

"I understand," Ching replied with a smile. "I shall take my leave. Goodnight, Shanta."

He left. Shanta gnashed her teeth in disappointment.

Damn me and my upbringing!

Mark was having a hard time getting away from Aiya.

"Leave me alone!" shouted Mark as he ran down the hallway.

"But Marky-poo, we were destined to be together," Aiya said chasing after him. "You can't fight fate!"

"Oh yeah! Watch me!" he replied turning a corner.

Mark kept on running down the hallway until he realized he had reached a dead end. He could see Aiya's shadow from around the corner Mark only had a few seconds to find a hiding place.

"Now I got you!" exclaimed Aiya looking down the dead-end hallway.

Mark was nowhere to be found.

Aiya was perplexed. "Huh? Where did you go, my lover?"

She looked around checking every possible hiding place. No such luck. Aiya sighed heavily and went back to Mark's room. As soon as it was safe, a camouflaged Mark reappeared and jumped down from the ceiling.

"That was close," he replied wiping his forehead.

Andrew got lost yet again. To him, this temple was a gigantic maze. He tried to retrace his footsteps, but soon found himself in the courtyard. The night breeze teased the trees, knocking some leaves off. The serene scene eased Andrew's heart as the leaves blew across the air like a swarm of fireflies. Suddenly, Andrew heard footsteps. He turned around to find Hibika approaching him. She was in a light pink kimono-style nightgown with wooden sandals. Andrew's heart skipped a beat at the sight of her beauty.

"What are you doing here?" she asked, glaring at him.

"I…got lost…" he answered, feeling ashamed.

"I don't buy it. You knew I was coming here and tried to get another peek at my body."

"As if! Look, what happened the other night was an accident."

Suddenly, Hibika threw her sandals at Andrew. Andrew dodged them but couldn't dodge a powerful blow to his stomach. He tumbled backwards before regaining his balance.

"What's…your deal?" Andrew asked, slowly standing up while clenching his stomach.

"I do not tolerate perverts," Hibika said boldly. "That includes you!"

"I'm not a pervert and I'm not going to fight you!" Andrew cried out.

Hibika didn't listen. She dashed towards Andrew and attacked him with punches and kicks. Andrew dodged as much as he could but was soon overwhelmed by Hibika's power. Andrew skidded across the ground. He struggled to get up. Hibika cracked her knuckles as she slowly approached Andrew.

"Give up, pervert," she said with a smug look. "You cannot defeat me, at the level you're at!"

That pissed Andrew off. He was getting sick and tired of being called pervert, despite acknowledging his mistake. He wanted to shut Hibika up so that he could get back to his room. Andrew got on all fours. Instantly, his arms and legs transformed into werewolf arms and legs and his eyes turned yellow. Hibika's body froze, sensing Andrew's powerful aura.

Andrew dashed towards Hibika, giving Hibika no time to react. Andrew extended his arm out to her but stopped inches from her face. Hibika stared into Andrew's yellow eyes. Fear took over her, as her heart raced and sweat rolled down her cheeks. Suddenly, Andrew's eyes rolled back, and he collapsed onto the ground. Hibika stared at the unconscious Andrew as his arms and legs returned to normal. She let out a huge sigh of relief as she fell to her knees.

Andrew woke up, finding himself in his room. He quickly sat up and looked at his window. He could see that the moons were still out. He gave a huge sigh of relief. Then, he looked towards the door and noticed Hibika resting her head on the side of his bed. Immediately, Andrew freaked out, falling out of his bed. That loud thud woke Hibika up.

"Oh, you're awake," Hibika said, rubbing her eyes.

Andrew quickly got up. "What the hell happened? How'd I end up here?"

"I carried you here," she said, as she headed for the door. "You're surprisingly light for a man."

Andrew's face turned bright red. Hibika opened the door and let herself out. But before she closed the door, she gave Andrew a warm look. It was like her opinion of Andrew started to change. Andrew stood there with a perplexed look.

As dawn approached, Mark, Shanta and Andrew got ready for their daily training. They arrived at the training area before Master Dao came out of his room. Mark and Shanta stretched their muscles and did a few warm-ups. Andrew, on the other hand, could barely do his stretches.

"Yo Drew, what gives?" Mark asked, noticing the bags underneath Andrew's eyes.

"Sorry, I didn't get much sleep," Andrew answered with a yawn.

"What did you do last night?" Shanta asked curiously.

Andrew sighed heavily. "I…sort of sparred with Hibika…

Mark's eyes widened. "You what?! How'd that go down?"

Finally, Master Dao opened his door, walking out to the training area.

"Are you guys ready to train?" he asked looking at them.

"Yes Master," they said in unison.

"Good, then let's begin," Master Dao said with a smile. "Three laps around the temple!"

Mark's mouth dropped.

"C'mon Cuz, you can do it," Shanta said as she slapped his back.

Minutes later, their legs started to feel numb and sweat dripped down their backs. Even Mark was having trouble finishing his laps. Shanta, on the other hand, seemed to be enjoying the training.

After an hour break, they began their meditation. This time, the meditation seemed easier. Andrew could almost feel his body rise into the air (mostly due to him sleeping). Even Mark was able to focus his mind.

"Excellent work," Master Dao said. "Get something to eat and we'll resume our training."

As they walked to the dining room, they saw Ching standing by Shanta's room. Shanta smiled as she ran towards him.

"Hey," she said as she hugged Ching.

Both Mark and Andrew raised an eyebrow.

"Are you free right now?" Ching asked. "I'm in the mood for a walk."

"Yeah, I'm free," Shanta said. She turned to Mark and Andrew. "You guys go on without me. I'm going to hang with Ching."

"Uh, okay…" Andrew said and walked off.

"I'm watch'n you, Cuz," Mark replied, giving Shanta an evil glare.

Both Mark and Andrew arrived in the dining room. They sat down, stretching out their legs. Instantly, Ching's servant-girls came over to them and served them.

Their mouths watered as they gazed upon the food. There were eggs, both scrambled and sunny side up. The roast Dehas (Macuan pork) were wrapped in a sweet honey glaze. There were roast Giras (Macuan chicken) hot from the oven and fresh Veyas (Macuan fish) from the sea. Of course, who could forget some of the Macuan vegetables, fresh from the greenhouse.

Both Mark and Andrew wolfed down their food, leaving not a single piece of food on the table.

"I'm stuffed," Andrew said rubbing his stomach.

"Me too dawg," Mark said also rubbing his stomach. Then, he gave Andrew a serious look. "Hey, do you think Shanta and Ching are going out?"

"Nah," Andrew answered. "It's way too soon. We've been here only three days."

"You're right," replied Mark. "But seriously, you think Ching got the hots for my Cuz?"

They both looked at each other for a moment.

"Naaah!" they said unison. They laughed.

Just then, Shanta ran into the dining room with a wide grin spread over her face. Mark and Andrew looked at her strangely, wondering why she was so happy.

"Check out the ice Ching gave me," she said showing them the huge diamond ring.

"DAMN!" Mark and Andrew both said in unison.

"Ching and I are going to get married after our training," replied Shanta with her hands on her cheeks. "I can't believe I'm getting married to a king!"

"Hold up!" Mark interjected. "Cuz, you don't know him. Haven't you heard of *taking it slow*?"

"Think about it," replied Shanta. "We're here for three months. That's plenty of time to take things slow. Besides, we are just friends."

"Huh?" Andrew asked. "How are you just friends when you are engaged?"

"Technically, we aren't engaged," Shanta clarified. "This ring is a real wedding ring. They don't do engagements here. See, after the training, Ching and I are going to get married. So, during our training, we'll slowly move from friends to boyfriend and girlfriend. Now, do you understand?"

Mark and Andrew both looked at each other and then at Shanta.

"Aren't you guys happy for me?" she asked still smiling.

They nodded with a surprised look on their faces. They couldn't formulate any more words.

"Well, I'm going to Ching's room to get a head start on our wedding plans," Shanta said as she walked off. "See you guys at the training area."

A few seconds later, Mark and Andrew looked at each other with the same surprised look.

"Well, I guess that answers my question," replied Mark.

"Uh-huh," Andrew said slowly.

Andrew headed out to the courtyard, where he could take a moment to enjoy the scenery. When he got there, he saw Hibika sitting underneath a tree with at least thirty Nebtan children gathered around her. He walked over there to get a closer look.

"The first word for today is apple," Hibika said to the children. "Repeat after me, Ap-ple."

The children began to sound out the word apple. After a couple of tries, the Nebtan children were able to say apple.

"Very good," Hibika said smiling. "Next word is…"

She looked to her right and saw Andrew standing a few feet from her with a smile on his face.

"Would you like to join us?" she asked, looking at Andrew.

"Yeah, sure," he said, sitting next to a little Nebtan girl.

He watched as Hibika continued to teach the children Earth words. A half-hour later, Hibika gave the children time to play.

"How's training?" she asked Andrew.

"Hard, but effective," answered Andrew.

There was a moment of silence as they looked around. Suddenly, Hibika looked at Andrew with apologetic eyes.

"About last night…" she began. "I'm…sorry for calling you a pervert and forcing you to fight me."

Andrew was speechless.

"A-Aren't you going to say anything?" Hibika asked, feeling embarrassed.

"I accept your apology, only if you'll accept mine," Andrew answered. "I, too, am sorry for my mistake."

Hibika smiled and nodded. Andrew smiled back. He looked at all the Nebtan children, who were playing tag.

"You're good with children," Andrew said, looking at Hibika. "You should be a teacher."

Hibika sighed. "I wish I could. As princess of my people, I can't do common work in public."

Andrew made a face. "So what? If that's what you want to do, then you should do it. It shouldn't matter if you're the princess or not."

"But, I…"

"Look, my friends and I were chosen to save our world. The odds may be against us, but there is still a way to win and we're not going to give up. So, don't give up on your dream either."

It was at that moment Hibika saw Andrew in a different light. Hibika's face grew hot. Her heart throbbed a little as she averted her eyes.

"You're a strange one, Andrew," Hibika replied.

Suddenly, the Nebtan children wanted Andrew to play with them. Andrew stretched out his hand toward Hibika, asking if she wanted to join him. As Hibika gently grabbed Andrew's hand, the Nebtan children began to chant and giggle at the same time.

"What are they saying?" Andrew asked.

"Oh, nothing," answered Hibika, feeling flushed.

Mark, Shanta and Andrew trained hard. They were determined to get stronger and faster. Master Dao decided to upgrade the training the following week. He gave them each weighted moccasins, shirts and wrists-bands. Then, he told them to deliver three big boxes. One box contained forty gallons of milk, the other contained thirty pounds of meat and the last box contained fifty pounds of vegetables. Master Dao told them to deliver to his best friend, who lived beyond the forest every four days. And so, they did, for the next three weeks.

"I feel like a sumo wrestler," Mark complained.

"How do you think I feel?" Andrew said sarcastically.

"Let's just deliver these boxes," replied Shanta.

Walking through the forest became a hassle by the third week. Master Dao increased the weights, as well as the boxes. Mark and Andrew struggled to carry their boxes, since they both got the heavier ones. Shanta, on the other hand, had improved her stamina and was able to carry the heavy box a little better than them.

"Just another mile guys," she said pointing to a small house at the end of the forest.

They reached the end of the forest with only a few yards to go. Sweat dripped down their backs as they walked to the house. Mark set down his box onto the front porch before he knocked on the door. Seconds later, Phansu opened the door. He was the same size as Master Dao and was also bald. He had thin gray eyebrows and dark brown eyes.

"Hello young'ns," he said with a smile.

"Hey Phansu, where shall we put them this time?" asked Shanta.

"Over in the kitchen," Phansu said directing them.

They set the boxes down onto the kitchen floor. They wiped the sweat off their faces.

"Would you like a drink of water?" asked Phansu.

They nodded. "Yes please."

Phansu went into the kitchen for a moment and came back with a tray with three cold glasses of water. Mark, Shanta and Andrew each took a glass and gulped the water vigorously. They wiped their mouths as they set the glasses on the table.

"Thank you," replied Shanta.

"You're welcome," Phansu said, with a smile. "Oh, I have something for each of you. I'll be right back."

Phansu walked off into a room. They looked at each other wondering what it was. A few minutes later, he came back with a small black box with gold trimmings around it.

"These are for you," Phansu said and opened the box. "You guys are ready to move on to the next stage of your training."

Their eyes gazed upon the shiny objects. They were amazed by the craftsmanship.

"These Nebtan bracelets symbolize your animal spirits," Phansu said. "They can help increase your strength, speed and many other things not known to me or Master Dao."

It was a golden bracelet, about an inch in width. On the center of each of the bracelets, were the Japanese symbol for wolf, panther and fox. Each bracelet had a small gem underneath the symbol.

They picked up their respected animal bracelets and slipped them onto their right wrists. Suddenly, their bracelets began to glow and surround them in an aura of light.

"What's happening?" Andrew asked in a frightened voice.

"The bracelets are acknowledging you all," Phansu answered.

The light faded. Andrew stared at his bracelet for a moment. His gem seemed to glow with power as he continued to stare at it.

"These bracelets are awesome," replied Shanta. "Thank you."

"You're welcome, Child," Phansu said smiling.

"We better bounce," replied Mark. "Master Dao is waiting for us to return."

Mark, Shanta and Andrew waved good-bye to Phansu as they walked back to the temple. They arrived at the temple with about five hours of sunlight. They found Master Dao sitting down on the ground meditating. Master Dao opened his eyes as he got up.

"What took you?" he asked them.

"We were talking to Mr. Phansu," answered Shanta.

"And I see he has given you the bracelets," replied Master Dao.

"Yes," Andrew answered.

"What's that got to do with us?" asked Mark.

"Everything," answered Master Dao. "Those bracelets will help you with your next task. I must warn you: this task may take a day or so. So, you might want to get plenty of rest. I'll see you all back here tomorrow at dawn."

Andrew walked with Hibika across the courtyard that night. The sky was clear, and all three moons were full. Even the pinkish trees glowed brightly with the night sky. Andrew wished he had brought his phone with him. This would be something to show Lily and the others. However, his phone got singed from that battle with Sparks. Suddenly, tiny fireflies began appearing, twinkling like little stars. Hibika looked all around her and smiled. Andrew's face felt flushed. Hibika looked so beautiful tonight. Andrew's heart raced as he averted his eyes.

"What?" Hibika asked.

"It's nothing…" Andrew managed to say without looking at her.

Hibika looked away in disgust. "I bet you were thinking of something dirty."

"I'm not perverted."

"Then why does your face look flushed?"

"You…look beautiful tonight!"

Hibika's face turned bright red. "You…really think I'm beautiful?"

Andrew's face also turned bright red. "Yeah…"

"That's the first time a man has ever said that to me."

Hibika embraced Andrew tightly. Andrew felt her plump breasts press up against his chest. She gazed into his eyes with a sad look.

"Master Dao told Ching, Aiya, and I your next task. I'll miss you. Please come back safe."

Her words pierced his heart. That voice and look reminded him of who he wanted to protect.

"I will," he said with a smile.

Mark sat in the steamy water, staring at the ceiling. Thoughts of Tracy circled his mind as he slowly sank further into the water.

Please be safe, Tracy...

Suddenly, he felt something grab his leg. Mark sprang out of the water and landed on all fours on the tiled ground. The water bubbled before it made a huge splash. Mark's eyes widened as a naked Aiya sprang out from the water.

"Wh-What are you doing in here?!" exclaimed Mark, covering his package.

"I wanted to spend some time with you, my lover," she answered sweetly. "Won't you let me express my love to you, before you go on your task?"

"How'd you...?"

"Master Dao told me. Mark, I love you and I want you to know that before you go."

She approached closer. Mark stepped back with every step she took. Soon, his back was against the wall. Mark got an eyeful of Ayia's fully developed body. It was like her baby face was plastered on a woman's body. Ayia pressed her body against his. Mark squirmed as he tried to ignore his hormones.

"Aiya, you're too young to be doing things like this," he said, looking the other way. "On Earth, I could go to jail for being seen like this with you."

Aiya stopped and blinked a few times. "But…I'm much older than you."

"Have you seen yourself in a mirror? Your face looks like a middle-schooler!"

Aiya grinned seductively. "But not my body…"

Aiya continued to rub her body against Mark. Mark finally had enough.

"Look, Aiya," he replied, grabbing her shoulders. "Don't waste your time on me. I'm sure there's a guy out there for you. Besides, I'm already with someone. Do you understand?"

Ayia wasn't listening. She was too busy looking down.

"It's…really…big," she said with wide eyes. "Let me touch it!"

"No, don't…!" Mark exclaimed.

Soon, the bathroom was filled with cries of pleasure and terror.

Ching walked Shanta to her room. Ching listened as Shanta told him stories of her childhood. He was amazed by the wondrous adventures she experienced. They laughed and talked all the way to her door.

"May I come in?" Ching asked.

"Do you always have to ask?" Shanta asked. "You've been in my room several times now. You don't have to be so formal with me. Relax, Ching: I won't bite."

Ching blushed as he walked in. They both sat on her bed and continued talking. As the night progressed, their bodies grew weary. Soon, Shanta was yawning with every sentence.

"Time for bed," Ching said. "You've got a long day ahead of you."

"Did Master Dao tell you?" Shanta asked with a sad look. "Sorry for not telling you."

"It's okay. Come on, in you go."

Shanta hopped into the bed. Ching pulled the covers over her, tucking her in. She looked up at him with a smile. Gently, he kissed her forehead. Shanta's face turned red as she covered her face. Ching smiled, gently pulling the covers from her face. Shanta's eyes darted towards the wall before she looked back at him. He was still there, looking at her with his handsome smile.

"Goodnight, Shanta. Please come back safe."

"I will."

Ching faced the door, getting ready to leave. Without hesitation, Shanta grabbed his hand. Ching looked back. Shanta quickly sat up. She leaned forward and kissed him. Ching's eyes widened as the warm kiss surged through his body.

The next morning, they arrived at the training area. They couldn't wait for their next task. Of course, they still had to wait for Master Dao to show up.

"I'm so psyched for this!" exclaimed Andrew.

"Me too!" replied Shanta.

There was silence. They both looked at Mark, who was in a daze.

"What's wrong, Cuz?" Shanta asked, lightly shaking him.

"I...don't want to talk about it," Mark answered in a low tone.

"What, did Aiya attack you again?" Andrew asked sarcastically.

Mark's eyes widened and got into the fetal position, chanting, "I'm a good boy...I'm a good boy...I'm a good boy..."

"Oh my God, did you...?" Andrew began.

"Hell no, Dawg!" exclaimed Mark, springing out of his fetal hole. "We didn't do the do! She just…"

"Choked your chicken?" Shanta interjected. "Girl got skills to be able to get you this worked up."

"It's that baby face of hers!" cried Mark, recalling last night's event. "It hides what a real woman looks like. Even her kimono does too…"

"We'll…discuss it later," Andrew replied, noticing Master Dao approaching.

Master Dao greeted them.

"Good morning, students. I hope you got plenty of rest. For your next task…"

The suspense was killing Andrew. He just wished Master Dao could tell them now instead of pausing in the middle of his sentence.

"I want you to…clean the temple," he said smiling.

Mark, Andrew and Shanta quickly fell to the ground.

"What!" Mark exclaimed angrily as he sprang up from the ground. "I didn't wake up this morning to clean a temple!"

"I was just kidding," replied Master Dao trying to calm Mark. "Your real task is behind those three doors over there."

He pointed to three huge doors with their animal symbols on them.

"Once you pass those doors, there is no turning back," Master Dao said. "I wish you all luck."

"Well guys, let's do this," replied Mark.

Shanta and Andrew nodded. They went to their respective doors and turned the knob. They took one look back at Master Dao before they went inside. None of them were sure what they were getting themselves into, but they were prepared for anything.

TEN

"Where am I?" Shanta asked herself, looking at her surroundings.

"This place looks like a desert…Wait a minute…I'm in a desert?!"

The sun began to beat down on Shanta's body. Shanta walked through the desert without a sense of direction. Her mouth began to feel dry, and she began to feel weary. Suddenly, the ground began to move. Shanta could see a snake-like trail coming towards her.

"What now…?"

A giant desert worm sprang out of the sand with its huge fangs ready to devour her. The worm aimed for Shanta but missed. Immediately, Shanta transformed. She attacked it with her Needle Storm attack. Her attack bounced off the worm's body and exploded in the sand. Shanta's eyes widened, for she knew she couldn't beat it. With super speed, she ran away from the worm in the other direction. The worm roared, creating a tidal wave of sand. Despite Shanta's efforts, the wave caught her, carrying her away.

Mark wandered through a dense forest trying to find civilization. He searched for hours and hours, but no luck.

"I'm gonna get Master Dao for this!"

Suddenly, Mark heard a growl in the bushes. He quickly transformed. He looked all around him. Mark spotted a pair of glowing yellow eyes in the bushes in front of him.

"Come out!"

Instantly, a baby panda standing on its two legs walked out of the bushes. From the looks of it, it wasn't in a cuddly mood.

"Man, why do I get the weird ones?"

The panda snarled as it dashed towards Mark. Mark dodged and countered with his Shadow Fang attack. The blow knocked the panda backwards, crashing into a nearby tree. The tree collapsed, knocking several other trees down.

"Who da man!" exclaimed Mark smiling.

The baby panda lifted the broken tree and threw it at Mark. Mark jumped into the air, preparing for an aerial attack. The panda looked up and opened its tiny mouth. Suddenly, a small ball of energy began to snowball. Soon, a huge blast came out of the panda's mouth. Mark's eyes widened as the blast came towards him. BAM! The blast hit Mark directly in his chest. He plummeted into several trees.

Mark rubbed his bruised head. "I'm getting my ass beat by a baby panda...and it sounds like he wants to finish the job!"

Andrew opened his eyes. He sat up for a moment. He realized he was in an alley. He got up and decided to look around. Andrew found a homeless guy sleeping in a pile of trash with a newspaper over his face. Andrew crept over, staring at the front page of the newspaper.

Bronx Times?! But how did I get back? And where are Mark and Shanta?

Andrew walked out of the alley and couldn't believe his eyes. He was back home. He recognized the street he was on and knew how far he was from home. Suddenly, a cold chill went down Andrew's spine.

Andrew reached his apartment. He noticed that the time was five o'clock on the huge wall clock near the elevators. The elevator ride seemed like eternity. He pulled out his keys from his pocket and unlocked the door. Andrew walked in. He saw Lily and William watching TV.

"Hey guys," Andrew said.

"How was school today?" Lily asked him.

Andrew paused before he answered, "It was great."

"That's good. I left your dinner in the fridge. Oh, and Rosa called earlier. She wanted to talk to you about something."

The same chill came back.

"Sounds like love is in the air," replied William smiling.

Andrew's face slight turned red. "I'll go see her now."

He ran up the stairs to the tenth floor, heading for her apartment door. He rang the doorbell. A few seconds later, Rosa opened the door. Andrew stared at her for a moment.

"What, is there something on my face?" she asked, looking at Andrew confused.

"No," Andrew answered forcing a laugh while scratching the back of his head. "Uh, Lily told me you wanted to see me."

"Yeah, I did. Can we talk outside?"

"Sure."

Rosa put on her shoes. They both walked to the park. The park was quiet today. Usually, kids from the apartments would play around this time. Something seemed off. Rosa led Andrew to the swings and sat down. Andrew sat down next to her.

"What did you want to talk about?" Andrew asked swinging a little.

She looked at him. "About us."

"What about us?"

Rosa paused. She stared at the ground with a sad look on her face. Andrew got off the swing and squatted next to her.

"Tell me, please?" Andrew asked.

Back at the temple, Ching and Hibika were sparring with their katanas. The sounds of metal clashing filled the air, as they moved across the training grounds and lightning speed.

"You have to do better than that, Brother!" Hibika exclaimed with a downward slash.

Ching quickly blocked Hibika's attack but was soon overpowered by Hibika's strength. Ching flew backwards, but quickly regained his balance. He was breathing hard. Hibika walked towards Ching, sighing.

"How are you going to protect Shanta with those lame sword skills?" she asked.

Ching bashfully looked away. "You're right…"

Hibika smirked. Then, she pointed her katana at Ching. "Ready to continue?"

Shanta arose from the sand, coughing. She quickly got up and dusted herself off. Suddenly, she realized she was standing by the front gate of a domed city.

"At least I'll get a bath," said Shanta de-transforming.

As she walked past the front gate, Shanta was amazed by the structure. Even though this city was highly advanced, it kept a primitive way of life. The buildings were made of stone and the streets weren't paved at all. The civilians were dressed in garments like what the Israelites used to wear back in the Old Testament. To her surprise, the civilians rode in hover wagons and had television screens posted on the taller buildings. It was like the Old Testament meets the future.

Shanta walked up to one of the civilians and asked if there was a hotel anywhere in the city. The man pointed to a hotel two buildings down and told her to get some clothes, since she stuck out like a sore thumb. Shanta went to the nearest clothing shop and bought a blue garment to cover herself. She reached the hotel with a puzzled look. It was a hexagon shaped hotel with a rectangular smokestack.

"Are you lost?" someone asked with a smirk.

Two guys, one tall and the other short, wearing raggedy blue garments walked up to her.

Shanta gave them an innocent look. "I'm okay."

"We can get you a room here if you do us a favor," said the tall guy grinning.

"I'm not that kind of girl," replied Shanta as she kneed the tall guy into the stomach.

The tall guy clenched his stomach with his eyes wide open. He couldn't formulate a single word. The short guy attacked. BAM! Shanta kneed the short guy in the face, giving him a nosebleed. The tall guy got up and began throwing punches at her. Shanta dodged his attack. She countered. The tall guy fell to the floor with a loud thud. The short guy was in so much pain he could barely stand up. Suddenly, she heard clapping.

"You're stronger than you look," he said, looking at her with a smile.

Shanta turned around to see a handsome young man the same height as Mark staring at her. He had short black hair, brown eyes, and a long face. His green garment made his mocha complexion show more.

"Who are you?" Shanta asked.

"The name's Barzus," he answered. "I'm an imperial guard at the palace. I saw you fight that worm creature, and I must say you're not too shabby. We could use someone like you to help defend our city.

"Sorry, not interested in joining you. Besides, I despise people who see me as a tool and not a person. You don't know what it's like to be feared and misunderstood."

"Heh, suit yourself," Barzus replied. "But let me tell you something: in this city, the only person we fear is the King. No one has ever stood up to him and probably never will. The number of worms has increased in the last month and yet the King does nothing for his people. He'd rather kill us all than lift a finger to help. I ask you again, will you help us?"

Shanta pondered for a moment. She sighed. "Lead the way."

Everything in the city seemed to be a mixture of the past and the future, yet poverty remained the same. Shanta's heart ached as she looked into the eyes of the people. She could feel their fear and their sadness. Their homes were like run down apartments in Bronx and the smell of death filled the air. Shanta decided to take off the garment, since it was itching. She gave it to a poor mother with her two children. The mother smiled and thanked her while the children ran up and hugged Shanta.

Shanta looked at Barzus with a serious look. "Let's get one thing straight: I'm doing this for them, not you. Got it?"

Barzus smiled. "Yeah, I got it."

This is ridiculous, Mark thought while he was hiding in a bush. *A baby panda that can fire energy blasts is chasing me. I feel so embarrassed.*

Suddenly, the panda jumped out of nowhere and grabbed Mark. Mark struggled to get free from the panda's grip. He began punching the panda in the stomach. The panda loosened its grip. Mark used his Shadow Fang attack to knock the panda into a tree. With super speed, Mark ran away from the panda. When he felt it was safe to take a breather, Mark slowed down to lean against a tree. Mark looked up: the baby panda was clinging to the tree.

"Aw hell nah!" Mark exclaimed as he tried to run away.

Suddenly, an arm grabbed him and pulled him into the bushes. Mark looked around. He was in a small cave covered by dense vines and tall bushes. He stood quiet as he heard the baby panda pass by. Minutes later, there was silence. Mark let out a sigh of relief.

"I'm glad I got to you in time," a voice said. "Otherwise, you'd be dead."

"Who said that?" Mark asked in confusion.

Mark looked down and saw a small girl with long black hair and red eyes, wearing a torn blue slip. She smiled at him, leading him deep into the cave. There was a small fire already made.

"You live here all by yourself?" Mark asked. "Where are your parents?"

The girl stared at the fire with a sad look. "They're dead. I've been alone ever since that panda came into my village and destroyed everything. Now, he's after me, the sole survivor."

Mark patted her head. "I won't let him hurt you."

"But what can you do? You barely escaped death. Why sacrifice yourself for me?"

The girl began to sob. Mark held her close to him. His warmth eased her sobbing.

"All my life, I've been afraid to do the right thing," he said looking at her. "I've watched my best friend and my cousin grow stronger while I'm lagging. To me, I'm the weakest one of the group. But now, I have several reasons to keep fighting. By the way, what's your name?"

"Reina's my name. What yours?"

"Mark," Mark answered and smiled. "Go ahead and cry. I know you've been wanting to for a while now."

Reina gripped Mark's sleeves tightly and cried. Mark patted her small head as her cries echoed in the cave. Minutes later, Reina was fast asleep. Mark laid her down and headed toward the entrance, determined to end both his inward battle and his battle with the baby panda.

"I love you, Andrew," Rosa said looking at Andrew.

Andrew was speechless.

"My love for you is real, but this place isn't."

"What? You are real."

"No, I'm not. If I was, then your friends would be here too."

"Why am I here?"

"To unleash a power that is deep within you. I don't know much, but that's what this dimension was created for."

Rosa got up from the swing and began to walk off.

"Where are you going?" he asked following her.

"It's time," she answered.

"Time for what?" Andrew asked, grabbing her shoulder.

Rosa looked at Andrew with her hazel eyes.

"It's time to kill you, Andrew," a familiar voice said.

Andrew turned around and saw the Meta Morphic Five standing behind him.

"This can't be happening," Andrew said with wide eyes.

"Don't worry: it'll be over soon," said Sparks as electricity dispersed from his body.

The others meta-morphed too, dashing toward Andrew. Quickly, Andrew transformed and attacked. It was five against one, but Andrew had to save Rosa from these goons.

Shanta, in her fox form, waited for the worms to attack. Sweat rolled down her furry neck as the blazing sun beamed down on her. All she could think about was taking a nice long bath and drinking a gallon of water. Suddenly, the ground shook. Four giant worms sprang out of the sand and attacked. Shanta dodged and used her Needle Storm attack. The attack bounced of their tough skin.

"Damn! How am I supposed to beat these things if my attack just bounces off them?" Shanta asked angrily.

SMACK! One of the worms lashed Shanta in the back making her skid across the sand. Shanta struggled to get up from that powerful blow. The four worms jumped into the air, preparing to devour her. She couldn't believe her life was about to end as worm food. Suddenly, gunshots made of energy knocked the worms down. Shanta got up and saw Barzus standing next to her with an energy rifle. He smiled at her before he dashed towards the dazed worms. Shanta quickly followed. Shanta dodged the first worm's attack and attacked it with her Needle Storm attack again. The attack bounced off the worm. Frustrated, Shanta dashed towards the worm. All she could think about was having more firepower. Suddenly, her tail split into three. She attacked the worm with her tails. The worm cried in pain as each tail began to burn through its tough skin. Then, Shanta's three tails combined into one large, fiery tail and bore a huge hole into the worm. The worm let out a painful cry before collapsing. At the same time, Shanta's tail returned to normal. Shanta took a moment to assess the situation.

"What just happened?" she asked, touching her tail.

Barzus approached her. "Nice work, but we have two more worms to kill."

Shanta nodded as Barzus dashed towards the next worm. Sand was kicked up wildly as the sounds of energy attacks and worms crying in pain filled the hot air. Both Shanta and Barzus picked up on the worms' movements and countered. With their combined strength, all four worms were destroyed.

"We make a pretty good team, don't we?" Barzus commented with a smile. "You sure you won't reconsider?"

"Sorry, my man's waiting for me back at the temple," Shanta answered. "You're cute, but I love Ching."

Barzus was confused for a moment but decided to let it go. Suddenly, the ground began to shake tremendously. A sand explosion filled the air as the king worm appeared before them. It roared angrily and attacked Barzus. Barzus stood frozen in fear as the king worm quickly approached him. SMACK! Sand flew everywhere. The king worm raised its mouth from out of the sand. However, its meal had disappeared. It looked to its left: Shanta was holding Barzus. The king worm roared with anger and jumped into the sand, charging towards them. Shanta was petrified. She knew her Needle Storm attack was useless against the king worm, and she didn't know what she did earlier to kill the smaller worm. But she couldn't let Barzus die either. She was confused and afraid to move. Suddenly, Barzus put up an energy shield around them, countering the king worm's attack. The king worm fell backwards, crashing into the sand. Barzus looked at Shanta with a disappointed look.

"What happened to you?" he asked. "I need you focused on the battle. We both got people to return to. So, let's finish this."

Suddenly, a sandy tidal wave appeared. Barzus quickly put up an energy shield, but the wave was too strong to deflect. The shield smashed into tiny pieces as the wave crashed into Barzus and Shanta. Seconds later, Shanta rose from the sand to find Barzus unconscious. Suddenly, the king worm appeared. It roared angrily as it leaped towards Shanta. Shanta ran towards Barzus, standing in front of him. She wasn't going to let his life end so quickly, even if it meant sacrificing her life. She began thinking about Ching, Mark, Andrew, and her family: how she would miss them. Suddenly, the gem on her bracelet glowed. It formed a light blue energy shield around her. The king worm collided with the shield and flew backwards, skidding on the sand. The shield faded. A light blue aura began to surround her.

"Bye-Bye worm," she said as her eyes glowed a light blue color.

Shanta extended both arms, with her hands stretched out sideways and fingers curved in. Suddenly, the sand began to circle around her.

"ENERUGĪ BAKUHATSU!!!" she shouted.

A huge blast of light blue energy flew across the desert splitting the sand as it headed for the king worm. The king worm tried to escape, but the blast was too big for it to dodge. The king worm shrieked in pain as the blast hit. A few seconds later, the king worm was nothing more than a pile of dust.

"That…was…fun," Shanta said breathing deeply.

Shanta felt faint and slowly collapsed. However, Barzus caught her before she hit the sand. Shanta slowly opened her eyes.

"Good job," Barzus replied with a smile. "You passed your test."

Suddenly, a door appeared in front of them. At first, Shanta thought the desert heat was getting to her, but soon realized the door led back to the temple. Shanta thanked Barzus for his help. She slowly got up and walked towards the door.

With no place to run or hide, Mark knew he had to fight the panda, especially to protect Reina. At super speed, the panda jumped from tree to tree. Mark stood there watching the panda move. He couldn't believe a small panda could move so fast. Mark soon got frustrated and tried to attack the panda. But every time he tried, the panda was one step ahead of him, quickly countering.

Gotta stay calm: focus on his movements with my ears, not my eyes.

Mark closed his eyes and listened for the baby panda's movements.
"SHADOW FANG!!!"

Mark split his shadow into several smaller shadows making it easier for him to hit the panda. SMACK! One of the shadows hit the panda, knocking it to the ground. Mark smiled with joy, since his plan worked. The panda got up, firing a huge energy blast at Mark. With no time to dodge, Mark extended his arms forward and blocked the blast with a shadowy wall. He could feel the blast pushing him backwards. Mark struggled to move forward as the blast got bigger and stronger.

Can't let it end like this. I won't let him get his paws on Reina. I won't back down!

 Suddenly, the gem on his bracelet began to glow. He used his shadowy wall to send the blast upward. Mark and the panda both watched as the blast ascended to the sky.

"Here's something I cooked up for you," he replied with his arms above his head and his hands crisscrossed. "It's time to kiss your ass good-bye! KAGE BAKUHATSU!!!"

Instantly, a purplish-black colored blast flew straight towards the panda. The panda tried to grab the blast, but soon realized the blast was too much for it. It shrieked in pain as its body was disintegrating. Seconds later, the panda's body disappeared without a trace. Mark fell to his knees and began breathing hard. He was exhausted. Then, he realized something.

"Oh snap! I just spoke Japanese and I don't know what the hell it means!"

Suddenly, a door appeared in front of him.

"I guess this is my ticket out of this place," replied Mark as he slowly got up.

"Mark!" a voice called out to him.

Mark turned around to see Reina running towards him. She quickly hugged him.

"Thank you," she said with a smile. "Thank you for saving me and putting an end to the terror that plagued my village. I watched most of the fight and can say you're not weak. You have proven to me how strong you are, when you fight with your heart. Always remember that feeling."

Mark patted Reina's head and smiled. "I won't forget it."

SMACK! Andrew fell face first into the ground. He struggled to get up. Sparks kicked him in the ribs, sending Andrew flying into the air. Big C appeared above Andrew and clubbed him in his back. Rosa watched helplessly as Andrew was getting tossed around. Andrew smacked the ground hard, making a huge hole in the playground. Dust kicked up into the air. The dust settled, revealing Andrew face first in the ground.

"Had enough ass-wipe?" Gyro asked with a huge grin on his face.

"I'm just…getting started," Andrew answered slowly getting up.

He dashed toward Gyro, tackling him to the ground. Andrew jumped into the air as soon as he heard someone approach him. Andrew kicked Big C in the face. Big C went down hard. Sparks attacked. Andrew countered with a punch to Sparks' face. Sparks flew backwards, but quickly regained his balance. Suddenly, Rampage's gorilla body tackled Andrew to the ground. He grabbed Andrew's foot and flung him upward. Rampage jumped into the air and bear-hugged Andrew.

"POWER DRIVE!!!" he shouted as they plummeted to the ground.

BAM! Andrew's entire upper body was buried in the ground leaving his legs dangling in the air. Rampage grabbed both of Andrew's legs and pulled him out of the ground like a vegetable. Andrew's whole body became numb. He couldn't even formulate a word.

"How do you like your meta-human guys?" asked Flameboy preparing to barbecue Andrew.

"Crispy," answered Gyro and laughed hysterically.

Flameboy raised both arms and shouted, "WAVES OF INFERNO!!!"

A stream of flames came towards Andrew. Andrew burned Rampage's arm with his Striking Claw attack, dodging the blast. Flameboy's attack incinerated a tree to the ground. Andrew countered, punching Flameboy in the face. He skidded to the ground, crashing into a car.

"HAILSTORM!!!" shouted Big C.

Instantly, thousands of tiny icicles came straight towards Andrew. Andrew tried to dodge, but the icicles ended up following him. BAM! SMACK! Andrew could feel each icicle explode on his body. Andrew crashed to the ground hard. He slowly got up, coughing up blood. Rosa rushed over to Andrew, trying to help him up.

"Stop your attacks," she cried to the Meta Morphic Five. "Don't you see he has had enough?"

"Step away bitch or I'll be forced to kill you too," replied Big C.

"Don't you…dare call her a bitch," Andrew replied angrily as he got up.

With the remaining strength in his body, Andrew charged forward. He began punching Big C in the stomach. Big C's jaw sank further and further with every blow. Suddenly, his body became weightless. He could almost see the rooftop. Andrew appeared above Big C and clubbed him in the back. Big C plummeted. The ground shook as the entire playground became a scrap yard. Andrew's body was exhausted. Each breath felt worse than the last. He wasn't sure if he could fight them anymore. Suddenly, Andrew's ears perked as he heard Rosa scream.

"Move and the girl dies," replied Gyro with one arm wrapped around Rosa's waist and the other shaped like a blaster, pointed at her head.

"Let her go," Andrew said angrily.

"Alright," Gyro said smiling as he pushed Rosa to the ground somewhere in the middle of him and Andrew.

"Rosa, run!" Andrew cried.

"GIGA DESTROYER!!!" shouted Gyro as he fired his blaster.

Rosa ran as fast as she could towards Andrew. Her heart raced as she stretched out her hand towards him. It was too late. The blast hit and went through her. Andrew's eyes widened as he watched Rosa fall to the ground. He ran towards Rosa, cradling her head on his lap. Blood soaked through her clothes and her body grew cold. A tear rolled down Andrew's face and splashed onto her cheek. Rosa looked at Andrew with half-open eyes and a small smile.

"Fight with both your heart and body…" she managed to say. "Don't be afraid of your feelings for the real Rosa…Deep down, she…"

That was the last thing Andrew heard from her. Rosa's head tilted to the right. Her body disappeared right before his eyes. Andrew could hear Gyro's laughter ringing in his ears. Andrew gnashed his teeth and clenched his fists tightly. Soon, the others began to laugh.

"You have grown stronger Andrew, but you're still weak," replied Sparks. "You can't even save the one you love."

Andrew muttered something under his breath.

"What was that?" asked Big C with one hand cupped over his ear.

Suddenly, the gem on Andrew's bracelet glowed. A bright red aura surrounded him. Andrew rose. The aura grew and his yellow eyes became blood red. The ground began to shake and split open. Andrew could see fear in their eyes.

"You bastards!" he cried. "You killed the only person I loved and now you'll die!"

Andrew extended both arms with one hand pointed upward, the other pointed downward and his fingers slightly curled.

"GEKIDO BAKUHATSU!!!" he shouted at the top of his lungs.

A huge red blast of energy flew across the playground, heading straight for the Meta Morphic Five. They couldn't dodge the blast. Big C stood in front of the blast and grabbed it with his bare hands. The blast began to push him back. Suddenly, Rampage stood behind Big C, becoming his anchor. The others did the same. Big C's veins pulsated as he continued to hold the blast. It was a stalemate.

"You think I'm done?!" exclaimed Andrew. "Guess again!"

He added more energy to the blast. The blast grew wider, pushing them all back. Big C's arms began to shake as the blast became cumbersome to hold. A direct hit! Soon, their bodies began to disintegrate. They cried for mercy, but Andrew was too enraged to hear it. Seconds later, the Meta Morphic Five was no more. Andrew fell to his hands and knees, breathing hard. The battle was over. Suddenly, the playground disappeared. Andrew quickly got up and watched as everything around him began to disappear.

What the…? Andrew asked himself as he de-transformed.

"Andrew," a voice called out to him.

"Who…are you?" he asked, looking around.

"Be not afraid, for I am your mother."

Andrew chuckled. "Sorry, but Lily is my mother."

Suddenly, the mysterious voice appeared. She had the same eye and hair color as Andrew. She was the same height as Andrew, but a little skinnier than him. She wore a white long-sleeved dress with a small pink flower in the middle. Andrew's eyes widened as he took a step back.

"I know you have never seen me, but I'm your biological mother," she said. "My name is Alice Bridges."

"If that's true, then who's my real father?" Andrew asked, hoping to stump her.

Alice cast her eyes down for a moment, before looking at Andrew. "Your biological father…is Jin Hidishi."

When Andrew heard Hidishi's name, he was pissed.

"There's no way I'm related to Hidishi!"

Alice gave Andrew a sad look. "I'm sorry Andrew, but you are. It happened eighteen years ago, in Japan."

Instantly, a table with two chairs appeared. Alice signaled Andrew to sit down. Andrew sat down first. Alice cleared her throat as she began her story.

"I was born in America, but moved over to Japan when I was five," she said. "My father was a rich businessman and owned a company in Japan, called Stonewell Inc. I met your father when I was about your age. He was handsome and mysterious. I thought he loved me, but he never did. All he wanted was my body and my family's fortune. When he found out I was pregnant, your father left me to survive on my own. Even my family disowned me. So, I secretly moved back to America to give birth to you. With no way of taking care of you, I put you up for adoption by leaving you at the doorsteps of St. Mary's Orphanage."

Andrew was awestruck and speechless.

Alice placed her hand on top of Andrew's. "I'm sorry for abandoning you, but if I hadn't, you wouldn't grow up to be the kind, caring young man I wanted you to be."

Andrew moved his hand and ignored her comment. He was solely focused on knowing the truth. "How did you die?"

Alice sighed. "Hidishi's men found me in my Brooklyn apartment, took me to an abandon warehouse, and killed me there. Hidishi figured I might say something to the FBI or CIA since I knew about his plans."

"What are Hidishi's plans?"

"I don't fully understand it myself. But listen to me, Andrew: you and your friends must stop Hidishi before it's too late. The entire world will be in utter chaos if you don't."

"Yeah, I know," Andrew replied. "That's the whole purpose of training." Suddenly, his eyes widened. "Wait, how'd you know about my friends?"

Alice smiled. "Silly boy: a mother always watches over her children. You have great friends."

Andrew had a hard time digesting everything Alice told him but kept his composure. "So, how do I get out of here?"

Alice pointed to the door standing behind Andrew. Andrew got up and ran towards the door. Suddenly, he stopped. He turned around and stared at his real mother. He still couldn't believe his eyes, yet he knew, in his heart, she was real.

"I love you, my son," Alice said with a tear rolling down her cheek. "I'm always watching over you."

Andrew gave Alice a small smile before he went through the door.

"What's taking Andrew so long?" Mark asked, tapping his foot.

"He'll be here," answered Shanta staring at the sky.

Suddenly, a weird light poked through the bottom of the door. Everyone turned around and watched as Andrew came out of the door.

"What took you, Dawg?" asked Mark, bumping fists with him.

"I had a run-in with my mom," Andrew answered.

Both Shanta and Mark looked at him strangely.

"I'm serious, my biological mom talked to me after I finished my training," he replied. "Even I'm having a hard time believing it…"

"Okay…did she tell you anything?" Shanta asked.

Andrew stared at the ground. Mark and Shanta looked at him, expecting an answer. Andrew knew it was going to be difficult to explain.

"Well?" Shanta egged Andrew on.

Andrew looked at Mark and Shanta once more. "She…told me that Hidishi is my real dad."

"Hell nah!" exclaimed Mark. "That can't be right."

"Are you sure?" asked Shanta.

"Positive," Andrew answered. "She told me Hidishi's drug-dealing plans started eighteen years ago and that we have to kill him now before he puts the world in chaos."

"Looks like we have to leave Macu ASAP in order to kill Hidishi and rescue the girls," replied Mark.

"You are still not done with your training," Master Dao interrupted.

"Say what?!" Andrew exclaimed.

"You may have gained a new power, but you still don't have full control of it. We start training tomorrow morning."

Andrew sighed. "Yes Sir…"

That night, Aiya wandered around the courtyard. She sat underneath a tree, staring at the sky. A smile spread over her face as she pictured Mark in her mind.

"I'm so glad Mark gets to stay a little longer. Maybe now I can win his heart. I'd better get back so I can make some plans."

"I don't think so little girl," answered a voice with yellow eyes.

Aiya looked up into the tree. She screamed. Mark heard Aiya's scream and ran as fast as he could. When he arrived, Aiya disappeared. Mark noticed Aiya's necklace lying on the ground, next to a strange footprint. Aiya was kidnapped, but by whom?

ELEVEN

"Kidnapped!" exclaimed Ching. "Who would do such a thing?"

Mark and the others were in a large meeting room, used by the royal family to discuss important matters and also make executive decisions.

"I don't know, but we'll find out," replied Mark, holding onto Aiya's necklace.

"No need," said Master Dao entering the meeting room. "It was the work of Nayo, dark warlord of the Gyus. I checked the soldier's footprint."

"Nayo?" asked Mark. "Who's that?"

"Nayo was once ruler of the Forest Region, until Ching's father defeated him in battle and took over," answered Master Dao. "But unlike Ching's father, Nayo was an evil ruler who made us all suffer. I helped Ching's father defeat Nayo and banished him to the southern side of the planet. The Gyus live in the Aqua Region, about thirty miles from here."

"Guess he plans on using Aiya as bait in order to get back the throne," Andrew said.

"Looks like this will be our training," replied Shanta. "Are you guys ready to fight?"

"You bet, girl," answered Mark. "Let's go kick some Gyu butt!"

The next morning, Mark, Shanta and Andrew set out to get Aiya back. With Ching, Hibika, (who were both wearing cool samurai outfits), and a thousand soldiers occupying them, it would be easy for all of them to get in the fortress and defeat Nayo. As they rode through the dense forest on horseback, they had to watch their backs since many creatures lurked around.

Hibika and Andrew lead the way, followed by four hundred soldiers. Next were Ching and Shanta with three hundred soldiers behind them. Finally, Mark brought up the rear with the remaining group of soldiers.

"Hey Hibika," Andrew asked looking at her, "how much further?"

"We should reach their fortress by nightfall," she answered still looking ahead.

Andrew could tell Hibika was angry. He was in the same boat as she was. He too wanted to save the person he loved. Andrew wasn't sure how they would get in, but he was determined to find a way.

Somewhere in the afternoon, they reached halfway through the forest. It was amazing how none of them wanted to take a break. Getting Aiya back kept them going. They came to a downward slope, which would take them to the fortress much faster. Suddenly, a gorilla-looking creature jumped out from the trees.

"Let me handle this one," replied Mark telling everyone to back off. "I've been itching for a fight."

Quickly, Mark transformed. Mark's speed and strength had improved dramatically. The creature was having a hard time keeping up with Mark. BAM! The creature's face was smashed in. Soon, it became weightless. Mark appeared above the creature and clubbed it in the head. The creature plummeted, shaking the ground.

"Stand back guys," said Mark, who was still in mid-air, but falling fast. "I'm gonna make roast creature. KAGE BAKUHATSU!!!"

The impact of the blast created a huge hole in the ground. Everyone watched the hole grow deeper and deeper. Mark landed safely onto the ground. The hole began to fill up with smoke. The smoke cleared. The creature was nothing more than a pile of ash.

"That was easy," replied Mark de-transforming.

"Your power has increased dramatically," replied Shanta. She slapped him on the back. "I'm proud, Cuz."

"We better continue," said Ching looking at the sky. "It will be nightfall soon."

The rest of the way was on foot. They walked down the slope and continued through the dense forest, until they reached a massive clearing. Andrew, Mark, and Shanta's eyes widened at the site. Just on the horizon was the sea. The rocky terrain had become a smooth path and the sky was crystal clear. Andrew could see the massive fortress in the distance. Everyone took the smooth path, passing various abandoned homes along the way. Soon, they stopped at the port. The port looked abandoned, despite having several boats tied to the docks. Ching pointed to the fortress, which was in the middle of the sea.

"Yo, that's too far to swim!" exclaimed Mark with wide eyes.

"It's low-tide, Mark," Ching replied. "We can walk across the hidden path."

Mark sighed as he followed the others across the hidden, stony path. Soon, they reached the foot of the fortress, as the stars and two moons began to appear. The front entrance was bigger than the courtyard and there were a lot of tall trees and average-sized bushes surrounding it. Everyone stopped a few yards away from the entrance. Ching and Andrew did a little scouting of the fortress in a nearby high tree. From the looks of it, the outside was heavily guarded. There were eighty creature-soldiers guarding the entrance.

"How do we get in?" Andrew asked Ching.

"We need a diversion," Ching answered, "a really big one."

"I think Mark and I could handle that," Andrew said smiling.

Andrew somersaulted off the tree, landing onto the ground.

"Mark, wanna cause some serious chaos?" Andrew asked him.

"You bet, Drew," answered Mark with a grin.

Quickly, Mark and Andrew transformed and headed for the front entrance. Mark took the lead and walked right up to the creature-soldiers.

"Wassup, my creatures!" exclaimed Mark.

The creature-soldiers looked at him funny before they attacked Mark. Mark smiled. Something pierced their hearts. Instantly, they dropped to the ground. Mark's Shadow Fang killed them in one silent shot. Andrew came out of the bushes and used his Striking Claw attack to break the gate open. The alarm went off.

"Nice going, Drew," replied Mark sarcastically.

"Shut up and fight," Andrew shot back, seeing a group of creature-soldiers coming towards them from the right side of the fortress.

"Looks like we have a little bit more on our plates," said Mark, seeing more creature-soldiers come from the left.

 The front entrance was covered with creature-soldiers. Armed with spears and swords, they inched towards them.

"It's now or never," Andrew said, "GEKIDO!"

"KAGE!" shouted Mark.

"BAKUHATSU!!!" they shouted in unison.

Their blasts combined, racing towards the gate. BOOM! The front entrance was nothing more than a wasteland, covered with crispy creature-soldiers. Even the fortress door was gone. Mark and Andrew both ran inside the fortress. To Mark's surprise, there wasn't anyone on the massive main floor.

"Guess we killed all the guards," he replied looking at Andrew.

"I don't think so," Andrew said. "I have a feeling this is a trap."

The others finally caught up. As they stood around the main floor, they noticed the decorations were like the temple, except that every floor in the fortress was covered in marble. Since there were three floors, Andrew decided they should split up in order to cover more ground.

"Ching and Shanta will look on the main floor. Mark, check the third floor. Hibika and I will check the second floor. We'll meet back here in an hour."

"Men, I want you to go outside and guard the entrance," Ching said to the soldiers.

They went their separate ways to find Aiya.

Ching and Shanta wandered down a wide hallway with many doors. They searched every door but found nothing inside of them. Ching turned the corner and found another hallway filled with many doors.

"This is hopeless," he said. "How are we going to find Aiya with these many doors?"

"I don't know, but we have to search them all," answered Shanta, who was beginning to give up also.

Suddenly, they heard a voice from behind. They turned around to see a creature-soldier signaling his companions to hurry. Ching and Shanta ran down the hallway. A large group of creature-soldiers burst out from one of the doors, blocking their path. They attacked Ching and Shanta. Quickly, Shanta transformed. She dashed toward the creatures with her claws ready. Ching also joined in on the fight, drawing his katana.

The battle was fierce. Ching struck several creature-soldiers with downward slashes. But as one fell, another one appeared in its place. Ching stepped back and stared down at his opponents.

Time to use that attack.

He flipped his sword, pointing the hilt upward while holding it in one hand. Ching dashed forward, disappearing from their sight. Seconds later, he reached the other side. The creature-soldiers turned around. Blood splattered everywhere. They cried in pain as their bodies began to fall apart.

"Kaze no Mai," Ching said as the last creature-soldier gurgled his last word.

Amazed at Ching's performance, Shanta got serious. She ran on all fours towards them. Suddenly, her tail split into three. Shanta leaped into the air, somersaulting over them. At the same time, her tails stretched out and began piercing their armor and vitals. Shanta landed as the creature-soldiers fell. This battle was over.

"You're…not a bad swordsman," replied Shanta catching her breath.

"And you move like lightning," replied Ching smiling.

Shanta felt flustered. "Oh, stop…"

They continued down the wide hallway, opening every door on either side of them. It seemed hopeless until Shanta opened a door leading to the basement.

"We better tell the others about this," she said looking at Ching.

Hibika and Andrew were having a hard time avoiding the creature-soldiers. No matter where they turned, creature-soldiers seemed to appear. Andrew and Hibika both led the creature-soldiers to a large, wide room. Soon, they were surrounded.

"I had enough with running away!" Hibika exclaimed, drawing her sword. "It's time to fight!"

Andrew stood there and watched as Hibika charged toward the creature-soldiers. Her moves were like water, fluent yet deadly. She began slicing and dicing them one-by-one. She did somersaults, flips, and moves Andrew had never seen before. But despite her efforts, more creature-soldiers appeared. Andrew stepped forward.

"Don't interfere, Andrew!" Hibika said, gripping the hilt tightly.

As much as he wanted to fight, he let her handle it. Hibika reached into her pouch and pulled out a small bottle of water. She poured some on the blade and threw the rest on the ground. Confused, Andrew watched Hibia take her stance. She pointed her blade downward, into the puddle of water and held the hilt with two hands. One of the creature-soldiers grew restless. He quickly attacked. Hibika swung. Instantly, a massive wave of water surrounded them. Hibika dashed forward, disappearing from Andrew's sight. She appeared in mid-air, with droplets of water flying off her. The glistening of the blade and her hair made Andrew blush. The watery wave disappeared, and all the creature-soldiers fell to the ground with very deep wounds. Blood soaked through the rug and stained the walls.

"Ame no Mai," Hibika said landing onto the ground.

 Andrew almost felt sorry for the creature-soldiers. They didn't know, as well as him, Hibika was a trained swordsman.

"We have to continue the search," said Hibika sliding her sword into the sheath, which was on her back.

Andrew nodded and quickly followed her down the hallway.

"Why do I have to be by myself?" Mark asked himself as he wandered through the third floor. "I wish one of the servant-girls knew how to fight."

Just then, one of the doors began to open. Quickly, Mark hid in another room with the door slightly open. He couldn't make out what the person was saying, but he knew the person was coming in his direction. The person walked past Mark.

He looked young. Judging by the amount of gray hair on his head, he was in his mid-forties and his body was muscular. He looked like he could kill an entire army with his bare hands. He wore red pants with black boots, black wristbands, and a red cape with matching mask.

"That has to be Nayo," Mark whispered.

Mark decided to follow him.

As Ching and Shanta were coming out of the hallway, Ching stopped.

"What's wrong?" asked Shanta, stopping also.

"Someone is coming," he answered. "I can hear footsteps."

"We better hide," she replied, grabbing Ching's arm and leading him to an open door.

Ching watched through the small crack in the door where Nayo was headed. Once it was clear, Ching opened the door. To their surprise, Mark came down the hallway also.

"What are you doing here?" whispered Shanta.

"I'm following Nayo," Mark answered.

"We already know where Aiya is," said Ching. "Nayo has put her in his dungeon."

"Let's go get him," replied Mark running past Ching.

Shanta grabbed the back of his shirt and pulled him down. "We're waiting for Hibika and Drew."

"Fine," replied Mark folding his arms.

A few minutes later, Hibika and Andrew came downstairs and joined the others. Mark told Hibika and Andrew where Nayo was keeping Aiya. They all ran down the hallway. However, something was off. Different sections of the hallway began to close. Despite their efforts, they were trapped like rats. Two large walls made of solid rock surrounded them.

"What do we do?" Hibika asked Andrew.

"We bust through," he answered.

"How?" asked Ching looking at Shanta, "That wall is made of solid rock."

"Piece of cake," replied Shanta as she transformed. "I'll break it."

They all stood back and watched as Shanta's Enerugī Bakuhatsu attack demolished the rock into a pile of pebbles. They continued down the hallway until they reached the door that led to the dungeon. They walked down the narrow staircase. The light became brighter and brighter. Their hearts raced with every step. Soon, they were going to fight Nayo and rescue Aiya. They arrived at the basement and were amazed by the structure.

Dungeons were supposed to be gross and scary, but Nayo's…was neat, beautiful, and huge. The whole room was covered in black marble with small torches surrounding the room. In the back of the dungeon was a small altar, where he kept his prisoners and sacrificed them. There were only two tapestries in the room, located on the sides of the room.

"What kind of dungeon is this?" asked Mark. "This looks like every other room in this place. For an evil guy, he doesn't know what scary and gross are. My grandma can make a better dungeon than this."

"Ah, I see that Aiya's friends have arrived," replied Nayo facing the altar.

"Come get an ass beating!" replied Mark angrily.

 Nayo turned around. "You must be Mark. Princess Aiya seems to talk about you a lot. I challenge you to a fight to the death. The winner will get Aiya. Do you accept?"

"Let's do this," answered Mark cracking his knuckles.

"Are you crazy? You can't fight this guy," Andrew said.

Mark gave Andrew a serious look. "I gotta, in order to save Aiya. One thing I learned from our last training is to never back down, even if the odds are against you. Aiya may get on my nerves, but that doesn't mean I have to let her get taken by this guy. She's still someone I want to protect."

Andrew smirked. "Fight well, man."

They fist bumped. Andrew signaled the others to get out of the dungeon. They stood near the staircase. Nayo took off his cape. He cracked his knuckles and his neck. Mark transformed, waiting for Nayo to attack.

"Let's see how fast you are," replied Nayo as he dashed towards Mark.

Nayo began his assault, throwing punches. Mark dodged every blow, countering with his own. Their hands were moving so fast, it looked like a bunch of blurs were between them. BAM! Nayo felt a blow to his stomach. He returned the favor with a punch to Mark's face. Both fighters stepped backwards before they charged towards each other once more. Their bodies were moving fast. None of the others could keep up with Mark and Nayo's movements. SMACK! Mark kicked Nayo in the cheek. Nayo flew backwards. He regained his balance, flipping a few times across the floor. He wiped the blood from his mouth and charged towards Mark. The battle was fierce. Both fighters were fast and strong. It was like their powers were even. None of the others knew who was going to win. SLAM! Mark crashed into the altar wall, leaving a huge hole in it. He slowly got up. Nayo appeared in front of him and began punching him in the stomach. Mark cried in pain with every blow. He grabbed both fists and kneed Nayo in the chin. With the palm of his hand, Mark pushed Nayo to the other side of the dungeon. He crashed into a wall before falling to one knee.

"You…fight well," replied Nayo as he got up.

"Yeah, I've got sweet skills," replied Mark grinning.

"Now it's time to show you my true strength."

"Funny, I was thinking the same thing."

Nayo extended both arms with his palms face up and fired a huge blast at Mark. Mark dodged. Part of the altar wall was destroyed. Nayo laughed evilly and continued to fire more. Mark dodged, flipping everywhere. Suddenly, two blasts appeared above him. BAM! A cloud of smoke began to fill the room. The smoke cleared. There was no sign of Mark. Nayo laughed evilly as he turned to face the others. Suddenly, his body froze.

"What?" Nayo asked with wide eyes.

He looked down and saw worm-like shadows wrapped around his legs. "But…how?"

"An illusion," answered Mark, rising from behind the damaged altar. "You destroyed my shadow clone while I quickly found a place to take cover. You may be strong, but you're so stupid."

More worm-like shadows wrapped themselves around Nayo. They raised him in mid-air, facing him towards Mark. Mark raised both arms into the air with his hands crisscrossed.

"Now, kiss your ass good-bye!" he shouted, "KAGE BAKUHATSU!!!"

Mark's blast hit Nayo head on. He cried in pain as the blast began to burn his body.

"This is for Aiya!" shouted Mark as he added more power to the blast.

The others watched Mark blast Nayo into the ceiling and onto the main floor.

"Who…da man…" replied Mark as he fell onto his hands and knees.

Shanta and Andrew helped up Mark before they walked up the stairs.

"Naruto would be proud of your Shadow Clone Jutsu," Andrew joked.

Mark smirked. Soon, they got to the main floor. They saw Nayo still standing. Most of his body was charred and blood oozed from his abdomen.

"Where's Aiya?" asked Mark trying to stand up on his own.

Nayo chuckled through the pain. "I never thought…I would lose to a mere child. Mark, you have…indeed won this fight. Aiya is in…a special prison cell, located on the third floor. Here, take this key."

He chucked the key with his remaining strength. They watched Nayo collapse to the ground, with a pool of blood surrounding him. Mark picked up the slightly charred key and hurried towards the third floor. The others followed. They searched every door.

"She's in there," Shanta answered pointing to a door with a tapestry next to it.

Mark unlocked the door and found Aiya on a bed, staring at the wall. She turned her head and looked at everyone with dazed eyes. She wasn't sure if it was a dream. Tears of joy ran down her cheeks as she ran towards Ching. Everyone gave a sigh of relief. Aiya noticed Mark behind everyone and quickly looked away.

"Aiya, you should be proud of Mark," said Ching, realizing her hesitation. "He saved your life by defeating Nayo."

Aiya covered her surprised look. "Why would he do that for me? He doesn't even love me."

"I did it because I care about you," Mark answered, stepping forward. "You're still someone I want to protect, even if you're annoying."

Tears rolled down Aiya's cheeks. She ran up to him and squeezed him tightly. Mark hated to be squeezed by her, but he let her hug him to her heart's content.

"C'mon, let's go home," said Mark, looking at Aiya with a smile.

TWELVE

Hours seemed like eternity to Rosa as she and Tracy waited patiently for some kind of contact. Suddenly, there was a knock.

"Dinner time," said a voice.

The door opened and two guards appeared with trays of food. The smell enticed them, as well as the appearance. For the first time, Rosa and Tracy were eating lobster and steak. Alongside the meat were buttered rolls, seasoned potatoes, fresh vegetables, and pitchers of juice.

"The boss must really like you two," said one of the guards. "Even we don't get all of this."

"What does your boss want with us?" Rosa asked.

"You'll find out soon enough," answered the other guard. "Just eat. We'll be back in an hour."

They left. Rosa stared at the food with a sad look. Suddenly, Tracy began grabbing a portion of her share and slowly ate it. Rosa watched Tracy wolf it down. A small smile came upon Rosa's face as she took back her remaining share.

"You really are brave, Tracy," Rosa said before she ate a piece of steak.

Tracy stopped chewing. "I'm not: I'm really scared. Yet, deep down, I believe that Mark and Andrew will save us."

Rosa thought about Andrew for a moment. Her face turned red as she looked down at her food. "Tracy…is it okay to love someone who doesn't love you?" Rosa asked.

"Andrew loves you," Tracy answered. "He's scared to admit it. Give him time and he'll say it."

"Has Mark ever said it to you?"

"Once, at the dance."

"How'd you respond?"

Tracy smiled. "Well, it was the first time a guy ever said that to me and meant it. So, I said it back to him and then kissed him."

Rosa was awestruck. "Wow, you're so bold! Wait, how many guys have you dated?"

"Only two, before Mark. Of course, they each lasted a short while. What about you? Did you ever have a boyfriend?"

"No…"

Tracy felt giddy. "Then that means Andrew's your special one! And I know he'll take good care of you."

"You think he would want an aggressive girl like me?"

"Andrew needs your strength to move forward. You can also stand up for yourself. I'm a little envious of that."

Rosa made a face. "What do you mean?"

"The reason my past relationships ended so quickly was because I couldn't stand up for myself. I was merely eye candy. It was around my Junior year that I started to take charge of my life and be aggressive. But even that couldn't protect me from danger. Mark's the only guy to ever protect me and try his hardest to make me happy."

Rosa couldn't believe her ears. For the first time, she truly understood Tracy and wanted to be strong like her.

"Right now, Andrew is fighting to protect you," Tracy said. "Doesn't that count as his declaration of love to you?"

Rosa smiled. "Yeah, it does."

Suddenly the door opened, and the same guards appeared. They signaled Rosa and Tracy to follow them. They walked through the interior part of the warehouse.

It was a two-story building. The inside of the warehouse was filled with many crates. Most of the workers were either packaging or sorting the crates and there were two overseers watching the workers' every move. There were many machines producing different products with workers operating them. There was a spare room where they kept junk or other drugs. Trucks came and left the docking bay as the fumes from the gasoline filled the air. On the second floor were three large rooms. On the far right was the cafeteria and bathroom. On the far left was Hidishi's office and on the lower right was the break room, where the Meta-Morphic Five hung out.

Rosa wasn't sure what was going on but kept a straight face. Even Tracy observed her surroundings. They reached an elevator at the front end of the warehouse and rode it to the second floor, where they walked to the left corner of the open hallway. There, a lonely door stood. One of the guards rapped on the door.

"Enter," a voice said.

The guard opened the door, leading Rosa and Tracy in. Suddenly, Tracy began to feel lightheaded.

What's this odd feeling?

"You okay, Tracy?" Rosa asked, letting Tracy lean on her.

"I'm fine…" Tracy answered with a small smile. *His aura…so much evil…*

"Welcome, guests, to my little hideout," Hidishi said. "Please, enjoy your stay."

He turned around. Their eyes widened as they gazed into his blood red eyes.

THIRTEEN

Tonight, was a night for celebration! Everyone at the temple cheered for Aiya's safe return. Even Master Dao couldn't let this celebration go unheard. Ayia stood in the center of the dining room, looking at all her friends and people. Aiya truly felt loved.

"Thank you all for your support," she said with a smile. "But please, don't just praise me. Praise Mark for defeating Nayo for my sake."

The crowd cheered. Four Nebtan men picked up Mark and began tossing him up in the air. Soon, the entire Nebtan crowd joined in.

"Jeez, what are we, chopped liver?" Shanta asked angrily.

"Yeah, I know the feeling," Andrew added before sipping his drink.

"I, for one, am proud of all of you," replied Master Dao with a smile. "You three have improved so much, I almost have nothing left to teach you."

"So, we're done?" Andrew asked.

"I said *almost*," answered Master Dao. "You still need a little more training."

Andrew sighed. Suddenly, there was a dinging sound from across the room. Everyone became silent and looked at Ching, who was tapping his glass with a fork.

"Everyone, may I have your attention? As you know, your King is at the age of marriage and has yet to find a bride."

Shanta's eyes widened as her heart raced.

"I come to you tonight to say that there's another thing to celebrate: our new Queen, Shanta."

Everyone's eyes fell upon her. Shanta turned bright red as their surprised looks became smiles.

"All hail Queen Shanta!" they shouted in unison.

"I don't know what to say…" Shanta replied, covering her face.

"Say you'll be my Queen," Ching said embracing her.

She looked up and smiled. "I will."

"So, Master Dao, does this count as our training?" Andrew asked, nudging him.

Master Dao cleared his throat. "Of course, it does! Now that Shanta will be Queen, she must know the entire Forest Region. Starting tomorrow, she'll head into the city of Raion to meet the other Nebtans."

"What?!" exclaimed Andrew. "There's more of you?"

"Did you think the entire Nebtan race lived in the temple?" Master Dao asked. "Silly boy, the entire Nebtan race is equivalent to the states of California, Texas, and New York combined. The temple holds at least three thousand Nebtans while the city of Raion has nearly two million Nebtans."

Andrew's jaw dropped. He never realized how large the Forest Region was.

"Just how far is the city from here?" Shanta asked.

"About half a day's trip," Ching answered. "The city is north of the temple and twenty miles away from the Mountain Region border. My best friend, Lin, is the mayor. I often visit him and bring back souvenirs for Hibika and Aiya."

"Why didn't you tell us about Raion?" Andrew asked.

"There wasn't much time in between training to take you there," Ching answered.

"What I want to know is why it's called Raion," replied Mark.

"Raion is named after the mighty warrior of Macu," Ching said. "Raion protected everyone, people and animals, from a wicked devil. Legend says that when Raion died, his spirit was placed into the hearts of two brave warriors. Whenever they called upon his name, Raion would appear to fight once more."

Shanta started to panic. "Do I need to wear something formal? And how will they know about me?"

"Settle down, Shanta," Ching said, chuckling. "Everything will be taken care of. Before I go to bed, I'll send Lin a message via hoot-tah. They're the fastest night birds in Macu."

"With that settled, can I move my things into your room?" she asked sweetly.

"Jeez, Shanta, you ain't married yet and you're eager to move in with him," replied Mark with a glare.

Andrew carried Hibika to her room on his back. She giggled and hiccupped as they got closer to her door. He sighed. He opened the door, laying her gently on the bed.

"You shouldn't have drunk that third drink, Hibika," Andrew said. "Try and get some rest."

"Andrew, I'm so hot," Hibika said, loosening her obi belt.

"I'm gonna go," replied Andrew, feeling flushed.

Andrew headed for the door. She grabbed his arm. He looked back, gazing into her eyes. Hibika crawled closer to him, letting her kimono loosen further. Soon, most of her breasts and panty were exposed. Andrew quickly looked away.

"Why are you not looking at me?!" Hibika exclaimed. "You've seen me naked! Why now do you turn away from me?"

"Hibika, that was an accident," Andrew replied, reasoning with her. "Look, you're drunk. You need to rest."

"Don't you dare tell me I'm drunk! You don't know me!"

"And you don't know me. I'm not the type of guy to take advantage of a drunk girl."

Hibika laughed. "You don't get it, do you?"

"Get what?" Andrew asked with a confused look.

"I'm in love with you, Andrew," Hibika declared. "I've come to realize this three days ago, when you went through that dimensional door for training. For the first time, I yearned to see you, to chat with you and…"

Hibika pressed her body close to him. "To even kiss you."

She perked her lips. Andrew's heart raced. It would be his first kiss and he didn't want to ruin that moment. He gently pushed her aside.

"I'm sorry, I can't do this," he said. "I'm…in love with someone else."

"Who is she?"

"Her name is Rosa."

"Do you even like me?"

"Yeah, there are things about you I like."

"Like what?"

"For starters, you're fighting skills. I've never met someone quite skilled like you. You're also great with kids. You really will make a great teacher."

"You really like me for those things?"

"Yes, as well as your kind heart."

Hibika squealed with joy. "Andrew, I love you!"

She jumped on him. Andrew fell backwards, making a loud thud. He rubbed his head and noticed Hibka was on top of him. She sat up and stared at Andrew seductively, with half of her kimono off her shoulder. Andrew turned bright red.

"Hey, something's poking me from behind," she said with a flushed face. "What is it?"

"That…would be me…" Andrew answered, looking away.

"Can I see it?" she asked, moving her hips along his body.

Hibika felt a sharp poke below. She moaned. Andrew desperately tried to suppress his hormones, but her movements and moaning didn't help. Hibika lay on top of him, leaning close to his ear.

"Andrew…" she said, whispering, "Make me into a woman."

That was the last straw. Andrew didn't care anymore. All he wanted was to satisfy this beastly desire. He wrapped his arms around her and began caressing her back. Suddenly, he heard a sound. It was low, but close. His eyes darted around but couldn't pinpoint it. The noise grew louder. His heart raced as he continued to look for the sound. Hibika moved her head closer to Andrew's ear. There was the sound: it was…Hibika's snoring. Andrew gave a sigh of relief. That was the closest he'd ever been with a girl. Minutes later, Andrew got Hibika into her bed.

She's cute when she sleeps, he thought with a smile.

Suddenly, she grabbed his arm.

"Please, don't leave me…" Hibika said in a low voice.

She yanked Andrew into the King-sized bed. Andrew quickly kept a safe distance from her. Still holding onto her hand, Andrew stroked the back of it. Hibika began to rest easy. Soon, she was fast asleep. Andrew yawned, as his eyes slowly closed.

She's sure a handful.

Mark watched Rei-Rei fall asleep in his lap. He stared at the dining room ceiling with a smile. He was glad for this experience. For the first time, he felt happy and strong. Suddenly, Aiya walked in.

"Did you need something?" Mark asked.

"I wanted to see how you were doing," Ayia answered. "May I sit down?"

"Go ahead."

She sat next to him. Silence filled the air for a moment.

"Mark," she said, breaking the silence, "I'm sorry for everything."

Mark's eyes widened. "What?"

"I'm sorry. I never wanted you to hate me. I do love you and I wish I was the woman you want to marry. I realize that I'm no match for your true love. So, I want us to start over, as friends."

Mark was shocked. Her words pierced his heart. It was the first time Aiya acted like an adult to him. He smiled.

"I never hated you," he said. "I don't know how to deal with aggressive girls. Even my girlfriend can be very aggressive."

"Really? Tell me more about her."

Mark smiled. "Her name is Tracy and she…"

Ching lay down next to Shanta. She buried her head in his chest as he embraced her. Their warmth was all they needed.

"I still can't believe this is happening," Shanta said with a smile.

"Me too," replied Ching smiling back. "I used to think I could never find happiness, until I met you."

Shanta blushed. "Same here. Ever since I got my powers, guys would be afraid to get close to me. You're the first guy to accept me for who I am."

Ching's face became flushed.

"Now that I think about it," said Shanta, sitting up, "what am I going to tell my parents? I totally forgot."

Ching sat up and kissed her head. "We'll figure something out. Right now, get some rest. Tomorrow will be a long day."

Shanta nodded and laid back down. She smiled as Ching soon followed. She leaned forward and gave him a long kiss goodnight.

Hibika woke up the next morning to find Andrew sleeping in her bed. She jumped out of the bed, letting out a yelp. Andrew quickly rose to find Hibika cowering in a corner.

"It's not what you think," he said getting out of bed. "You were drunk and fell asleep. You even asked me to stay with you in your sleep."

Suddenly, those memories came flooding back to her. She calmed herself. She stood up and fixed her kimono.

"Are you…mad at me…?" Hibika asked. "I did some things I shouldn't have."

Andrew smiled. "I'm not mad. I'm quite glad you told me your feelings."

"So…we're still friends?"

"Of course. Now, let's get ready for this trip."

Hibika smiled. "Yeah, sure."

An hour later, Andrew and the others gathered at the front entrance. Horse-drawn carriages were already prepared. Mark, the eager one, got into one of the carriages, along with Master Dao, Rei-Rei, and Aiya. Andrew and Hibika sat in the second carriage and Ching and Shanta were in the third one. The drivers snapped the reins. The horses neighed and began trotting towards the gate. The gate opened as the horses continued to move towards the winding road.

Mark and Rei-Rei looked out the carriage window, taking in the scenery. Aiya looked at Mark with a small smile and quickly looked out the window on the opposite side.

In the other carriage, Ching and Shanta continued to discuss their wedding plans, as well as their future.

"I'm telling you, my parents won't accept our marriage," Shanta said.

"I don't understand why," replied Ching.

"Ching-darling, it's one thing if I was becoming the Queen of England, but Queen of an unknown race is a little farfetched with my parents. Besides, on Earth, our marriage has no meaning. You and I must be twenty-one in order to be considered adults."

"I did read in an Earth book that certain countries or states vary with that age law. We could always move to the state of Georgia. I hear they have nice weather and friendly people."

"Ching, you know that wouldn't fly with my parents."

Ching smiled. "I know. I was trying to make a joke."

Shanta giggled. "Appreciate the thought. Look, after this whole battle is over, why don't you live on Earth for a while?"

"But…I can't leave my people."

"Isn't Hibika next in line for the throne? Let her rule in your place. I know she'll do a good job."

"I'll…think about it," Ching replied.

The carriages stopped at a large stone gate. Two security guards, wearing samurai armor, approached the drivers. The drivers showed them their documents. The security guards nodded as they signaled another security guard to open the gates. The gates slowly opened. The carriages proceeded. Everyone was in awe.

The city of Raion spanned most of the lower portion of the Forest Region. It was divided up into three sectors: poor, middle, and rich. It was like the city Shanta visited during her training, minus the sand and sand worms.

Crowds of Nebtans lined the streets as the carriages slowly proceeded towards City Hall. Some waved, while others chanted, "Hail to the Queen!"

"This is way too much for me," Shanta said, trying to stay calm.

Ching placed his hand on top of hers. "It'll be okay. I'm here with you."

Shanta smiled. "Thanks."

They arrived at the steps of City Hall with a large crowd following them. Soon, they were surrounded by Nebtans and journalists.

"Does this always happen to you?" Shanta asked, feeling uneasy.

"Yeah," Ching answered, waving to the crowd. "Even I'm not used to this."

City Hall was a large three-floored building. The inside had marble floors, oak furniture, and white walls. It was the glass dome ceiling in the middle that made the building stand out. Most of the workers were dressed in formal kimonos while all the guards wore samurai armor.

Ching led them to the third floor, where Lin's office was. He knocked on the door before he opened it.

Lin's office was like the Oval Office, except there weren't any flags or pictures of former presidents.

"Ching, you finally made it!" Lin exclaimed as he got up from his seat. He greeted the others. "Hey, I'm Lin, Mayor of Raion."

Lin was the same height and age as Ching. His long black hair was in a ponytail and his dark brown eyes were full of energy. He wore a blue embroidered fire dragon kimono and wooden sandals.

"Lin, these are my sisters, Hibika and Aiya," replied Ching, introducing everyone. "This is Master Dao, his grandson, Rei-Rei, Andrew, and Mark. And this is Shanta, your future Queen."

Lin blushed at the sight of Shanta. Quickly, he wrapped his arm around Ching's neck with a grin.

"Ching, you sly dog. You never told me our Queen is such a beauty."

Shanta felt flush. "I'm not that beautiful."

"On the contrary, my Queen," said Lin, "You're much more beautiful than the former Queen."

"Are you saying my mother was ugly?" Ching asked angrily.

"No, I'm not," Lin answered quickly. "It's just that we Nebtans haven't had a queen in quite some time. Hasn't Ching told you about his parents?"

"No," Shanta answered.

"Ching, I know it's a touchy subject, but you have to let her know," Lin replied.

"I agree with Lin, Brother," Hibika chimed in. "Shanta deserves to know."

Ching sighed. "Fine, I'll tell you all what I know."

Ching cleared his throat and began his story.

"Both my parents, the former King and Queen, were killed in the last Nebtan war against father's rival, Uni," Ching said. "I don't know the details, since I was only ten, but I do know that we won the war. Mother was a bold and kind woman. Everywhere she went, she had the respect of the other kings."

Hibika chimed in. "She always spoke her mind. Even Father loved that about her."

"I still remember accompanying mother on a visit to the Plains Region," Ching continued. "She took on several of the Plains Region's creatures all on her own. Even her bodyguards were amazed at her swordsmanship. In fact, she was the one who taught me and Hibika how to wield our katanas."

Hibika smiled. "Yes, Mother was a wonderful teacher. Even to this day, neither Ching nor I could ever beat her."

"She was also a great cook too!" Aiya interjected happily. "Sometimes, she would feed everyone at the temple one of her famous dishes."

Ching and Hibika laughed. Shanta watched them for a moment. She could see loving and sad emotions festered deep within them. She gave them a small smile. "Thank you for sharing your past with me."

Ching smiled back. "You're truly welcome."

"Yup, this Queen will truly make a difference here," Lin said with a smile.

"So, are you going to give us a tour of the city?" Aiya asked.

"Of course, Princess Aiya," Lin answered. "I'm just waiting for my wife to get here."

"How is Kusha doing?" Ching asked.

"She's just great," Lin answered with a grin. "Expecting our first child soon."

"That's wonderful," Hibika replied with a smile. "Is it a boy or a girl?"

"Don't know yet," Lin answered. "But it doesn't matter to me. I'll still love the child the same."

Suddenly, a knock came upon the door. The door opened, revealing Kusha. Kusha was the same height as Shanta. Her long black hair glistened in the light and her blue spots matched her blue eyes. Judging by her small face, she looked to be about Hibika's age. She wore a red silk kimono with embroidered cherry blossoms and a pink obi belt.

"Sorry I'm late," she said in a sweet voice. "I had to stop to get some food."

Lin introduced everyone to Kusha. Kusha smiled as she bowed slightly. Hibika and Ayia both stared at Kusha's stomach. Kusha noticed and giggled.

"Don't worry girls, it's not as bad as you think. You'll understand soon."

"Well, let's get going," said Lin, leading the way.

They all boarded the limousine-carriage, powered by mechanical horses.

The interior was elegant. There were cushioned seats and wool carpeting. A mini bar in the center of the carriage was filled with various alcohols and beverages and there was a small pantry next to it, filled with various pastries and snacks.

"Help yourself to a drink and cake," Lin said, sipping on his Nebtan martini.

"Wait, are you old enough to drink that?" Mark asked. "Aren't you our age?"

"Mark, you realize we're on another planet, right?" Shanta answered, giving him a glare. "Nebtan law is completely different to ours."

"Oh yeah, sorry about that," replied Mark with a forced chuckle.

Andrew shook his head and took a bottle of water from the bar. The carriage trotted along the smooth street. Occasionally, Lin would point to a building he had been to, trying to act like a tour guide. And where he didn't point and talk about, Kusha would fill in.

The ride seemed endless and magical. In the rich sector, there were various trees and tall buildings. Shops were everywhere, having at least two small plazas every four blocks.

The middle sector was more residential than business. There were townhouses, ranch-style, and even Victorian-style houses. Tall apartment buildings were scattered everywhere, and convenience stores were on every second street corner.

Truly, Raion reminded Andrew of New York. Suddenly, his mind turned elsewhere. He began to think about Rosa and his family, how he missed them. Although he knew the time gap between Earth and Macu was great, he still was anxious to return to Earth.

"Andrew," a voice called out to him.

He turned his head and saw Hibika staring at him.

"Yes, Hibika?" he asked with a smile.

"We're almost to the poor sector," she answered.

Andrew looked out the window and his eyes widened.

The poor sector was very similar to third-world countries. Small shacks filled the area with a small river running through it. Many Nebtans gathered around small fires, trying to keep warm. Nebtan women washed their clothes in the river, while some of Nebtan men told their tales to the Nebtan children.

"The last war made the poor sector skyrocket," Lin explained. "We do everything we can for them. However, our resources are getting thin and there is corruption within Raion, especially with officials."

The carriage rode through the sector. Millions of eyes watched with suspicion and fear. Suddenly, the carriage stopped. The door opened and Shanta burst out. The Nebtans were in shock.

"My Queen, you can't do that," Lin said, stepping out.

The Nebtan crowd began to boo and hiss. One Nebtan even threw a piece of trash at Shanta. Shanta quickly caught it and laid it on the ground. Ching stepped out of the carriage. Instantly, the crowd became quiet. They all bowed in unison.

"My fellow Nebtans," Ching said in a loud voice, "I come here to tell you of my marriage and to introduce you to your new Queen, Shanta."

The crowd looked at Shanta, talking amongst themselves.

"Hello," Shanta said in a shy voice.

"What was that?" one of the Nebtans asked, cupping his ear.

"I said, hello!" she shouted.

"Hello!" the crowd shouted back.

Shanta walked towards the crowd. They looked confused and began talking amongst themselves. She stood a few feet away from them and cleared her throat.

"As you know, I'll be your new Queen. To be honest, I don't know anything about your race. I've never dated or married into royalty before."

The crowd wasn't sure what Shanta was getting at, but they continued to listen.

"Look, I don't have a single clue what to say to you," replied Shanta nervously. "You all have been through a lot and deserve better. Just like my home on Earth, there's too many people suffering because of corrupted officials. Seeing you guys reminds me of my purpose. I can't promise you anything, but I'll do my best to protect you and give you what you need."

The crowd stared at Shanta. They could see a glimpse of the previous Queen within her. In their hearts, they decided to give Shanta a chance. Suddenly, a handclap from way back was heard, followed by more handclaps. Soon, the crowd cheered loudly for their new Queen. Shanta looked back to see both Ching and Lin clapping along with the crowd. The crowd bowed to Shanta, paying their respect to her. Shanta's face turned red.

"Your wife knows how to draw in a crowd," Lin said to Ching with a grin.

"That she does," Ching said bashfully.

An old man, with blue eyes, long stringy hair, and yellow stained teeth, broke away from the crowd and snuck back to his shack. There, he met with a shadowy figure.

The figure wore a black, hooded ninja outfit with gold trimmings around the neck. He carried a katana on his back and his blood red eyes matched his waistband.

"What news do you bring?" said the shadowy figure.

"The new Queen is here in the poor sector," answered the old man.

"So, Ching finally has a bride," the shadowy figure replied with a grin. "I must tell the master about this."

"What about my payment?" asked the old man, sticking his hand out.

"Oh right, your payment..." answered the shadowy figure.

He drew out his katana. He took one swipe at the old man and drew back his katana. The old man stood still with wide eyes. Suddenly, the room turned upside-down. A loud thud soon followed as the room began spinning. The spinning stopped. The old man's eyes widened as he stared at his headless body. His eyes engraved that picture until his eyes glazed over.

"Shadow demons never keep their promises," said the shadowy figure with a laugh.

FOURTEEN

Afer three weeks of planning and visiting Raion, today was the big day.

Mark and Andrew couldn't wait to see Shanta get married. Even before they woke up, the servant-girls hung their purple garments with yellow capes in their closets.

Now Andrew has been to many weddings, but this wedding was different. Besides the fact they were on a different planet, they also were in a different time period.

After breakfast, Mark and Andrew took a bath and put on their wedding garments. They looked like Buddhist priest. Mark and Andrew walked over to Ching's room to see how he was doing. They entered his room. There, twenty servant-girls prepared him for his wedding. It was like watching a car being made on an assembly line. First, he was given a bath. Next, they put on his wedding garments, as well as the finest cologne on the planet. Finally, the girls kissed Ching on the cheek for good luck. They all escorted him to the courtyard.

"So, this is how a king gets prepared for a wedding," Andrew said with his eyes wide open.

"I wish those girls would kiss me on the cheek for good luck," replied Mark folding his arms.

Mark and Andrew followed Ching to the courtyard, where the wedding took place. They couldn't believe how beautiful the chapel was.

The altar itself was big enough to hold the bride, groom, priest, and some of the bridesmaids and groomsmen. It was a white two-step altar with Macuan roses hanging everywhere and in the center was a wooden pulpit made of a strong Macuan tree.

"Hey Ching," Mark asked, touching his shoulder. "You ready to do this?"

"Indeed, I am Mark," Ching answered with confidence.

"I know you and Shanta make a great couple," Andrew said.

"Yeah, and your kids will be very strong," replied Mark with a smile.

Ching felt flushed. "Thank you for your support."

"I wonder what's taking her so long," Mark asked, folding his arms.

"You know how girls are," Andrew said, touching Mark's shoulder. "They love to spend hours getting themselves ready."

"Well, she better hurry up, I'm getting hungry," replied Mark, rubbing his stomach.

Suddenly, one of the servant-girls ran towards Ching. She stopped in front of him with her hands on her knees and her head down, trying to catch her breath. She whispered something into Ching's ear. Ching's eyes widened as he heard the news.

"What is it?" Andrew asked with a concerned look.

Ching paused for a moment with his fists clenched tightly. "Shanta has been kidnapped."

"What!" exclaimed Mark, "by whom?"

"From what she told me, it was the work of a shadow demon," Ching answered. "It must've snuck into the temple without my guards noticing it."

"But why would it take Shanta?" Mark asked with his hand on his chin.

Suddenly, a shadow demon appeared a few feet in front of the altar.

"If you want to see your Queen again, you must defeat my master," he said to Ching, Mark and Andrew.

"Where is he?" Andrew asked angrily.

He pointed to a mountain to the right of them.

"Why can't bad guys live closer to people?" asked Mark, realizing how far it was from the temple.

"You have until the next full moons to rescue her or else," he said.

"Or else what?" asked Mark, raising a fist.

"Trust me, you don't want to know," he said as he quickly disappeared.

Silence filled the air for a moment.

"What do we do?" asked Ching with a worried look. "I can't risk sending my men into the Shadow Region."

"How far is it from here?" Andrew asked looking at Ching.

"It is in the far east," answered Ching. "I would say about two hundred miles. We have three days until the next full moons."

"Mark and I will rescue Shanta and bring her back," Andrew said, touching Ching's shoulder.

Mark took off his wedding garment, revealing his training outfit.

"You had that on the whole time?" Andrew asked with a surprised look.

"A brotha gotta be prepared for anything," answered Mark, tightening his belt. "Now let's go kick some serious ass."

"If you haven't noticed, I don't have my training clothes underneath my wedding garment," Andrew said. "Give me a minute to change."

"Hurry up, every second wasted reduces our chances to saving Shanta," Mark called out as Andrew ran towards the temple.

Shanta woke up to find herself in a prison cell. She looked down at her hands and ankles, realizing she was chained to a wall. Suddenly, a shadow demon appeared on the other side of the prison cell. Shanta jumped back, scared to death.

"Comfortable, my Queen?" he asked nicely. "You should be since you'll be here for a while."

"Who are you and what do you want with me?" Shanta asked angrily.

"I'm a humble servant of my master and my master wants you," the demon answered.

I know I'm pretty, but this is ridiculous, she thought.

"Oh, I made sure your husband-to-be knew where you were," he replied. "Just so you can watch him die by the hands of my master."

"Not if I kill your master first," replied Shanta.

Shanta transformed. But as she got close to the cell door, her strength began leaving her. Shanta de-transformed as she fell to ground. The demon chuckled with delight as Shanta slowly rose from the ground.

"Looks like you're not going anywhere," he replied. "Those chains are connected to the wall made of Gukai, a material capable of draining life energy. But don't fret: your friends will come soon."

The demon laughed as he disappeared into the floor. Shanta sat up with her arms wrapped around her knees.

Ching, she thought as a tear rolled down her cheek.

Andrew and Mark ran as fast as they could to the mountain. With their minds focused on saving Shanta, breaks were out of the question. As the sun began to set, Andrew and Mark reached the foot of the mountain. They sat by a nearby dead tree, trying to find a way in.

The Shadow Region was a place crawling with various shadow demons. Until the master showed up, the Shadow Region was considered an uncivilized area, where it was survival of the fittest. According to Master Dao, the shadow demons are evolved forms of low-level demons from Hell. They used to have an Interdimensional Gateway, just like the Nebtans, to communicate with Hell. Sadly, they were banished to the region and the gateway was destroyed by the King of Hell himself.

Mark pointed to an opening a few feet from them. Even though it was being guarded, they had to take the chance. Mark quickly used his camouflage technique to cover both him and Andrew. They walked towards the opening, passing every guard. Once inside, Mark and Andrew ran down a lit narrow hallway. At the end of the hallway, they were in a grand lobby. They looked around the room and were amazed by the structure.

"This place looks like Nayo's crib," whispered Mark. "What, do they share the same decorator?"

Mark was right. It had the same black marble rooms on all three floors, as well as the same kind of tapestries on the walls. The only thing different about this place was that it is crawling with shadow demons.

The sounds of shadow demons approaching filled their ears. They quickly hid behind a group of metal statues.

"We have to be careful," Andrew whispered to Mark. "The slightest sound will alert every shadow demon here."

"You know I'm careful, Dawg," Mark whispered with his hand leaning on the side of the metal statue.

Suddenly, the metal statue fell over. The sound of metal crashing echoed throughout the hideout.

"Uh…oops," replied Mark shrugging his shoulders and grinning.

Andrew raised an eyebrow. Suddenly, Mark and Andrew were surrounded by shadow demons. They looked at each other and then at the shadow demons.

"You ready?" Andrew asked Mark as he rose from the ground.

"I've been ready," answered Mark. "Besides, these guys are a piece of cake."

Back at the temple, Ching was worried about Shanta. He hadn't eaten or slept for the whole day. He just sat by his window and stared outside, hoping Shanta would return. Suddenly, one of the servant-girls knocked on the door while she opened the door. Ching looked at her for a moment before he stared at the window once more. The servant-girl asked Ching a question in their native tongue. Ching looked at the girl and answered the girl back with a sigh. The servant-girl stared at Ching for a moment with a frown. She left the room quietly. Ching placed his hand on the window and continued to stare outside.

"Please come back to me, my love," he whispered to himself.

BAM! Both Mark and Andrew were knocked down hard. They got up slowly. The shadow demons dashed towards them. Mark and Andrew dodged most of the attacks, but there were too many shadow demons fighting them.

"Now, who said they were easy?" Andrew asked sarcastically, looking at Mark.

"I'm sorry!" Mark answered, blocking one of the demon's punches. "Sheesh, is this *Make Fun of Mark Day*?"

Andrew ignored Mark's joke as he continued to fight the demons. Despite the odds, Andrew wasn't going to give up. He began attacking the shadow demons all at once. Mark joined in. He used his Shadow Fang attack to distract the demons while Andrew used his Striking Claw attack to finish them off. The battle was intense, but they pressed on. Blood splattered everywhere and the cries of the shadow demons filled the air. Minutes later, every shadow demon was killed. Mark and Andrew bumped fists before they ran to the second floor.

Suddenly, a huge blast stopped them in their tracks. Mark and Andrew looked up and saw the shadow demon they had met earlier, standing on the rail of the second floor.

"You have to get pass me in order to fight my master," he said before he jumped off the rail.

He drew out his katana, raising it over his head. SLICE! Mark and Andrew dodged his attack as the blade demolished a piece of the ground. The demon picked up the katana from out of the ground and began his assault. With no way of defending himself, Andrew dodged the blade as best he could. SLASH! The blade cut him on his right arm. Andrew somersaulted over the demon and used his Striking Claw attack. The demon back-flipped over Andrew's attack: squatting on the wall for a couple of seconds. He charged at Andrew once more.

"SHADOW FANG!!!" shouted Mark.

Andrew moved over to the right as Mark's attack was about to hit the demon. Quickly, the demon slashed the shadow in two. The attack exploded behind him as he kept his eyes on Mark.

This isn't good, thought Mark still looking at the demon.

"It's time to end this battle once and for all!" exclaimed the demon as he charged at Mark.

Mark froze. He only had seconds before he was sliced and diced. Andrew had to do something. Mark closed his eyes and waited for impact. SNAP! Mark opened his eyes and saw that the blade was broken in two. He looked to his left. The broken blade was in Andrew's hand. The shadow demon stood there in awe with the broken katana still in his hand. Mark looked back at the demon with a grin. He began punching him in the face. BAM! Mark uppercut the demon into the air. Immediately, Andrew used his Gekido Bakuhatsu attack. The demon cried in pain as the blast began to burn his body. Seconds later, the demon was no more.

"Let's find Shanta before we have to fight more demons," replied Mark as he led the way to the second floor.

The second floor seemed quiet. They looked to their left and then their right. They found no one in sight. Andrew wanted to say they destroyed every demon here, but he had a feeling it wasn't true. Mark and Andrew walked down a long hallway filled with many doors.

"I got that weird feeling," replied Mark looking at every door they pass.

Suddenly, every door around them opened simultaneously. The first five doors began to shower them with arrows while the next five doors tried to barbecue them. Suddenly, a huge piece of the ceiling tried to crush them. Mark and Andrew managed to escape unharmed. The last five doors were a piece of cake. They tried to slice them with sharp blades, but Mark and Andrew dodged the blades easily. Mark and Andrew took a minute to catch their breaths.

"I hate…rescue missions…" replied Mark sitting on floor.

"C'mon…we have to…find Shanta…" Andrew said leading the way.

A few minutes later, Mark and Andrew reached the end of the hallway. To their surprise, they still had to climb several flights of stairs in order to reach the third floor. They were in for a surprise.

"I hope that isn't the master," Andrew said pointing to the creature guarding the third-floor door.

"It looks more like his pet," replied Mark trying not to sound scared.

It looked like a mix between a dragon and a serpent. It had green scales and yellow hair. Its wingspan was at least twelve feet long and its body was about thirty feet long with a skinny arrow-shaped tail. Its ice blue eyes stared at Mark and Andrew while its razor-sharp fangs drooled with saliva.

"I-I think he-he's hun-hun-hungry," Andrew stuttered nervously.

"And here I thought he had a drooling problem," replied Mark nervously.

The creature rose and fired a huge fiery blast at them. Mark and Andrew both dodged the blast. They dashed towards the creature. The creature flapped its mighty wings, creating a powerful gust of wind. They flew backwards, crashing into the walls. Mark got up and used his Shadow Fang attack to pin it down. The creature flew upward into the very high ceiling, dodging the attack. It nose-dived straight towards Mark. Mark froze for a second before he jumped out of the way. The impact of the dive created a hailstorm of rocks. Mark and Andrew dodged the oncoming rocks, but there were too many. SMACK! BAM! Mark and Andrew both felt the rocks knock the wind out of them. They hit the ground hard as the oncoming rocks began to pile up on them. Soon, their bodies were covered in rubble. The creature hissed in delight, deciding to barbecue them. It fired a huge fiery blast at them. The explosion demolished most of the third floor, creating a huge smoke cloud. The smoke cleared. The creature's eyes widened. Standing in front of it was a shadowy dome, just inches from the edge.

"It's time to kiss your ass goodbye!" shouted Mark as the dome began to disappear.

"GEKIDO!" Andrew shouted.

"KAGE!" shouted Mark.

"BAKUHATSU!!!" they shouted in unison.

Both their blast flew across the floor and headed straight for the creature. The creature took flight. Instantly, Mark and Andrew redirected their blast upward. Try as it might, the creature couldn't dodge their blast. The blast made contact. The creature cried in pain as its body began to disintegrate. Seconds later, the creature was no more.

"We rock!" Andrew exclaimed, bumping fists with Mark.

"Now we can rescue Shanta," replied Mark.

"I hope so," Andrew said folding his arms.

Shanta's strength was slowly leaving her. She tugged furiously on her chains, hoping she could break them and escape from her cell. She was out of breath. Try as she might, the chains wouldn't budge from their places. Shanta fell to the ground, panting. She stared at the ceiling in her cell. Thoughts of hopelessness filled her mind as her lips began to frown. Suddenly, the ground began to shake.

"Was that an earthquake?" Shanta asked herself, covering her head.

The wall cracked and crumbled. The chains fell from their posts, clanging as they hit the ground. She could feel her strength returning. Shanta smiled as she broke the chains with her bare hands.

"I guess all that training paid off," she said amazed by her strength. "Well, I better get out here."

Shanta transformed. She ripped the cell door open with her claws.

"Now to get out of this dump," replied Shanta, running out of the dungeon.

"Hey Drew, I was thinking," said Mark as they ran down the stairs.

"Yeah, what?" Andrew asked.

"Maybe we can avoid fighting the master."

"How?"

"By getting out of here before he finds us. I figure Shanta found a way to get out and is trying to find us."

"Well, you have a point."

They turned a corner. They headed for the stairs, leading to the main floor. Suddenly, the ground shook. A huge piece of the ground collapsed in front of them. A shadowy blur jumped out of the hole and landed on the other side.

"I think the master found us," replied Mark looking at the tall shadow.

The shadow stepped forward, revealing himself. Mark and Andrew both stood there with their fists clenched tightly.

He was about seven feet tall and had massive muscles. He wore some kind of samurai outfit made of Macuan metal. The helmet was bucket-shaped with two horns pointing upward.

"You two have ruined my plans," he said angrily. "Now, you have to die."

"Bring it on!" shouted Mark and dashed forward.

Mark began punching the master. To Mark's surprise, the master blocked his punches with one hand. Andrew joined in. To his surprise, the master was able to block both their punches with one hand. Suddenly, he vanished. Mark and Andrew both looked around trying to find him. SMACK! BAM! Mark and Andrew were hit from behind. Their faces met the ground as they skid. They got up quickly and dashed at him once more. This time, they both cranked up their speed. They bounced off walls trying to confuse him. It didn't work. He knew their every move and countered them instantly. Mark and Andrew both crashed into the ground hard, cracking it. Pain surged through their bodies as they struggled to get up. The master picked them up by their necks and slammed them onto the ground. Instantly, the ground collapsed.

Shanta ran up the stairs to the main floor. Suddenly, the ground began to shake again. Shanta covered her head while she continued to climb the stairs. She arrived at the main floor. There was a huge dust cloud in the air.

What happened? she thought as she tried to see through the cloud.

Suddenly, Shanta noticed Mark's claw lying underneath a pile of rubble. She knew they were in trouble. She looked a little over to her right and faintly saw the master.

"NEEDLE STORM!!!" shouted Shanta.

The master cried in pain as the attack pierced his armor. He tried to look for the culprit but couldn't see through the dust cloud. SMACK! Shanta kicked the master in the head. The blow knocked off his helmet. Shanta continued to attack the master. The dust cloud faded. Shanta's eyes widened.

"Who…are you?"

"My name is Uni," he answered. "You're stronger than I thought."

Uni's face was handsome. He looked like he was in his late twenties since his jet-black hair didn't show any signs of gray in it. He had a small face with smooth skin and his eyes were ice blue.

"You can't be him," Shanta said still looking at him. "You're supposed to be old, like Ching's father."

"I'm but a few Nebtans that stop aging after they reach their late twenties," Uni replied. "That genetic trait is long gone now, thanks to the last war. I'm the sole survivor."

"What do you want with me?"

"I need a son to take my place when I die. There is a disease plaguing my body. I don't have much time to live. I chose you because you are strong. I knew you would be the perfect mother for my son."

Shanta raised her hand. "Hold up, I'm getting married to someone else and becoming Queen. I can't have your kid! That's called cheating and I don't do that stuff!"

"Then, you must die!" exclaimed Uni charging towards Shanta.

BOOM! Rocks flew everywhere. Shanta and Uni shielded themselves from the oncoming flying rocks. Shanta looked to her left to find Mark and Andrew standing with tiny rocks hovering around them.

"My Cuz won't be a baby momma!" exclaimed Mark while raising a fist.

"About time you guys got up…" muttered Shanta.

"Time to give him a beat down, Bronx style," Andrew said cracking his knuckles.

Shanta led the assault. She began punching Uni with everything she had. Mark joined in. When it looked like Uni was worn out, Andrew stepped in to finish the job. To their surprise, Uni was able to block all their punches and kicks. SMACK! POW! BAM! Mark, Shanta and Andrew skidded onto the ground.

"This guy is too strong," replied Mark getting up.

"We need a plan," Andrew said trying to get up.

"I think I got one," replied Shanta smiling. "Just follow my lead."

Shanta used her Needle Storm attack to blast the walls around Uni. The attack created a huge dust cloud. Uni saw through their plan. He counterattacked. Shanta, Andrew, and Mark felt like rag dolls as their bodies tumbled across the ground. Mark got up and used his Shadow Fang attack. The worm-like shadows quickly grabbed Uni. Uni smirked as he broke free. Instantly, he vanished. Mark looked around. BAM! Mark felt a hard blow to his back. His body became weightless as he headed straight for a wall. Mark regained his balance a little too late, crashing into the wall. Andrew stepped in to help but saw Uni's knee connect with his chin. Andrew flew upward, crashing into the ceiling. Shanta watched as Andrew plummeted to the ground. She froze in terror. Uni slowly approached her with a stern look. Both Mark and Andrew could barely move. This was it for Shanta. She shut her eyes tight, quivering. Suddenly, Uni's body became heavy, and his breathing became shallow. Soon, his vision became blurry.

No! Not now…

Shanta opened her eyes. Uni was down on one knee, struggling to breathe. Mark summoned his strength and used his Shadow Fang attack. Uni saw the shadow a little too late, dodging it. Blood ran down his armor as he covered his wound with his left hand. Still unable to defend, Uni tried to escape. It was too late. Andrew used his Striking Claw attack to pierce his chest-plate. Andrew pulled out his hand and watched as blood oozed out of Uni's chest. Uni staggered backwards, pressing his back against the wall. Blood drooled from out of his mouth as he clenched his chest.

"If I die, you all are going down with me," he choked out.

"I've gotta bad feeling," replied Mark signaling Shanta and Andrew to get out of here.

"DESECRATION!!!" shouted Uni with an evil grin.

Suddenly, his body began to glow. With every second wasted, Uni's body began to glow brighter. Mark, Shanta and Andrew ran down the main floor hallway. BOOM! Uni exploded. The blast crept up behind them as they turned corners. They found the main entrance and headed for it as fast as they could.

"The heat from the blast is getting closer towards us," replied Mark running for his dear life.

"We're almost there," Andrew said pointing to the entrance door.

They went through the entrance door, finding a place to take cover. They watched as the whole mountain began to crumble inward. They all gave a sigh of relief as they sat on the ground.

They arrived at the temple the next day. Everyone was happy to see us, even Ching. Mark and Andrew immediately headed for the dining room for a well-deserved meal. Afterwards, the servant-girls treated their wounds. Meanwhile, Shanta and Ching were in Ching's room discussing the wedding ceremony.

"Are you sure want to get married tomorrow?" Ching asked. "You just came back from battle and…"

"I'm totally sure, Ching," answered Shanta with a smile. "I won't let anything stop this wedding from happening."

Ching was awestruck. He knew he had found the right bride.

"I won't argue," he said looking into Shanta's dark brown eyes. "By the way, was your wedding dress to your liking?"

"Well…" she began and said, "I was thinking of a different kind of dress."

"What do you mean?" Ching asked looking confused.

"Don't worry, you'll see it tomorrow," answered Shanta tapping his hand gently.

Today was the big day. This time the ceremony was held much earlier. Mark and Andrew waited for Hibika and Aiya while Ching waited by the altar.

"You two look handsome," said Hibika looking at them.

"You two look awesome," Andrew said looking at Hibika.

Hibika and Ayia were both wearing a long blue sleeveless dress with a small slit on the right side and matching hi-heeled shoes. They each wore a diamond bracelet on their left wrist and their hairs were up in a bun.

"Where's Shanta?" asked Mark looking around.

"She'll be here soon," answered Aiya. "She had to find her veil."

"Sorry I'm late," said Shanta sort of running towards the others in her wedding dress.

"That dress is hot, Cuz," replied Mark.

Shanta's wedding dress was like Hibika and Aiya's dress, but it was backless, and the slit was on the left. Her hair was also in a bun and her veil was made with fine pearls and sheer fabric. Mark and Andrew noticed the ice on her. Besides the diamond ring, Shanta had diamond earrings, a diamond necklace and a diamond bracelet on her left wrist.

"Now to get you and Ching married," Andrew said looking at Shanta.

Mark signaled the Nebtan band to play the wedding march. First, one of the servant-girls walked out throwing flower petals down the aisle. Next, Rei-Rei came out holding the rings on a pillow. Finally, Mark and Aiya and Hibika and Andrew, as bridesmaid and groomsman, came out arm-in-arm. They stood in their respected places. Everyone in the chairs stood up and faced the back. Shanta walked down the aisle slowly with her veil covering her face. The diamonds shined brightly as she walked towards the altar.

"Doesn't she look beautiful," said Master Dao, who was standing behind the pulpit.

"What are you doing there?" asked Mark. "You better get back to your seat before the preacher comes."

"Uh, Mark," said Ching, "Master Dao is the preacher. He has married most of my people for years."

"How many years…?" Mark muttered.

"I heard that," replied Master Dao angrily.

"I didn't mean it," said Mark with a forced laugh.

Master Dao gave him a nasty look. He cleared his throat and began the ceremony. "We are gathered here today to join Ching and Shanta in holy matrimony. If there is anyone in audience who does not want them to get married, speak now or forever hold your peace."

Silence filled the air.

"Okay, then let us begin," said Master Dao breaking the silence. "Shanta, do you take Ching to be your husband? To have and to hold for richer or poorer, in sickness and in health, until you both shall live?"

"I do," answered Shanta.

"Do you Ching take Shanta to be your wife? To have and to hold for richer or poorer, in sickness and in health, until you both shall live?" asked Master Dao.

"I do," answered Ching.

"The rings please," said Master Dao smiling.

Rei-Rei stepped forward and gave the rings to both Shanta and Ching.

"Ching, place the ring on Shanta's finger and repeat after me," said Master Dao. "With this ring…"

"With this ring…" Ching repeated as he placed the ring on Shanta's finger.

"I thee wed," said Master Dao.

"I thee wed," repeated Ching.

"Repeat after me," said Master Dao looking at Shanta. "With this ring…"

"With this ring…" Shanta repeated as she placed the ring on Ching's finger."

"I thee wed," said Master Dao.

"I thee wed," repeated Shanta.

Hibika and Andrew smiled at each other for a moment before they looked at both Shanta and Ching. Master Dao signaled Rei-Rei to get the broom behind the back row. Seconds later, Rei-Rei returned with a large broom.

"To show the strength of your love, you must jump over the broom at the same time," replied Master Dao receiving the broom from Rei-Rei.

He placed the broom onto the ground and told the bridesmaid and groomsmen to stand aside. Ching and Shanta stepped down and stood behind the broom. They looked at each other for a moment and jumped over the broom simultaneously. Everyone clapped and cheered.

"Well, it's the moment you two have been waiting for," replied Master Dao as he stepped down from the pulpit. "With the power vested in me, I pronounce you husband and wife."

Ching lifted the veil and locked lips with Shanta. Everyone stood up and cheered. As Ching and Shanta walked down the aisle, everyone began throwing rice. Luckily for Mark and Andrew, the reception was in the dining room. They were awestruck by the decoration for the reception.

The tables were moved over to the far-left corner, facing horizontally. Next to the tables, just ten feet away, was the food. Macuan fruits and vegetables were in a clear sectioned tray. Fried Giras were in a blue bowl, roast Dehas, were in a red pan, and Veya fillets were in a purple pan. There was also rice and some Macuan fruit punch. On the far right, only a small space was where the DJ played the music. The remaining space was for dancing. Believe it or not, but Nebtans love to dance. They look like they don't, but they have some of the hottest Nebtan music.

Of course, Mark and Andrew headed for the food while everyone else was either talking or dancing. After wolfing down their food, Mark and Andrew decided to talk to Shanta and congratulate her.

"Congrats, Cuz," said Mark slapping her on her back.

"Thanks," Shanta said.

"I know you two will be happy together," Andrew replied and sipped some more of the punch.

"Hey Andrew," asked Hibika as she came towards him. "Want to dance?"

"Sure," Andrew answered smiling.

"Uh, Hibika," asked Mark grabbing Andrew's shoulder. "Can I talk to Drew for a moment?"

"Okay, but don't take too long," she answered.

Mark pulled Andrew over to a quiet spot in the dining room. He gave Andrew a concerned look.

"What's wrong?" Andrew asked.

"You and Hibika: since when are you two such good friends? Before, you used to keep your distance, but now it seems you two are hittin' it off."

"Look, Hibika told me how she felt about me."

"What ya say?"

"I told her that I have feelings for Rosa and I wanted to be friends."

"How did she take it?"

"She took it well."

"That's good," replied Mark as he pushed Andrew to the dance floor. "Now, I'll let you two dance the night away."

Later that night, Mark and Andrew told Shanta they were leaving first thing in the morning.

"Are you sure about this?" Shanta asked. "You gotta stay for my coronation."

"I wish we could," Andrew answered with a stern look, "but we need to save Rosa and Tracy. Who knows what my father has done to them."

"I understand how you feel," replied Shanta, "but you can't go back to Earth without a plan. Your dad will kill you before you get to the front door."

Andrew clenched his fists tightly. Tension grew thick with each passing second.

"Look, let's go to her coronation," said Mark nervously. "Time hasn't passed as much as we think. We've been here only two and half months, which is equivalent to seven Earth days…I think. Anyway, what's one more day?"

Andrew sighed deeply. "Fine…"

Suddenly, they heard a gasp. They turned around and saw Hibika and Aiya standing behind them.

"What are you guys doing here?" Mark asked.

"We came to tell Shanta about the coronation…" Hibika started but trailed off.

"We didn't mean to intrude in your conversation," Aiya added. She stared at Mark. "Are you going to stay for the coronation?"

"Yeah," Mark answered with a smile. "Wouldn't miss it."

FIFTEEN

William was watching TV while Lily was cooking dinner. Suddenly, the doorbell rang. William lowered the volume. The doorbell rang again. He got up off the couch and walked over to the door. He peeked through the hole and saw two men, one tall and one short, in suits.

"Mom, run!" he shouted.

The two men barged in, breaking the door down. They drew out their guns and began firing. Bullets flew in and out of William's body. He stared at his bloody hands as he fell to his knees. He leaned up against the wall. He slowly became lightheaded and dizzy. Blood streaked along the wall as William's body hit the floor. His eyes glazed over as his last breath left him. A small pool of blood formed around him, staining the carpet. The two men rushed over to the kitchen to find Lily. They pointed their guns, searching high and low. They decided to split up and search the whole apartment. The tall man searched through the terrace. Suddenly, he heard a noise. He turned around, staring at the table. He crept slowly. He flipped up the tablecloth and found Lily hiding underneath it. The tall man grabbed her arm and dragged her across the floor. He stood her against the living room wall. The shorter man soon entered the room.

"Nice job," he said with a grin.

"Let me go!" Lily cried struggling to get free.

"Shut up bitch!" the other guy exclaimed.

He slapped her across her face. Lily felt dizzy for a moment. Tears began to run down her cheeks.

"Why are you doing this?" she asked sobbing.

"Orders are orders," answered the tall man.

He fired. Lily's eyes widened as she felt a sharp pain in her chest. She clutched her chest tightly as she fell to her knees. Blood soaked through her clothes as her breathing became shallow. Suddenly, the room began spinning. Lily collapsed. The life in her eyes grew dim with each passing second as muffled sounds filled her ears. And then, silence.

"That takes care of them," the tall man said smiling.

In Manhattan, Mike was rechecking the inventory list at the chemical plant. He marked the paper with a check for every chemical that was there.

"Everything is here," he said checking off the last chemical on his list. "Now to go home and get some sleep."

Mike yawned as he walked to his office, located on the second floor. He picked up his jacket and hat. With his hand on the switch, Mike was about to turn off his office lights. Suddenly, five guys dressed in suits stood by the door. The leader was the only man dressed in red. Mike stepped back towards his desk.

"You guys shouldn't be here," said Mike reaching for the phone. "Leave now or I'll call the police!"

BAM! One of the guys shot Mike in the hand. Mike covered his wound with his other hand and slowly stepped backwards towards the fire alarm. Another guy shot the fire alarm.

"Why are you doing this?" asked Mike, feeling frightened. "I didn't do anything to you."

"But you have," answered the leader. "You and your family let that foster kid stay alive. Now, our boss wants you and your family dead. Don't take it personally. We're just doing our job."

A hailstorm of bullets hit Mike. Blood splattered across the wall and on the floor. The lifeless Mike collapsed to the ground, surrounded by a pool of blood.

"Mission complete," replied the leader with a smile.

Shanta woke up to Ching's sweet voice. She stretched out her arms as she sat up. Ching smiled as he stared at her in all her morning beauty.

"I look ugly, don't I?" Shanta said, fixing her bedhead.

"No, you're still beautiful," Ching answered. "Are you ready for your coronation?"

"A little. I'm a bit nervous about this."

"Don't worry, I'll be there with you."

She kissed him. "Thanks, sweetie."

Shanta got out of bed and took a bath. Ching helped her dress in her Queen attire. Although it was nothing more than a purple heavy kimono with embroidered pink flowers, it still was difficult for Shanta. Ching quickly summoned several servant-girls to help with Shanta's makeup. After an hour of preparation, Ching couldn't believe his eyes.

Standing before him was not only his wife, but his people's new Queen. There wasn't much foundation on her, since her skin was flawless, and the purple eye shadow brought out her dark brown eyes. The light shade of pink lipstick matched the flowers on her kimono and her hair remained down.

"Wow," Ching managed to say.

Shanta's face turned red. One of the servant-girls helped Shanta walk in her new wooden shoes. Ching got himself ready. He wore the same purple kimono, except there was an embroidered Yin-Yang symbol on the back.

The servant-girls led them to the Grand Hall, where major events take place. Shanta and Ching held hands, occasionally glancing at each other. The servant-girls opened the bronze doors. Everyone inside stood up and cheered as they walked down the long aisle. Shanta blushed, waving to the huge crowd. Both Andrew and Mark smiled, giving her a thumbs up. Shanta and Ching stood at the bottom of the altar for a moment. While everyone sat down, Ching walked up the steps and stood next to Master Dao, who was holding a silver crown. The crown was exactly like Ching's, except it had a small blue diamond in the center.

"My fellow Nebtans," Ching began, "we are here today to witness the coronation of our future Queen, Shanta."

Everyone clapped, along with a few cheers. Master Dao handed the crown to Ching. Ching approached Shanta with a smile.

"Kneel please," he said.

Shanta knelt.

"Shanta, repeat after me," said Ching. "I, Shanta…"

"I, Shanta…"

"Queen of the Nebtan race…"

"Queen of the Nebtan race…"

"Will rule over my people with kindness and defend them with all my strength."

"Will rule over my people with kindness and defend them with all my strength."

Ching placed the crown on her head. "I, Ching, King of the Nebtan race, declare you, Shanta, Queen of the Nebtan race."

Shanta rose and faced everyone. Everyone stood up and cheered. As she walked down the aisle, everyone began to kneel. Shanta wasn't much for being the center of attention, but she sure was having a blast with it. For the first time, she truly understood how Miss America felt.

One of the servant-girls opened the door for her. Shanta quickly left the room. Ching followed. Soon, everyone was excited to meet and greet their new Queen. Andrew and Mark watched as Shanta became an instant celebrity.

"My Cuz, the Queen," said Mark, pretending to tear up. "I'm so proud of her."

Andrew chuckled. "Guess this means we're her bodyguards."

Mark chuckled. "Guess so."

That night, Andrew and Mark prepared themselves for the morning. They both sighed, knowing that their fantasy trip had to end.

Morning came almost suddenly. They got dressed, wearing their training outfits, and ate their final Nebtan meal. As Mark and Andrew were heading out, someone jumped onto Mark's back.

"Hey! You guys didn't think you would really leave without me, did you?" Shanta said laughing.

Shanta was also packed and wore her training outfit.

"But aren't you supposed to stay here with Ching, now that you're Queen?" Andrew asked.

"Yeah, how'd you get Ching to let you leave, Shanta?" Mark added.

"Well…" Shanta said with a smirk on her face, "you know what a little persuasion can do."

"Oh, you nasty!" exclaimed Mark.

"Ha-ha-ha-ha…SIKE! Ya'll knows it's not that type of party!" Shanta exclaimed. She calmed down. "But for real, I'm coming. Ching and I talked about it, and he agrees that it's for the best. He knows that I'll be back soon. Besides, you guys know that you don't stand a chance without the Big Shanta! Ha-ha-ha-ha-ha…"

Mark made a face. "Ah, ha-ha…shut up!"

Shanta gave Mark a smug look. "Aw, don't hate."

"Alright you guys, please stop," Andrew said breaking the small argument. "Now let's go. The gateway is back in the forest. Let's get there before nightfall."

"Ok…" Mark and Shanta both said sighing.

They left the temple, saying goodbye to their newfound friends. Both Ching and Hibika stood with the other Nebtans and waved. Andrew and Hibika looked into each other's eyes. Andrew wanted to say something to Hibika, but hesitated. Suddenly, Rei-Rei ran up to Mark and hugged his leg. Mark knelt to pat his head.

"Th…Tha…thank…y-you…" said Rei-Rei slowly. He gave Mark a huge smile.

Mark smiled and said, "You're welcome, Kid."

"Rei-Rei's first words," said Shanta with a smile. "Mark gave Rei-Rei the courage to speak."

"Mark, I also want to thank you," replied Aiya stepping forward.

"What do you mean?" asked Mark sounding concerned.

Aiya stopped in front of Mark. She looked into his eyes and tiptoed, leaning forward. They locked lips. Everyone was shocked, even Mark.

"Duh…duh…duh…" Mark managed to say after they unlocked lips.

"I know you love someone else on Earth, but I just wanted to know how it felt to kiss you," said Aiya looking into Mark's eyes. "I hope your lover gives you the same love I want to give you."

Mark just stared at her saying, "Duh…duh…duh."

"Uh, Mark says thank you Aiya," Andrew replied dragging Mark out of the temple. "Thanks for everything."

Mark, Andrew and Shanta walked down the pathway through the forest. The sun poked through the trees lighting their way towards the gateway. From the looks of it, the gateway was already waiting for them.

"Well guys, you ready to go home?" Andrew asked, looking at them.

"Let's do it," answered Mark with a smile.

They took one last look around the forest before they went through the gateway. None of them were sure what to expect on Earth, but they knew they were ready.

On a very early Sunday morning, Hidishi was in his office reviewing his profits with the staff manager. The sun began its journey towards the sky, shining brightly on Hidishi's desk. It made enough light for the staff manager to see Hidishi's mouth.

"Your cocaine shipment has reached Mexico, Sir," said the staff manager looking at the clipboard. "We should be receiving the money by tomorrow."

"Excellent," said Hidishi with a smile. "What about my opium shipment?"

The staff manager flipped a couple of pages. "The Russians demand for a lower price for the opium."

Hidishi leaned forward a little with his hands folded and said, "If the Russians want my opium so badly, why don't they raise some taxes?"

The staff manager didn't answer.

"Listen to me…Kenny," said Hidishi, looking at the staff manager's nametag. "I don't care how poor the country is. If they want my drugs, then they must pay for it. Otherwise…"

Suddenly, one of Hidishi's men came in.

"Sorry for interrupting," he said. "We just finished taking care of the foster family."

"Excellent," replied Hidishi. "What about the kid?"

"Well…he wasn't anywhere in the house or at the plant," the man answered. "We are still looking for him and his friend."

"You better or else," Hidishi said angrily. "Now, get out of my sight!"

The man left the room quietly. Hidishi focused his eyes back on Kenny.

"Tell me Kenny," he asked, "how much money has this corporation made this year?"

Kenny flipped over to the last page on the clipboard. His eyes widened as he stared at the numbers.

"Well, how much Kenny?" Hidishi asked.

"Ninety m-m-million dollars SSSirrr," said Kenny stuttering.

"Excellent," said Hidishi smiling. "You may go Kenny."

Kenny left the room. Hidishi turned his chair around, facing the window.

"So, you think you can hide from me?" he asked as though he was talking to Andrew. "Sooner or later, I will find you..."

They arrived back to Madam Renee's Fortune House that Sunday morning.

"We're home," replied Mark looking around the room.

"How was the trip?" asked Madam Renee hovering towards them.

"Great," Andrew answered. "We learned a lot and trained hard."

"Fighting mostly creatures and shadow demons," added Mark.

"I'm even Queen of the Nebtans," replied Shanta showing Madam Renee the diamond ring.

Suddenly Madam Renee's smile turned into a frown.

"What's wrong?" asked Shanta looking concerned.

"Andrew…I have some bad news…" she answered looking at him.

Andrew's heart raced.

"Lily and William…are dead," Madam Renee sadly. "The neighbors heard gunshots and quickly called the police. By the time they arrived, both Lily and William were found dead. They also killed Mike while he was at work, making it look like a robbery."

Andrew clenched his fists tightly. Tears roll down his cheeks. Lily, Mike and William weren't Andrew's blood family, but they were still his family. Pissed, Andrew punched a huge hole into the wall.

"Hidishi will pay," Andrew said raising a fist. "Hidishi will pay!"

Rosa woke up to the sound of the two guards talking. She tapped Tracy on the shoulders as she tried to listen to the guards' conversation.

"What is it, Rosa?" Tracy asked, slowly waking up.

Rosa put a finger to her lips, signaling Tracy to hush. She signaled Tracy to come over by the door and listen to the conversation.

"No way, they still haven't found that kid yet?" asked the first guard.

"Nah, it's like he disappeared," answered the second guard. "Even his friend vanished."

"Thank goodness Andrew and Mark are both safe," whispered Rosa looking at Tracy.

"But where could they be?" Tracy asked.

Andrew paced back and forth, trying to keep his cool. Besides taking Rosa, Hidishi killed Andrew's family. Andrew was so pissed, he couldn't think straight. All he wanted to do in that moment was to kill Hidishi and rescue Rosa and Tracy.

"Don't worry, Dawg, we'll get him," replied Mark, trying to cheer Andrew up. "But we have to find his hideout first."

"Not to mention we have to figure out how many guards are there," added Shanta.

Andrew ignored them and looked at Madam Renee.

"I need you to pinpoint Hidishi's location." Andrew demanded.

"Of course," Madam Renee answered calmly. She began focusing her mind.

"Hidishi's hideout is a warehouse in Mott Haven," said Madam Renee. "It is off Willis Ave and East 138th Street. That's all I can give you. Somehow, I'm being blocked by another force."

"That's all I need," replied Andrew, as he headed for the door.

Mark quickly blocked his path.

"Yo, calm down," said Mark with a stern look. "I'm as pissed off as you are. However, you don't have any way of getting there. And do you have a plan, once you're there?"

Andrew looked away. "I'll think of something."

Mark punched Andrew in the face. Andrew fell backwards, landing on his butt.

"I hope that woke you up," Mark said angrily. "The Drew I know is much more level-headed than that."

Shanta quickly helped Andrew up. "You're not alone in this: we're all here for you."

Tears rolled down Andrew's eyes. "I'm sorry…"

Shanta hugged him. Soon, Mark joined in. Their warm embrace helped Andrew come back to his senses.

Madam Renee smiled. "Don't worry you three: I'll take you there."

"How?" Mark asked. "Your chair can't carry us all."

"Stupid boy, I'm going to teleport you there," Madam Renee answered with irritation in her voice.

"I…knew that…" replied Mark, feeling embarrassed.

"Alright guys let's do it!" exclaimed Shanta.

Madam Renee raised both arms. Soon, they began to feel lightheaded and transparent. They disappeared.

"Good luck to you all," she said with a smile.

The Meta-Morphic Five waited patiently for Hidishi to give them an assignment. They sat in the cafeteria, eating and drinking. Flameboy rested his head on the table, napping. Drool stained his sleeve as he snored. Suddenly, a voice came onto the loudspeaker.

"Will the Meta-Morphic Five please come to Hidishi's office," replied the voice.

"Finally, some action," said Big C slamming his fist into his other hand.

Gyro slapped Flameboy's head. Flameboy sprang up from his seat. He quickly rubbed his eyes.

"Boss wants us," said Gyro snickering.

Flameboy quickly followed the others. As they walked to Hidishi's office, Sparks stopped suddenly. He stared at the workers below.

"Something wrong, Sparks?" asked Rampage.

"It's nothing," he answered smiling.

"Okay," said Rampage. He continued walking.

That boy is here, thought Sparks. *I can sense his presence.*

Near the corner of East 138th Street and Willis Ave, Mark, Shanta and Andrew planned their next move. Mark reported only four guards were guarding the entrance. Shanta led the first attack.

Shanta walked over towards the guards swinging her hips to and fro. The guards stopped marching and stared at Shanta's incredible body.

"Can you guys tell me how to get to Fenton Ave from here?" she asked, batting her eyelashes and giggling.

"Sure baby," one of the guards answered. "If you go down East 138th and get on I-278, you should reach Fenton Ave in an hour and ten minutes."

"I was wondering if you could take me there since I don't have a car," replied Shanta leaning closer towards the guard.

"I'll take you in my car," replied the guard grabbing Shanta's butt.

Shanta wanted to punch him but kept up her seductive composure. "What about you guys?"

The other guards nodded frantically. All the guards followed Shanta into the car. Both Andrew and Mark were awestruck.

"She's good," replied Mark.

Andrew and Mark went inside the warehouse, sneaking behind crates.

"I like the décor," whispered Mark. "It gives this place that drug-lord feeling."

"This isn't the time to joke around," Andrew said with a stern look. "We have work to do."

Mark and Andrew snuck past the overseers and hid behind huge pile of crates. They knew the only way to rescue Rosa and Tracy was to get to the second floor. Suddenly, Mark pointed to a staircase on the other side of the warehouse.

"How do we get to the stairs without getting noticed?" Andrew asked him.

"We don't," Mark answered with a smile. "But you will. I'll distract them while you find Rosa and Tracy."

"Can you handle all these people?"

"It's just those two big guys I gotta worry about. Besides, the workers will be too frightened to fight me. I got this, dawg."

"Have fun."

Andrew watched as Mark had jumped from behind of the crates and transformed in front of them. The plan worked. All the workers were running scared while the two overseers attacked Mark. Andrew snuck past them and headed for the staircase. On the second floor, guards were waiting for him. Instantly, Andrew transformed. He attacked them with ease. Seconds later, every guard was knocked unconscious. Hidishi's office door opened, revealing the Meta-Morphic Five. Andrew flipped over the railing and landed on top of the two overseers on the main floor.

"We have a problem," Andrew said pointing upward.

"Oh great, they're here," replied Mark looking upward.

One-by-one, the Meat-Morphic Five flipped over the railing and landed onto the main floor. Each of them rose like a wave. They stared Mark and Andrew down.

"I'm surprised you two made it this far," Big C said with an evil grin, "but you won't defeat us."

"Think so?" asked Mark with a smile.

"We know so," answered Big C. "Sparks, finish them off."

"With pleasure," Sparks replied, meta-morphing as he cracked his knuckles.

He vanished. Even though Mark and Andrew couldn't see him, they could sense his presence. Andrew turned around and blocked Spark's punch. Mark countered for Andrew: punching Sparks in the face. The blow knocked Sparks backwards. Sparks quickly regained his balance.

How did they become so fast and strong in a week? No one is faster than me!

Sparks charged at Mark and Andrew. Flashes of light scattered across the floor. The remaining Meta-Morphic Five stood there amazed by Mark and Andrew's fighting skills. Even they couldn't believe how strong Mark and Andrew had become after a week. SMACK! Sparks flew backwards, skidding on the ground. He crashed into the wall. He coughed up blood. Sparks got up slowly, leaning against the wall.

"Had enough?" Andrew asked him angrily.

"I won't be defeated by the likes of you!" Sparks exclaimed, spitting blood to the side.

"Need help?" Big C asked. "You look like you need it."

"Sure," Sparks answered with an evil smile, "let's kill these brats together!"

"Not without me," replied a familiar voice.

Mark and Andrew turned their heads to find Shanta, in her fox form, running up towards them.

"What took you?" asked Mark.

"Those guards actually tried to take me to Fenton Ave," she answered. "They also tried to feel me up, so I kicked their ass. Now, let's kill these goons so you two can rescue Rosa and Tracy."

Despite it being five against three, Mark, Andrew and Shanta still had the upper hand.

Shanta ended up fighting Rampage. Despite his gorilla body and power, he was no match for Shanta. Shanta blocked or countered his moves. Angry, Rampage let his gorilla side take over. He threw crates at her and stomped the ground hard, creating small waves of concrete. Shanta dodged and dashed forward. She kicked Rampage in the face, knocking him off balance. Rampage hopped backwards. Shanta got behind him lightning fast. She kneed him in the back. Rampage's spine cracked as he went flying into the air. Shanta jumped into the air. She clubbed him in the stomach. Rampage plummeted hard into the ground, making a huge hole on the main floor. He couldn't move at all. He de-morphed.

"That takes care of you," she said as she landed onto the ground.

Meanwhile, Mark blocked both Gyro's and Flameboy's assaults. No matter how fast they were Mark was able to block. Mark vanished. They looked around the main floor, trying to find him. BAM! Both Flameboy and Gyro felt a powerful blow from behind. They skidded across the ground.

"That's it!" cried Gyro as he transformed both hands into mechanical blades.

Gyro swung his arms in different directions, trying to slash Mark. Mark dodged, countering with his Shadow Fang attack. Gyro went flying, crashing into a wall. His body left an impression as he slid down the wall. Suddenly, huge flames headed straight for Mark. Mark jumped into the air. He back-flipped onto a pile of crates.

"Prepare to burn!" shouted Flameboy. "WAVES OF INFERNO!!!"

"Kiss your ass goodbye!" shouted Mark. "KAGE BAKUHATSU!!!"

Both blasts met in the middle. The ground cracked and was scorched by the intense heat. It seemed to be anyone's win. Mark's gem glowed, adding more power to his blast. It sent both Flameboy's, as well as his blast, to Flameboy. Flameboy couldn't dodge. He took the blast head on. He cried in pain as the blast began to slowly disintegrate his body. Seconds later, Flameboy was no more.

"That was easy," replied Mark sarcastically.

Gyro jumped into the air, firing blasts at Mark. Mark dodged. The blasts hit the wall and ground, turning it into Swiss cheese. Mark used his Shadow Fang attack. The worm-like shadow extended towards Gyro. Gyro dodged. The shadow ricocheted from the wall and headed towards Gyro once more. Gyro dodged again. The shadow split into thin strands, covering more area. Gyro's jaw dropped as the thin strands fused together. The shadow swallowed Gyro whole. Gyro tried to escape, but the shadow grew smaller. Mark grinned as he snapped his fingers. The shadow exploded. All that was left of Gyro was his right mechanical hand.

"Need some back up, Dawg?" asked Mark, looking at Andrew.

Andrew didn't answer, as he blocked both Sparks' and Big C's punches.

"Don't let your anger cloud your judgement…" Mark muttered.

Andrew jumped into the air. He used his Striking Claw attack. Even though they blocked Andrew's attack, Sparks and Big C still were badly bruised by it. Andrew landed onto the ground. He attacked them head on. Big C and Sparks couldn't block Andrew's assault. Both of their bodies felt the intense blows. They flew backwards, tumbling onto the ground.

"Shanta," Andrew said looking at her, "find Rosa and Tracy. Mark, let's double team these guys."

"I've been waiting for you to say that!" exclaimed Mark with a smile.

Big C and Sparks began to laugh.

"What's so funny?" asked Mark raising a fist.

"You may be stronger than us when we are separate, but not strong enough to defeat us when we are united," Sparks answered.

"You catch that, Drew?" asked Mark looking confused.

 "Not really," Andrew answered, looking confused.

"You shall see our awesome power!" exclaimed Sparks.

Instantly, their bodies began to glow. The light was so bright Andrew had to cover his eyes. The light faded. Mark and Andrew both stood there with their eyes wide open.

"What do you think?" he asked, looking at Mark and Andrew with an evil smile.

"What…are you?" Andrew asked, staring at him.

"The name's Big Sparks," he answered folding his arms.

Big Sparks was at least seven or eight feet tall. He wore blue jeans and black boots. His muscles were massive. He could take out at least a hundred men with one punch. Big Sparks' head was the same size as Big C's, but he had Sparks' hair color and narrow eyes.

"This ain't good," replied Mark.

"I don't care," Andrew said angrily. "We have to defeat him!"

SIXTEEN

Shanta continued to look for Rosa and Tracy on the second floor. She checked the cafeteria and the training room. She noticed a door without a sign on it. Shanta walked over towards it and turned the knob.

Locked.

She stepped back and kicked down the door. Shanta de-transformed so that she wouldn't scare the girls. The room was dim and smelled of food.

"Are you guys in here?" she called out.

"Yeah, we're over here," answered Rosa stepping forward.

"Who are you?" asked Tracy, also stepping into the light.

"I'm Shanta, Mark's Cuz," answered Shanta. "I'll explain everything to you later. But right now, we must get out of here."

BAM! SMACK! Mark and Andrew both skidded on the ground, crashing into a wall. They slowly got up, coughing up blood. Big Sparks charged towards them. Try as they might, they couldn't touch him. Big Sparks blocked their punches, as well as their attacks. Mark and Andrew stared at Big Sparks, as their breathing became shallow.

"You two look tired," said Big Sparks. "Let me give you a jumpstart."

He shocked Mark and Andrew. One hundred thousand volts of electricity surged through their bodies. Andrew could feel his body going numb. Mark and Andrew de-transformed and collapsed to the ground face first. Andrew tried to get up but couldn't move his legs. He looked down. He noticed that his bracelet was scorched, and the gem had fallen out, landing a few feet away from him. Andrew looked at Mark's bracelet and saw the same thing.

Andrew knew they couldn't win. Without their bracelets, they were powerless.

"Ready to give up?" asked Big Sparks looking at Andrew.

Andrew didn't answer. Nothing he could say could change the situation. His heart raced as he felt death standing before him. Suddenly, he heard a familiar voice calling out his name. It was like the voice of God reaching out to him. He looked up and saw Rosa calling for him. Rosa smiled, wiping the tears from her eyes. Andrew smiled back. Mark woke up to Tracy calling for him. He sat up and looked at her with a smile. She smiled back.

"Looks like Shanta found the girls," Andrew said, looking at Mark. "We can't give up now, not when the girls' lives are at stake."

"You're right, Dawg," replied Mark. "We can't go out like this. You know I got your back, no matter what."

Andrew nodded and slowly got up. "Let's give them an ass beating."

"Bronx style," added Mark getting up also.

They bumped fists. Suddenly, their gems began to glow. Fear and confusion flooded their minds as the light became more intense. Rosa, Tracy, and Shanta weren't sure what was happening. They covered their eyes from the blinding light. The light faded. Mark and Andrew were no more. There was only one person standing in their place.

"How…how did you two do that?" asked Big Sparks with his eyes wide open. "Only we can fuse together!"

"I don't know," a different voice said, "but now my chances of defeating you have gone through the roof. Let me introduce myself. I am Raion, the Japanese Lion."

Raion was a foot shorter than Big Sparks. All he wore were blue jeans with ripped hems and a white tank shirt. His caramel-colored body was muscular, his mane was a brown color, and his eyes were green. Raion's ears were triangular-shaped. He had huge claws and feet and a long tail with a small bush of hair at the end. His face was the same shape as Pansā, except that his nose was a bit bigger. Even when he didn't smile, his top fangs stuck out.

"Hey Shanta," Rosa asked with her eyes wide open, "what just happened?"

"I'm…not sure," answered Shanta with her eyes wide open.

Suddenly, Shanta began to remember what Phansu had said about the bracelets.

"These Nebtan bracelets symbolize your animal spirits. They can help increase your strength, speed and many other things not known to me or Master Dao."

Shanta rubbed her chin. *Somehow the bracelets fused Mark and Andrew into Raion. What new power have Mark and Andrew received in their fused form?*

"Ready to fight?" Raion asked Big Sparks.

"Let's dance," Big Sparks answered.

He charged toward Raion. Big Sparks started his assault with several punches. Raion blocked every single one. Raion countered, punching him in the stomach. The blow knocked the wind out of Big Sparks. He stepped backwards clenching his stomach. Big Sparks growled angrily and dashed forward. He turned it up a notch. Flashes of light scattered across the floor. They were destroying everything. Booming sounds filled the air. All Hidishi's crates were destroyed, as debris scattered everywhere. The ground itself was full of large craters and cracks. Even the ceiling began to show signs of cracks. SMACK! Big Sparks flew backwards. He crashed into a wall, making a huge imprint of his body. He got up, a bit dizzy, but he charged toward Raion again. Raion attacked Big Sparks first. Big Sparks felt every punch Raion threw at him. His right eye began to swell, and his body was turning black and blue. Big Sparks fell to the ground hard. He tried to get up, but his body was too bruised to take another beating. Raion watched as Big Sparks struggled to get up. Even though he could finish him off right there, somewhere in his mind, Raion decided to test his newfound strength. Finally, Big Sparks rose with one arm raised halfway and the other just dangling on his side.

"I will not…be defeated…by you," he managed to say.

He leaped backwards. Raion realized he was preparing to make a huge attack. Unfazed, Raion stood there, waiting. Big Sparks began to power up, causing a lightning storm to develop outside. A jolt of lightning came crashing down on him, recharging his energy. He extended both arms outward with his palms facing Raion, and his thumbs crisscrossed. Electricity surged around his body. His hands began to form a ball of pure electricity.

"SHOCK WAVE!!!" shouted Big Sparks.

The blast came towards Raion. He grinned, deciding to try out a new attack.

"ROAR OF THE BEAST KING!!!" he shouted.

A huge blast came out of his mouth and flew across the ground. Raion's blast collided with Big Sparks' blast. Both blasts were equal in power. Suddenly, Big Sparks' blast began to diminish in size. It was like Raion's blast began to absorb his. Big Sparks couldn't dodge. He didn't want to die just yet. He stretched out his arms and grabbed the enormous blast. He felt himself being pushed back. Try as he might, his strength wasn't enough to make a difference. Big Sparks crashed into a wall. He cried in pain as the blast began to crush him, slowly disintegrating his body. Seconds later, Big Sparks was no more.

"I can't believe he defeated the Meta-Morphic Five," replied Tracy looking at Raion.

"He had help," replied Shanta angrily. "What am I, chopped liver?"

"Are you guys alright?" Raion asked, looking at them.

"We're okay," answered Rosa. Then, she asked, "Uh, are you either Mark, Andrew or both?"

"I am neither Mark nor Andrew," he answered. "I am Raion. I have both of Mark's and Andrew's characteristics, making us one person."

"Can you separate?" asked Tracy, hoping the fusion wasn't permanent.

"Yes, I can, but I still have unfinished business," Raion answered, looking at Hidishi's office door from the first floor.

Hidishi's office door opened, revealing Hidishi himself. He walked over to the middle of the second floor with an evil grin.

Hidishi was tall and wore a dark blue Armani suit with a white tie and black leather shoes. Hidishi had a long face, long jet-black hair in a ponytail and his blood red eyes were filled with evil. Raion really didn't see how Hidishi could be Andrew's father, but he could feel Andrew's rage.

Raion stared at Hidishi with his green eyes waiting for him to try something. Tracy began to get that same feeling again as she stared at him. She could see a shadowy figure with wings and bloody red eyes standing behind him. Her body froze and sweat rolled down her cheek. Suddenly, Raion noticed Hidishi holding a nine-millimeter gun in one hand and holding a detonation device in the other.

"Everyone, get out of here now!" Raion shouted. "He's gonna blow this place up!"

Immediately, the girls rushed for the stairs. Hidishi appeared in front of Rosa. He grabbed her by the waist and held the gun to her head. Rosa gasped.

"Surrender now or the girl dies," said Hidishi, pressing the gun closer to her skull. "You can't win. Even if you save the girl, you will die."

"Guess we have no choice," Raion said.

SMACK! Shanta kicked Hidihsi in the head, causing him to let go of Rosa. Quickly, Hidishi raised his gun at Rosa. Raion appeared in front of him and used Andrew's Striking Claw attack to pierce a hole into Hidishi's stomach. To his surprise, Hisidhi already held the gun to Raion's other arm. He quickly pulled the trigger. The sound of the gunfire filled the stale air as blood splattered everywhere. Raion pulled his arm out of Hidishi's stomach as he staggered backwards. He watched as Hidishi slowly fell backwards, hitting the ground. A small pool of blood began to form around Hidishi.

"I'll…see you…in Hell," Hidishi managed to say and pressed the detonation button.

A huge explosion demolished the warehouse. Rosa, Tracy and Shanta watched as the warehouse began to burn to the ground. Shanta pointed to a shadow walking out.

"He survived," she said smiling.

Raion walked out of the warehouse clenching his wounded arm. He separated. Mark and Andrew both de-transformed before they collapsed onto the ground. Tracy and Rosa ran towards Mark and Andrew and cradled their heads. Smoke filled the air, as the snapping sounds of embers flooded their ears. Soon, the building collapsed. The battle was over.

Mark and Andrew woke up in a hospital with IVs in their veins. Andrew slowly looked over to his right. Rosa was sitting in a chair next to him. She was asleep on the edge of the bed, with her head was resting on her arms. Andrew smiled a little. She looked cute when she slept.

"What just happened?" asked Mark, looking at Tracy.

"Don't you guys remember?" asked Shanta.

"All I remember is bumping fists with Mark," Andrew answered looking at Shanta. "The rest is a blur."

"I can't believe you guys don't remember saving us," replied Rosa waking up.

"At least we saved you," Andrew shot back.

"Only a minute and they already are arguing," muttered Mark shrugging his shoulders. "Ouch! Why is my arm hurting?"

Andrew looked at his wounded arm. "What happened?"

"You were shot a few hours ago," answered Tracy. "You two killed Hidishi."

"Hidishi is dead?" Andrew asked, with a surprised look. "I don't know how we did it, but I'm glad he is dead."

"Ya damn right," replied Mark with a smile.

"So, when were you gonna tell me you can transform into a werewolf?" asked Rosa, staring at Andrew as if she was interrogating him.

"I was going to tell you, but I…" Andrew started, looking away.

"Was scared to tell you," Mark replied, finishing Andrew's statement.

"Is that true?" she asked, looking at Andrew.

Andrew nodded.

"At least you are honest about it," said Rosa. "You guys need some rest. We'll come back tomorrow to see how you two are doing."

Mark and Andrew watched the girls leave. Andrew closed his eyes and slowly drifted off to sleep. As they slept, their tattoos slowly began to heal them.

SEVENTEEN

That night, a mysterious woman was walking through the halls of the morgue. She was a tall, beautiful woman in her thirties. Her olive skin was wrapped around a curvy, athletic body. Her long, dark brown hair draped over her back and was filled with thick cowlicks. She was voluptuous: even her blue mini dress couldn't hide them.

The mysterious woman made it to the end of the hall. She stared at the double doors through her tinted shades. She smirked as she entered the morgue. She looked around and saw no one. She grinned, as she took her time scanning each door. Soon, she stopped at a door and read the label. The label said Jin Hidishi. Happy, the mysterious woman opened the door and pulled out the large, silver tray. Laying on the tray was Hidishi's body. Aside from the huge hole in his stomach and a severed left arm, Hidishi's body was intact...and naked.

The mysterious woman leaned in close and whispered in a Southern accent, "Time to wake up, Sugar."

Hidishi's eyes widened. He sat up and stared at the mysterious woman. "What are you doing here?"

The mysterious woman giggled. "Nothing in particular, Sugar: just making sure the plan is still on track.

Hidishi looked away. "There's been a slight setback, but I can assure you the other entities are intact.

The mysterious woman quickly grabbed Hidihi's throat. He was gasping for air.

"Listen to me, Sugar: I don't give a damn about setbacks, I care about results," she said, in a calm voice. "So, I'm giving you another chance, or I'll kill you myself."

Hidishi was scared. He clenched his fist tightly and gnashed his teeth. "I understand."

"Great!" the mysterious woman squealed. "Now, let's take lil 'ol you to get healed up."

She touched his chest. Instantly, they vanished.

Two weeks later, Andrew's relatives had a funeral for Lily, Mike and William. It was a cloudy Friday afternoon in May at St. Peter's Cathedral. Andrew wore a black suit and tie with a white collared shirt and black shoes. Mark, Rosa, Shanta and Tracy came with Andrew to support him in his time of sorrow. Andrew's relatives decided to have the funeral outside, since it was easier to pay their respects and bury them afterwards. The grass in the cemetery was freshly cut and there were only three trees in the whole cemetery. Rows of tombstones laid everywhere. Andrew couldn't believe the number of people buried.

As the priest began the ceremony, Andrew began to think back at all the good times Lily, Mike, William and he shared. He still remembered all of William's corny jokes, and he knew he would miss Lily's cooking. Andrew was going to miss hanging out with Mike. He remembered going to his first baseball game with him, when he was eight. Mike took Andrew to see the Yankees beat the Red Sox. That was the best game Andrew had ever seen, especially when Derek Jeter made his forty-second homerun.

Andrew began to remember Alice. He knew that she was his real mother and he had just met her. But he couldn't help but feel sorry for her. To think Hidishi would go as far as to kill the mother of his child, just so he can keep his drug business going. Andrew also began to feel sorry for all the parents who had to bury their kids, who were involved with gangs or in the drug business themselves. He began to wonder if he was worthy of protecting this city. How could he protect a city if he can't protect the ones he loves? What if another drug-lord decided to come after Rosa and he couldn't save her? What then? Andrew was sick and tired of fighting. Too many people were dying, and he couldn't stop it, even with the power of Ōkami.

As the gravediggers began to bury his family, Andrew began to cry. As much as he wanted to hold back the tears, he couldn't. Rosa held his hand and let him cry on her shoulder. His friends could see his pain and sorrow.

After the funeral, everybody went inside the church for the reception. Andrew stayed outside and stared at his family's tombstones. He didn't feel like eating or talking to anyone. A gentle breeze blew across the cemetery as the clouds began to darken. Suddenly, it began to rain. Andrew was soaking wet, but he didn't care. He let the rain hide his tears. He continued to stare at the tombstones, clenching his fists. Suddenly, someone tapped his shoulder. Andrew turned around with his fist ready. It was Rosa holding an umbrella. Andrew lowered his fist while gazing into her hazel eyes.

"Leave me alone Rosa," he said softly, looking away. "I don't wanna talk."

"Good, then listen," Rosa replied. "Andrew, I know what happened to your family is heartbreaking and unforgiveable. But that doesn't mean you have to give yourself pneumonia. Please come inside and get something to eat. Everyone is worried about you."

Rosa reached out for Andrew's hand. Without thinking, he backslapped her hand.

"Don't you see I want to help you?" snapped Rosa.

"I don't want your help!" Andrew shouted. "Just leave me alone! I don't want to fight anymore! I can't protect everyone anymore! I'm…a failure…"

"No, you're not! You can still protect the weak and helpless."

"No, I can't! Hidishi may be dead, but someone else can always take his place. I don't have the strength to keep on fighting."

"You just don't get it, do you? This city needs you. I need…you…"

She trailed off as her face grew hot. Andrew's eyes widened when he heard those words. She was right. He was given these powers because he was needed. Andrew's distant look grew close as he stared deeply into her hazel eyes. He placed his wet hand onto her cheek.

"Thanks…for caring," he said softly and smiled. "Rosa, I…"

Rosa placed her finger on his lips. She stared deeply into Andrew's green eyes, slowly removing the umbrella from her head. Her hair and clothes were wet, but she didn't care either. She held him close, wrapping her arms around his strong back. They both slowly leaned forward.

"Andrew!" Mark called out as he ran towards them.

Rosa and Andrew quickly separated. She quickly picked up the umbrella, placing it over them.

"So that's where you two were," replied Mark trying to get underneath the umbrella. "How ya feeling, Drew?"

"Better, thanks to Rosa," Andrew answered looking at her.

"Well, you two better get inside before you guys catch pneumonia," said Mark and ran back into the church.

They waited a few minutes until Mark was almost inside and walked to the church together, underneath the umbrella.

On an island, on the outskirts of Japan, was a large building. It was five stories high and took almost half of the island. It was in the shape of a step pyramid. The main floor was twice as long and wide as the other floors and had huge windows. The second through fifth floors had the fewest windows but had the most security. There were four machine guns posted on the corners of the second and fourth floors and two cannons with 180° rotation posted on the walls of the third floor. Over to the right, was a small airport. In it contained a private jet and four transport jets. Over to the left was a small harbor containing two large hi-powered ships and a private yacht. This was Hidishi's main base.

Inside, was a different story. The main floor was huge. In front, was a long wide hallway with three elevators and a staircase at the end. On the right, was a security desk with screens from every hallway on every floor. The floors were tiled, and the walls and ceilings were painted white. It was like being in a hospital.

In a room on the third floor, was a short man with stringy black hair in a ponytail, round thick glasses, and a huge nose. He sat in his chair, pondering. Suddenly, the intercom came on.

"Professor Yen, please report to the Developing Room."

Yen grinned as he rose from his chair. He hurried towards the elevator and typed in a password on the computer's small keyboard. The elevator doors closed. The ride was smooth and quiet. Seconds later, the doors opened. Yen scurried down a long hallway. He stopped at a wide door, marked *Developing Room*.

The Developing Room was the biggest room of all the floors. Half of the room was used for research and development and the other half was used for training. The right side of the room was filled with meta-humans in huge water containers and workers monitoring them on giant computers. The left side of the room had a huge room, marked *Training Room*, with a monitoring room right above it.

"What's the situation?" Yen asked the nearest worker.

"The latest meta-human is almost complete, Sir," the worker answered. "We're monitoring the progress of the new drug."

"Excellent. That kid's DNA was a great choice for this drug. I'm going to check on the other meta-humans in the Training Room. Keep me posted."

The worker nodded and went back to work. Yen walked over to the Training Room's monitoring room. There were only two meta-humans training, with several workers monitoring them.

"How are they?" Yen asked a worker.

"They're failures, Sir," the worker answered. "Their speed, power, and agility are all at low levels. They are already at their limits, and we've started training five minutes ago."

Yen frowned. "Scrap them."

The worker nodded and pushed a button. Instantly, the Training Room became hot. The meta-humans tried to escape, but quickly realized the doors were shut tight. The temperature rose drastically as their bodies began sweating profusely. The worker monitored the temperature gauge as it rose to two hundred degrees. Suddenly, one of the meta-humans caught on fire. He cried in pain as he tried to smother the flames. Soon, the second meta-human caught on fire. The worker watched their silent screams as the flames spread. With a temperature reading of five hundred degrees, both meta-humans stopped moving. The flames burned them into dust. The worker pushed another button, cooling the Training Room. Minutes later, the room cooled, leaving a pile of ash on the ground. Instantly, a cleaning crew arrived onto the scene.

"Well, back to the drawing board," Yen said and left the room.

The next day, Andrew packed up his things as he prepared to move in with Mark and his family. He felt like a little kid sleeping over at his best friend's house. Luckily, Mark's parents had a spare room, which was next door to Mark's room. It took about two trips total to gather Andrew's belongings. Andrew stared at his new home for a moment. It was a new kind of experience and was going to get some use to. Andrew unpacked his things and began to fix up his new room. He was about halfway done when Mark handed him the phone.

"It's Rosa," he whispered. He closed the door behind him.

"Hello?" Andrew said.

"Hey Drew, how's it going?" answered Rosa.

"It's a'ight so far. I'm halfway done with my room."

"That's good. Hey…you wanna hang out later?"

"Sure, what did you have in mind?"

"I was thinking of watching a movie. So, meet me at the theater at seven tonight."

"Okay, I'll see ya later," Andrew said before he hung up the phone.

Suddenly, Mark knocked on the door. Andrew opened it.

"So…?" Mark asked, hoping Andrew would share the good news.

"So…what?" Andrew asked, continuing to fix up his room.

"Don't play, Dawg. What did Rosa want?"

"She wanted to hang out with me: that's all."

"Dude, she's obviously trying to get with you," replied Mark shaking Andrew's shoulders.

"Okay! Okay!" Andrew cried. "I'll try to make my move."

"Now that's what I wanted to hear," replied Mark slapping Andrew's back.

Ching was in the meeting room, listening to his advisors. At least, that was what he was portraying. He constantly nodded with distant eyes. His mind was focused on Shanta. He yearned to hear her voice, to touch her. He sighed.

"Is something wrong, my King?" one of the advisors asked.

"I grow tired of these meetings," Ching answered.

"You must be thinking about Queen Shanta again," Master Dao replied as he walked in. "Our Queen would want you to rule the Forest Region with strength and passion, not laziness."

"But I…"

"Then why not visit her?"

"If it's all right with everyone..."

Ching looked around the room. All his advisors nodded in agreement. They wanted their strong King back.

Ching smiled. "Then it's settled, I'll leave tomorrow morning."

"Better make it four days from now," replied Master Dao. "Have you forgotten about your two-day public meetings in Raion?"

Ching averted his eyes in embarrassment. Master Dao chuckled and slapped Ching's back.

"I'll tell Madam Renee the news. You get back to your meeting, Ching."

Hibika and Ayia walked around the courtyard with the Nebtan children. The sun shined brightly, and the gentle breeze cooled their skins. Everyone gathered next to a large tree and watched the grass sway in the breeze.

Aiya sighed. "I wish Mark was here…"

"Mark needs his space, Aiya," Hibika said. "Honestly, you need to forget about him."

"Like you're over Andrew! I know you miss him too."

Hibika felt embarrassed. "I-I do not!"

Aiya giggled. "You're hopeless. And to think I was so close to becoming a woman."

"Wait, you and Mark were about to…?"

Aiya grinned. "Mark's really big! I don't think it would've fit, but I was willing to try."

"Andrew's big too…from what I felt…"

"You did it with Andrew?"

"No! I was on top of him…and his thing kept poking me from behind…"

Aiya was intrigued. "Why were you on top of him?"

Hibika's face turned bright red. "Enough of this! The children don't need to know about this."

The Nebtan children booed and spoke in Japanese.

"What's going on?" Ching asked, walking towards them.

"N-Nothing!" Hibika and Aiya stuttered in unison.

Ching ignored their suspicious looks. "Anyway, I wanted to tell you that I'm going to Earth four days from now."

"That's not fair!" replied Aiya with a frown. "Can't we tag along?"

"Hibika can come, but you have to stay," Ching answered.

"Why me?!" exclaimed Ayia.

"You're too young to venture on Earth," Hibika answered. "Besides, Ching probably has business to deal with on Earth, right?"

Ching gulped. "R-Right!"

"So, it's settled," replied Hibika. "Four Earth days from now, Ching and I will head to Earth. I'm so excited!"

Rosa and Andrew went to Bay Plaza Cinemas to watch *I Really Know What You Did Last Spring.* It was the scariest movie Andrew had seen in ages. Even the sound effects were tight. Andrew munched happily on his popcorn with his eyes glued to the screen. Although he didn't like some of the actors, he liked how they died. Rosa tried to stay calm, sipping slowly on her drink. She glanced at Andrew and smiled. It was her first time spending alone time with him. She wished this night could last forever. Suddenly, the killer jumped from out of the bushes. With a long knife, he swiftly slashed the clueless actress' throat. Blood squirted everywhere as she convulsed on the ground. Rosa yelped and quickly grabbed Andrew's arm, pressing her head into his chest. Andrew blushed as he lifted her head up. She looked at Andrew with her hazel eyes.

"Are you scared?" Andrew whispered to her.

"Not when I'm with you," she whispered back. She gave him a warm smile.

Andrew smiled back and slowly leaned forward to kiss her. Finally, Andrew was going to make his move without any interruptions.

"Andrew," a familiar voice called out.

It was Madam Renee. Andrew hung his head low.

"What's wrong?" Rosa whispered to him.

"It's nothing!" Andrew exclaimed, forcing a laugh.

Rosa sat back in her seat and stared at the screen. Andrew heart sank as he sank further into his seat.

"Sorry for interrupting, but listen closely," said Madam Renee. *"Ching and Hibika are coming over to Earth four days from now. They wanted to understand more of Earth customs and traditions. Try to make them feel welcome."*

Andrew immediately freaked. He couldn't have Hibika around him, especially when Rosa was around. What a way to ruin a great night.

"You have to tell Rosa about Hibika before she thinks you and her are a couple," Mark said.

"Even if I tell her, Rosa wouldn't speak to me ever again," Andrew replied.

"If she cares about you, she'll understand."

"So, what do I tell her? Should I tell her that I saw Hibika naked?"

"You saw Hibika naked?" asked Mark, changing the subject. "Why didn't you tell me? Was her body banging?"

"Can we focus on the problem here?" Andrew asked Mark trying to keep his mind out the gutter.

"I don't know what to say, dawg. Only you can figure it out. In the meantime, tell me how your date with Rosa went."

"It wasn't a date. And I was about to kiss her when Madam Renee interrupted me."

"You were gonna kiss her during a scary part?"

"Uh, yeah! There I was, watching the movie when suddenly Rosa grabbed my arm and pressed her head into my chest. I gently lifted her head and gazed into her eyes. Well, you know the rest."

"Don't worry, Drew, you'll get to kiss Rosa," said Mark and muttered, "Hopefully before she finds someone else…"

"I heard that!" Andrew exclaimed and threw a pillow at Mark's face.

Three days later, Andrew went back to school. Who knew he had so much work to make up? All his teachers asked how he was feeling, since they heard about the incident on the news. Even Andrew's classmates asked the same question. Well, school hadn't changed at all.

During History class, Andrew listened to Mrs. Telhim's lecture. It's not that he never listened: all he wanted to do was to get back to a normal life. Even Emily was surprised how alert Andrew was. After class, Emily greeted him.

"How are you, Andrew?" she asked with a concerned look.

"I'm okay, Hime," Andrew answered with a small smile. "I'm…just trying to have a normal life."

"I understand. I'm glad you came back."

"Me too, Hime."

The remainder of his classes were boring, but his day was cool. Andrew felt like a celebrity. No matter where he walked, he was greeted and was given support for his loss. Even the bullies had sympathy for him.

After dismissal, Andrew went to his locker. All he wanted to do was prepare himself for that big arrival. Suddenly, Rosa walked up to him. She seemed a little disappointed.

"Welcome back," she said, "How's your classes?"

"The way I remember them…boring," Andrew replied. "Listen, about last night, at the movies…"

"It's okay," Rosa said quickly. "I know you're not ready to go past being friends. I must admit, I wasn't ready either. Do you…want to…stay as friends?"

Andrew felt his heart shatter. He wanted to say no, to tell her how he truly felt about her. But he knew his life was too complicated to explain to Rosa right now. All he could say was yes. Rosa gave him a small smile. Andrew watched her walk away.

"That was harsh, Bro," Josh said, walking up to him. "You need to find someone else."

"Thanks for the support," replied Andrew, trying to hold back his frustration.

"Hey, just looking out for ya."

Josh walked off. Andrew pressed his forehead against his locker. Suddenly, Mark came up and put his hand on Andrew's shoulder.

"Is Hibika's arrival getting to you?" he asked.

"No, but I feel it might soon," Andrew answered. "C'mon, let's go over to the Fortune House and wait for Hibika and Ching to arrive."

Mark and Andrew went to the basement of the Fortune House, where they found Madam Renee waiting by the Inter-dimensional Gateway.

"How long till they come?" asked Mark looking at his watch.

"Five minutes," answered Madam Renee still staring at the gateway.

"Hey Mark, ya think Aiya tried to tag along?" Andrew asked, looking at Mark.

"I hope not," he answered. "I don't want her around me while Tracy is around."

"Gee, how do you think I feel?" Andrew asked sarcastically.

Suddenly, the door opened, revealing Shanta.

"Sorry I'm late," she said as she walked down the basement stairs.

"You're just in time," replied Mark. "Two minutes left before they arrive."

"So, Andrew, have you told Rosa yet?" asked Shanta.

"Well…not exactly," Andrew answered looking at the ground.

"What did you do?" she asked angrily.

"It's not Andrew's fault," answered Mark defending him. "Rosa was the one who wanted to be friends."

"See, she told me that she wasn't ready to go past being friends," Andrew added. "So now, we're just good friends."

"Rosa is full of sh-" said Shanta but was cut off.

Suddenly, the gateway began to glow. Three shadows walked out of the gateway with sacks over their backs. The light faded. Everyone saw Ching, Hibika and Master Dao standing in front of the gateway.

"What are you doing here?" asked Mark looking at Master Dao.

"I came to learn more about Earth, as well as see an old friend," answered Master Dao. He kissed Madam Renee's hand.

"You're such a charmer," replied Madam Renee giggling a little.

"I'm surprised Aiya didn't tag along," Andrew said looking at Hibika.

"We already told Aiya that Mark needed some space," replied Ching.

"Hey Baby," said Shanta hugging Ching. She kissed him passionately.

"That's new," said Mark staring at Shanta and Ching kissing.

"Ooh, Master Dao," replied Shanta after unlocking lips, "there's something I have to tell you about the bracelets."

"What is it, my child?" Master Dao asked.

"The bracelets gave Mark and Andrew the power to fuse into a super-being."

"So, the bracelets can fuse people together?"

"Yes, but when Mark and Andrew separated, they didn't remember anything."

"I see. I wish I had an answer, but I don't. Mark, Andrew, where are your bracelets?"

"They…uh…got destroyed," answered Andrew feeling embarrassed.

"Destroyed?!" Master Dao shouted. "How could you two let your bracelets get destroyed?!"

"It wasn't our fault," Mark butted in. "Check this out: Big C and Sparks fused together and started to beat the crap out of us. He also scorched our bracelets. Even though Drew and I were powerless, we still weren't going to give up. One minute I'm bumping fists with Drew, and then the next minute the warehouse is on fire."

"That must mean the gems are inside both of you," said Master Dao. "You two can fuse, without the bracelets, into…what do you two fuse into?"

"Into Raion," answered Shanta.

"The mighty lion?" asked Ching with a surprised look.

Shanta nodded. "Guess the tale is true, huh?"

"But why can't we remember beating Big Sparks?" Andrew asked looking at Master Dao.

"Maybe you can," replied Master Dao.

"What do you mean?" asked Mark.

"Maybe your gems can playback the battle for you," Master Dao answered. "Now that your gems are a part of you, you two can activate its memory banks."

"How?" Andrew asked.

"Try concentrating?" suggested Shanta.

Mark and Andrew both closed their eyes, relaxing their minds. Soon, they could see the battle. Mark and Andrew couldn't believe how Raion looked. Even Andrew was surprised by the way Raion killed Big Sparks with his Roar of the Beast King attack. Then, Mark and Andrew finally saw Hidishi. Even though he was Andrew's father, Andrew was happy to see him die in the fire. Mark and Andrew opened their eyes.

"Did it work?" asked Shanta.

They both nodded.

"So, how long are you guys staying here?" Andrew asked.

"Three weeks," answered Ching. "We plan to learn more about Earth, especially here in the Bronx. I heard they have wonderful food."

"Hey Andrew," asked Hibika, "I would like to know more about your movie houses. Could you take me there?"

"Sure," Andrew answered. "Wanna come, Mark?"

"A'ight," answered Mark. "What are we gonna see?"

"I was thinking of seeing *Three Skateboarders*," Andrew answered. "I heard it's a good movie. But first, we gotta dress Hibika in Earth clothes. No one wears kimonos in this country."

Minutes later, Hibika was dressed like an Earthling. She wore blue jeans, a pink T-shirt with a silver star in the middle and white shoes. Although Hibika was concerned about hiding her spots, Mark quickly told her that she would blend in, since Earthlings like to get various tattoos and show them off.

"We better get there before they're sold out," replied Mark heading for the stairs.

"We'll be back around eight or nine," Andrew said as he and Hibika went up the stairs.

"Have fun, you three," Shanta said as she waved goodbye to them.

Shanta found this to be a good opportunity to let her family meet Ching. She still had mixed reviews in her mind but pressed forward. She unlocked the front door and led Ching inside. Ching was amazed by the structure and the interior. Suddenly, he heard footsteps. He turned around and saw Mrs. Shepherd walking down the stairs.

"Mom, this is Ching…my boyfriend," Shanta said with a smile.

"But I thought we are…?" Ching asked.

"I'll explain later," Shanta muttered, cutting him off.

Mrs. Shepherd approached Ching, slowly studying him. Ching stood still as his eyes nervously followed her.

"He's cute, but looks aren't everything," Mrs. Shepherd said. "What do you do, Ching?"

"I'm King of the Nebtan race," Ching answered proudly.

Mrs. Shepherd looked puzzled. "Excuse me?"

"I live on the planet Macu, thirty light years away from Earth," Ching explained. "I rule a section of the planet, called the Forest Region. It is inhabited by my people, the Nebtans."

She looked at Shanta. "Is this where you went for training?"

Shanta nodded. "Mom, he's a great guy. Everyone there loves him and…they made me their Queen…"

Shanta showed Mrs. Shepherd her wedding ring.

"Mrs. Shepherd, I love Shanta with all my heart and wouldn't do anything to hurt her," Ching said. "I came here to receive your blessing. My only wish is that my parents were alive to see your daughter."

Mrs. Shepherd sighed. Although she was familiar with Shanta's powers, this was going to take a while to sink in.

"Wait til your father gets home," she said, sitting down on the couch.

"Have you told him about my powers?" Shanta asked.

Mrs. Shepherd shook her head. "Other than me, your sisters know."

"You didn't tell me you have sisters," Ching replied. "How many?"

"Two younger sisters," Shanta answered. "Their names are Bozenka and Desireé. Right now, they're on vacation with my grandmother in Jamaica."

"Ja…mai…ca?"

"It's a small island in the Caribbean. One day, I'll take you there."

Suddenly, the doorknob turned. The door opened, revealing Mr. Shepherd. He was a tall mocha-colored man with short black hair, a thick black mustache, and dark brown eyes. He wore a navy-blue suit with a red tie and a white dress shirt.

"Hey guys…" his voice trailed off. "Who's this young man, Honey?"

"Dear, come sit down," Mrs. Shepherd said, patting the couch. "You're going to need to."

Mr. Shepherd sat down with a worried look. Thoughts ran through his head as he stared at both Shanta and Ching. "Can I ask something?"

"Yes, Daddy?" Shanta asked.

"You're not pregnant, right?" Mr. Shepherd asked bluntly.

"Daddy!" exclaimed Shanta. "No, I'm not! You taught me better. Let me explain..."

Shanta explained everything to him. Mr. Shepherd sat there in a daze as her explanation of her powers, Ching, and her mission slowly sank in.

"So, let me get this straight," said Mr. Shepherd. "My daughter can transform into a werefox, because a mysterious lady gave it to you when you were young. And your mission is to stop a drug lord from taking over this world. My nephew, Mark, and your friend, Andrew, also have the same powers and mission. To get stronger, you go off to another planet, where you meet Ching and later get married to him and become the next Queen of the Forest Region. Is that correct?"

Shanta nodded her head nervously. She could feel his disapproval coming through. Mr. Shepherd sat there with his eyes closed. Tension built up in the living room. Even Ching was nervous to say anything. Mr. Shepherd stared at Ching. Ching stared back. Mr. Shepherd folded his arms and sighed heavily.

"You better take good care of her, or else…" Mr. Shepherd said.

Everyone gave a sigh of relief.

"You approve of him, Daddy?" Shanta asked.

"I shouldn't, but his eyes speak the truth," Mr. Shepherd answered. He glared at Ching. "Remember this, Ching: until Shanta is the legal age to get married, you two are boyfriend and girlfriend here on Earth. That also means no naughty stuff in my house either. I'm watching you two."

"Daddy!" Shanta exclaimed, feeling embarrassed.

Ching nodded. "I understand, Sir. Thank you."

"You're more than welcome to stay here, Ching," Mrs. Shepherd replied. "We have plenty of spare rooms."

"Thank you," Ching said with a smile. "Thank you for everything."

The line at the movies was packed. As they waited in line, Andrew saw this fine Spanish chick staring at one of the movie posters. She looked familiar. The girl turned around. Mark and Andrew both freaked.

"Why did she have to be here, now?" Andrew asked Mark.

"We better hide Hibika before Rosa sees us," replied Mark trying to get in front of Hibika.

"Why do I have to hide from Rosa?" asked Hibika, looking at Rosa.

Rosa was heading towards them. Their hearts and minds raced. There were only seconds to come up with a plan.

"I'll explain later," said Andrew. "Look at those movie posters over there. Mark and I will pay for your ticket."

"Whatever you say," she said walking over to the movie posters.

Rosa walked up to Mark and Andrew and bumped fists with them.

"You guys here to see *Three Skateboarders*?" she asked, looking at Mark and Andrew.

"Yeah," Andrew answered.

"Well…it's sold out," said Rosa, giving Andrew a sad look.

"I guess Mark and I will have to see another movie," Andrew said looking at Mark. He signaled Mark to keep an eye on Hibika.

"Where's Tracy?" Rosa asked Mark.

"Tracy isn't here," answered Mark, choke-holding Andrew. "I wanted to hang with my boy, Drew."

"I understand," Rosa replied. "I guess you need to have some boys' night out too.

"Yeah…" Andrew said.

Suddenly, Hibika stood next to Andrew, grabbing his arm.

"Andrew, can we see that movie next time?" she asked, pointing to a romance movie poster.

Rosa stood silent for a moment. Thoughts raced through her mind as she stared at Hibika. Andrew could tell she was surprised, but mostly angry. She looked like she was going to snap.

"So, who is this slut?" Rosa asked in a jealous rage. "All this time, you wanted me while having her on the side. What, you need to sow your seeds that bad?"

"What!" Andrew exclaimed. "That's so not true! Let me expl-"

"Liar!" she replied, bursting into tears. "I never want to see you again, you two-timer!"

Rosa cursed Andrew out in Spanish as she stormed out of the cinemas. Even though Andrew didn't know what she said to him, he knew it wasn't good. Andrew looked at all the people watching him with disappointed eyes. Even the old ladies were angry. Andrew felt so embarrassed, he left too. Mark and Hibika soon followed. They found Andrew standing by the curb staring at the sky.

Mark placed his hand on Andrew's shoulder and asked, "You a'ight, Dawg?"

"Just heartbroken…" Andrew answered, sighing.

"I didn't mean to ruin your relationship with Rosa," Hibika replied in a sad voice.

"It's not your fault," Andrew said. "I should have told her you were coming."

"I'm proud of ya Drew," replied Mark with a smile.

"Proud of what?" Andrew asked with a confused look.

"You went from chump to player in one night," he answered, laughing.

"Shut up," Andrew said shoving Mark a little.

"Andrew, why did Rosa call me a slut?" asked Hibika looking confused. "What does it mean?"

"Trust me, you don't want to know," Andrew answered.

EIGHTEEN

Andrew felt miserable. Even though he looked like he was paying attention in his Chemistry class, he was really thinking about Rosa.

"I never want to see you again, you two-timer!"

It seemed to play in his head over and over. Mrs. Gills called on Andrew several times. Someone tapped on his shoulder. It was Josh.

"Yo, the teacher wants you," he whispered.

Andrew looked at Mrs. Gills, who was pointing to the board. He scanned the equation on the board and solved it.

"Correct," Mrs. Gills replied. "But next time, answer me when I call you."

"Yes, Mrs. Gills," Andrew said with a sigh.

After dismissal, Andrew went to his locker to exchange his books. All he wanted was to get a chance to explain to Rosa who Hibika was. He chuckled, knowing that possibility was impossible. Suddenly, Andrew saw Rosa walk past him.

"Hey, can we talk?" he asked, walking beside her.

She didn't answer. Rosa walked a little faster before she turned a corner. Andrew heard Rosa yelp, followed by a loud thud. Andrew quickly ran. He turned the corner. His eyes widened and his jaw dropped. He couldn't believe Rosa was flirting with Brian Tanka, captain of the football team.

Brain is a tall guy with brown hair and blue eyes. Andrew knows the guy is buff and handsome, but he has a brain the size of a walnut. Andrew could easily beat him with the power of Ōkami.

Andrew stepped back and headed for his locker. Suddenly, a hand tapped Andrew's shoulder. Andrew turned around and saw Mark standing behind him.

"I see Rosa is using the *get Andrew jealous* trick," he replied looking at Rosa hug Brian.

"Well, it seems to be working," Andrew said turning red with anger.

"Don't blow a fuse, Dawg," replied Mark. "Besides, she did bump into him. He was just being nice."

"Being nice?" Andrew asked furiously. "Brian doesn't do nice!"

"Brian's a jock, but I don't think he's a complete jerk," DJ replied, butting into the conversation.

"I agree, DJ," said Mark, nodding.

"Fine, I'll let it go," replied Andrew with a deep sigh.

On Macu, a warrior was training with Phansu. Despite his small size, he progressed through his training faster than Mark, Shanta and Andrew. Three days later, Phansu gave the warrior a Nebtan bracelet with the Japanese symbol of Saru, the Japanese monkey. The warrior smiled and headed for the gateway. With newfound strength, courage and a Macuan bamboo stick, he was determined to help them.

Madam Renee had a vision that night. In the vision, there were two shadows fighting Raion and one shadow was fighting alongside Raion. As Madam Renee took a closer look at the bigger shadow, beads of sweat dripped down the side of her face. Suddenly, the big shadow revealed Hidishi, holding an Earth engulfed with flames. His psychotic laughter echoed through her head. Madam Renee woke up in a cold sweat. She clenched her chest. Her breathing was shallow as she stared at the wall.

"Hidishi is back," she whispered to herself, "and this time, he will rule the Earth."

"It's great to have you back, Mr. Hidishi," said one of his employees.

Hidishi, in a sandy toga with dark brown sandals, entered the building. As he walked to his office, many of his staff members reported damage to the warehouse, as well as profit sales.

Hidishi's backup corporation was located near the Jersey Shores. It was shaped like the old warehouse, except it was much larger and had a lot more floors and rooms.

"Excellent," said Hidishi putting on a new suit. "Get Professor Yen on the phone."

"Right away Sir," replied one of his staff members.

Hidishi opened the office door and admired the changes to it. He loved how his black marble desk stood in front of the window and the bookshelf was moved over to the right side of the room. He even loved the standing lamps with light control.

Hidishi walked into his office and sat in his big leather chair with polished oak arms. His secretary notified him Professor Yen was on Line One. Hidishi pushed the flashing button and picked up the phone.

"I need a favor," he said. "I need a new meta-human, much stronger than the Meta-Morphic Five."

"That can be arranged," replied Yen. "When do you want her?"

"ASAP," answered Hidishi before he hung up.

Meanwhile, Mark and Andrew were trying to get their homework done. Whoever said Algebra was easy was lying. Andrew couldn't figure out how to do inverse functions. Even Mark had trouble helping Andrew. After working on inverse functions for a half hour, they decided to take a break. They went downstairs into the kitchen and got themselves a snack.

"Algebra is mad hard," said Mark. "I'm surprised I passed it with a C. Maybe Rosa can…oh, sorry."

"It's okay," Andrew replied. "Let's not worry about her. You think Shanta could help?"

"Probably," Mark answered. "I think she's taking Calculus this year."

Andrew's jaw dropped. "What?! I didn't know Shanta was that smart. Wait, does she even go to our school?"

Mark chuckled. "Yeah, she does. She just takes Honor classes. That's why you never see her in the halls."

Andrew was impressed. "And all this time I thought she went to a different school. Guess there's more to Shanta than meets the eye."

Shanta stared at her Economics book with dissatisfaction. Nothing was sticking. She sighed and stared at the ceiling.

Why can't Economics make sense? This is the only class I hate. Maybe I could ask Rosa for help. No, she's on a date with that jock. Seriously, why would she even go on a date with Brain? I know why she's doing it, but I still think it's a bad idea. Anyway, back on topic! Damn, if only I knew someone who could explain this chapter to me...

She heard a knock. "Enter."

Ching opened the door. "How are your studies coming along?"

Shanta sighed. "Slow. I hate Economics."

"I can help you with that."

"Ching-darling, I don't think…"

Ching looked at the book for a moment. "Supply and Demand is easy stuff."

"How? I don't get it."

"Let me explain," he said before he cleared his throat. "Supply refers to how many of a certain good or service is available for people to purchase, and Demand means how many people wish to buy that good or service. For example, let's say that a brand-new Macuan vegetable is about to come out. The farmers must decide how many vegetables to grow, so they are not stuck with too many. They then must decide how much to charge for the vegetable, that would be its price. They would need to charge enough for the vegetables to cover the costs of creating the vegetable, advertising, and shipping to stores. Since they also wish to make a profit on the vegetable, they will also want to figure that cost as well. If the price of the vegetable is too high, people may not be able to afford it or decide it is not worth the price and there will be too many or an oversupply. If the price is too low, costs will not be covered, and little profit will be made even though the vegetable may sell very well. The farmers would lose money and may even have to close."

Shanta's eyes widened with amazement. She never realized how talented Ching was ruling his people. She was glad for falling for a wonderful man.

Ching stopped and looked at her. "Is something wrong?"

Shanta felt embarrassed. "Nothing. Please, continue."

Ching cleared his throat and picked up from his last statement.

Rosa went out with Brian to the *Gardenia* in White Plains, a city like the Bronx, except it was much cleaner and friendlier. The hostess took them to their seats. Of course, Brian tried to be a gentleman by seating Rosa first. A waiter came over to take their orders.

"So, what will you have?" Brian asked, looking at Rosa.

"I'll have the spaghetti with meat sauce," answered Rosa still looking at her menu.

"I'll have pollo con broccoli," he replied looking at the waiter.

"Anything to drink?" asked the waiter looking at them.

"Soda," answered Rosa.

"Soda too," added Brian.

The waiter left. Silence filled the air. Rosa decided to ask Brian some questions, just so she could get to know him better.

"So, Brian, where are ya from?" she asked, looking at him.

"Minnesota," he answered looking at Rosa. "I moved to the Bronx two years ago."

"Well, I've been here all my life. Do you play any other sports, other than football?"

"Nah, I love football. What about you? Play any sports?"

"I enjoy playing flag football."

"That's cool. Great, our food is here."

"Good, I'm starving."

They ate quietly. Brian couldn't stop looking at Rosa. Even though Rosa loved the attention, she felt uncomfortable. She looked around the restaurant and tried to think of something else to talk about while she ate.

After dinner, Brian took Rosa to a quiet place, just off the highway. They got out of the car and looked at the starry night sky. Again, Rosa felt uncomfortable around him. She could feel him staring at her, as her eyes stayed glued towards the sky.

"You're pretty cute," Brian said boldly. "I'm surprised you don't have a boyfriend."

Rosa looked at Brian. "I've got other priorities."

"Saving yourself for Andrew?" he asked with a smirk.

Rosa gasped and averted her eyes. "It's not like that…not anymore…"

Suddenly, Brian put his arm around Rosa. "Oh well, his loss."

Rosa felt embarrassed as she tried to get free, but his grip was too strong. He looked into Rosa's hazel eyes, leaned forward and tried to kiss her.

"I don't kiss on the first date," said Rosa as she struggled to get free.

"Just relax, Baby," Brian said as he tried to kiss her again.

"Stop it! Let go of me!" she yelled at the top of her lungs.

Huh?

Andrew dropped his pencil on top of his Algebra book. His green eyes stared out the window.

I could have sworn I heard Rosa's voice. Nah, I'm just imagining things.

He went back to his work. He stared at the equation but couldn't focus on solving it.

I have a gut feeling she's in trouble. Should I go?

Andrew shook his head. *No, she wanted to date Brian. I won't interfere. But…?*

He growled angrily and got dressed. He opened his window and jumped out, landing onto the wet lawn. Andrew quickly transformed and tried to pick up Rosa's scent. He sniffed the air while heading towards her apartment. He found it! Andrew grinned as he raced towards the highway.

"Let go Brian!" Rosa shouted as she struggled to get free.

"Let me get your mind off of Andrew," he said pinning Rosa to the hood of his car.

SMACK! Rosa kicked Brain in the crotch. The blow paralyzed him, as he held his jewels for dear life. Rosa ran. Brian quickly regained his strength and ran after her. He quickly caught up to her. He grabbed Rosa's arm and spun her around. Rosa could feel her circulation being cut off. Out of anger, Brain raised a fist at her.

"I think the lady wants you get off of her," Andrew said grabbing Brian's arm.

Brian turned around, ready to knock Andrew out. He stood there, frozen in terror. Andrew growled. Brian could feel his pants getting soaked. He screamed at the top of his lungs. Andrew let him go. Brian ran towards his car. The car started and quickly drove off at top speed. Andrew smirked at his accomplishment.

"I didn't ask for your help," Rosa said angrily.

"I didn't come here to start a fight," Andrew said turning around. "I came here to save you from that maniac. Look, I'll take you home since your ride left in a hurry."

"I don't want your help."

"Stop being so stubborn! Just climb on my back and I'll take you home." Rosa looked away. "Fine…"

She climbed onto Andrew's back and wrapped her arms around his furry neck. Andrew ran as fast as he could to her apartment. Since most people were in their apartments, it was safe for Andrew to take her to the main door in wolf form. She climbed down. Andrew turned around, ready to leave. Rosa grabbed his arm.

"Thanks…" she said, smiling a little.

"You're welcome," he replied before he ran off.

Hidishi sat in his conference room with Army generals from Mexico, Russia, and China. He stared at them with his hand on a small metal case. From their body language, they were ready to negotiate.

"Inside this case is the meta-human drug I've been developing," he began.

Hidishi opened the case. Inside the molded foam was a small vial, containing a light purple liquid. The general's eyes widened with awe as infinite possibilities ran through their minds.

"This is my offer," Hidishi said, shutting the case. "I will give three crates full of these vials for a total of six billion."

"That's ludicrous!" exclaimed the Mexican general. "Mexico can't afford that!"

"Then you shouldn't be here," said the Chinese general with a smirk. He looked at Hidishi. "Before I give you an answer, how can I be sure you're not tricking me?"

Hidishi smiled. "My meta-humans are the real deal. Do you recall an incident at a local high school here?"

They nodded.

"That was my meta-humans' handy work," he said. "Gentlemen, all that power can be yours. Imagine: soldiers that can quickly heal in the heat of battle and don't forget the various abilities they will acquire. Six billion isn't a lot, compared to what your government spends."

The generals looked at each other. This was an opportunity they couldn't pass up.

"Where can we transfer the money?" asked the Russian general.

Hidishi grinned with delight.

Andrew got home, jumping through his open window. Suddenly, he saw Mark, who was already in his room. From the looks of it, Mark was irritated.

"Where were you?" Mark asked. "I asked you for your calculator an hour ago."

"I was…out," Andrew answered, de-transforming.

"Don't tell me, you went to go see Rosa."

"Not exactly…" Andrew replied with his stare cast on the floor. "I went to help Rosa from Brian. He tried to attack her."

"Did ya beat him up?"

"No, I just scared him. But check this out: Rosa thanked me for saving her."

"Well…it's a start," replied Mark rubbing his chin. "Anyway, can I borrow your calculator?"

The small warrior came out of the gateway with a sack full of clothes and stared at familiar faces with a smile.

"Welcome to Earth, Rei-Rei," said Master Dao.

"So, this is Earth," said Rei-Rei looking around the room. "It looks small and dusty."

"No Rei-Rei, you're on Earth, but in an Earth building," replied Hibika.

"Where is Mark?" he asked. "I want to talk to him in his language."

"Mark will be here tomorrow," answered Madam Renee.

"I see Phansu gave you the Nebtan bracelet of Saru," replied Master Dao. "Now you can help Mark and the others fight."

It was a boring Thursday at school. Andrew felt like sleeping in every one of his classes. Even Mark had that same feeling.

During Bio class, Rosa didn't say a word to Andrew. It was like she didn't know him. Andrew occasionally glanced at her while listening to Mr. Frider.

Last night probably didn't mean anything to her.

After Bio class, Andrew went to his History class where he could talk to Tracy. Even Tracy wasn't speaking to him. She quickly gave him the cold shoulder. Andrew figured Rosa told Tracy about Hibika. He sighed and sank into his chair. He knew he had to tell Rosa the truth. After dismissal, Andrew headed for Rosa's locker. It was too late: Rosa had already left.

Andrew walked home with Mark. He tuned out Mark's voice as his mind raced.

"Earth to Drew!" Mark shouted.

Andrew snapped back to reality. "What?"

"Shanta called me last night," he said looking at Andrew.

"About what?"

"About Rei-Rei being here on Earth. Weren't you listening?"

"Sorry, had a lot on my mind."

"Look, Rosa will come around soon. The more you worry, the more worried I get. Right now, let's focus on meeting Rei-Rei."

Andrew nodded. "You're right. Besides, I'm sure he's dying to see you."

Meanwhile, Rosa and Tracy were also walking home from school.

"Rosa, can you slow down?" asked Tracy, trying to catch up with Rosa. "You're walking too fast."

"Sorry Tracy…I just have a lot on my mind," replied Rosa stopping.

"You're thinking about Andrew. I think you need to forgive him."

"So, you're taking his side? I can't believe you."

"I'm not taking anyone's side. I just think you need to forgive him. If you cool your jets, you might see what I mean. Did you even figure out who this girl was? For all you know, she could be one of Andrew's cousins or someone from the funeral. Give the boy a chance to explain himself."

"I don't know if I can forgive him," Rosa said sadly while staring at the ground.

Mark and Andrew arrived at the Fortune House later that afternoon. Rei-Rei, who was wearing blue shorts and a white T-shirt, immediately ran up to Mark and hugged him. Mark carried Rei-Rei on his shoulders as they walked down the basement stairs.

"Looks like you guys made it," replied Shanta smiling.

"Mark, Rei-Rei has a surprise for you," said Master Dao with a smile.

"What's up Mark," said Rei-Rei with a smile.

"He can talk?" Mark asked looking surprised.

"I taught him myself," replied Master Dao. "And he can also meta-morph."

"Now I can help you beat the bad guys," Rei-Rei said.

"Welcome to the team," Andrew said patting his head.

The phone rang in Hidishi's office. He picked it up and pushed the flashing button.

"Mr. Hidishi, your meta-human will be there tonight," said Professor Yen.

"Excellent," said Hidishi with a huge grin on his face.

During lunch, Madam Renee told Mark and Andrew about her vision. At first, they didn't believe it, but Andrew remembered a guy at school talking about working for Hidishi and how the pay was great.

"We have to stop him, once and for all," Andrew whispered to Mark. "Or else every kid here will be working for him."

"I hear ya Drew, but we don't know where his corporation is," replied Mark before he drank some of his milk.

"Maybe Madam Renee can find it," Andrew said. "In the meantime, we must keep this to ourselves. We don't know who works for Hidishi."

Mark and Andrew headed for the Fortune House. They arrived with everyone waiting for them.

"So, what's the plan?" Mark asked as he walked down the stairs.

"I have found Hidishi's corporation," answered Madam Renee. "It's near the Jersey Shores, on a street called Port Carteret Drive."

"We just need to infiltrate the building and stop his operation there," replied Mark.

"I don't think it's that simple," Andrew butted in.

"What do you mean?" Mark asked.

"I've been thinking about this for a while, and I believe Hidishi has another corporation somewhere else, in a place we would never look," Andrew replied.

"Huh?" asked Mark looking confused.

Andrew sighed while shaking his head. "What I'm saying is that Hidishi's main corporation must be in Japan while this small one is in the Jersey

Shores. We should split up into two groups in order to stop Hidishi's operation for good."

Everyone was impressed by Andrew's deduction.

"How should it be split up?" asked Shanta, looking at Andrew.

"Mark and I will take the corporation here while you and Rei-Rei will take the one in Japan," Andrew said.

"We will help too," Hibika said rising from her seat.

"Alright, but you two have to stay out of trouble," Andrew replied. "Hidishi is very strong."

"We understand," replied Ching. "I will go with Shanta and Rei-Rei while Hibika will go with you and Mark."

"Agreed," said Madam Renee, "Tomorrow will be the final battle. Get some rest all of you."

That evening, Mark gave Rei-Rei a small tour around the Bronx. Rei-Rei oohed and ahhed as he saw the different kinds of buildings.

"Can we go in there?" he asked, pointing to a nightclub.

"That's no place for kids," said Mark, feeling embarrassed. "That place is for adults only."

Mark drove further down the road. Rei-Rei saw a giant building with the name *Silverman's Gym* written on the roof.

"Can we go there?" Rei-Rei asked.

"Yeah, sure," said Mark pulling into the parking lot. "I got a membership here."

They went inside. They were amazed to see how many people go there. *Silverman's Gym* was packed with exercise bikes in the front, weightlifting machines on the right, and free weights on the left. Their aerobics classrooms, the largest part of the gym, were in the back.

"This is a gym," said Mark before he realized Rei-Rei disappeared. "Crap, where'd he go?"

Rei-Rei stood by the free weights watching muscular men lift them. He looked at the rack with free weights and saw a hundred-pound free weight sitting on the bottom rack. Rei-Rei stretched out his hands to pick it up. Suddenly, one of the muscular men stopped him.

"You shouldn't be here," he said to Rei-Rei. "You better go find your mommy."

"Okay Mister, but I want to lift some weights too," Rei-Rei said.

The man chuckled. "You need me to spot you?"

Rei-Rei walked over to the hundred-pound free weight and picked it up with one hand. The man's eyes widened in both amazement and horror as Rei-Rei tossed it around like a toy. The man slowly stepped back with beads of sweat on his brow. Suddenly, Mark walked up to Rei-Rei.

"There you are," said Mark.

"Look Mark, I can lift one hundred pounds," said Rei-Rei with a smile.

"Awesome, but we have to go," said Mark. "Master Dao will kill me if I don't bring you back by nine o'clock sharp."

"Okay," said Rei-Rei as he put down the weight and walked with Mark to the front entrance.

"There's…something in the water," the man replied nervously, wiping the sweat from his brow.

Hidishi examined his new meta-human. She was strong, sexy, and deadly. She wore a red tank top, a black skirt and black hi-top sneakers. Her blonde hair was long and straight, complementing her seductive, ice blue eyes.

"Katherine, I presume?" asked Hidishi looking at her file.

"Call me Kat," she answered.

"Okay, Kat," said Hidishi looking at her and then back at the file. "I have a job for you. I want you to get rid of some pests for me. Can you handle it?"

"Of course," answered Kat with a smile. "I love to exterminate pests."

"Good," he said. He showed her a picture of Rosa. "I want you to capture her. She is the bait for these pests."

"It will be done," she replied, walking out the door.

Rosa was in her room looking out the window. She kept on thinking about Andrew with Hibika that night at the movies.

"What does she have that I don't have?" she asked herself.

She looked at herself in the mirror and began groping her breasts, remembering how big Hibika's were. She even thought that her butt was smaller than Hibika's. And to top it off, Hibika's spot pattern on her cheeks and arms really made her very beautiful. Frustrated, Rosa lay on her bed, staring at the ceiling. She began to wonder why she cared about Andrew in the first place.

"Jerk…" she said angrily, burying her face in her pillow.

Suddenly, memories of nearly kissing Andrew seemed to play back in her head. Rosa imagined how it would feel to kiss him. She imagined Andrew's lips pressed against hers and his arms wrapped around her body.

Maybe…Tracy is right…

Suddenly, a loud thump came upon the wall, next to the window.

"Who's there?" Rosa asked, jumping out of her bed.

BAM! Kat bust through the wall. Rosa screamed at the top of her lungs as she frantically headed for the door. Kat flipped over the bed, blocking Rosa's path.

"You're coming with me," she said with an evil smile.

She grabbed Rosa, stuck a note on the wall and jumped out the window.

NINETEEN

Andrew woke up early the next morning to the sound of the phone ringing. Andrew hesitated because he didn't know anyone who would call at this time.

He picked it up. "Hello? Hey Ms. Sanchez…What? Rosa's been kidnapped? When did this happen…Last night…They left a note…I'll do everything I can to find her…"

Andrew hung up the phone in anger. He rushed into Mark's room and woke him up. Andrew told Mark everything Ms. Sanchez told him. Immediately, Mark jumped out of his bed and changed into his training clothes. Andrew went to his room and did the same. They went downstairs and left a note on the kitchen table. They headed for the door. Suddenly, they heard footsteps. It was Mr. and Mrs. Rivers, coming downstairs to get some coffee.

"Where are you two headed this early in the morning?" asked Mrs. Rivers.

"We were going to…." Mark answered but trailed off.

"Where Son?" asked Mr. Rivers.

"Ms. Sanchez called this morning to tell me Rosa was kidnapped last night," Andrew butted in.

"Oh no!" Mrs. Rivers gasped. "We better call the police."

"No, the police won't help," replied Andrew. "It's my father's doing."

"Andrew, Mike's dead," replied Mr. Rivers, with a concerned look. "Besides, Mike wouldn't hurt a fly."

"He's right," Mrs. Rivers chimed in. She looked at Andrew and Mark with a worried look. "What's really going on?"

Andrew sighed heavily. He knew this day would come. He glanced at Mark, who was glancing at him.

"I think it's time to tell them," Andrew said to Mark.

Mark stepped forward. "I know you're gonna think we sound crazy, but we have to save the world from Andrew's real dad, who's a drug-lord."

Mr. and Mrs. Rivers both raised an eyebrow.

"It's true!" Mark whined. "Andrew found out who his real mom and dad are and now has to face off against his real dad to save the world."

"Son, you need help," said Mr. Rivers. "I knew you had an active imagination, but this is going a bit too far."

"But…" replied Mark.

Andrew grabbed Mark's shoulder. "We better show them instead. They're not buying anything we're saying, aside from Rosa being kidnapped."

Mark nodded. Mark and Andrew stepped back and transformed in front of Mark's parents. Their eyes widened as they stared at Mark and Andrew's transformations.

"My word!" gasped Mrs. Rivers.

Mr. Rivers, on the other hand, was speechless. He stared intently at their transformations, trying to understand what just happened.

"Now do you believe us?" Andrew asked.

They nodded nervously. Mark and Andrew quickly de-transformed.

"I don't know when we will be back, but we will come back in one piece," said Mark looking at his parents. "Let's go, Drew."

Mark and Andrew ran towards the door. Suddenly, Mrs. Rivers called out to them. They stopped and looked back at her. She slowly approached them.

"We will pray for both your safety," said Mrs. Rivers.

She embraced both Mark and Andrew. It was warm and sincere. They smiled as they embraced her back. Mrs. Rivers looked at Mark and Andrew one last time. Mark wiped the tear in his eye. Andrew tapped Mark's shoulder.

"To the Mazda, Robin," he said to Mark and ran out the door.

"Why do I have to be Robin?" asked Mark, following Andrew. "I'm the one driving."

Tracy woke up in a cold sweat. She clenched her chest, struggling to breathe.

What was that feeling? It was so dark and ominous. I could literally smell death. But why did I see Rosa in my dream? What's wrong with me?

She got out of bed and headed to the bathroom. She splashed cold water on her face. She stared at her reflection as water dripped from her chin.

Those weird visions came back again. I thought I got rid of them.

Suddenly, a deep chill went down her spine. She gasped as she fell to her knees, clenching herself.

I sense that dark presence again. But I also sense Rosa. What's going on?

Rosa woke up to find herself tied up to a chair in Hidishi's office. She saw him staring outside his window.

"Why have you taken me prisoner again?" asked Rosa looking at Hidishi angrily. "Do you like me or something?"

"I only captured you to lure your friend Andrew here," Hidishi answered as he sat in his chair. "I want him to join me as I take over this wretched planet."

"Why Andrew? What is he to you?"

"Andrew…is my biological son."

Rosa's eyes widened. "That…can't be true…"

Hidishi chuckled. "I'm afraid it is, child."

Rosa glared at Hidishi. "Andrew will never join you! He will defeat you!"

"Then, let him try…" Hidishi said with an evil grin.

Everyone at the Fortune House was ready in his or her fighting gear.

Mark and Andrew noticed Shanta was also wearing her training clothes except she was wearing a black karate belt instead of a white one.

Ching decided to wear his warrior outfit. Hibika wore blue jeans with a baby blue tank top and a pair of white shoes. She carried her katana on her back and kept her hair down.

Rei-Rei wore dark green sweatpants with a dark green V-neck sleeveless shirt and black moccasins. He cut his long hair and made it spiky. He even carried his bamboo stick on his back.

Andrew told everyone Rosa was kidnapped by Hidishi. Everyone gasped. This gave them more reason to fight.

"Everyone remembers the plan?" Andrew asked, looking at everyone.

They all nodded.

"Wait!" Mark suddenly exclaimed. "Before we go, I thought we should have a team name."

Everyone sighed.

"Can't this wait, Mark?" Andrew asked. "We need to go."

"Don't worry, I came up with one."

"What?"

"The Bronx Beast."

Everyone remained silent.

"What? It's not a bad team name," Mark said.

"How about Yajuu no Bronx?" suggested Ching.

"What's that mean?" Shanta asked with a confused look.

"It's Japanese for Mark's team name," he answered.

Everyone nodded in agreement. Mark sighed heavily, but even he liked the name.

"Alright!" exclaimed Mark with a grin. "Let's do this, Yajuu no Bronx!"

Everyone cheered, raising fists in the air. They all separated into their groups. Madam Renee raised both arms towards Andrew's group and instantly transported them to the Jersey Shores. Then, she transported Shanta's group to Japan.

"Good luck," she whispered to herself.

"Don't worry," replied Master Dao with his hand on her shoulder. "Those kids will defeat Hidishi."

"I hope so, for the world's sake," replied Madam Renee.

Mark, Hibika and Andrew arrived at the corner of Port Carteret Drive, a safe distance from Hidishi's corporation. By the looks of the place, it was heavily guarded. Workers came in and out of the front gate, by swiping their card.

"How do we get in?" Hibika asked.

Suddenly, Mark had an idea. "Drew, I'm going to summon a shadow wall to camouflage us from the guards, like I did when we rescued Shanta."

"Go for it," Andrew said.

Mark closed his eyes and focused his mind. The shadow wall rose and covered them. It began to blend in with the surroundings. They were invisible. They waited for a worker with a card to approach the gate. Minutes later, a young Hispanic woman, with long black hair and dark brown eyes, approached the gate. Mark, Hibika, and Andrew raced towards the gate as the woman went in. With seconds to spare, they passed through. They followed the woman to the main door, where she had to swipe her card again. Once inside, Mark snatched the woman and dragged her to an empty hallway. He deactivated the wall and covered her mouth with his hand.

"Please, don't scream," he whispered. "We're not going to hurt you."

The woman nodded. Mark moved his hand from her mouth. She looked at them nervously. Andrew noticed her name tag. Her name was Amalia.

"Can you tell us where Hidishi's office is, Amalia?" Andrew asked.

Amalia nodded. "It's on the third floor. Why?"

"Hidishi kidnapped my friend and plans to destroy this world," he answered with a serious look.

"I...don't follow..."

"Just get out of here, while you can."

"Yeah, we want you and your co-workers to live," added Mark.

Amalia nodded and ran off.

"So, we have to reach the third floor before anyone sees us, right?" Hibika asked.

Mark and Andrew nodded. Suddenly, they heard footsteps. From the sound, they had seconds to escape. It was too late. A guard spotted them at the other end of the hallway. They ran. The guard sounded the alarm. Soon, there were thousands of guards chasing them. Quickly, they scattered down separate hallways. The guards did the same.

Andrew transformed and began attacking the guards. One-by-one, the guards fell to the ground. Quickly, Andrew headed for the stairs. More guards showed up, blocking his path. He pointed his Gekido Bakuhatsu attack at the ceiling. The blast made a huge hole, causing part of the second floor to crash down. The guards cried in terror, fleeing. With no one to stop him, Andrew leapt through the hole to the second floor.

Mark had already made it to the second floor. His Shadow Fang attack knocked out most of the guards as he pressed forward. Mark punched the ground. A huge hole developed, stopping the guards right in their tracks. Mark smiled as he headed for the third-floor staircase.

As he ran down the hallway, Mark noticed another part of the building where trucks were being loaded with huge crates.

"So that's where Hidishi keep his drugs," he replied to himself. "And it looks like they're gonna send them out today. I better tell Drew about this."

Mark and Andrew arrived on the third floor. To their surprise, Hibika was standing there waiting for them.

"What took you guys?" she asked.

"We…had to fight…our way through…" Andrew answered trying to catch his breath.

"How…did you…get here so fast?" asked Mark, also catching his breath.

"I took that thing over there," Hibika answered, pointing to the elevator.

"Lucky you," Mark said sarcastically.

"C'mon guys, we have a job to do," Andrew said running down the hallway.

"Drew, there's something you should know," said Mark catching up to him.

Andrew stopped. "Mark, we don't have time for…"

"Hidishi plans to ship out his drugs today while we fight him!" Mark interjected. "We must destroy that warehouse before they're shipped off."

"Where is it?" Andrew asked, looking at him.

"It's outside of this building, but there is a back door on the main floor to get there," Mark answered, pointing to the directory.

Andrew looked down the hallway and spotted Hidishi's office. He looked down at the ground.

"We'll rescue Rosa later," said Mark. "Right now, we must stop those trucks from reaching the hands of kids and adults. Besides, Hidishi won't kill her just yet."

Andrew looked up at Mark and said, "Lead the way."

Tracy felt a voice calling out to her. She stared out the window of the subway train as it traveled underground.

Where am I going?

The subway doors opened as more people flocked into the car. Tracy stared deeply into her own world as people talked amongst themselves and more people came in.

Suddenly, the train stopped and called out to her stop. Tracy quickly got off and followed the voice in her head. She walked aimlessly around South Bronx, watching people pass her by. The sounds of cars honking and people talking couldn't drown out the voice as Tracy slowly reached her destination.

Shanta, Ching and Rei-Rei arrived on the island. They could see the main corporation standing on a huge hill. They walked through a dense forest with patches of moonlight shining down. The sounds of the wildlife had them on edge. They weren't sure what to expect. Suddenly, a creature with glowing red eyes jumped out from the bushes. It was a buff man with eight octopus arms.

"What the hell is it?" Shanta asked looking into its red eyes.

"It must be a scout to warn others if there are intruders," answered Ching drawing his katana.

"Let's kill it," replied Rei-Rei and quickly transformed.

Rei-Rei's transformation was cute. He was covered in brown fur and had longer arms. His hands, feet and ears were twice as big as his and were a light peach color. And with a long skinny tail and huge dark brown eyes, Rei-Rei truly looked like a monkey.

Rei-Rei drew out his bamboo stick and dashed toward the creature. The buff man launched his tentacles. Rei-Rei dodged, jumping into the air. He whacked the buff man with the stick, knocking it down.

"TAKÉYARI!!!" shouted Rei-Rei as he drove the bamboo into the ground.

Instantly, thousands of tiny spear-shaped bamboos rose out of the ground. The buff man dodged but could keep up with the attack's speed. The attack pierced the buff man's body, turning it into Swiss cheese. The buff man died instantly. Shanta and Ching both looked at Rei-Rei with their eyes wide open. They couldn't believe he defeated the guy without breaking a sweat.

"Where did you learn that move?" asked Ching, still looking surprised.

"Phansu showed me," answered Rei-Rei with a smile.

"Phansu really knows some moves," replied Shanta.

"We can't waste any more time," replied Rei-Rei placing his bamboo stick into the hilt on his back. "Andrew expects us to destroy this building."

Shanta led the way. They ran through the forest until they reached the front gate. They hid in some bushes.

 "So how do we get in?" Shanta asked, looking at the guards guarding the front gate.

"Maybe I could distract them while you two get inside," answered Rei-Rei.

"No way, it's too dangerous," she replied looking at him.

"Just trust me on this one. I wasn't given the power of Saru for nothing."

"Okay…but be careful. Ching doesn't want to be the one to tell Master Dao we let you get yourself killed."

"Since when was I in the conversation?" asked Ching looking at Shanta.

"Never mind that," she said and looked at Rei-Rei. "Ready?"

Rei-Rei gave Shanta a thumbs up and ran towards the front gate. He flipped over the gate and waved at the guards with a smile. Instantly, the guards attacked Rei-Rei. With lightning speed, Rei-Rei dodged their gunfire. He jumped into the air with his arms extended outward.

He grinned. "COCONUT BARRAGE!!!"

Thousands of small energy balls the size of coconuts instantly appeared and surrounded Rei-Rei. He extended both arms forward, firing them all at once. The energy balls hit the guards, knocking them all to the ground. It was like watching fireworks explode on the ground. Rei-Rei landed onto the ground. He looked and saw all the guards knocked unconscious. Suddenly, the machine guns on the second and fourth floors began firing at Rei-Rei. He dodged the gunfire. Rei-Rei saw Shanta, in her fox form, running towards the entrance with Ching following behind her.

"Nice going Rei-Rei," said Shanta passing him. "Let's get going!"

Rei-Rei soon followed, while dodging the gunfire. Once inside, they took a moment to admire the décor and look at the directory.

"This map doesn't show a factory," replied Rei-Rei looking at the directory.

"Then the factory must be underground," said Shanta. "We have to use the elevator."

"What's an elevator?" asked Ching looking confused.

"That's an elevator," she answered pointing to it. "Rei-Rei, push that button right next to the elevator."

Rei-Rei pushed the button. Suddenly, humanoid security drones came out of the staircase and walked towards them.

"I'll hold them off while you two get that elevator open," replied Ching holding onto the handle of the katana.

Still holding onto the handle, Ching ran up to the drones. SLASH! Ching drew out his katana slicing one of the drone's arms off. The other drones began shooting at him. Ching dodged their gunfire while slashing the drones one-by-one. Soon, every drone became nothing more than a pile of scrap.

"The elevator is open," replied Shanta waving to Ching.

Ching ran towards the elevator and hopped inside. Rei-Rei and Ching both watched in awe as the elevator doors closed. Shanta put her hand over her face in embarrassment. Suddenly, the computer asked for a password. Instantly, Rei-Rei and Ching drew out their weapons.

"Put your weapons down," Shanta said with her hand still over her face. "It's only a computer asking for a password."

"What's a com-pu-ter?" asked Rei-Rei.

"It's a machine capable of storing a lot of information," Shanta answered. "Some computers need a password in order to gain access for certain information."

"So, what's the password?" asked Ching

"I don't know," answered Shanta, looking at the keypad and screen next to the elevator panel. "Maybe Hidishi is the password," suggested Rei-Rei.

Shanta typed in Hidishi's name on the keypad and pressed enter. The computer took in the password. Suddenly, the bottom part of the elevator panel opened revealing four buttons. Shanta pressed the button marked *B1* and waited for the elevator to move. She told Rei-Rei and Ching to stay on the sides of the elevator, just in case more drones appear and start firing.

The elevator moved downward. Then, it stopped suddenly. The elevator door opened. Instantly, a hailstorm of gunfire was aimed at the elevator.

"We have to do something," replied Shanta as she pressed her body closer to the elevator wall.

"I've got an idea," replied Rei-Rei. He looked at Ching. "I need you to give me a boost."

Rei-Rei climbed onto Ching's shoulders. He used his tail to grab the vent cover. He drew out his bamboo stick and placed the end of the stick onto the ceiling.

"TAKÉYARI!!!"

Thousands of tiny spear-shaped bamboo sticks fell from the ceiling, piercing the drones' heads. Every drone exploded, making a huge smoke cloud.

"Nice one," said Shanta exiting the elevator.

Rei-Rei and Ching soon followed. The smoke cleared. Shanta, Rei-Rei, and Ching realized they were on the first level of the factory. They stared outside a huge window showing workers working on developing the meta-human drug.

"There has to be a way to reach the development room," replied Ching still staring out the window.

"There's a staircase over there leading to the developing room," Shanta said pointing to a staircase outside the window. "But how do we get there?"

"Maybe this hallway might take us there," suggested Rei-Rei pointing to a staircase marked *Second Level Staircase*.

They headed for the staircase and went downstairs to the second level. Though it seemed to be unguarded, there were four laser rifles posted on the corners of the ceiling.

"Anyone got a plan?" asked Shanta.

Rei-Rei and Ching shook their heads.

Suddenly, a guard spotted them from behind and sounded the alarm. The whole room began flashing red. Quickly, Shanta attacked the guard, knocking him out. Soon, drones with machine guns appeared. Shanta tried to find an escape route, but they were soon surrounded. They heard footsteps. A bead of sweat rolled down Shanta's cheek as the footsteps got louder.

"Welcome to my research facility," he said, appearing before them. "I'm Professor Yen. Every meta-human you have faced, I created. And you're just in luck: I have one who needs a new training partner."

Just then, the meta-human stepped forward. He stared at them with his green eyes and had an evil grin on his face.

"It can't be," replied Shanta with her eyes wide open. "It just can't be."

TWENTY

Mark, Hibika and Andrew reached the hallway, leading to the warehouse. They carefully walked down the narrow hallway, making sure no one was following them. Mark peered through the window in the door to see if the coast was clear. He nodded as he opened it slightly. They quickly sneaked past a few warehouse workers and hid behind some crates.

The warehouse was huge. There were thousands of crates stacked against the walls and the windows were filled with dust. Only forty trucks were allowed to load from the warehouse at the same time.

"Looks like they're loading the trucks with the drugs," Andrew said watching the workers. "We have to stop them before more kids are on the streets selling drugs."

"I hear ya, but how?" asked Mark looking at him.

"Leave it to me," said Hibika with a smile.

Hibika rose from behind the crates. She walked up to the workers.

"What the hell is she thinking?" Andrew asked Mark while his eyes watched Hibika approach the workers.

"She said she had a plan," Mark answered also looking at Hibika.

Hibika smiled at the workers and asked in a sexy voice, "Can you direct me to the bathroom? I seemed to have gotten lost."

All the workers stopped what they were doing and stared at Hibika. She giggled and bent over to look at a crate with her hands behind her back. Her cleavage caught their eye. All the workers were flushed with excitement.

"I'll show you where it is," replied one of the workers.

"No, I will," said another worker shoving the other worker.

Soon, all the workers began to fight. Hibika watched as the small fight began to escalate into a brawl. She ran over to where Mark and Andrew were hiding.

"How did you do that?" asked Mark.

"I saw it in a movie," she answered giggling.

"Good job, Hibika," Andrew said and looked at Mark. "Let's finish the job."

"You got it," replied Mark with a smile.

Mark and Andrew quickly transformed. They attacked the workers. With the workers easily knocked out, Mark and Andrew began to attack the loading bay.

"These drugs aren't gonna reach the hands of kids!" Andrew exclaimed as he destroyed the crates.

"Ya damn right!" replied Mark as he destroyed the parked trucks, from the inside, with his Shadow Fang attack.

Soon, the loading bay was in ruins. Debris was everywhere. Andrew and Mark fist bumped. Suddenly, they heard a scream. They turned around and saw a teenage girl holding a gun to Hibika's head.

"My, My, you've been busy," she said with a smug look.

"Let her go, whoever you are," Andrew said with his claws ready to attack.

"The name's Kat," she replied.

Suddenly, a familiar voice came on the intercom.

"You may have stopped most of my trucks from delivering my drugs, but you still can't stop me," said Hidishi, through the intercom.

"We will defeat you!" Andrew exclaimed angrily. He looked at Kat. "Let her go. It's us you want."

"Very well," said Kat pushing Hibika to the side, "but let me slip into something more comfortable."

Instantly, Kat transformed. Her transformation made her look twice as sexy. Kat's body was covered in yellow-brown fur, and she had a skinny bushy tail. She had razor sharp claws, her pointy ears moved up to the top of her head and her yellow eyes were oval-shaped. Kat's nose became smaller and triangular, with whiskers sticking out and her upper lip was shaped like a curvy "W".

Kat ran towards Mark and Andrew at full speed. She punched them both in their stomachs. Mark and Andrew staggered backwards with their hands clenching their stomachs. Mark dashed forward. Mark went for a straight jab. Kat blocked and countered. Her uppercut sent him into the air. Kat leaped into the air and clubbed Mark in the stomach. Mark plummeted diagonally, crashing into the ground. She landed onto the ground, dusting herself. Furious, Andrew dashed forward and began punching her. To his surprise, she dodged every blow. BAM! Kat punched Andrew in the stomach and followed up with an uppercut to the chin. Andrew felt weightless for a moment, but soon smacked the ground with his back. Kat looked at them, smiling evilly.

"It was nice knowing you two," she said raising her hand in the air summoning a ball of energy. *Huh?*

Suddenly, Kat vanished just as Hibika swung. Hibika looked around but couldn't find her. She held the hilt tightly. She heard a buzzing noise from above. Hibika swung upward, slicing the energy ball in two. The two halves flew past her, exploding onto the ground. Kat reappeared in front of Hibika and threw more energy balls. Hibika dodged, slowly inching towards her. Hibika swung upward. Kat dodged, leaping backwards. She wiped her cheek and saw blood on her hand. Kat grinned as she fired a huge energy ball. Hibika stuck her katana into the ground. She made a hand sign with her right hand. Instantly, a baby blue aura surrounded her. She picked up the katana with her left hand and swung.

"IWA NO MAI!" Hibika cried out.

The swing created a tidal wave of rock and concrete. The wave cut the ball in half. The ball exploded. SMACK! The backlash hit Hibika. Hibika flew backwards, crashing into a wall. She was bruised everywhere, even her clothes were slightly ripped. Mark and Andrew rose and decided to turn it up a notch.

"KAGE!" shouted Mark.

"GEKIDO!" Andrew shouted.

"BAKUHATSU!!!" they shouted in unison.

Both their blasts intertwined into one huge blast. Kat crossed her arms over her face and waited for impact. The blast hit Kat. Smoke filled the area. The smoke cleared. It destroyed everything around her and made a gaping hole in the loading bay.

"Was that your best attack?" she asked them, dusting herself off. "Let me show you two an attack! LIGHTNING SPEAR BARRAGE!!!"

Suddenly, thousands of tiny light energy spears came crashing down.

"Seriously?!" exclaimed Mark, as he dodged the attack. "Do all the bad guys know an electric attack?!"

Mark and Andrew continued to dodge the lightning attack as best they could, but there were too many. They screamed in pain as each spear sent out ten thousand volts of electricity into their bodies. They collapsed to the ground like rocks. Andrew and Mark de-transformed. They struggled to get up. Kat stood there, laughing with delight.

"This…looks like…the end," Mark managed to say to Andrew.

"It's…not over yet…" Andrew said to him. "Not when Rosa is still in Hidishi's hands."

Tracy stared at the Fortune House's door. All she kept on thinking was why she was here. She slowly reached out for the knob. She turned it and opened the door.

"Hello?" she asked, slowly walking in.

No one answered. Tracy looked around nervously: making sure no one would attack her. Suddenly, she saw a small light coming from a door. She slowly approached it, opening the door. It was the door that led to the basement. Tracy sneaked down the creaky steps. Suddenly, she heard a voice.

"So nice of you to join us, my dear."

She walked the rest of the way normally. Since she was spotted, there was no point in sneaking around. She looked and saw Madam Renee and Master Dao.

"Who are you?" she asked.

"My name is Madam Renee," Madam Renee answered, "and this is Master Dao."

"Were you the one who called me here?"

"Indeed, it was I."

"Why?"

"You have a very special gift, Tracy. It's almost time for you to awaken."

"Who is she?" Master Dao asked.

"This is Tracy, Mark's girlfriend," answered Madam Renee.

"You mean…?"

Madam Renee smirked. "Yes."

"What are you talking about?" Tracy asked. "Why am I here?"

Suddenly, Madam Renee and Master Dao sensed Mark and Andrew were in danger. Soon, Tracy sensed it. She collapsed to her knees.

"What was that?" she asked, shivering.

"That was Mark and Andrew," Madam Renee answered. "They need our help. It's time, Dao."

Master Dao nodded. "Let's go, Renee."

"Stay here," said Madam Renee, looking at Tracy. "I'll explain everything later."

Tracy nodded nervously. Madam Renee and Master Dao both closed their eyes. Seconds later, they vanished.

Mark and Andrew struggled to get up. Kat raised her arm, summoning an enormous energy ball.

"It's time to say goodbye," she said with an evil smile.

BAM! Kat was hit with a blast of energy. She skidded across the ground, crashing into the wall. Mark and Andrew looked at the smoke cloud with wide eyes. They quickly turned their heads as the footsteps grew louder. They could see two shadows approaching them.

"Think they're friendly?" Mark asked him.

"I hope so," Andrew answered.

"Are you okay?" a familiar voice asked.

"We're kinda pinned to the ground," Andrew answered bluntly. "What are you and Master Dao doing here?"

"To give you two a helping hand," answered Master Dao. "I'll have you two up in no time."

He placed his hands just a few inches above their backs. Suddenly, a warm energy began surging through their bodies. It almost felt like being at a spa. They closed their eyes as their wounds quickly healed. Minutes later, Mark and Andrew were up.

"You da man, Master Dao," replied Mark with a smile.

"Stay focused you two," said Master Dao. "That meta-human will get up soon."

Kat rose, destroying the debris with her powerful aura. Mark and Andrew looked at each other.

"Let's do it," said Mark.

"RAION!!!" they shouted in unison.

A bright light illuminated the warehouse. The light faded. Mark and Andrew became Raion once more. His eyes were filled with anger and his fists were ready to fight. Raion told Master Dao to heal Hibika while he took care of Kat.

"Ready for round two?" Raion asked Kat.

Kat didn't answer, but instead dashed forward. Soon, they were nothing more than blurs. Flashes of light scattered across the floor and quickly escalated into the air. Both their intense energies began to further destroy the warehouse. It already had gaping holes in the walls and in the ceiling. SMACK! Raion clubbed Kat in the back. She plummeted, crashing down into the ground. Kat slowly rose and charged at Raion once more with one arm extended forward. Raion dived towards her with one arm extended forward also. SLASH! Kat and Raion both received claw marks across their chest. They both landed on the ground and continued the fight.

"Raion has gotten stronger from his last fight," replied Madam Renee, watching him fight.

"I see," said Master Dao, helping Hibika up.

"I never thought I would see Raion up close," said Hibika with a smile.

SMACK! Raion punched Kat in the face. Her face caved in as her body was sent flying into the wall. Kat left a huge imprint of her body, as she slid down the wall to the ground. She slowly got up, with her body leaning against the wall. Her body was covered in bruises. Even her clothes were torn. Raion stared at her with his green eyes. Furious, she jumped into the air with both arms extended forward.

"I will kill you!" she shouted. "LIGHTNING SPEAR BARRAGE!!!"

"Not likely," Raion said. "ROAR OF THE BEAST KING!!!"

Their blast met. It began destroying the ground beneath it. Slowly, Raion's blast absorbed Kat's attack. It struck her. Kat screamed in pain as the blast pushed her backwards into the ceiling. He added more power, causing part of the ceiling to crumble around her. Despite her efforts to push back Raion's blast, the blast was too strong. Her body slowly disintegrated with each passing second. Soon, Kat was no more. Hibika, Master Dao, and Madam Renee approached Raion.

"Are you guys okay?" Raion asked.

"We're fine," answered Madam Renee. "You must find Rosa before Hidishi decides to kill her."

"No need to," a familiar voice said. "I have her right here."

They all turned around. They saw Hidishi standing next to Rosa, who was handcuffed to a steel beam.

"Let her go, Hidishi!" Raion exclaimed angrily while raising a fist.

"Not until I kill you all," he replied with an evil smile. "You don't know who you are dealing with."

I was afraid of this, thought Madam Renee. "Raion, let us help you. Hidishi is more powerful than you."

"I don't want you all to get killed," said Raion. "I can handle him."

"Then I guess we have no choice," she said looking at Master Dao.

Suddenly, Madam Renee and Master Dao both began to glow. Everyone looked away, as the light got brighter and brighter.

"What's happening?" Raion said as the light illuminated the warehouse.

TWENTY ONE

Standing in front of Shanta was a duplicate of Andrew. The only difference was that he is part man and part wolf. He had wolf ears on top of his head, long brown hair, green oval-shaped eyes, razor sharp fangs and claw-like fingers. Even his bushy tail was brown in color. He wore blue sweatpants and a white T-shirt that was tucked inside his sweatpants.

"What kind of sick joke is this?" she asked looking at Yen.

"Oh, this isn't a sick joke," answered Yen. "This is a genetically enhanced Andrew that I created from a blood sample given to me from his very first battle. He is ten times stronger than Andrew himself and will help us conquer this world."

"Not if we stop you first," replied Rei-Rei pointing his bamboo stick at Yen.

"Guards, take them to the Training Room," Yen said smiling. "Monitor their progress. I want to know how strong our young warriors are."

The drones began pushing Shanta, Rei-Rei and Ching towards the Training Room. Once inside, the drones locked the door and stood outside.

"Welcome to my Training Room," said Yen from the Monitoring Room, high above the Training Room.

"Just you wait, Yen," replied Shanta raising a fist, "we will get you and destroy this place."

"Ooh, I'm scared," Yen shot back. "Let the training begin!"

A panel door opened. The clone stepped out, walking towards Shanta and the others.

"My name is Senko," he said stopping a few feet from them. "I may look and sound like your friend, Andrew, but I can assure you that I will kill you all without mercy. I hope, for your sake, you all are stronger than you look."

Senko dashed forward at Shanta and the others, vanishing. He reappeared on the other side of the room. The backlash from his speed knocked them down. Shanta got up and used her Needle Storm attack. Senko stood his ground and took the attack directly. To her surprise, her attack didn't faze Senko at all. Senko dusted off his T-shirt and laughed. Rei-Rei gnashed his teeth and quickly charged at Senko. Rei-Rei thrust his bamboo stick several times. Senko dodged the assault. Try as he might, Rei-Rei couldn't touch Senko. Senko countered. Rei-Rei felt Senko's fist connect with his chin. Rei-Rei flew high into the air. He quickly regained his balance and used his Coconut Barrage attack. Senko dodged, inching closer towards Rei-Rei, who was plummeting fast. Shanta's tail split into three and began to attack Senko. Senko dodged as Rei-Rei landed onto the ground. Both Shanta and Rei-Rei dashed toward Senko. Senko blocked their combined assault and countered. He grabbed Rei-Rei by his tail and slammed him into Shanta. Both of them flew backwards, crashing into the wall. The wall cracked as pieces of debris fell upon them.

"Pathetic," said Senko.

Ching drew out his katana. He dashed forward. Senko back-flipped as Ching swung. SMACK! Both of Senko's feet connected to Ching's chest. Ching staggered back. Senko dashed forward, closing in on Ching. Ching read his movement and dodged. Quickly, Ching flipped his katana upside-down, pointing the hilt upward.

"KAZE NO MAI!" he exclaimed as he vanished.

For a split second, Senko couldn't detect Ching. Senko dodged, but a little too late. Blood splattered everywhere as Ching reappeared behind Senko.

Senko clenched his chest and grinned. "I commend you for cutting me, but it'll be your last."

Meanwhile, Yen got a call from the mysterious woman.

"You want me to initiate the plan now?" he asked with a surprised look.

"Why not, Sugar?" asked the mysterious woman. "Even with these minor setbacks, the plan is still doable."

"I already have a meta-human army ready to carry out *Operation: New World*."

"Wonderful, Sugar! I expect great results from you, so please make sure your end is in order."

"I understand," he said and hung up.

Yen looked back at the screen. Senko was still toying with them. Yen grinned with delight and quickly spoke to a nearby worker.

"Have the meta-army gear up for transport. Tonight, we initiate *New World*."

"Yes, Sir," replied the worker and began calling the transport room.

"STRIKING CLAW!!!" shouted Senko as his hand began to glow.

He swung. Ching jumped into the air with his sword raised over his head. Ching swung his sword vertically as he plummeted back to the ground, trying to cut Senko down to size. Senko vanished. Ching looked around, keeping his guard way up. Senko reappeared behind Ching. SMACK! Senko kicked Ching in the back, sending him flying towards the Training Room walls. Ching quickly regained his balance, but it was too late. Senko was one step ahead. Ching blocked with his katana, but still felt the piercing blow from Senko's Striking Claw. Blood splattered as Ching spun out of control. He crashed into the wall face first.

"Pathetic," Senko said.

Shanta and Rei-Rei finally got free from the debris. Shanta gnashed her teeth as she saw Ching on the ground, with severe damage to his armor.

"You hurt my man!" shouted Shanta. "ENERUGĪ BAKUHATSU!!!"

The huge blast flew straight towards Senko. Senko extended his arms forward. The impact pushed Senko slightly, but he was able to get a grip of the blast. He sent it into the ceiling. The blast exploded, destroying half of the ceiling. Shanta and Rei-Rei's eyes widened as Senko dusted off his hands.

"Is that the best you got?" he asked, looking at them with an evil grin.

"Oh yeah, take this!" shouted Rei-Rei. "SEISMIC WAVE!!!"

Rei-Rei pounded his small fist into the ground, creating a huge wave of energy. The wave flew straight towards Senko at lightning speed. Senko froze for a moment before he jumped into the air, dodging the huge wave. He watched as the wave destroyed the Training Room wall and most of the ground. Shanta dashed forward. Instantly, she appeared in front of Senko. Her foot connected with his chin. Senko flew upward. Shanta leaped into the air and bear-hugged Senko. She spun them around as they plummeted. BAM! They crashed into the ground. Debris flew everywhere and a huge dust cloud filled the air. Shanta landed onto the ground. Senko back-flipped out of the cloud. The dust settled.

"Nice one," Senko said, "but you won't be so lucky next time."

He wiped the blood from his mouth. He jumped into the air and began firing blasts at Shanta and Rei-Rei. They dodged them as best they could, but Senko's blasts were coming down too fast. It was like dodging rain. Senko's blasts knocked them down to the ground. Shanta and Rei-Rei struggled to get up. Senko laughed with delight, slowly walking towards them.

"I have to say, you two have proven you are worthy fighters," he said raising his glowing hand, "but now you two must die."

This was the end. They could see their life flashing before their eyes.
SLASH! Senko felt a sharp pain across his back. He turned around and saw
an armor-less Ching holding his katana, with blood on his forehead and on
his left side. Senko knew he wounded Ching but didn't think he'd have the
strength to attack. Senko dashed forward and attacked. Ching defended but
couldn't keep up with Senko's assault. Senko slashed Ching across his
chest. Ching staggered back as he clenched his chest. Blood soaked
through his clothes and ran down his fingers. Senko punched Ching in the
face. The blow knocked Ching backwards. Ching skidded across the
ground, crashing into the wall. Shanta could see Ching's bruised body
through the dust cloud. Ching wasn't moving. Shanta clenched her fists
tightly and gnashed her teeth. Out of anger, she charged at Senko and
began an assault of punches and kicks. Senko dodged and quickly
countered with a hard right to the stomach. Shanta gasped for air as Senko
roundhouse her to the other side of the Training Room. Shanta lay on the
ground for a moment, twitching. She slowly got up, leaning closely against
the wall.

"We have…to stop Senko…" she told herself out of anger. "Ching did his
best to damage him. Now, it's our turn."

"We can't let Senko win.," replied Rei-Rei looking at Shanta. "Andrew is
counting on us to finish this mission. I won't let him down!"

Suddenly, both their gems began to glow. Senko's body froze. Shanta and
Rei-Rei looked at each other, realizing what was happening. Their bodies
began to glow, illuminating the Training Room.

"What's that weird light?" Yen asked covering his eyes.

The light faded. Standing in the Training Room was a large creature. It was
about seven feet tall. It was covered in white metallic armor with black
stripes and stood on all fours. Its head was shaped like a fox, but broad
around the nose and had a monkey-like tail. Its claws were about a foot

long and it had blue eyes. Its ears were small, and its fangs were razor sharp. To top it all off, a cannon was mounted on its back.

"Who…are you?" asked Senko with his eyes widened in terror.

"I am Tora, the Japanese Tiger," answered the creature.

The ground shook as Tora walked towards Senko. Senko froze for a moment and jumped into the air. He began blasting Tora, but his blasts didn't affect her. They bounced off her armor, destroying the walls.

"My turn!" she roared. "NEEDLE STORM!!!"

Suddenly, hidden panels on her front legs opened and fired a hailstorm of white energy shaped like needles. Senko dodged but couldn't keep up. The attack hit Senko hard. He felt every needle explode on his body. He dropped to his knees. Smoke rose from his body as Tora walked slowly towards him.

"Had enough?" she asked looking at Senko.

"I won't give up to the likes of you," he answered looking up at her.

"Then feel my wrath," replied Tora. "SEISMIC WAVE!!"

Tora stomped the ground with her front leg, sending a bigger wave of energy towards Senko. Senko knew he couldn't dodge it. He crossed his arms over his face and braced for impact. SMACK! The wave knocked Senko backwards, making him skid on the ground. He crashed into the wall. Senko rose slowly, gnashing his teeth.

"I will not be defeated by you!" he shouted. "Take this! SENKO FIRE!!!"

A huge orange-red blast shot towards Tora. She stood there for a moment, aiming with her cannon.

"TORA CANNON!!!" she shouted as she fired a huge light blue blast.

Both blasts collided, destroying the center of the room. Debris fell from the ceiling and the ground crumbled. Soon, Senko's blast was overpowered. Senko knew he lost. He accepted his fate. Senko screamed in pain as the blast pushed him into the wall. Suddenly, the walls in the Training Room began to crumble. Yen and several workers fled from the Monitor Room. Seconds later, Senko and the Training Room were no more. Tora stared at Yen with her blue eyes. He knew his time was up, but he couldn't help but laugh.

"You may have stopped me from creating more meta-humans, but you haven't stopped Hidishi from taking over the world," he said chuckling.

"What do you mean?" asked Tora.

Yen smirked. "You can destroy this place, but it won't do you any good. Even as we speak, a meta-human army is flying to their destinations!"

Yen laughed hysterically as the lab was beginning to shake. Soon, the lab caught fire. Tora picked up Ching with her mouth and ran out of the lab. She looked back. Yen was still laughing while the fire surrounded him. BOOM! The lab was no more. Tora ran down the hallway. Soon, she realized she had to separate in order to get out of the building. Tora separated. Shanta carried Ching while Rei-Rei helped guide them out.

"Five minutes until self-destruct sequence is activated," replied a voice on the intercom.

"Where is the elevator?" Rei-Rei asked Shanta as they ran down the hallway.

"It's there," answered Shanta pointing to it.

Rei-Rei pressed the elevator button. Nothing happened. He pressed it several times.

"Three minutes until self-destruct sequence is activated," replied the voice.

"The elevator doesn't work anymore?" asked Rei-Rei, with a confused look.

"But this is the only way to get back up," replied Shanta. "They must've done this in order to keep contaminates from spreading."

"I have an idea."

"What is it?"

"Just stand back and watch."

Rei-Rei used his Seismic Wave to attack the ceiling. Instantly, the ceiling collapsed. Shanta looked through the huge hole and saw that it led all the way to the main floor. They leaped through the hole, jumping from one steel beam to the next. Minutes later, they reached the main floor.

"One minute until the self-destruct sequence is activated," replied the voice again.

They burst through the doors and ran over to a huge hill. The building exploded, scattering pieces across the island. Shanta covered Ching's body as some of the debris fell over to where they were hiding. Rei-Rei peeked over the hill to see if there was anything left of the building.

"Mission completed," said Rei-Rei with a smile.

"Ching! Wake up, Ching!" shouted Shanta as she tried to wake him.

Ching opened his eyes slowly and smiled. "Did…we win…?"

"Yes," she answered, with tears rolling down her cheeks.

"I wonder if Madam Renee knows we have completed the mission?" asked Rei-Rei, looking at Shanta.

"I hope so," answered Shanta, still looking at Ching. "I don't want to be stuck here while Andrew and Mark have all the fun."

"Now that we can fuse, we can defeat Hidishi," he replied.

"You guys fused?" Ching asked, trying to sit up.

Pain surged through his body. Shanta gently laid him back down.

"When you were knocked out, Rei-Rei and I fused into Tora, the tiger," answered Shanta.

"I see," he said, staring at the sky. "At least Mark and Andrew aren't the only ones now."

"I wonder how they're doing," replied Shanta looking up at the sky.

TWENTY TWO

The light faded. Standing in front of everyone was Master Dao and Madam Renee's true forms.

"Master Dao? Madam Renee?" Raion asked with a surprised look.

"Allow us to introduce ourselves," said Master Dao, "I am Ganit, Protector of the Universe."

"And I am Rina, Guardian of the Earth," added Madam Renee.

Ganit stood to be six feet tall with huge muscles and six fiery wings. He had long black hair in a ponytail, three dark brown eyes, and a long face. He wore a silver chest-plate with matching round shoulder-pads, blue skintight pants. His brown Viking boots were made of wolf fur and had two small black wristbands. Ganit carried a huge sword. The length of the blade was nine feet tall, and the width was three feet wide. The metallic grip handle was three feet tall and had a crystal pommel disk.

Rina was the same height as Hibika and had a slender curvy body. She had long white hair with short-parted bangs, blue eyes, and an oval-shaped face. Even her two white wings were heavenly. Rina wore a white/blue short-sleeve dress that stopped at her knees with two slits, and matching knee-high boots. She had small triangular shoulder-pads and a small necklace with a diamond-shaped gem linked to it. She carried a golden scepter with a light blue crystal resting on top of it. The crystal itself was double-terminated with a thick gold band around its center.

"What do you mean?" asked Hibika.

"We became the people you knew as Master Dao and Madam Renee," answered Ganit, looking at Hibika. "If we told you who we were, none of you would be here now saving the world."

"I believe the others have finished their mission," said Rina. She used her scepter to transport Shanta, Rei-Rei and Ching to the warehouse.

Instantly, they appeared. They looked around and were confused at who was standing next to Hibika and Raion. Rei-Rei looked into Ganit's eyes for a moment. Suddenly, he realized who it was.

"Grandpa!" he exclaimed, hugging him.

"Listen to me Rei-Rei," said Ganit looking down at Rei-Rei. "I am not your grandfather: I'm a Seraph, a heavenly being. Your real grandfather died when you were very young. Before he died, he asked me to take care of you. So, I decided to become your grandfather and take his place."

"You'll always be Grandpa to me," replied Rei-Rei.

Rei-Rei's words pierced Ganit's heart. Ganit smiled as he hugged Rei-Rei.

"What about the real Madam Renee?" Shanta asked.

"Madam Renee was a fortune teller with psychic powers," answered Rina looking at Shanta, "and used them to help others. Why do you think there are so many spare rooms in the Fortune House? Madam Renee took care of orphans and the homeless. She used her powers to help them find homes or jobs. Before she died, she wanted me, an Archangel, to continue her work for her. So, I became Madam Renee and used my powers to help people and to watch over the Earth. That's how I met Andrew, Mark and you. I knew you three could save your world from a powerful man like Hidishi. You three have kind hearts, not found in many people these days and the courage to overcome any obstacle."

"Why did you send us to Macu?" asked Shanta remembering the gateway.

"In order to train with Ganit," answered Rina. "Ganit gave me the gateway to communicate with him. We have been best friends since the beginning of time. I knew that Macu's time difference would give you an edge over Hidishi's meta-humans and would teach you how to work as a team. I see my plan has worked."

Rina walked over to Ching, who was still badly wounded. She placed her hands on his chest. Soon, a warm energy surged through his body. Ching's pain subsided as his wounds began to heal. Shanta smiled as Ching's facial expression became calm. Minutes later, Rina was done. Ching slowly opened his eyes. He sat up and quickly felt his chest. His wounds were gone.

"Raion, let Rina and I handle Hidishi," replied Ganit. "Separate and conserve your energy. Let Andrew and Mark rescue Rosa."

Raion nodded and separated. Andrew ran towards Rosa, freeing her from her shackles. Everyone, except for Rina and Ganit, left the warehouse. Hidishi watched as his prey got away.

He shrugged his shoulders. "As much as I want to kill them now, you two have caught my interest. So, will you two entertain me for a while?"

Hidishi's aura sent shivers down their spines. Hidishi walked slowly towards them with his usual evil grin.

"Ready Rina?" asked Ganit with a grin.

"Let's do it," answered Rina grinning back.

Rosa and Andrew were having another argument. Everyone watched in embarrassment.

"I didn't want your help," she said looking at him.

"Who else would have saved you?" Andrew asked angrily.

"They would."

"Why do you hate me?"

"You lied to me! You played with my emotions!"

"That's not true Rosa," said Hibika, trying to stop the argument.

"What do you know?" Rosa asked angrily. "Andrew is like every other guy here: all they want is a girl with big boobs and a big ass! He never cared about me. He just wanted to get some of this."

SMACK! Hibika slapped Rosa across the face. Rosa stared at Hibika with her hand over her bright red cheek.

"Listen and listen well," said Hibika angrily. "From the time I knew Andrew, all he thought about was you. I admit that I love Andrew. Despite that, all he thought about was you! Andrew loves you, not me! He is willing to risk his life for you. I understand that you feel Andrew…oh, what's that word you Earthlings use…oh yeah! You feel like Andrew *played* you. But he didn't."

Suddenly, everything became clear. Like a ton of bricks, Rosa's heart sank. She realized how wrong she was.

"Andrew wasn't lying…?" Rosa asked herself. "I feel so stupid."

Rosa stared at Andrew with tears rolling down her cheeks. She hesitated, feeling scared that he wouldn't forgive her. But she decided to put that feeling aside and ran towards Andrew. Rosa wrapped her arms around him, burying her head in his chest.

"I'm so sorry," she managed to say through her sobbing.

"It's okay Rosa," Andrew said softly as he gently lifted her head. He wiped her tears. "I'm the one who didn't tell you sooner."

"But still, I…" replied Rosa, but was cut off by Andrew's lips pressed against hers.

Andrew finally kissed Rosa, the girl who he used to take a bath with and play on the monkey bars with, when they were younger. Andrew wrapped his arms around her waist while she wrapped her arms around his neck. It was the happiest moment in his life.

"Get a room," Mark said sarcastically.

BAM! A huge smoke cloud blasted out of the warehouse. They all covered themselves from the oncoming dust and debris. The smoke cleared. Ganit and Rina were in trouble. They both were on their hands and knees, struggling to get up. The others knew they had to help them.

"Stay here guys," Andrew said to Rosa, Hibika and Ching.

"Be careful," replied Rosa with a worried look.

"I will," Andrew said before he kissed her for good luck. "Let's go, Yajuu no Bronx!"

Quickly, Mark, Shanta, Rei-Rei and Andrew all transformed and headed towards the warehouse. They saw Hidishi still standing with a ripped suit.

"Let's fuse guys!" Andrew shouted.

"RAION!!!" Mark and Andrew shouted.

"TORA!!!" shouted Shanta and Rei-Rei.

Raion and Tora dashed forward and attacked. Hidishi dodged their assaults and countered with his own. SMACK! Raion went down hard. Tora dodged Hidishi's powerful kick and used her Needle Storm attack to even the score. Hidishi dodged. He jumped up into the air. He fired two huge blasts at her. Tora dodged the first blast but was hit by the second. She skidded on the ground, crashing into a wall. Raion got up and quickly vanished. Hidishi vanished too. Their speeds were even for a moment as flashes of light scattered across the warehouse. Hidishi turned it up a notch. Soon, Raion couldn't keep up. BAM! Raion was knocked to the ground. Tora slowly got up and head-butted Hidishi in the stomach, knocking him into a broken stair rail. The broken rail pierced through Hidishi's stomach. Blood soaked through his clothes.

"Nice one Tora," said Raion with a smile. "Now, the battle is over."

Suddenly, Hidishi began to laugh. "You don't know who you're dealing with. I am not a human, but a devil!"

Hidishi broke off the rail and pulled it out of his stomach. His body hovered above the ground. Seconds later, Hidishi's wound was healed. He stared at the two warriors and grinned evilly.

"Now, I will show you my true form," he said.

He began to change as his aura swirled around him.

"This isn't good," said Raion as black wings began to sprout out of Hidishi's back.

TWENTY THREE

The sky was filled with transport planes that day, as they flew towards various countries. Although Hidishi owned six transport planes, each plane could hold up to fifty meta-humans and two crates. For Hidishi's plan, each transport plane carried five crates of the meta-human drug, a forklift, twenty meta-humans and one meta-human captain.

 Each meta-human soldier, dressed in blue, green, or black coveralls, was equipped with a backpack (consisting of a passport, a change of clothing, and US currency). Only the captain wore red and didn't carry a backpack.

The plan was simple: once the planes landed at their destinations, one group would transport the crates into the trucks, set up by Hidishi's clients. As for the other group, they received information about the world leaders gathering for a UN meeting.

Hibika, Ching and Rosa could see a weird light flashing through the holes of the warehouse. They weren't sure what was going on, but they had a feeling it wasn't good.

"I can feel a dark presence growing inside the warehouse," Hibika replied staring at it.

"I feel it too," said Ching also staring.

"Please be careful Andrew…" Rosa whispered to herself.

Tracy sat on the steps of the Fortune House's basement, contemplating. Questions ran through her mind as she stared at the floor.

Why is all of this happening? What am I supposed to do? Are Mark and the others okay?

Suddenly, a flash of light came from the corner of her peripheral. She turned her head and stared at the glowing gateway. Fear took over as her body trembled. She could see a shadowy figure slowly approaching her. Tracy shut her eyes and cowered in the corner of the steps.

"Haven't been here in a while," a voice cheerfully said.

Tracy opened her eyes. It was Aiya.

"Who…are you?" Tracy asked nervously.

Aiya looked at Tracy. "I'm Aiya. Who are you?"

"Tracy."

"You're Tracy?! I've heard so much about you."

Aiya quickly hugged her. Tracy pushed Aiya aside, staggering back. She looked at Aiya with fearful eyes.

"H-How do you know me?"

"Mark told me about you. Did Mark forget to mention me to you?"

Tracy was confused. Standing in front of her was a little girl, who not only came out of the gateway, but also knew Mark.

Aiya continued. "Look, I came all this way to find you. I wanted to introduce myself, seeing that I, too, love Mark."

"Hold up, you can't have him!" Tracy exclaimed spontaneously.

"I know that now. Before, I didn't care who else loved him. I came here to give you some advice."

"What advice?"

"Treasure him. Mark trained hard for your sake. Even though he saved me once, he really was focused on saving you. Don't ever let him go."

Tracy couldn't believe her ears. She never realized what trials Mark and the others went through just to save her and Rosa. Even though she didn't know Aiya, she believed her words.

"I will," she replied with a smile.

"Good," Aiya said, smiling back. "Now, I can go back home. By the way, how is everyone?"

"They're fighting."

"I know how it feels to be left behind."

"Then, what do I do?"

"Just believe they will return safely."

Tracy nodded. "Will you stay with me?"

Aiya smiled. "Only for a bit."

"How do you like me now?" Hidishi asked, completing his transformation. Everyone stared at Hidishi's devil-like look. He grew to be about seven feet tall with massive muscles and purple skin. His black hair grew longer, and his eyes were completely blood red. Hidishi had claw-like fingers and feet, a long reptile-looking tail and devil-like wings that were six feet in length. His face stayed the same except he grew fangs that stuck out. Hidishi wore the same suit pants, but it was ripped at the hems and waist.

"Be on your guard everyone," said Rina. "Hidishi's power has grown to a level beyond your comprehension."

"I can feel it," replied Raion looking at Hidishi with clenched fists.

"Do you people honestly think you can stop me?" asked Hidishi looking down at them. "I have enough power to destroy this planet. Surrender now and I will make you all my personal slaves."

"No way," Raion said sarcastically. "You don't have good health benefits."

"And we can't get days off," added Tora.

"Then, I have to kill you all," Hidishi said shrugging his shoulders.

Hidishi raised his arm and fired a huge blast at the warriors. They leaped backwards, landing a few feet away from Hidishi. Raion dashed forward. Tora followed. Raion began punching Hidishi in the face and Tora blasted Hidishi with her Tora Cannon attack. The blast created a huge smoke cloud. The smoke cleared. Hidishi was still standing without a scratch on him.

"That's impossible!" exclaimed Raion with his eyes wide open.

"We didn't even make a mark on him," replied Tora with her eyes wide open.

"Was that the best you got?" Hidishi asked looking at Raion and Tora. "Here, let me show you two how it's done! DARKNESS WING!!!"

Suddenly, his wings expanded. They shot out black waves of dark energy. Rina jumped in front of Raion and Tora and created a huge barrier made of pure light energy. The impact of the blast pushed the barrier a bit.

"Are you okay?" asked Tora looking at Rina.

"I'm fine," she answered, leaning on her scepter. "Don't worry about me. You two are the only ones who can stop him. Ganit and I will help you the best way we can."

"Then let's attack Hidishi again," said Raion. "This time, we all attack at once."

All of them looked at Hisidhi. They attacked him head on. Raion led the attack with several punches, distracting Hidishi. Ganit ran towards Hidishi's tail. Tora aimed her Tora Cannon at Hidishi's legs. Rina transformed her scepter into a golden sword, aiming for Hidishi's head. Hidishi smirked, quickly realized their plan. He snapped his fingers, blowing them away with his dark energy. They quickly dispelled, flying backwards. They crashed into the ground. Raion quickly rose and leaped towards Hidishi.

"STRIKING CLAW!!!" he shouted, extending his left arm towards Hidishi.

"Your attack is no match for mine," replied Hidishi, also extending his right arm. "DEVIL'S CLAW!!!"

Hidishi's claw-like hand began to glow bright purple. BAM! Both claws met, dispersing energy throughout the warehouse. The ground began to shake as they both tried to overpower the other's attack. SNAP! Raion's left arm fractured. Hidishi slammed Raion into the ground with his glowing hand. Blood dripped down Raion's wounded arm as he struggled to get up.

"Time to say goodbye!" Hidishi exclaimed, pointing towards Raion.

"GIGA STRIKE!!!" shouted Ganit, slamming the tip of his blade in the ground.

Instantly, a wave of energy, bigger than Rei-Rei's Seismic Wave attack, quickly headed straight for Hidishi. SLASH! The wave sliced through Hidishi's wrist, disconnecting it. Hisidhi cried in pain as blood gushed out. Ganit raised his sword once more. Hidishi fired two red beams from his eyes. Ganit blocked the beams with his sword, but the impact knocked him backwards into a wall. Rina jumped into the air, right in front of Hidishi's face.

"LIGHTSWORD SLASH!!!" shouted Rina as her scepter transformed into a golden sword once again.

Her attack slashed Hidishi's right eye. Hidishi cried in pain as he covered his wounded eye with his right hand. Rina jumped into the air again and used her attack once more to slash his chest. Blood splattered everywhere.

"That's enough!" Hidishi cried. "DARK FIEND!!!"

A shadowy fiend came from out of the shadows and covered Ganit and Rina. They looked around. There was no escape. Suddenly, they both were being electrocuted. Hidishi could hear their screams.

"This is my most favorite attack," he said with an evil smile. "Not only does the attack cover you in total darkness, but it also gives you a nasty shock."

"Stop this, you bastard!" cried Tora. "TORA CANNON!!!"

Hidishi grinned at the blast and deflected it with his right hand. Tora's eyes widened.

"Try this on for size!" shouted Hidishi. "DARK FIEND!!!"

Another shadowy fiend appeared and covered Tora in total darkness. Tora cried in pain as the shock began to numb her body. The shadow disappeared. Both Shanta and Rei-Rei lay on the ground, face first in their human forms. Even Ganit and Rina were unconscious. Hidishi regenerated his hand and healed his wounds. Raion slowly got up with his wounded arm dangling to his side.

"Hidishi, why are you doing this?" he asked, looking at him. "What do you hope to gain?"

"I'm doing this to gain the power I richly deserve!" Hidishi answered. "Allow me to explain, I grew up in the bad streets of Japan. My father worked in the factories while my mother was a teacher. They didn't make much money and housing was extremely high. Even though I was an only child, I still had to fend for myself. I learned how to hustle, kill, and steal from a drug-dealer around my neighborhood. I was considered his best friend or "dawg" as you people here say. One day, another drug-dealer came into my neighborhood and challenged my friend to a gun duel. My friend called his friends, and the other guy called his friends. Soon, the streets rang with gunfire. I watched in terror as my best friend died on the street with four shots in his chest. Later that night, the same group that killed my friend did a drive-by in our neighborhood. The next morning, I found out both my parents were killed in that drive-by. From that day on, I was determined to kill my killer. Two years later, I had my revenge. But after all that, I soon realized I wanted more. That's when I was given this power from the devil himself. Only he understood my pain and weakness. From that day forward, I decided to use my street smarts to rule this world."

"And you killed Andrew's mother for this plan?"

"Yes, because she knew everything. After Andrew was born, I told her I wanted no part with her and the child. That night, as she was taking out her stuff from my house, she overheard a conversation I had with one of my men. She realized that I was going to rule the world by killing off every human with a new race of people."

"Meta-humans."

"Imagine every human with powers that haven't been awakened. I can make the poorer people rule the richer people by tapping into their hidden powers. Thanks to Yen and his meta-human drug, I can create a utopia where humans are our enemies and our slaves. Join me and you can have everything you desire."

"I have everything right here," replied Raion. "I know this world isn't perfect, but I love it just the way it is. Besides, I won't join someone who plans on enslaving humans that I love and care about."

"If that's your decision, then perish!" exclaimed Hidishi. "DARK FIEND!!!"

The attack instantly covered Raion. Raion struggled. The attack delivered a shock stronger than any of Hidishi's previous Dark Fiend attacks. The shadow disappeared. Covered with cuts and bruises, Mark and Andrew lay on the ground face first in their human forms. They tried to get up, but their bodies were too paralyzed and bruised to move. Soon, the others woke up from their unconscious state. They realized they couldn't move either.

"What did I tell ya!" Mark joked. "Every bad guy we faced knows an electric attack. No originality."

"Still, we can't give up," Andrew said, trying to get up.

"I hear ya," said Mark also trying to get up. "You know I got your back, Dawg."

"Me too," said Shanta.

"Me three!" replied Rei-Rei.

Finally, the numbness subsided.

"Thanks guys," Andrew said standing up with all his weight on one leg. "We must stop him no matter what the cost. We're doing this for our family, friends and the whole planet."

The others stood up. Suddenly, the Japanese symbols for their animal spirits began to glow brightly on their chests. They looked at each other as their bodies began to glow.

"What's going on!" exclaimed Hidishi looking at them.

Instantly, they shot up into the air like rockets. Blue, red, green and purplish-black colors with the heads of their animal spirits streamed downward towards Hidishi. Hidishi blocked the lights with an energy shield. They pierced through the shield and his stomach. Hidishi cried in pain and coughed up blood. He clenched his wounded stomach as he slowly turned his body around to face them. They were in their were-animal forms.

"Face it Hidishi, your time is up!" Andrew proclaimed.

"Yeah, it's time for you to kiss your ass goodbye!" Mark chimed in.

"I'm not done yet!" exclaimed Hidishi with a smile. "Even if you defeat me, my meta-human army has already unleashed the drug into the water treatment plants. Face it, you lost!"

Rina could feel a tremendous change in the Earth's energy. She closed her eyes and began to see people in various countries transform after drinking the water. Although the spread was on a low scale, it needed to be stopped.

"He's right about one thing," Rina replied to the others. "The drug is already in the water and people are starting to change."

Hidishi laughed hysterically as he heard the terrifying news. He laughed so hard he'd forgotten about his wound and began firing blasts at them.

"Die, all of you!" he managed to say through his laughter.

Dodging his blasts was like dodging rain: they were struck down. The warehouse couldn't stand anymore. Steel beams crashed onto the ground, making loud thuds and cracking the concrete floor.

"Shanta! Rei-Rei! I want you two to get Ganit and Rina out of here," Andrew said staring at Hidishi. "Mark and I are gonna end this battle."

"You two can't stop him," replied Shanta, looking at Andrew. "You need Tora's help."

"No!" cried Mark. "Drew knows what he is doing and I'm with him one hundred percent! Have faith in us, Cuz!"

Shanta smirked at Mark as she hugged him.

"Be careful, you two," she said as she and Rei-Rei picked up Ganit and Rina, leaving the crumbling warehouse.

Mark and Andrew looked at each other.

"Ready?" Andrew asked Mark with a grin.

"Let's do it!" answered Mark, grinning back.

"RAION!!!" they shouted in unison.

Hidishi immediately powered up. Raion stared at Hidishi with his green eyes. Pieces of concrete began to hover around Hidishi as he extended his arms forward, facing Raion.

"You are prepared to die for these humans?" asked Hidishi as a black ball of energy began to form in front of his hands.

"These humans are my friends," Raion answered. "I'll do whatever it takes to defeat you!"

"Stupid meta-human!" shouted Hidishi. "NEGACANNON!!!"

He fired a gigantic blast of dark energy at Raion.

"STRIKING CLAW!!!" shouted Raion, as he extended his right arm toward the blast.

The blast impacted Raion's right claw. Everyone shielded themselves from the oncoming debris. The smoke cleared. Everyone could see the fight clearly. Hidishi and Raion struggled to gain the upper hand. Waves of energy dispersed into the air and the ground trembled. Hidishi added more power to his blast, pushing back Raion.

I can't give up, thought Raion, struggling to push back the blast. *My friends and this whole planet are counting on me to defeat Hidishi.*

"Give up Raion, you are no match for me," said Hidishi adding more power to his blast. "I will rule this world whether you like it or not."

"I won't let you!" said Raion angrily. "I may be a meta-human, but I won't let you harm my friends or this planet! This is for everyone you have killed or hurt!"

Suddenly, Raion's claw began to glow bright red. Images of Rosa, Tracy, Shanta, Rei-Rei, Ching, Hibika, Aiya, Ganit, Rina, Lily, Mike, William, Alice, Ms. Sanchez, Mr. and Mrs. Shepard and Mr. and Mrs. Rivers appeared in his mind. Soon, his glowing hand began to pierce through the blast.

"This is impossible!" exclaimed Hidishi with his eyes wide open. "I'm stronger than you!"

"No, I'm stronger, because of my family and friends!" Raion roared. "Take this! RAGING STRIKING CLAW!!!"

Raion leaped into the blast with his glowing claw, slicing through it like an arrowhead slicing through the air. Hidishi added more power, trying to push Raion back. It was too late.

"I've won!" yelled Raion.

Raion pierced through Hidishi's chest and through his heart. Hidishi cried in pain. Blood gushed out from Hidishi's back. He slowly looked down at Raion and smirked. Suddenly, Hidishi coughed up blood. Raion pulled his arm out of Hidishi's chest. Hidishi collapsed to the ground, making a huge dust cloud. The dust cloud cleared. Raion stared down at Hidishi's lifeless body. Raion separated. Mark and Andrew bumped fists.

"The world is saved," said Mark looking up at the afternoon sky.

"I couldn't have done it without you…Dawg…" Andrew said slapping Mark's back.

"Yeah, I know," said Mark sarcastically. "But don't say dawg again: you sound terrible saying it."

"I'll keep that in mind," Andrew said chuckling.

Suddenly, they saw Hidishi's fingers twitch. They jumped back. Hidishi stared at Andrew with a smirk.

"You…did well…Son…" he managed to say.

"I don't need complements from my father," Andrew replied angrily.

Hidishi smiled. "Glad to know…you still see me…as your father."

"I don't, but I can't fight DNA."

Hidishi laughed until he coughed up blood. He stared at Andrew once more. Soon, his eyes became glassy. He let out his last breath. His body turned black and crumbled, resembling sand. Andrew stared at Hidishi's remains with clenched fists. He was happy that the battle was over, but deep down, he wished he could've had more time with him, at least under better circumstances. Mark put his hand on Andrew's shoulder.

"You finally found out the truth about you. You're now free from those shackles."

Andrew nodded. "Yeah…"

The others approached them. Although they were happy, they still had another mission ahead of them.

"The world isn't safe yet," replied Rina with a concerned look.

"The spread has picked up," said Ganit looking at Mark, Shanta, Rei-Rei and Andrew. "We must stop it."

"Oh no! I almost forgot!" cried Shanta with her hands on her cheeks.

"What's wrong?" Andrew asked looking concerned.

"We still haven't stopped all the meta-humans from killing all the world leaders," she answered. "I forgot to mention it since we were fighting Hidishi."

"When did this happen?" asked Mark.

"While Rei-Rei, Ching and I were in Japan," answered Shanta. "Part of Hidishi's plan was to kill all of the world leaders with meta-humans and start a war."

Suddenly, Rosa's cell phone rang. She looked at the screen and saw Tracy's number flash.

"What's up, Tracy?" she asked, answering the phone.

"I don't know how to explain this," Tracy replied, "but I'm at some creepy house with a little girl and had a vision about an army of guys in coveralls taking over the UN."

"A vision…?"

There was silence on Tracy's end.

"Tracy…?" Rosa asked.

"Oh, sorry," Tracy answered. "It's just that the news is now speaking about my vision."

Rina smiled. "Now, all the players are here."

Ganit looked at Rina and knew exactly what she had in mind. Rina raised her arms as she closed her eyes. Instantly, Tracy appeared before everyone. Tracy, who was still on her cell, looked around. She quickly realized she wasn't at the Fortune House.

"H-how did I get here?" she asked nervously.

Mark hugged her, calming her down. "You were brought here by Rina, Honey."

"Who?"

"By me, Child," Rina answered, stepping forward. "I brought you here because I have chosen you to become the next Guardian of Earth."

Everyone, except for Ganit, was in shock. They couldn't believe Tracy was a candidate as Earth's Guardian. Mark wanted to laugh, but he could tell Rina was being serious.

"Why her?" asked Mark calmly.

"She has amazing spiritual powers, not seen in many humans," Rina answered. "Her powers even surpass my own. From the time she could talk, she was able to sense spiritual energy and even learned how to heal. Tracy truly has what it takes to be a Guardian."

Mark looked at Tracy. "Is this true?"

Tracy felt embarrassed. "It is. I didn't know how to tell you."

Mark kissed her forehead. "It's okay, I'm cool with it. I guess that would explain why you were so calm about everything. So, you can heal people? Think you can give me some sex-"

"Not now, Mark!" Andrew exclaimed, knowing where he was taking it. "Focus on the task at hand, please."

"Before that, I have a few questions for Mark," Tracy replied angrily. "Why didn't you tell me about Aiya?"

"H-How did you two meet?" Mark asked with a frightened look.

"I met her at the Fortune House," she answered. "She came out of the gateway, searching for me. She told me everything."

His misadventures with Aiya played back in his head. *Crap! I'm so dead…*

Tracy looked at him and smiled. "She also told me how you trained so hard for my sake. She gave me advice, telling me to treasure you. To think, a little girl was giving me advice. But she's right. I do treasure you, Mark. And I know you treasure me."

She kissed him, holding him close. Mark wrapped his arms around her. They unlocked lips.

"Next time, don't hide things like that from me, okay?" Tracy asked with a smile.

Mark nodded. "By the way, where is she?"

"She returned home. But she did say she'll come and visit soon."

"I don't mean to interrupt, but we do have a mission to complete," Rina replied, butting in.

Rina stepped forward and handed her scepter to Tracy. Instantly, the scepter began to glow, surrounding Tracy in that same aura of light. The light faded. Tracy looked down and saw that she was wearing the same exact outfit as Rina. Tracy's face turned bright red as she tried to cover herself. Mark was awestruck, knowing how sexy she was in that outfit.

"Now that the scepter has recognized you, Ganit and I can proceed with our plans," said Rina.

"What plans?" Andrew asked.

Rina looked at everyone with a sad look. "Our plan is to stop the spread of the drug while you guys stop the meta-humans at the UN. Ganit and I are going to combine our powers and cover the Earth in immense spiritual energy, capable of destroying the drug. It won't heal the infected, but it can at least prevent future ones."

"So…you're telling us you ain't coming back, right?" Shanta asked with a serious look. "That's why you both made Rei-Rei and Tracy new Guardians."

Everyone was in shock. Rei-Rei ran up to Ganit and hugged him tightly. Tears rolled down his cheeks as he sobbed. Ganit knelt and patted Rei-Rei's head with a smile.

"I must do this, Rei-Rei," he said. "It is for the better of mankind. I know you'll do a better job than me."

"But…" Rei-Rei began. "I understand…"

"Tracy, I want you to teleport everyone to the UN while Ganit and I prepare," Rina said.

"But…I never teleported before," Tracy replied nervously.

Rina smiled as she pointed at the scepter. "Let the scepter help you. Just think about the UN's location and the scepter will do the rest."

Ganit looked at Rina before he looked at everyone. "Well, this is goodbye, my friends. I'm glad to have met you all. You all will make fine, strong men and women."

"I agree, Ganit," Rina replied. "I, too, am glad to have met you all. It was short, but well worth every minute. Let's go, Ganit."

Instantly, they vanished. For that moment, it felt surreal. But soon, reality settled in.

"I know how everyone feels, but now is not the time," Ching said, breaking the silence.

"I agree, Brother," Hibika replied. "Let's go to this UN place and stop those meta-humans."

"Let's go, guys," Tracy said, raising the scepter in the air.

The scepter glowed. Instantly, they vanished.

TWENTY FOUR

"**H**oney, I love you, but you do realize this isn't the UN, right?" Mark said sarcastically.

A gentle breeze blew across the hot sands of the Sahara.

"Don't you start with me, Mark Rivers!" exclaimed Tracy angrily. "I'm not used to teleporting. Don't make me hit you with this scepter."

"Sorry…"

"That's better. Now, let me try again."

Tracy raised the scepter in the air and closed her eyes, focusing on the UN's location. The scepter glowed brightly. Instantly, they vanished.

In the depths of space, Ganit and Rina faced the blue planet with their minds and hearts ready. They stood on opposite ends of the Earth and took a deep breath. A fierce aura of light surrounded them as they powered up. Soon, both sides of the Earth were lit up by the shining light.

Guard them well, Tracy, Rei-Rei, thought Rina with a smile as the Earth was being slowly covered in a bright blue aura.

No one noticed Tracy and the others' sudden appearance. With all the commotion going on inside the building, they were able to sneak in.

Inside, the sounds of gunfire and screams filled the air. Blood and corpses were everywhere as the small meta-human army massacred everyone in sight. Soon, they reached the large auditorium, where all UN meetings were held. Inside, all the world leaders were hiding under their respected tables. Suddenly, a tall man wearing a red coverall stepped forward.

"No use hiding," he said with a smile. "You're all going to die. I suggest you surrender and let us do our job."

"Not on my watch," a voice replied.

Red looked around the auditorium and spotted Andrew and the others standing at the very back of the room.

"I don't know how you got in here, but you're all going to die," he said.

He snapped his fingers, signaling his men to attack.

Crap, we can't fight in here, Andrew thought as the men charged towards them.

Tracy raised her scepter in the air and closed her eyes. Instantly, everyone vanished. Every world leader got up from under their tables, looking around the room.

"Have we…been saved?" asked the French leader.

No one answered.

Ganit and Rina continued to focus their energy on the Earth. The Earth was only one-fourth covered in the bright blue aura. Sweat ran down their faces as their breathing became hard.

"Hang in there, Rina," Ganit thought-spoke to Rina.

"You too, Ganit," Rina thought-replied.

The battle was fierce as Andrew and the others struggled to defeat the meta-human army. Thanks to Tracy teleporting them outside, everyone had freedom to go all out. Rosa and Tracy hid behind a limo and watched the others fight bravely.

"These guys are a lot stronger than the previous meta-humans," Tracy said with a worried look.

"Maybe you can do something about that," Rosa replied, looking at the scepter. "You're a Guardian, remember?"

"But…"

"Just try, okay?"

Tracy gripped the scepter tightly. Nervously, she stood up. Doubt ran through her mind. She looked at Rosa, who was cheering her on. Tracy raised her scepter in the air. Suddenly, the sky began to turn dark. Everyone stopped fighting as they saw lightning flash across the sky. Mark looked over his shoulder and saw an aura surrounding Tracy. Streaks of lightning came crashing down on everyone. Mark and others dodged. Soon, the lightning struck the meta-human army. They cried in pain as their bodies became numb. They all collapsed, with smoke rising from their clothes. It was a powerful attack, but only five out of the twenty meta-humans were instantly killed. The remaining meta-humans slowly rose and began their assault.

Mark and Andrew quickly transformed into Raion and attacked the first five meta-humans. To his surprise, they all were speed-type meta-humans. They crisscrossed past him, forming an orbital. Raion couldn't touch them. They attacked. He could feel all their blows all over his body. In seconds, Raion collapsed to his hands and knees. The meta-humans paused for a second before they quickly dashed forward. Raion grinned. Shadowy spikes rose from the ground. They dodged, running past him. Raion tried again. They broke through and attacked him. Cuts instantly appeared on Raion's body. He staggered backwards. He looked back and saw one of the meta-humans in mid-air. Raion's body froze. He knew he couldn't dodge. Suddenly, the meta-human began to slow down. Raion took this opportunity to attack. Quickly, Raion leaped forward and used Raging Striking Claw. Blood splattered everywhere as the meta-human was torn apart. The remaining four saw their comrade's body fall in different places. Confused and filled with anger, they dashed forward. Soon, they could feel their bodies begin to slow down. They slowly turned around with shocked looks. They saw Tracy pointing her scepter at them. Suddenly, they felt great pain. They slowly looked down. Their bodies were being slowly ripped apart by Raion's Raging Striking Claw. What felt like eternity only lasted for a few seconds. Their bodies hit the ground with a pool of warm blood surrounding them.

"Thanks, Tracy," Raion said with a smile. "You saved my butt."

"No problem," Tracy replied, feeling embarrassed.

Shanta and Rei-Rei transformed into Tora. They, too, fought five meta-humans. To their surprise, they had an elemental group, consisting of twin girls and triplet boys. Their synchronization was perfect. They all dashed toward Tora at once. Quickly, they jumped into the air. Tora danced across the parking lot, dodging Wind, Water, Fire, Earth, and Lightning combinations. She tried to counter, but they were a step ahead. SMACK! Tora was hit hard. She skidded across the parking lot. She shook off the attack, but the next Wind/Water attack came at the last second. Her body froze. Suddenly, the attack was destroyed by Raion's Roar of the Beast King. Tora appreciated the help but wanted to finish the fight herself. Raion stood back and watched Tora get serious.

"Let's go!" she shouted as an onslaught of elemental combos came crashing down on her.

BOOM! The ground cracked and debris flew everywhere. Even Raion leaped out of the way as smoke rose into the air. The smoke cleared. A bamboo dome stood with barely a scratch or crack on it.

"NEEDLE STORM MAXIMUM!!!"

Instantly, a hundred-foot storm of energy needles formed, attacking the elemental group. The storm raged violently as they tried to dodge and counter. On the outside, Tora waited patiently for the results. She could hear their cries and several dings as they countered. The storm cleared. Only Lighting and Water were left. They clenched their fists tightly as they stared at their dead siblings. Suddenly, the sky grew dark with lightning flashing. Tora looked around and noticed that the ground was wet. Lightning pointed his finger at Tora. Instantly, a bolt of lightning came crashing down. Tora leaped, but it was too late. The bolt of lightning quickly traveled through the wet ground and hit Tora's left back leg. The shock knocked her down hard. She lay on the cold, wet ground as Lightning and Water slowly approached her.

"Die, in the name of our dead siblings!" exclaimed Water as her right hand became a watery blade.

Tora grinned. Instantly, bamboo spears sprouted from the ground. Water created an ice shield. The bamboo spears broke as they collided with the shield. Water threw ice shards at Tora. Tora dodged but was cut on her right shoulder. Blood ran down her front leg as she struggled to stand. Water and Lightning laughed with delight as they slowly approached her. Tora fired her Tora Cannon. Lightning deflected it. The blast flew towards the back parking lot. Burning cars flew high into the air from the explosion. Tora was at a loss: she didn't know how she would win. Suddenly, she saw a blast from her peripheral. Lightning blocked the blast but was pushed back. Water looked left: she saw Tracy firing the blast.

"Now's your chance, Tora!" Tracy exclaimed, focusing on Lightning.

Tora nodded. Bamboo spears rose from the ground. Water countered, slicing them down. She looked around, but Tora wasn't in sight. Water looked up. Tora grinned as her Tora Cannon came crashing down at them. With no way of blocking, both Tora and Tracy's blasts collided. The ground trembled and debris flew everywhere as smoke rose. Tora landed, breathing hard. The smoke cleared. Not a trace of Water and Lightning remained.

"Not bad, for a Guardian," said Tora with a grin.

Tracy felt flushed.

Only one-fourth left, Ganit thought as he watched the Earth become three-fourths covered in the light blue aura. *I just hope those kids can stop those meta-humans.*

The sounds of metal clashing filled the air as Ching and Hibika fought against four meta-humans, who were enhanced versions of Gyro. Red stood back and watched with glee as both Ching and Hibika struggled to keep up with his men, who were excellent swordsmen. SLASH! Blood oozed out from Ching's left arm.

"Brother!" Hibika cried as she blocked another strike from one of the meta-humans.

"Focus!" exclaimed Ching as he dashed towards a nearby meta-human.

Ching swung, but the meta-human countered and kicked Ching in the stomach. Ching staggered backwards while keeping his katana up. The meta-human leaped into the air with the blade over his head. Ching looked up and quickly dodged the aerial attack. The ground split open and debris flew everywhere. Ching noticed that the meta-human's blade was stuck into the ground. Quickly, Ching charged toward the meta-human and stuck his blade into his chest. The meta-human cried in pain as the blade sank deeper into him, piercing through his heart. He dropped to his knees and his head hung low. Ching pulled out his katana from the corpse and flicked the blood from the blade. He looked over to his right: Hibika managed to kill one too, with several cuts on her. With only three left, they needed to come up with a plan.

"Hibika, I think it's time to use *that* attack," Ching called out.

Hibika nodded as she ran towards Ching. The three meta-humans stood there in confusion, but soon followed. Hibika and Ching stood back-to-back as the meta-humans dashed towards them. Ching and Hibika vanished. Suddenly, the meta-humans' bodies were frozen as a ten-foot yellowish circle with white Nebtan words engraved on it appeared from under them. They stared at the ground for a moment before they saw Ching and Hibika on opposite ends of the circle. Ching and Hibika's legs were spread apart, with their left leg in front. The blade was pointed downward as they held their katanas on their right.

"DANCE OF THE NEBTAN FLOWER!!!" they shouted in unison.

They vanished. The meta-humans cried in pain as the bodies were being ripped apart. By the end of the dance, both Hibika and Ching flicked off the excess blood from their blades as the three meta-humans collapsed to the ground. Blood spread over the ground, filling up the cracks. All that was left was a red flower pattern in the ground with the three dead meta-humans in the center.

Side note: compared to the other dances, it was considered the slowest and most beautiful. It was a series of synchronized steps moving in and out of the circle, creating a flower pattern using the enemy's blood. Mastering this dance took years.

Red was furious. He spread his arms wide. Instantly, the dead meta-humans turned into small silver orbs and swirled around him.

"What's going on?" Raion asked Ching as he, Tora, and Tracy approached him and Hibika.

"I don't know," Ching answered with a serious look.

Suddenly, the orbs flew into Red. Red laughed hysterically as the ground trembled and debris floated upward. Tracy's legs trembled with fear as she felt the enormous power Red was emitting.

"Prepare for your demise!" Red shouted with an evil grin.

He flicked his wrist with his index and middle fingers pointed upward. Instantly, a whirlwind sprang up from the ground and blew them to the other side of the parking lot. They crashed into cars, denting doors and smashing windows. Raion and the others struggled to get up, seeing that they were exhausted from their previous fights. Suddenly, fire, water, and lightning came crashing down on them. But with quick action from Tracy, they were spared from certain doom. The ground cracked beneath Tracy as she struggled to hold up the energy dome around her and her friends. CRACK! The energy dome began to crumble. Tracy tried to reinforce it, but it was too late. The three elements fused and crashed onto them. The explosion scattered everyone across the parking lot. Rosa, who was hiding on the other side of the lot, watched as her friends flew everywhere. Tears rolled down her cheeks as she thought the unimaginable. Suddenly, a pillar of light shot up from the other side of the damaged lot. Cars flew everywhere, crashing into nearby cars. The light faded. Tracy stood tall with a serious look.

"Impossible!" Red exclaimed. He fired another Wind/Earth/Water attack.

Tracy began walking towards the elemental attack. She whacked it with her scepter, redirecting it upward. The attack shot up into the sky and exploded like fireworks. Tracy continued walking towards Red with a light blue aura surrounding her. This was a side to Tracy not many people got to see. She was so focused on protecting her friends that she didn't realize her powers were literally destroying everything around her. Cars began to turn to dust as the ground broke up into tiny pieces, floating upward. Red stood frozen in terror as he stared into her cold, emotionless green eyes.

"No, wait! Stop!" he exclaimed, stepping back. "Have mercy on me!"

Suddenly, a pillar of light shot up into the sky and surrounded Red. He became weightless and floated towards the middle. Red looked up and then down. In the sky was a round gate with a cross engraved on it. On the ground was also a round gate, but with a demon's eye engraved on it.

"HEAVEN'S JUDGEMENT!" exclaimed Tracy.

Instantly, Red plummeted towards the demon gate. The gate opened with black shadowy arms springing out. They grabbed hold of Red and began tearing his flesh. Red's cries filled the air. Soon, Mark woke up.

"What the…?" Mark asked, slowly sitting up. "Tra-Tracy?"

Tracy slowly turned around, staring at Mark with those same emotionless eyes. Mark ran towards her but felt her aura pushing him back.

"Stop this at once! This isn't right."

"I'm protecting my friends. I don't want to lose them."

"We're okay," Mark replied, pointing to the others. "See, everyone is okay. Please, come back to me."

Tracy didn't respond. Instead, her aura grew stronger, pushing Mark back. Determined to save her, Mark slowly pushed his way to Tracy. He grabbed her shoulders as he stared into her eyes. Without thinking, he kissed her, holding her close. Slowly, that loving kiss began to suppress Tracy's power. The pillar of light faded. Red was no more. They unlocked lips and Tracy stared at Mark with her warm, loving green eyes. She collapsed from exhaustion into Mark's arms. Mark gave a sigh of relief as he held her close. Soon, the others approached them.

"Glad to see you're okay" Rosa said to Tracy, who was still unconscious. "Remind me never to piss you off."

Suddenly, two comets streaked across the sky. Andrew and the others watched the comets head somewhere west. Their only explanation was that Ganit and Rina finished their job, but at a hefty price.

TWENTY FIVE

Tracy woke up to find her friends surrounding her. Mark gently helped her up as Andrew explained the situation.

"I have a feeling those comets we saw were Ganit and Rina," Andrew said. "They appear to be west of here."

"That's too vague," replied Rosa. "They could be anywhere, even another state."

Andrew looked at Tracy. "I know you just woke up, but do you think you could locate them and take us there?"

Tracy hesitated. She wasn't sure if she had the strength to teleport everyone. Suddenly, Mark placed his hand on her shoulder. He could tell she was worried.

"I have faith in ya," he said with a smile.

"But…" Tracy replied. "I nearly went rogue. I…"

Mark kissed her forehead. "You can do it. I trust you."

Tracy smiled. She looked at Andrew. "I'll do my best."

Everyone stepped back, giving Tracy space. She closed her eyes and began to focus. At first, all she could sense was her friends. Her forehead wrinkled up as she continued to focus. Soon, she was able to sense further. She slowly distinguished people and animals as she continued her search. Suddenly, her eyes opened.

"I think I found them," she said with beads of sweat on her forehead. "It's faint, but I can sense them."

"Rest a bit, honey," Mark replied, wiping the sweat off her forehead. "You don't have the strength to teleport yet."

"No! I need to do this now. If I wait, I won't be able to find them again."

"But…"

"No buts! We go, now!"

Tracy raised her scepter as she closed her eyes. In a blink, they vanished.

In a desolate area of California, was a huge crater the size of three football fields. Tracy and the others reappeared thirty feet from the crater with confused looks. Rosa signaled everyone to follow her. They reached the edge. They all looked down and were shocked at what they saw. Inside the crater, were two infants, wrapped in Ganit and Rina's clothing.

"Well, aren't they cute," said Mark.

Ching went down into the crater. The others quickly followed. He sat next to the infants and held them in his arms. Shanta stood next to him with a smile. She never realized how handsome Ching looked with children. Ching looked at Shanta, smiling back.

"What are we going to do with them?" Rei-Rei asked.

"I was thinking of raising them as my own," Ching answered. "But only if Shanta says it's okay."

Shanta eyes widened. "But I'm not ready to have kids. I can't even breastfeed."

Ching chuckled. "Don't worry, Shanta. They'll be raised on Macu. From time to time, you can visit them. I know how school is important to you."

"Yes, but…"

"No buts. You finish school and then we can discuss the future."

"Crap!" exclaimed Mark.

"What?" Andrew asked.

"I just realized that finals are coming up. Now that the world is saved, we gotta focus on our finals. I haven't even studied."

Andrew hung his head low. "I so haven't studied either…"

Tracy giggled. "Boys, have you forgotten you have three smart women in your group?"

Mark grabbed Tracy's hands. "Baby, will you please tutor me?"

"Naturally," Tracy answered with a smile.

"I-I'll help you, Drew…" Rosa replied, as her face began turning bright red.

"Thanks…" said Andrew, blushing.

Shanta sat in her Economics class, waiting for the teacher to arrive. Her mind was focused on Ching's decision.

I can't be a Mom now. Well, they're not really my kids, but still…

Rosa sat next to her. "You okay, Shanta?"

Shanta came back to reality. "Huh? What?"

"You okay?"

"I guess…"

Rosa whispered. "Still thinking about yesterday?"

Shanta nodded. "I, too, want what's best for Rina and Ganit. But I don't think me becoming a mother would help."

"I understand how you feel. But you forget: you and Ching aren't alone. They got Ching's family, your family, Andrew, Mark, Tracy, and me. You'll make a great mom."

Shanta gave a small smile. "Thanks. I guess I don't want to be another high school mom."

"You'll make the right choice," said Rosa. "Just go with your gut."

Shanta stared at her desk. *My gut, huh?*

Andrew and Mark couldn't believe their ears as news about their fight spread through the school.

"Dude, did you see the news last night?" Josh asked them. "Turns out the X-Men are real, yo."

Mark and Andrew blinked.

"I'm serious," he replied. "There was some footage taken from a nearby news chopper. Dude, it was like watching an action flick. I was so root'n for the sexy chick with the scepter."

"That's my gir-" Mark started, but Andrew quickly covered his mouth.

"What?" Josh asked with a confused look.

"He was trying to say that's my girlfriend's hero," Andrew answered with a forced laugh.

"That's cool," Josh replied. He quickly spotted DJ and Emily. "Yo, over here!"

"Don't yell, Josh," Emily said angrily.

"Did you guys catch the news?" DJ asked.

"Josh just told us," Andrew answered with a bead of sweat rolling down his cheek.

"I heard that they're some people in third-world countries with powers," DJ said. He leaned closer. "Does this mean America will be attacked?"

"DJ, stop your nonsense," replied Emily. "America will be fine."

"Maybe America has some too," Josh said. "After all, those guys did save us."

As the conversation got deeper, Mark and Andrew slowly inched away, making their escape.

Their walk home was silent. The birds chirping and cars zooming filled their ears on that sunny afternoon.

"You think it's cool for DJ and them to know about us?" Mark asked, breaking the silence.

"I don't know," Andrew answered. "I just don't think the world is ready for us yet."

"Maybe..." replied Mark as he crossed the street.

Tracy sat on her bed, staring at her scepter. In the dark corner of her room, it shined brightly. Questions raced through her mind. She knew that her life had changed, but she wasn't sure how to adapt to the change. Suddenly, a knock came upon her door. Tracy quickly put the scepter under her bed. The door opened. It was her mother.

"Tracy, are you okay?" Mrs. Hamilton asked.

"I'm fine, Mom," Tracy answered.

"That's good."

Mrs. Hamilton paused. "I got a call from your father. He said he'll be late, due to the incident yesterday."

"Dad's running tests again?"

"He is a forensic scientist. He said there were several corpses lying around."

Tracy mumbled. "Next time, we do a cleanup."

"What?"

"Oh, nothing," Tracy answered, forcing a laugh. *Better wait to tell them when this incident blows over.*

Ching and Hibika carried Ganit and Rina to the hot spring. They each filled a small tub with warm water and slowly dipped them in. Ganit and Rina cooed and giggled as they splashed warm water around. Ching and Hibika smiled as they bathed them.

Afterwards, they took the infants outside to enjoy the gentle breeze. They cooed as their big eyes wandered. Ching looked up at the sky with a smile.

"Thinking about Shanta?" Hibika asked.

Ching nodded. He looked down at Ganit. "I wonder if this is how Shanta and I will be."

"I think so."

Ching smiled. "Looks like Rina is fast asleep."

Hibika looked down and saw Rina's tiny hands grip her clothing. Rina's eyes were shut, and she had a faint smile. Hibika smiled.

You deserve some rest, little one.

Weeks passed as Andrew and the others studied for their finals. For once, they felt like normal high school students. Then, finals rolled around. It was a hot day in June as students gathered into their classes to take their exams. With pencils and their minds ready, the exam began. The week itself was a battle for everyone as some students had exams back-to-back. After it was all said and done, the school gave a sigh of relief.

The bell rang loudly that Friday afternoon as students flooded the streets and school buses, desperate to leave.

"I'm so glad Finals are over," said Mark, stretching out his arms.

"Me too," replied Andrew with a grin.

"Hey, how'd you guys do?" DJ asked, walking towards them.

"I think I did okay," Andrew answered. "Algebra is no joke."

"Tell me about it," Mark added.

"Glad to see you guys survived," Josh said, entering the conversation. "So, what plans you got for summer?"

"Family vacation to Florida," DJ answered.

"Not sure," Mark replied, rubbing his chin. "I might be home for the summer."

"Same here," Andrew added. "What about you, Josh?"

"I'm going to Europe with my family," Josh answered with a grin. "Might find me a European chick and spend some alone time with her."

"You're hopeless," DJ replied, shaking his head in embarrassment.

"Who's hopeless?" Emily asked, walking into the conversation.

"This idiot," DJ answered, pointing to Josh.

"Figured," replied Emily with a disgusted look.

"Got any plans for the summer, Hime?" Andrew asked.

"No, I'll be at softball practice for our final game of the season," Emily answered with a sad look. "And I was hoping to spend some time with my boyfriend too."

"I'm sure you will," replied Andrew.

Mark looked at his watch. "Yo, Drew, we gotta go."

Andrew nodded. "Later guys, see you at Graduation next week."

Rosa and Tracy waited at the park for another five minutes. Rosa tapped her foot with her arms folded.

"They're late, as usual," she said.

"Now, now," Tracy replied with a forced chuckle.

Suddenly, Andrew and Mark ran towards them.

"Sorry for being late," said Andrew. "DJ and the others were talking to us."

"Whatever," Rosa said. "Anyway, how'd you guys do?"

"I believe we passed," answered Mark, "thanks to both of your tutoring."

Tracy and Rosa both smiled.

"Has Shanta called?" Andrew asked.

"Not that I know of," Tracy answered, shaking her head.

"Maybe Shanta's occupied," Mark suggested. "She has been distant lately."

"It must be because of Ching's decision to raise Ganit and Rina," said Rosa. "The last time I spoke to her, she seemed really bothered by it."

"I think we should talk to her," replied Andrew. "She can't deal with this alone."

"Spoken like a true leader," said Mark with a grin.

Shanta lay on her bed with her face buried in her pillow. Her thoughts were saturated, regarding her future with Ching. It wasn't that she couldn't see herself having children with him, but the fact that it would start sooner. She was afraid, plain and simple. Suddenly, she heard the doorbell ring. She got up and went to answer the door. She opened it and was surprised to see Andrew and the others at her doorstep.

"What are you guys doing here?" she asked.

"We came to see you," Andrew answered. "May we come in?"

Shanta let them in. They looked around the house for a moment before sitting down on the couch.

"Cuz, we know what's wrong," Mark said. "Rosa told us."

"It's not a big deal, guys," Shanta said nervously. "I can handle it."

"No, you can't," Andrew said, standing up. "You're afraid about it."

"No, I'm…"

"Stop lying, Girl," Tracy interrupted. "Ching loves you enough to raise Ganit and Rina while you were at school. I don't fully understand the time gap between Earth and Ching's planet, but that's a lot of time to raise them. At least show the man you love him back."

"It's…not that easy…" replied Shanta staring at the floor.

"Are you worried that you'll be like those teen moms?" Rosa asked. "Have you forgotten what you've accomplished?"

Shanta looked at everyone with wide eyes. Rosa was right. Not only had Shanta completed high school, but she also became Queen. That was more than what most people have accomplished. She soon realized she wasn't afraid of becoming a stereotype but facing her destiny. For the first time, Shanta realized how complete she felt when she was on Macu. Tears rolled down her cheeks. Rosa quickly hugged her, letting Shanta cry.

"It's okay to be afraid of your destiny," Rosa said, gently stroking the back of Shanta's head. "Everyone is like that. But once you know what it is, you should dive straight into it. Right, Drew?"

Andrew nodded. "I, too, was afraid of my destiny. I thought I would end up not knowing who I really was. And even when I learned the truth, I was afraid. But you guys showed me that I'm me and that you all like me for me."

"Everyone has a purpose in life," Tracy said. "But we have the choice to live it or run from it. Shanta, we want you to live your destiny."

"Cuz, I know I don't always say cool things to you, but I want you to live your life standing by Ching's side, as Queen," Mark replied. "You were destined to be Queen and rule with that kind heart of yours. So, go rule the Forest Region with Ching and help him raise Ganit, Rina, and your future kids. I know you can do it."

Shanta wiped her tears and looked at everyone with a smile. "Thank you, all of you."

Tracy got home to find both of her parents at home, which hadn't happen for a long time. Mr. Hamilton, a tall mocha-colored man with black hair and dark brown eyes, looked at his daughter and smiled.

"What's up, Daddy?" she asked with a confused look.

"I'm proud of you," he said.

"But I haven't received my results yet," she said.

"That's not what I'm talking about."

"Then…what?"

"I saw the footage of the UN incident at work. At first, I thought it was some kind of hoax, but after watching several times, I realized you were there."

Tracy's eyes widened. "Daddy, I…"

"It's okay, you don't need to explain. You have a God-given purpose your mother and I wouldn't understand. All we ask is that you be careful."

Tracy hugged Mr. Hamilton. "Thanks, Daddy."

"Now, about this Mark person…" Mr. Hamilton started.

A week went by fast. The sun shined brightly, and the humidity rose that Saturday morning. Crowds of people flocked towards the stadium bleachers. Despite the heat, a breeze managed to cool people down. It was a perfect day for graduation. As the crowd began to settle down, a tall lanky man with round glasses and thin brown hair entered the stage. He walked up to the podium and cleared his throat.

"Please rise as our graduates walk to their seats."

Everyone stood up. They cheered as the graduates walked. Some even whistled and chanted. The graduates waved and smiled as they sat down. Minutes later, the crowd quieted down. The principal introduced the Valedictorian. She quickly walked up to the podium. Mark was surprised.

"I didn't know Tracy was Valedictorian," he whispered to Andrew.

"Me either," Andrew whispered back.

Everyone listened closely to her speech.

"I have to admit, I have no idea what to say," Tracy said with a silly grin. "But after some thought, I figured it out. This speech is probably the shortest speech in our school's history."

Everyone looked at each other and then back at her. She took a deep breath.

"Everyone is born with a purpose. Some know what it is right away and work towards fulfilling it. Others take a while before they fulfill that purpose. I have come across various people who are like the latter. They never realized how precious they were to me and this world until they first found their purpose. Some needed a friend to stick by them while others needed to hear a word of encouragement. I stayed clueless to my purpose until that fateful encounter. And now that I've found it, I will show it to the world one day. I say to everyone here: don't be afraid of your purpose. Fulfill it to the best of your ability. No one else can do it, but you. Thank you."

Silence filled the air for a moment. Tracy could feel embarrassment surrounding her. Suddenly, a hand clap broke the silence. Seconds later, several more hand claps. Soon, everyone was clapping their hands. Tracy smiled and quickly walked off the stage. The principal got back on the podium and started the next section.

"I will now start handing out the diplomas," he said with a smile.

One-by-one, the principal called out the graduate's name. The crowd cheered as each graduate walked up the stage, shook the principal's hand and walked off the stage with their diploma. Some even chanted the graduate's name. Andrew felt nervous as it soon became his turn.

"You a'ight, Drew?" Mark asked.

"Yeah, I guess," Andrew answered with a sad look. "It's just…I wish Lily, Mike, and William were here to see this."

"Me too. But you're not alone, Dawg. You got me, my parents, Shanta, Tracy, and Rosa cheering for you. Well, I'm up."

Mark rose and headed for the stage. Andrew could hear Mr. and Mrs. Rivers cheering. Even Tracy was loud. Finally, it was Andrew's turn. He rose and slowly headed for the stage. He looked around and saw Mark, Tracy, Rosa, and Shanta cheering. Soon, he heard their families cheering for him. He smiled as he picked up the pace. He got onto the stage and shook the principal's hand, receiving the diploma in the other. Suddenly, he heard a faint voice. He looked straight into the crowd and saw Lily, Mike, and William cheering for him. He blinked. They vanished. Andrew smiled as he walked back to his seat.

Thanks, for everything.

Back in Japan, the mysterious woman entered the condemned area that once was Hidishi's main headquarters. She wandered through the debris, with her phone in her hand. She was searching for something. Her phone began to beep louder and louder. Soon, the mysterious woman came across a boarded-up entrance, just a few yards away from where the lobby used to stand. She cleared the debris and yanked the entrance door off its hinges. The entrance door flew and landed on a lush patch of grass.

"This looks promising," she said with a grin.

The mysterious woman went down through the entrance. It was a long, winding staircase. Soon, she reached the bottom. She looked around. The lab and training room were in shambles. The mysterious woman investigated the lab further, checking every nook and cranny. Suddenly, she stumbled upon a large safe. Using her strength, the mysterious woman ripped opened the safe and gazed upon its contents. Inside, were two vials and a thin stack of papers. She picked up the vial and examined it. The mysterious woman grinned evilly.

"Professor Yen did a wonderful job making this," she said. "Onward to the next phase…"

Three days after Graduation, Andrew and the others all met up at the Fortune House.

"Just like old times," said Mark heading towards the basement.

"For you guys," replied Rosa. "This is my first time."

"Tracy, Rosa, you ready for an adventure?" Shanta asked.

"We've been ready," Tracy answered with a grin.

They all headed towards the basement. Rosa stared at the gateway, as the others slowly walked through it.

"Don't worry, I got ya," Andrew said holding her hand.

They went through. In seconds, they were on Macu. After some traveling, they finally reached the temple. Rei-Rei greeted them. He was taller and toned, but still had his black spots. At first, the gang didn't recognize him. But after staring at his face, they knew it was him.

"Hey guys, long time no see," Rei-Rei said with a smile.

"You've grown, Rei-Rei," said Shanta. "You're almost my height and you got a cute, toned body. You must have the Nebtan girls all over you."

Rei-Rei felt embarrassed. "I've just been training. I'm still too young to marry."

"How's it going?" Mark asked, bumping fists with him.

"Terrible," Rei-Rei answered nervously. "I can't find Ganit and Rina."

Everyone's eyes widened.

"Where did you last see them?" Andrew asked.

"In the temple," Rei-Rei answered. "I babysat them while Ching and Hibika were out for a conference in Raion."

"Why didn't Aiya help you?" Mark asked.

"She was busy dealing with a dispute between a farmer and servant-girl," Rei-Rei answered.

"They couldn't have gone far," said Rosa. "I mean they're only infants."

"Actually, they're toddlers now," replied Rei-Rei. "You guys have been gone for two years in our time. They can walk and talk."

"Great, so we gotta find toddlers now," said Mark sarcastically. "Don't tell me: they can use their powers too."

Rei-Rei sighed heavily. "For children, who don't remember their past lives, they sure picked up on their powers pretty quickly."

Mark slapped his forehead. "Great…"

"Well, if they can use their powers, then maybe I can pinpoint their location," said Tracy.

"Please try, Tracy," replied Rei-Rei. "I'm still learning how to sense spiritual energy."

Tracy closed her eyes and focused her mind. She could feel the auras of her friends, but soon could feel other auras. She searched further and deeper.

"Found them," she said, opening her eyes. "They're a mile away from us."

"That's not too far," said Andrew. "Let's go!"

Ganit and Rina roamed around the dense forest, laughing. They ran round several trees and tried to catch Macuan butterflies.

"Dis fun!" Ganit squealed.

"Yay, fun!" Rina chimed in.

Suddenly, they heard a strange noise. They stopped and looked around.

"What dat?" Rina asked, clinging to Ganit.

Ganit shook his head. "Don know."

"Ganit, me scared."

"Me protect you, Rina."

"Promise?"

Ganit smiled. "Promise."

Suddenly, a large creature jumped out from the bushes. They took a good look at it. It was literally a humanoid version of a Boar. It grunted as it slowly approached Ganit and Rina. Ganit got in front of Rina with fists ready. He fired several energy balls. However, they all missed. Boar laughed as he cracked his knuckles.

"Time to die, kiddies."

Ganit held Rina close to him, as Boar stepped closer to them. Suddenly, Boar was struck down. Boar skidded across the ground. He looked up and saw Shanta, in her fox form, standing in front of Ganit and Rina.

"Don't you dare touch them," she said before she vanished.

Boar quickly rose and looked around. BAM! He felt a blow to his chin. Boar's body rose into the air. Shanta reappeared behind him. Shanta's foot connected with Boar's neck, sending him flying. He plummeted, crashing into the ground. Boar coughed up blood. His body became heavy as he tried to stand. He looked up and saw Shanta standing in front of him. She grabbed his neck and slowly lifted him up in the air. Boar struggled to breathe as his feet kicked wildly.

"Are you going to leave my children alone?" Shanta asked angrily.

Boar grunted yes. Shanta released him. Boar ran away. Shanta de-transformed.

"Are you alright?" she asked them.

Ganit and Rina both nodded.

She hugged them tightly. "I'm glad you're both safe."

"We missed Mommy," Rina said smiling.

Shanta's eyes widened. "You…think I'm your mommy?"

Rina nodded. "You always Mommy to us. Daddy always talk about Mommy and show Mommy's picture to us every day."

"You staying, Mommy?" Ganit asked, looking at her with his big dark brown eyes.

Shanta began to tear up. She realized how important they were to her. That fight proved that. She could even hear herself say *her children*. The others were right, she was their mother now.

"Yes, Ganit, I'm staying," she said with tears rolling down her cheeks.

Rina wiped Shanta's tears. "No cry, Mommy, no cry."

The others finally caught up with Shanta. They watched as Shanta interacted with Ganit and Rina.

"That's my Cuz," said Mark with a smile.

"She finally has accepted her destiny," Tracy replied, also smiling.

EPILOGUE

Four years have passed since their fight with Hidishi. All seemed well
with the world, but even that was a lie. More and more people had lost their
jobs and new viruses had plagued the world. Taxes had risen while wages
sunk. Many businesses across the globe had shut down and more and more
foreclosure signs appeared in front of houses. Even the Stock Markets cried
for help as red arrows fill their electric boards. People demanded leadership
from their President, yet their congressmen were the one pulling the
strings. They had become greedy, blinding themselves to the people's cries.
They allowed new shady groups and government programs to rise and take
control, brainwashing desperate people. Even now, bills were stuck in
limbo because no one in government could come to an agreement.

The Bronx hadn't changed much. Although there were fewer drug-dealers
prowling the streets, many more homeless people appeared. There had
been several incidents where the homeless were arrested for stealing and
even killing. They had a new mayor running the place. Some people never
knew that she was a meta-human, but they knew she was trying her best to
run the city.

Meta-humans have spread across the globe. Many people have accepted
them, but like racism, there are those who opposed them. On September
20th, 2011, ten thousand meta-humans were killed in Times Square during a
parade. It was known as The Cleansing. To counteract further deaths, a
secret organization, known as Sanctuary, stepped in and rescued many
meta-humans. These meta-humans learned how to control their powers and
became agents for the organization. Since then, the world was at peace
(sort of). So, what are our heroes up to…?

Andrew sat in his new office at the Fortune House, typing up an article. According to Mr. Rivers, who is a real estate agent, Madam Renee left a will. In it, Andrew was given ownership of the Fortune House. Naturally, Andrew and Rosa moved in, along with Mark and Tracy. It was a great idea during their college years.

There was a knock upon the door. The door opened, revealing Rosa. Andrew gave her a small smile before setting his eyes back onto his computer screen.

"Guess what?" Rosa answered with a grin.

"What?" asked Andrew, still typing.

"I got the job at the law firm. You know, the one two blocks down from the Fortune House."

Andrew stopped typing. Excited, he got up and kissed her. "That's great! I knew you'd get it!"

"Thanks," Rosa replied, feeling bashful.

Rosa walked over to the computer and peeked at the monitor. Andrew sighed heavily.

"Writing this article has been stressful," Andrew said. "My boss demands way too much."

Rosa snickered. "Well, you are writing for *Esquire*, one of the most popular magazines in New York. I got faith in you."

"Thanks."

"Why don't you take a small break and eat something with me?"

Andrew smirked. "Sure."

Shanta sat under a tree in the courtyard with Ganit and Rina sitting beside her. She was reading to them. They smiled and rested their heads on her shoulders as a gentle breeze blew. Shanta stopped and looked up, noticing Ching approaching her.

"Having fun?" he asked with a smile.

Shanta smiled back. "I was just about to finish the story. Is something wrong?"

Ching shook his head. "I was just checking up on you."

"You did that ten minutes ago."

"Really, I hadn't noticed."

Shanta slowly rose, revealing a large belly. "Silly man, the baby isn't due for another two months. Besides, Ganit and Rina are also looking after me."

Ching chuckled. "You're right."

"You just miss me," she said, hugging him. "I miss you too."

She kissed him. Ganit and Rina covered their eyes.

"Yucky," they both said in unison.

Shanta and Ching laughed.

"You'll understand one day," Ching said as he patted their tiny heads.

"Darling, don't you have a conference to go to?" Shanta asked.

Ching's eyes widened. "Oh no! I totally forgot!"

Shanta giggled as she held his hand. "Don't worry, I'll go with you. After all, the Queen must stand by the King."

"But what about…?"

"Aunt Hibika and Aunt Aiya can look after the little ones."

"I guess you're right. Well then, let's go."

Tracy was on her break when her cell phone rang.

"Hello?"

"Hey Baby," said Mark.

"Hey, what's up?"

"We got the house in Savannah and my transfer is a go."

Tracy squealed. "I'm so proud of you!"

"Yeah, who knew RKL Enterprises had another warehouse? Transferring jobs will be a breeze. What about you? How did your job take the news?"

Tracy sighed. "Not too well. At least they know I'll be in good hands. Memorial Health is a great hospital to work at. So, have you told Andrew yet?"

Mark sighed heavily. "No, not yet."

"Mark Rivers, how could you?" asked Tracy, feeling a little disappointed. "Andrew's a brother to you. He deserves to know."

"I know, but we've all been busy."

"That's not an excuse."

"I know…Well, I'll let you go. I'll call you later tonight, during my break."

"Okay. Have a good shift tonight. Love you."

"Love you too, bye," Mark said before he hung up.

Tracy put her phone into her pocket. She started to look a little sad. *I just hope we all can see each other again, even after all these changes…*

A gentle breeze blew across Andrew's hair as his eyes were fixed on three headstones. Gray clouds filled the sky as a lonely crow flew by. The crow's cry filled Andrew's ears as his eyes continued to stare at the people, he once called his family. He let out a sigh and smiled.

"Time sure flies, huh?" he said.

Andrew knelt. "Lily, Mike, William: it's been five years since the burial. To be honest, it's the first time I'm seeing you guys like this. Why? I was scared. That day, I felt like giving up everything. I couldn't bear losing anyone else. Although I never told you guys, Mike and Lily, about my powers, I felt powerless."

He smiled as he looked up. "But thanks to Rosa and everyone, I was able to overcome my fears and move forward."

Silence filled the air as Andrew sat down on the dry grass. The scent of rain filled Andrew's nose as he saw darker clouds slowly approaching.

"I wanna tell you guys my adventure," he said looking back at the headstones. "I knew I was adopted, but I wanted to find out for myself who I really was. It turns out I was the son of an infamous drug-lord and teenage mother. But the real kicker was confronting my father in order to save the world. See, he was a meta-human who couldn't stand humans and wanted to create a utopia for only meta-humans. And to stop him, I too became a meta-human. Well, I wasn't alone. Mark and his cousin, Shanta, also became one and together we saved the world with our new friends, Rei-Rei, Ching, and Hibika."

Andrew continued his story, telling them about the crazy adventures on Macu and about Ganit and Rina. His heart was at ease as he continued to talk. Suddenly, he gave them a serious look.

"In a way, you should be glad you're not here," he said. "These past five years has been filled with darkness. Homes are being foreclosed, jobs are getting scarce, and that war out in the Middle East is still going on. On top of that, the introduction of meta-humans has brought racism back to the surface. Some days I wanna crawl in a hole and hide."

He smirked. "But you guys taught me to never give up. Oh, I almost forgot: our team has disbanded. As much as I want them to stay, it's for the best. Shanta is ruling the Nebtans with Ching, Rei-Rei is guarding the universe, and both Mark and Tracy have moved to Savannah to start their own lives.

I don't know what the future holds for us, but I believe we'll get together again."

Andrew dug deep into his pocket and pulled something out. He opened his hand, revealing a silver ring with an average-sized diamond in the center. He pointed it towards the headstones.

"Guys, I'm going to ask Rosa to marry me. I know that in today's world, it'll be hard to start and raise a family. But when I look into Rosa's eyes, I feel that I can do anything. I just wish you could be here to see the look on her face."

Andrew stood up and placed the ring back into his pocket. "Well, I better go. It was great talking with you. I miss you guys and hope you guys are doing well. Wish me luck!"

He walked slowly, heading for the entrance. Suddenly, from out of his peripheral, he saw a bright light. He turned around. A ray of sunlight poked through the gray clouds. It shined brightly over the headstones, giving them a glittery look. Suddenly, Andrew's eyes widened, and his heart was filled with joy as faded images of Mike, Lily, and William appeared before him. He rubbed his eyes. They vanished. A tear rolled down his cheek as he smiled.

Andrew headed back to the entrance, where Rosa was waiting for him.

"How was the reunion?" Rosa asked.

Andrew smiled. "Relieving."

"Were you crying?" Rosa asked, wiping his tears.

"A little," Andrew answered. "At least I know they're okay up there."

"I'm glad to hear that," Rosa replied with a smile.

Rosa held Andrew's hand. Andrew smirked as they walked to his car.

9 7989 886 13909